PRAISE FOR THE NOVELS OF
CATHERINE SPANGLER

TOUCHED BY FIRE

"*Touched by Fire* is a blazing-hot romantic fantasy thriller
that is impossible to put down. Catherine Spangler puts her
readers into the twisted mind of a psychotic killer right
along with her heroine. It is an experience that one won't
soon forget." —*ParaNormal Romance Reviews*

TOUCHED BY DARKNESS

"Dark, edgy, and incredibly sensual, *Touched by Darkness*
is a spellbinding contemporary fantasy thriller . . . A unique
and enthralling series debut that is not to be missed!"
—*ParaNormal Romance Reviews*

"I loved the entire concept . . . and give this author high
marks for originality and creativity. Fans of Spangler's
sci-fi fantasy are going to be mesmerized by this sensual
new series." —*The Best Reviews*

"The talented Spangler returns in a complex and intriguing new s   ntinels."
—*Romantic Times* (four stars)

Berkley Sensation Books by Catherine Spangler

TOUCHED BY DARKNESS
TOUCHED BY FIRE
TOUCHED BY LIGHT

Anthologies

DEMON'S DELIGHT
(with MaryJanice Davidson, Emma Holly, and Vickie Taylor)

TOUCHED BY
LIGHT

Catherine Spangler

BERKLEY SENSATION, NEW YORK

THE BERKLEY PUBLISHING GROUP
Published by the Penguin Group
Penguin Group (USA) Inc.
375 Hudson Street, New York, New York 10014, USA

Penguin Group (Canada), 90 Eglinton Avenue East, Suite 700, Toronto, Ontario M4P 2Y3, Canada
(a division of Pearson Penguin Canada Inc.)
Penguin Books Ltd., 80 Strand, London WC2R 0RL, England
Penguin Group Ireland, 25 St. Stephen's Green, Dublin 2, Ireland (a division of Penguin Books Ltd.)
Penguin Group (Australia), 250 Camberwell Road, Camberwell, Victoria 3124, Australia
(a division of Pearson Australia Group Pty. Ltd.)
Penguin Books India Pvt. Ltd., 11 Community Centre, Panchsheel Park, New Delhi—110 017, India
Penguin Group (NZ), 67 Apollo Drive, Rosedale, North Shore 0632, New Zealand
(a division of Pearson New Zealand Ltd.)
Penguin Books (South Africa) (Pty.) Ltd., 24 Sturdee Avenue, Rosebank, Johannesburg 2196,
South Africa

Penguin Books Ltd., Registered Offices: 80 Strand, London WC2R 0RL, England

This is a work of fiction. Names, characters, places, and incidents either are the product of the author's
imagination or are used fictitiously, and any resemblance to actual persons, living or dead, business
establishments, events, or locales is entirely coincidental. The publisher does not have any control
over and does not assume any responsibility for author or third-party websites or their content.

TOUCHED BY LIGHT

A Berkley Sensation Book / published by arrangement with the author

PRINTING HISTORY
Berkley Sensation mass-market edition / June 2009

Copyright © 2009 by Catherine Spangler.
Excerpt from *Breaking Midnight* by Emma Holly copyright © 2009 by Emma Holly.
Cover art by Larry Rostant.
Cover design by George Long.
Interior text design by Kristin del Rosario.

All rights reserved.
No part of this book may be reproduced, scanned, or distributed in any printed or electronic form
without permission. Please do not participate in or encourage piracy of copyrighted materials in
violation of the author's rights. Purchase only authorized editions.
For information, address: The Berkley Publishing Group,
a division of Penguin Group (USA) Inc.,
375 Hudson Street, New York, New York 10014.

ISBN: 978-0-425-22637-7

BERKLEY® SENSATION
Berkley Sensation Books are published by The Berkley Publishing Group,
a division of Penguin Group (USA) Inc.,
375 Hudson Street, New York, New York 10014.
BERKLEY® SENSATION and the "B" design are trademarks of Penguin Group (USA) Inc.

PRINTED IN THE UNITED STATES OF AMERICA

10 9 8 7 6 5 4 3 2 1

If you purchased this book without a cover, you should be aware that this book is stolen property. It was
reported as "unsold and destroyed" to the publisher, and neither the author nor the publisher has
received any payment for this "stripped book."

This book is dedicated to, and in memory of, Janet Underwood. Jan, you've been one of my "bestest" friends for most of my life. I miss you so much. I know you've found a song to sing, a glass of good red wine, and some great—if slightly off-color—jokes in heaven. Love always.

Acknowledgments

If you're wondering why I always have such a long list of acknowledgments in my books, it's because so many wonderful people generously give of their time and knowledge to help me make the information in my stories as accurate as possible. You didn't really think I knew all this stuff, did you? My deepest gratitude and thanks go out to the following:

Nikki Duncan, fellow author, for doing a follow-up on the San Antonio Zoo and for providing additional pictures.

Edward Heasley, for once again sharing his gun expertise and for being such a great uncle.

The real Tami Lang, for inspiring the same-name character in this book and for her kindness to my father.

Craig Mallinson, owner of the real Red Lion Pub in Houston, for sharing the pub's amazing list of single malt liquors.

Angi Platt, fellow author, for scoping out the San Antonio Zoo and area cemeteries and for taking lots of pictures.

Melissa Schroeder, another great author, for answering questions about SeaWorld and San Antonio in general.

Linnea Sinclair, still another wonderful author and a former PI, for her great course on private investigators and for answering my questions.

Hank Stern, my brilliant father and math professor, who helped with math terminology.

My awesome support group: Angelica Blocker, Linda Castillo, Robyn Delozier, Beth Gonzales, Jennifer Miller, Carole Turner, and my wonderful husband, James. Some of you read pages and kibitzed, others offered encouragement and wine. Thanks!

Roberta Brown, for friendship and expert career guidance.

Cindy Hwang and Leis Pederson, for their unending patience and editing brilliance.

Thank you all. Walk in Light.

Glossary of Terms

Atlantis—A mystical, magical culture that some believe actually existed in the North Atlantic Ocean, bordering parts of what is now the eastern U.S. coast. It is also believed that Atlantis had an extremely advanced culture, and destroyed itself through civil war and the misuse of its great Tuaoi stone.

Belial—The cunning, evil leader of a rebel Atlantian faction, Belial advocated human slavery, human sacrifices, and the dark side of magic. His group gained control of the Tuaoi stone and orchestrated the destruction of Atlantis.

Belian—A follower of Belial (also known as the Sons of Belial). Adhering to their leader's original dark practices, Belians are now reincarnating in human form on Earth, and wrecking violence and havoc on its inhabitants. They thrive on chaos and terror and blood offerings to Belial. Although they occupy mortal bodies, they have superhuman abilities. They operate from the four lower spiritual chakras, and can shield their presence from Sentinels.

Belian Crime Scene (BCS)—The scene of a Belian crime. A Sentinel investigates the scene, absorbing the psychic energies left behind by the Belian, in order to track it down.

Belian Expulsion (BE)—A forced exile of a Belian soul to Saturn for spiritual rehabilitation. It requires the joint efforts of a Sentinel and the High Sanctioned.

Chakras—The seven spiritual centers of the human body, starting in the lower abdomen and moving upward. Each corresponds to a physical part of the body and also to a specific color. The first four are the lower chakras and are grounded to the Earth. The last three are the higher chakras and are linked to the Creator and the spiritual realm.

Conduction—The process in which a Sentinel and a conductor link spiritually through the seven chakras; most specifically, the sixth chakra and third eye. This amplifies the psychic energy the Sentinel has absorbed from a Belian crime scene and helps to identify the Belian. The process also raises powerful sexual energies and has a physical component—sexual intercourse, which further enhances the psychic energies. Often several conductions are required before the Belian's shields are breached.

Conductor—A regular human who is psychically wired to link with some Sentinels, and to magnify and enhance the Sentinel's psychic tracking abilities. Conductors are relatively rare, and a good conductor/Sentinel match is even rarer. A matched conductor is always the opposite sex of the Sentinel, and there's a powerful sexual attraction between them.

Crystal Pendant—A pink quartz crystal edged in silver, it's worn by many Sentinels. Attuned to the great Tuaoi stone and to the Sentinel's personal energy, it helps focus and magnify psychic energies, and with shielding.

High Sanctioned—Those entities (souls) that were the high priests of the temple of The One on Atlantis. Generally, they don't occupy physical bodies, but act more as spirit guides for Sentinels. They assist with Belian expulsions.

Initiate—A fledgling, a young Sentinel who is still learning how to shield energies and use the Sentinel powers.

Law of One—The spiritual law and belief followed by most Atlantians, it acknowledged a higher Supreme Being and placed the focus on the Light, and positive energies.

Psychic Signature (PS)—The energy patterns left behind by a Belian, more pronounced if a violent crime has occurred. A Sentinel collects and absorbs these energies, and pieces together clues and mental pictures to help identify the Belian.

Sanctioned—Spiritually advanced Atlantian entities who served the high priests in the temple of The One. They occupy human bodies and are the overseers and the decision makers in the day-to-day Sentinel operations on Earth.

Saturn (Burning/Experience)—Saturn, the "grim reaper," rules the moral and karmic lessons souls must experience and overcome. Also called the "karmic initiator," Saturn is where Belian souls are sent until they learn their spiritual lessons. It is not a pleasant experience—more like purgatory.

Sentinel—An Atlantian soul reincarnating into a human body to track down Belians and dispense karmic justice. Like Belians, Sentinels are mortal but possess superhuman powers. They operate out of the three higher chakras, making it difficult for Belians to sense their presence. They often use conductors to help them identify Belians.

Sexual Surge—The raw, powerful surge of sexual energy that occurs at the beginning of a conduction, when the lower chakras open and pull in earth-based energies—which most resemble the vibratory levels of Belians. This surge helps the Sentinel get a better fix on the Belian.

Shielding—Using psychic energies to create a spiritual shield that blocks the presence of either a Sentinel or a Belian.

The One—The Atlantian term for God/Supreme Being.

Third Eye—A spiritual center that is linked to the sixth chakra and the pineal gland, and represented by the color indigo, the third eye enhances "seeing" and "hearing" on an ethereal level. A Sentinel, often with the aid of a conductor, works through the third eye to track Belians.

Tuaoi Stone (The Great Crystal)—A huge spear of solid, multifaceted quartz crystal, the Tuaoi stone was housed in a special temple on Atlantis. It provided all power, as well as a means of communicating with The One, and was ultimately used to destroy Atlantis. It now lies at the bottom of the Atlantic Ocean, its power undiminished.

White Brotherhood—(Does not refer to race or gender.) This was the Atlantian priesthood established for the perpetuation of the Law of One. They had the ability to transport themselves in thought or body wherever desired. Many of them have incarnated as Sentinels, the Sanctioned, and the Higher Sanctioned.

PRELUDE, BOOK 3

To love is to live love—not the answer of desire or of amorous affection, but is all in one—for love is law, law is love.

(Edgar Cayce Reading 900-331)

Corpus Christi, Texas, Current Day
From the private journal of Sanctioned Adam Masters

BUDDHA said, "Everything changes, nothing remains without change." Even though the pattern created in Atlantis has endured for thousands of years, it's now shifting, as is the balance of power—and not for the good.

The Darkness is growing stronger. The Belians now entering the Earth are more dominant, more cunning. If I'm right about this current situation, it is an alarming sign that the Belians are finding new ways to entrench themselves. It will become increasingly more difficult to cast them from the Earth, into the fires of Saturn. We'll have to find new ways to fight them. We must change, or become nothing.

I believe the Light will prevail, but it will require a new infusion of energy. It's no longer enough for Sentinels and conductors to come together for the sole purpose of tracking evil. They must do more than ride the sexual explosion through the base chakras. They must bond, and create a wave of love that will reverberate out into the Universe. For the Divine Law is love. Love will empower the Light.

My meditative visions show I have my own role to play in this, and not solely as a Sanctioned. I must deal single-handedly with the current threat. Asking my Sentinels to take down one of their own, especially one whose powers encompass both Light and Darkness, is not an option.

An unprecedented occurrence in the history of the Sanctioned has provided one person—a human conductor—who can help me. She's brilliant, courageous, obstinate, highly uncooperative, and would rejoice if I vanished from the Earth. She is my match in every way, and adds another level—a very intriguing one—to this unexpected challenge.

It's crucial to act quickly, so I'll be seeking her out this week. I pray for the divine intervention that will be necessary to convince her to help me. Quick thinking will also be essential to stay one step ahead of her. Ah, but I'm looking forward to seeing her again.

Until then, in my meditations I will continue to visualize the Earth and all the souls who dwell on it surrounded by the Light.

The Sentinels will prevail.

ONE

Yea in thine experiences through the earth ye, too, have seen the light and lost thy way.

(Edgar Cayce Reading 1301-1)

THE phone call came at 3:37 that afternoon. *It truly didn't qualify as one of those life-altering calls,* Julia told herself. Not really, not compared to . . . say . . . the unexpected death of a loved one. Or a major catastrophe—like an earthquake, or a tsunami, or 9/11.

Yet the call had tilted her mundane world off its axis. Worse were the nightmare memories it had resurrected . . . *"Don't resist me, Julia, or I'll kill you,"* William Bennett said as he rammed himself into her. *Not that she could have fought at that point—he'd beaten her too badly. . . .*

Julia jerked herself back to the present. And here she'd been thinking she was finally putting it all behind her. She slugged back the rest of her bourbon. Managed to set the glass back on its paper coaster, despite the Herculean urge to hurl it against the wall.

"Can I get you another one, Dr. Reynolds?" Miriam, who happened to be both the bartender and one of the top students in both Julia's number theory and thermal physics courses at the University of Houston, took the empty glass.

Miriam's hair was styled into stiff spikes, the color du jour alternating sections of green, red, and blond. Heavy eye makeup accentuated her green eyes; one pierced eyebrow and multiple silver rings in each ear added to her distinct style. Julia just wasn't hip enough to know if it was Goth or punk, or whatever the latest look was.

Not that Julia was up with any of the current trends. She'd buried herself in teaching, with a strong minor in the art of becoming a hermit, in twelve short years. She certainly wasn't a spokesperson for the stylish and fashionable.

"Yes, I want another one," she told Miriam. "Make it straight up." No melting ice diluting this drink. Maybe then the bourbon would deaden the pain.

"Sure." Miriam turned to make the drink, hesitated. "Are you okay, Dr. Reynolds? You seem . . . upset."

Upset? Julia battled back the hysterical urge to laugh. Try *terrified . . . panicked . . . barely holding on to her sanity.* What would Miriam think if her staid, unemotional math professor suddenly lost it in the middle of the Red Lion Pub? Could make for an interesting story.

Get a grip, Julia told herself. She drew a deep breath, managed to shake her head. "I'm fine, Miriam. Just enjoying a few drinks."

Miriam's disbelief was clearly etched on her face, but she turned and walked off behind the polished mahogany bar. Julia raised a shaking hand to her throbbing temple.

"You're such a liar, Julia," came a voice from behind her.

Her head snapped up, and adrenaline shot through her like neutrons in a particle analyzer. God, she knew—*and hated*—that odd, rasping voice. Her body went rigid, while her heart decided she must be running a three-minute mile and went into frenetic overdrive. Her cool logic and acute analyzing ability evaporated in the muddle of shock and incredulity.

No! Not now. She fixed her gaze on the gleaming brass

beer tap behind the bar. Willed that voice to be the result of her overstressed state—although she knew her current luck was on the crappy side of negative one. "Go away," she said.

He didn't reply, but she felt the air shift as he settled onto the barstool beside her. Felt that disconcerting energy buzz that always arced between them, felt the spike in her normally dead-as-dirt libido. Felt the beckoning warmth emanating from his body, in direct opposition to the power and danger he radiated.

She refused to look at him. If she couldn't see him, he wasn't really there, right? But that didn't convince her clamoring senses, which had gone on full alert. His scent drifted to her—expensive, woodsy, totally male. That damned electricity continued bombarding her. Her nipples hardened and she grew damp between her legs. *Damn him.*

"I said *go away*," she snapped. "Does it work better if I say it three times? Go away, go away, go away. *Go. Away!*"

"That's six times, actually. And no, you can't will me away. Besides, I came from Corpus just to see you."

Her shoulders slumped. "Great. Exactly what I needed today."

"I take it you've had a tough day."

"It just got worse," she muttered.

Miriam returned then, before Julia could bring herself to look at Adam. The young woman set the drink down, her gaze going to him, her expression surprised. He was quite striking, and since the bar wasn't crowded, there was no reason for him to be sitting beside Julia. She was dowdy and ordinary, not in high demand as a flirtation partner.

"Can I get you something?" Miriam asked.

"I'll take a Glenmorangie scotch, if you have it, straight up."

Miriam nodded and left. Julia clutched her drink, considered slamming it down in one gulp.

"It would be nice if you would look at me." His rough voice washed through her like a nuclear shock wave.

She turned her head, glared into cool, midnight eyes. "What are you doing here, Adam?"

He stared back, as always, calm, intelligent, and—as she well knew—utterly ruthless. His ebony hair was short, meticulously combed back from his high forehead. His features were harsh, aristocratic, with the exception of a surprisingly sensual mouth. The expensive black Italian suit was a perfect foil for his ultraconservative and auto-cratic persona, while the single diamond glittering in his left ear seemed incongruous.

"I need your help, Julia."

This man had the ability to make her crazy, to evoke emotional responses that ran the gauntlet from sexually aroused to enraged. He threatened her on levels she didn't even want to acknowledge, especially after today's devel-opments.

"And *I* need a new identity and a new life in another country," she retorted. "Sorry, but you'll have to find as-sistance for your woo-woo endeavors elsewhere. I'm cur-rently occupied with other matters."

She took a gulp of her drink, almost choked as the burn spread down her throat. "And how did you know I was here anyway?" She returned her glare to him. "Playing stalker? Isn't that beneath you?"

"Ah, Julia, you're as blunt and entertaining as ever. I'm not stalking you, merely keeping track of you."

Tracking, stalking—basically the same thing. She'd al-ready been there, done that, twelve years ago. "Listen psycho-Sentinel, what I do with my life and my time is none of your damned business. Go away and leave me alone."

His expression remained neutral. That was another thing she despised about him—his utter lack of emotional reaction. But then, he wasn't really human. "Actually, I'm a Sanctioned, as I have previously explained. And you *are* my business, Julia. I'm responsible for every Sentinel and conductor in Texas."

"News flash—I am *not* a conductor. Not in thought or deed. Been there, done that. I helped you track down a crazed bomber and watched my sister get sliced up by that bastard. I'm done. And if I correctly understand the Sentinel code of honor, you can't force me to help you. So go back to your cave."

"I'm not leaving, Julia. Like I said, I need your help."

To hell with that. He could sit there all afternoon and watch her get soused, for all she cared. Miriam returned with Adam's drink and Julia took the opportunity to finish hers. "I'll take another."

"Not unless I'm driving you home," Adam said.

His arrogance upped her inner rage level. "The odds of that happening are about the same as solving Fermat's Last Theorem."

His ebony brows arched. "Hasn't that been done?" He sipped his scotch, his fingers long and elegant around the glass.

Damn, the man has to be brilliant as well as annoying. "It's still being debated, and it's taken well over three hundred years to get this close. You are not driving me *anywhere*."

"Then we'll settle the tab," he told Miriam.

She hesitated, glanced to Julia for confirmation. *Not a problem.* There were hundreds of bars in the Houston area, and any that were sans Adam Masters would do for Julia's purposes. Better that she was closer to home, anyway. Then she could call a cab if she needed to.

She nodded at Miriam. "It's all right. Be sure you pad the total a few times over. He can afford it."

She fumbled for her cane, glad Adam had sat on her left side and hadn't thought to confiscate it. It was a good thing for him that using the cane to get as far away from him as possible was a higher priority than smacking his hard head with it. She slid off the barstool, balancing her weight on her good leg, as Adam gave Miriam a fifty-dollar bill and told her to keep the change.

He moved to block Julia as she started toward the door. "We're not done here."

"We'll have to agree to disagree on that one." She started around him.

He didn't touch her—they both knew that often had undesirable repercussions. But his next words stopped her cold. "I know William Bennett will be released from Huntsville Prison in two days."

So did she; that cold, impersonal call earlier this afternoon had dropped the bombshell. And wasn't the Texas Department of Criminal Justice considerate to inform victims when their tormentors were let loose, not to mention its annoying habit of releasing violent prisoners simply because of overcrowding?

She swayed on her feet, pounded by an emotional barrage. *"I've been waiting for you, Julia." The man stepped from the kitchen of her home in Kingwood. He moved toward her, an ordinary-looking man with a monster's soul. "You've been going out again, Julia," he said in a soft voice. "Even though I told you not to. I was watching. I saw you flirting with those men. Why did you disobey me, Julia?"*

It took a major effort to push back the memories, to pull together her scattered psyche and deal with Adam. She managed an attempt at levity. "You really know how to make a girl feel safe and secure, you know that?"

His eyes were cold pools of black menace. "I *will* keep you safe. You can count on it."

From psycho-Sentinel to macho-Sentinel—make that macho-*Sanctioned*. "It's not your problem." She turned and made her way out, cursing the fact that her bad leg made her about as fast as a giant Galapagos tortoise on a slow day.

"The hell it isn't," he muttered.

Although he moved silently, she was acutely aware of him following her. Her entire body tingled, and she could feel the hairs on the back of her neck rising. He'd told her the reaction was caused by an electromagnetic current that formed between matched Sentinels and conductors and an ensuing sexual surge through the chakras. She'd told him that was a bunch of crap, with no scientific basis whatsoever. Even though she now knew better.

There was no denying the heart-pounding, visceral reaction she always had when he touched her. And when he'd kissed her at the Dallas/Fort Worth airport . . . Surely her reactions had to be exacerbated by the fact that she'd been celibate for twelve years. Deprivation could do strange things to people.

So could desperation. As she reached her car and fumbled inside her purse for her keys, Adam was far too close for comfort. She didn't need his unsettling presence. Especially not after that cataclysmic phone call.

She didn't find her keys, but she did find the grip of her trusty Beretta Tomcat. Taking that as a stamp of approval from fate—*the bitch*—she discreetly slid it out.

"Julia, we must talk," Adam said. "I have a situation that is extremely serious." Then he touched her, damn him, gripping her shoulder. She felt the sparks down to her toes, and everywhere in between.

"I have a better idea." She turned, shrugging free of his hand and sidling a few steps away, keeping the gun behind her. He started after her, but froze when she swung out the Beretta and aimed it at his chest.

"Back off, Adam." She clicked off the safety.

"Isn't that a little childish?" he asked, not appearing the least concerned.

Actually, it was probably incredibly stupid; she knew that with his thoughts alone, he could control her body like it was a marionette. But she was beyond caring. She dropped the gun due south toward a crucial target. "Maybe I'll shoot lower."

Adam shrugged. "That's not much of a threat to a man who hasn't had sex in a few hundred years."

"*What?*" Startled, Julia found herself momentarily distracted. All the Sentinel men she'd met had been ultramasculine, overflowing with testosterone and machismo. Adam was so intense and so forceful, he certainly fit the mold.

Besides, if she wasn't mistaken, that was a sizable erection her gun was aimed at.

"Could have fooled me," she said.

"Yeah," he said dryly. "Me, too."

ADAM had to force himself to keep his attention on Julia and that damned gun instead of his raging hard-on. It was a unique experience for him—both the difficulty in focusing and the explosion of sexual desire. Until now, he'd always maintained complete control over his mind and his body.

He sure as darkness hadn't experienced so much as a glimmer of sexual awareness for more lifetimes than he could count—until Julia Reynolds had walked into his private investigations office in Corpus Christi a little over six months ago. When they'd shaken hands, he'd experienced a one-two knockout punch from the realization she was a matched conductor—for *him*, a *Sanctioned*—and the ensuing stirring of a sexual surge.

His well-ordered place in the Universe had been upended ever since then.

She continued to challenge and surprise him, another rarity. But now he shelved his bemusement for a later time and forced himself to focus on the imminent threat of a .32 caliber-sized injury that might leave his voice an octave higher than it currently was. With minimal mental effort, he paralyzed Julia's trigger finger, then exerted invisible pressure against her arm, forcing it down at her side.

"Damn it!" she said furiously, her right shoulder jerking as she tried to move her arm. "Why do you always have to do that? Go around freezing things, or levitating things, or doing some sort of supernatural crap, stuff that goes against every known law of physics?"

"Obviously there are some unknown laws of physics, then, aren't there?" he pointed out reasonably. He demonstrated with a flick of his hand that released the gun from her helpless fingers. It hit the pavement with a metallic thud.

Her eyes narrowed. "I don't consider magic tricks, voodoo, or forcing people against their will at all scientific. Just sneaky and underhanded. Your forte, I believe."

But he knew that despite her caustic words, she had accepted the existence of Sentinels and Belians, as well as the fact that both were reincarnated Atlantians. Just as he knew her reactions to him and the situation were based in part on the horrendous assault she'd endured twelve years ago. That and her fear of not being in control. He understood her very well, even though he wasn't sure what it was about her that struck such a chord inside him.

She couldn't be called pretty, although she had flawless skin and a razor-sharp intelligence that gave her brown eyes an intriguing glow. But her face was too square, her eyes minimized behind tortoiseshell glasses, her wavy brown hair cut to chin length with no effort at style—all making her appear ordinary. She didn't wear makeup and favored earth-toned pantsuits that did little to enhance her voluptuous figure.

A lot of beautiful women had come on to him during his lifetimes, but none had affected him sexually, like Julia did. That was caused by the Sentinel/conductor energy, a link that dated back thousands of years to Atlantis, he reminded himself. Except as a Sanctioned, he shouldn't be affected by it. Yet he was.

"There is nothing sneaky or underhanded about my

actions," he said. "I entered the pub, sat next to you, and explained that I need your help. *I'm* not the one who pulled out a concealed weapon and threatened castration."

"You've been stalking me. Having me watched like a common criminal. You should be—"

"Julia, be quiet and listen to me. I didn't come here to match wits or verbally spar with you."

She tossed her head, started to speak, but a flick of his hand froze her vocal chords. "No," he said firmly. "You will not speak, and you *will* hear me out."

Panic flared in her eyes and she stiffened. But then she drew a deep breath and let her body relax against the car. *Smart lady.* Adam had paralyzed her vocal chords once before in Dallas, so she knew what was happening and that there would be no permanent damage. Her eyes, however, clearly telegraphed her fury. He wouldn't be leaving any sharp or dangerous objects within her reach any time soon.

He stepped closer to her, sensed the increased pounding of her heart. "I wouldn't be here if I didn't feel the situation was crucial," he told her. "One of my Sentinels has disappeared, and I'm unable to get a clear reading on him. I don't know what's happened to him, but I have to find out. You're the only person I know who might be able to help me."

"I've called the police," came another voice.

That statement jolted Adam's attention away from Julia. He turned to find the bartender standing there, her open cell phone in her hand. Her gaze was locked on him like a nuclear missile on a target. Behind her was a man in suit pants, dress shirt, and tie, with a name tag on the shirt pocket—probably the pub manager.

Adam groaned inwardly. The Universe was definitely throwing curveballs today. He stared back at the bartender, not pleased with the suspicious expression in her eyes. *She can't possibly suspect anything about my true identity,* he told himself. Yet a warning flickered through his senses. *Great.*

"The police are on their way," the man behind her said, his voice shaking slightly. "Move away from the lady."

Hearing sirens in the distance, Adam knew he only had a moment more to try to convince Julia to help him. He returned his attention to her, his gaze drilling hers. What he was about to do went against his normally ironclad code of never forcing compliance from a conductor, yet he felt the desperate situation warranted it.

"I'm sorry, but I'm hoping you can see something that will help," he said, taking Julia's right hand with his left. He opened the channel to Matt's energy. She gasped, her body jerking as if zapped by a jolt of electricity. He felt the energy transfer, saw the flickering flashes in her eyes.

The sirens grew closer. While he could manipulate minds and events, he only did so when absolutely necessary—which meant he was out of time. With a frustrated growl, he released Julia's hand. She blinked, opened then closed her mouth. Then she swung her left arm—the one he'd neglected to immobilize—and hit him in the face with her purse.

Pain smashed through his nose. He could practically feel the agony ripping through axons and synapses and screaming into the neurons of his brain. Times like this made inhabiting a human body a bitch. "Julia!" he snapped out, mentally slapping her with enough force to shove her against her car. "Stop it now!"

Damn it. His nose hurt like hell. He pulled out a handkerchief, forcing the pain back to a dull throb, and began blotting the blood. He eyed her in disbelief. "That was totally uncalled for." Even if he had just forced a vision on her.

She struggled to move, but he kept her pressed against the car. Her chest heaving against her burgundy jacket, she glared at him. She tried to speak, but nothing came out, since he hadn't released her vocal chords.

He drew a deep breath—through his mouth—and

reached for control. He could never—*ever*—harm an innocent. Julia might be a pain in the rear, and she'd definitely injured him, but she was both human and an innocent. He could heal the nose, but not now. The sirens were very close.

He stepped back, looked toward the bartender and the manager. "Please note that the lady attacked me, not the other way around. However, I won't be pressing charges." He glanced at Julia. "You and I will be talking *very* soon."

He strode away. He didn't release her until he was at his Mercedes. With one last look at her, he got in, started the car, and pulled out. He passed two police cars headed for the pub and shook his head.

Well, that had certainly gone well. But whenever Julia was involved, he could count on unpredictable reactions and outcomes.

The lady was definitely a challenge.

But she was about to learn she was no match for him.

THE voices were incessant, a cacophony of disjointed words and sounds ricocheting in his mind. He felt like a shattered mirror, splintered into a thousand excruciating shards. Where was he? Where was Susan? God . . . no . . . she wasn't dead. *She couldn't be!*

But she is . . . she is, whispered a voice, the words a knife, stabbing, stabbing, stabbing. Plunging into his heart, slicing at his humanity. Shredding his sanity.

The voice grew stronger, cutting through the melee of noises, like a bullet ripping through flesh. *Where was your One, your god, while she writhed in agony?* it taunted. *While she cried out to you to save her?*

Where was The One? Where? Where? The words echoed as if he were in a void.

Help me! he tried to shout, but no words came out, only a guttural sound that couldn't be coming from him. There was no response, only the odd hissing of the taunting voice.

It snaked through him, wrapped around his decimated heart, slithered into his dying soul.

And the Light went out.

He would make them pay! Reaching out a hand toward the nearest blurred figures, he released the force of his pain.

TWO

Julia walked into her house, both her leg and her head throbbing. To add to her misery, she didn't even have a good alcohol buzz, much less the numbness of a drunken stupor. And didn't she deserve—hadn't she *earned*—that oblivion? Damned straight, she had. And damn Adam Masters for interfering.

If not for him, she could be totally inebriated, blissfully unconcerned with William Bennett's imminent release and the inexorable nightmare memories.

She could also be totally unaware of her traitorous body; of the stirring sexual needs that had been absent these past twelve years. Needs that should be even further subjugated by the memories, but instead had flared to life the moment Adam sat next to her. *The bastard*.

And maybe she could even forget the awful vision that had filled her mind when he took her hand and opened his energy to her—oh yes, she'd known exactly what he was doing. Images of chaos and pain and destruction had roared through her with a terrifying ferocity that would have knocked her off her feet—if she'd hadn't been plastered against her car, compliments of Adam's mental manipulations.

The smug, arrogant, chauvinistic, overbearing, stubborn, infuriating bastard.

And hadn't it been fun dealing with the police and Miriam and the pub manager after Adam left? She should have pressed charges against him, should have started the process to issue some sort of restraining order against him. Except . . . she had attacked him, not the other way around.

Remembering the blood pouring from Adam's nose, the utterly calm and deliberate way he'd stared at her as he blotted it, as he shoved her against her car without lifting a finger, she felt a rush of guilt. She'd never been a violent person, had never hit anyone in her life—until today. That was Adam's fault, too, another transgression to add to the long list of grievances against him.

Still, she didn't feel very proud of herself. Two wrongs *never* made a right. She went to the bathroom and got four ibuprofen tablets. She would have preferred the narcotic kick of Vicodin, although she rarely took it. But, ever practical, she reasoned that might not be a good idea since she'd had two drinks before Adam had butted in.

After she'd bloodied him and dealt with the police, she'd aborted her plan to drink elsewhere and had come home. To a house that had been her haven these past years, but at this moment, felt more like a tomb.

Stop it! she told herself. That was the shock, fear, and alcohol talking. She'd always been pragmatic and rational, steady and completely predictable. Dramatics had no place in her well-ordered life. Nor did self-pity.

She got a glass of water, swallowed the ibuprofen, collected her purse and briefcase, and went to her study. Cataclysmic events notwithstanding, as long as she was sober, she might as well grade math papers.

Plus she needed to call her sister, Marla—and later, her parents. They should know about William Bennett. Her cat, Sir Isaac, was curled on a stack of periodicals on her desk. He stirred when he saw her, stretching and coming to his feet with a high-pitched meow.

He was a large, long-haired Siamese, a stray who'd taken up residence on Julia's doorstep right after she'd returned from Dallas six months ago. Her sister had gotten a pregnancy and a gorgeous husband from the Dallas adventure, if you could call tracking down a maniac killer and suffering knife wounds an adventure; Julia had gotten a cat. She'd never been one for pets, but Sir Isaac had had other ideas.

He padded across the desk and butted his head against her arm, demanding to be petted. "Hello, Ike," she said, stroking him. "How was your day? Any phone calls informing you that a violent rapist was being released early from prison? Any visits from an obnoxious man with superhuman powers?"

Sir Isaac responded by trying to rub his entire body against her and almost falling off the desk. She moved in closer. "I didn't think so. Lucky you. Want to trade places with me?" He gave her his cool, superior stare. Of course he didn't; he was no fool.

She set her purse and briefcase on the desk, eased herself into her chair. Sir Isaac got lowered to the floor. With an indignant meow, he meandered from the room. Julia fished her cell phone from her purse, remembered she'd turned it off after the phone call from the Texas Department of Criminal Justice. She had an absolute limit of one phone call like that, hopefully per lifetime, although zero was preferable.

She clicked on the phone and saw that Marla had called three times. Guess the TDCJ had shared the good news with her, too. She dialed Marla's number.

Her younger sister picked up after one ring. "Jules, where have you been? I've been trying to get you all afternoon."

Caller ID was a wonderful thing. "I'm sorry. I had my phone turned off." Julia felt a sudden tightening in her chest. "Marla, did you get a call from—"

"From the system that's supposed to uphold justice and theoretically protect the innocent? Yes, I did. The idiots."

Julia blew out a shaky breath. "Yeah, well, I can tell you it made my day."

"God, I can imagine. You want me to come over for a while?"

Marla knew better than anyone what Julia was feeling, since she'd been there. She'd tried to come to Julia's defense when William Bennett attacked, getting broken bones and a ruptured spleen for her efforts. Then she'd been forced to watch while he'd beaten and raped Julia. Great memories for sisters to share.

"No. I'm fine," Julia lied.

"Like I believe that. Listen, I don't mind coming over. It might be my last chance for a while. Somehow Adam found out about Bennett's release, and he called Luke. Luke's on his way back from Dallas as we speak. He probably won't let me out of his sight once he gets here."

Julia had no doubt about that. Marla's husband was a Sentinel, over six formidable feet of reincarnated Atlantian, pure testosterone and protective instincts. His purpose on Earth was to track down Belians and keep the innocent safe. He'd most likely chain Marla to his side once Bennett was released, not necessarily a bad thing. Julia didn't hold out much hope that Luke would take out Bennett, though; Sentinels weren't vigilantes unless Belians were involved.

"No, really, I don't need you to come over," she said. Her sister was six months pregnant and had no business driving across Houston at night. "I'm going to have to deal with the fact that Bennett is loose in the world sooner or later. Besides, I've got my tomcats—the Beretta and Ike."

Marla gave an unladylike snort. "So Sir Isaac is now a killer attack cat?"

Julia looked into the hallway, where Ike was sprawled on his back, paws in the air. "He's getting there. Speaking of Adam, I saw him today."

"Oh, really? I didn't know he was in Houston. Did he come by your office at the university?"

"Actually, he tracked me down at the Red Lion Pub."

"Oh." Marla paused, and Julia could almost feel her surprise—more probably shock. Julia never—okay, rarely—went to bars. "Well . . . That's very interesting. Wasn't the last time you saw Adam at the wedding?"

"Yes, it was." Then there had been three wonderful months without his irritating presence in her life.

Julia had a sudden memory of Adam at Marla and Luke's wedding and reception. He'd been very arresting in a dark gray pin-striped Armani suit and a maroon silk tie, the diamond in his ear catching the light. He'd also been incredibly annoying; his midnight gaze tracking Julia as she did her best to avoid him. Later, he'd been surprisingly graceful when he danced with Marla, and had charmed their unsuspecting parents.

No, none of that. No positive thoughts about Adam Masters. He was a sneaky bastard and at the top of Julia's persona non grata list. "I guess all good things must come to an end," she muttered.

"This is definitely a day for surprises," Marla said. "What did Adam want?"

"Oh the usual . . . that he needs me to help him. I'm the only one he knows who can do it, etc., etc. Something about a missing Sentinel."

"A missing Sentinel? Oh, man, that's not good."

"Of course it's not, and I'm really sorry about it. But then the jerk tried to force a vision on me, mentally slammed me against my car, and paralyzed my vocal chords—again." *And I probably broke his nose.*

"*What?* What do you mean, *again*?"

"Second time on the vocal chord thing. He did it in Dallas, too."

"Oh, that. Luke did that to me once. These guys really have an unfair advantage over us mere mortals. What about the forcing a vision and slamming you against the car?"

"He didn't really slam me, just shoved me firmly," Julia admitted grudgingly, still feeling bad about Adam's nose. "But he deliberately forced the vision on me. The first vision in Dallas was by accident, and the subsequent times he convinced me I had to do it for the good of humankind. This time was totally against my will."

"Sounds like something Adam might do, all right. He didn't hurt you did he?"

"No, not really." Another guilty twinge. Darned if she wasn't going to have to apologize to him the next time she saw him—which she suspected would be in the very near future.

"Great," Marla said. "So, did you see anything in the vision?"

The so-called visions were something Julia had begun experiencing twelve years ago, after Bennett had attacked her. It was as if the assault had thrown a switch in her brain; she'd begun seeing things before they happened. Not a flood of events, but the occasional precognitive flash, usually about someone she knew.

Then Adam had discovered that if he took her hand and channeled energy patterns he'd internalized, she could see a future event related to that particular energy.

Adam said it was because she, like her sister, was a conductor, an opposite-sex human psychically wired to link with Sentinels and enhance their psychic tracking abilities when they were hunting Belians. Just like that, Julia had become a valuable commodity to the Sentinels in their search for a bomber terrorizing Texas.

She'd helped catch the bomber, but she didn't intend to

spend her life "seeing" horrendous events and experiencing unimaginable evil. Nor did she want anything to do with Adam Masters and the unsettling sexual energies his presence stirred. She'd been sexually active before the attack, but since then had felt no desire to experience that type of intimacy with a man again—and most certainly not with Adam Masters.

Besides, there were other conductors available and all too willing to help the Sentinels in their quest to dispatch evil Belians to Saturn for "rehabilitation." Since conducting usually involved sex—incredible, mind-blowing sex, she was told—many conductors didn't seem to mind the trade-offs.

However, according to Adam, there weren't a large number of conductors, plus a conductor had to be a specific match to a Sentinel's energy. And wasn't it wonderful that Julia just happened to be a precise match for him—an anomaly, because Sanctioned weren't on Earth to perform conductions. *Not.*

And not my problem, she tried to tell herself. She had her own demons to battle, even more so now that her attacker would soon be free.

She returned her attention to Marla's question. "What I saw in the vision wasn't very specific. I think it was a theater of some sort, filled with people. It looked like they were rioting, or stampeding to get out. They were screaming, hitting, and trampling each other. But I don't know where it was, or what set off the panic. It was just . . . chaos." Still seeing the mayhem in her mind, she shivered.

"Oh, well, that's helpful."

Marla's vintage sarcasm eased some of Julia's tension. She smiled. "That's me, all right. Helpful—a Girl Scout, through and through."

"So what are you going to do about Adam?"

The tension returned. "I don't know. But I'm sure I'll be dealing with him tomorrow, or sometime soon. For tonight, I'm going to have a long soak in the tub, then go to bed."

"Good plan. When in doubt, hit the tub, and go heavy on the scented bath salts. Throw in a few drinks—oh wait, you've already been at the Red Lion. Maybe skip the drinks. You could eat chocolate instead, and you could sharpen the bottom of your cane—in case you need to stab Adam with it."

Julia laughed, allowing her body to relax. "I can always count on you to give me great advice."

"That's what sisters are for."

"Of course." Julia thought of how Marla had charged to her defense twelve years ago, of the horrendous injuries she'd sustained. "Thanks, sister. And, Marla, I'm so glad you have Luke and a baby on the way. You deserve to be happy."

"So do you. Jules, what happened wasn't your fault. It's time to stop blaming yourself. Time for you to be happy, too."

"I am," Julia protested. *Happy in an "everything under complete control and strict order" kind of way.* "You know I love teaching."

"There's more to life than going to work every day, Jules. But we'll have to talk about this later. I hear Luke's motorcycle pulling into the garage. I'd better go. I love you. Call me tomorrow. We'll talk about . . . the other situation—and come up with some kind of game plan. I still can't believe they let that bastard out."

How could Julia keep forgetting she needed to deal with Bennett's release? Adam had her so aggravated and distracted, he was diluting her focus on the *real* threat to her sanity. She firmly told herself that Adam didn't even rate being a distraction.

"I'll call you," she told Marla. "I love you, too." She clicked off, sat there a moment. She was exhausted, but knew she was too wired to sleep.

With a sigh, she pushed up from the chair and grabbed her cane. She started for her bedroom and the adjoining master bath, then turned and picked up her phone. Digging in her purse, she pulled out her Beretta. The phone and gun were both going into the bathroom with her. God, would she ever feel safe again?

And, even though she'd had two bourbons earlier, she was also getting a glass of wine to drink while she was in the tub. No, null that. She was taking the *entire* bottle of merlot in with her.

If she was going to experience hell on Earth, at least she'd be buzzed while she burned.

THE hot water and Epsom salts eased her throbbing leg and aching muscles, but two glasses of merlot hadn't done squat to take the edge off the fear or blur the memories. Lying back against the vinyl tub pillow decorated with a poodle print—a gift from Marla—Julia gave in to the tears, something she rarely allowed herself to do.

Reynolds women were made up of stern stuff, always forged ahead in life, regardless of pain or hardship. But today's events had been beyond even Julia's stoic endurance. She clenched her eyes shut, felt the slow, hot slide of tears over her cheeks. Told herself it was a damned good thing that these ultraspecial days came along only once every twelve years or so.

The faint stirring of the air, or maybe it was the hairs standing straight up on her exposed arm, jolted her to a state of hyperawareness. Something wasn't right . . .

"Good evening, Julia."

Her eyes shot open, but couldn't quite focus. Feeling as if her heart had just become a battering ram against her chest wall, she came upright with a gasp.

Adam sat on the closed commode with elegant indolence, his arm resting on the vanity.

"What—" Julia sputtered, her attention momentarily derailed by the wineglass slipping from her hand and smashing on the ceramic tile floor. A red stain spread across the beige surface.

"We still need to talk," Adam said.

She'd never been a slow thinker, and she rapidly processed the facts. He'd broken into her home and into her bathroom—she knew she had locked that door. He'd invaded not only her privacy, but her personal space. All while she was naked, adding insult to injury.

Sudden, blinding fury roared through her, obliterating sanity and reason. She was going to kill him.

She jolted over the edge of the tub, reaching for the gun she'd laid nearby, but it skidded from her reach, as did the phone. She twisted toward her cane, which was propped by the tub; it levitated out of reach and drifted toward Adam.

"You son of a bitch!" She got her hand around the neck of the merlot bottle, but it was wrenched away from her slippery fingers and scraped across the tile to him. All the while, he sat there, seemingly relaxed, as if he hadn't just telekinetically moved four items.

Her chest heaving, she stared at him, dark and dangerous in black slacks and a black silk shirt, his calm facade a deceptive cover for his merciless nature. His cool gaze swept over her, eyes burning with power and an alarming possessiveness. Her anger receded, giving way to a frission of fear and another, more feminine reaction. Oh, God, she was naked.

She grabbed the shower curtain and yanked it as far forward as she could. Then she drew her knees toward her chest, ignoring the painful protest in her left leg. Mortification swept through her.

"I think it's a little late for that," he drawled from the other side of the shower curtain.

Her anger resurged, now indignant outrage. "You sorry, arrogant bastard!"

He ignored her outburst. "We have a situation calling for extraordinary measures."

"Oh, this goes *far* beyond that. Stalking, paralyzing, breaking and entering—"

"And what would you call fracturing my nose?"

She heard the edge in his voice. She'd crossed the line with that action, so he hadn't hesitated to cross a personal line with her. Some of her anger dissipated, but damned if she would apologize to him now.

"I'd say it wasn't nearly enough," she muttered, thinking she should have castrated him while she had the chance. "Get out, Adam."

"I don't think so. We *are* going to talk tonight, Julia."

In her mind, she saw a stadium-type scoreboard and Adam was winning, three to one. And she was too wrung out to battle him head-on. "I won't talk unless you get out of here and let me get dressed first."

"I rather like having you at a disadvantage. It makes things more manageable."

She glared at the shower curtain. "What, you can't handle me under normal circumstances?"

"Julia, there's nothing at all usual and customary about you."

"Look who's talking. Lots of normalcy in the Sentinel realm."

"Touché." There was a hint of amusement in his voice. It always surprised her when he displayed a sense of humor. After a moment of silence, he said, "If I give you a few minutes of privacy, will you agree to have a calm, rational conversation with me?"

"I'm always calm and rational." Okay, except around him.

"We're not even going to debate that one. But I'll wait for you in the living room. Let me do something first."

There was the sound of glass clinking, then a soft thud. "Step on the towel when you get out," he said. "Most of the glass is now to the side, but this will protect you from any stray shards. Don't keep me waiting too long." She heard the bathroom door close.

She peeked around the shower curtain, although she knew he was gone, because the vibrant energy that always crackled around him was absent. The bathroom was empty. One of her bath towels was folded double and on the floor by the tub.

Surprised by his consideration, she pulled herself up, using the handicapped bar she'd had installed when she moved in nine years ago. A wave of dizziness hit her, brought on by too many things—news of William Bennett's release, too much to drink, Adam Masters barging into her home and seeing her nude. A winning combination, guaranteed to unbalance any woman.

And if he'd been put off by her rounded figure and generous thighs, then wasn't that just too bad?

The thought sent a surprising twinge of regret through her. She wasn't a vain woman, had long ago accepted that Reynolds women tended toward plump bodies and plain looks. Since the attack, she had made no attempt at makeup or any other vanity. It shouldn't bother her that a sophisticated, savvy man like Adam Masters might find her unattractive.

Maybe the visual of her in the tub would be off-putting enough to make him go away. She suspected the statistical odds of that were slim. He wasn't here because of her looks. Drawing a deep breath, she held on to the bar until she was steady.

She stepped from the tub, careful to stay on the towel, and began drying off. *This is totally unfair*, she thought. After everything that had happened today, she still had to deal with Adam.

Fate was definitely in full bitch mode.

* * *

MIRIAM White sat at the desk in her bedroom, her laptop open before her. But it wasn't the computer that had her attention; it was the fifty-dollar bill in her hand, the one given to her by the man who had upset Dr. Reynolds so badly earlier today.

Miriam currently had Dr. Reynolds for two senior-level classes in math and physics, and she'd also taken her courses in previous terms. She'd never seen her professor rattled by anything. The woman was always calm, composed, and in total control of her class. She was brilliant and an excellent instructor, and Miriam admired the hell out of her.

She'd been surprised to see Dr. Reynolds at the Red Lion Pub six months ago; even more astonished when the professor asked her questions about a really hot guy who'd been in the pub several days earlier. Then Dr. Reynolds had taken an unexplained leave of absence before returning to finish teaching the course. Miriam had thought it very strange at the time.

Now, six months later and into the fall semester, Dr. Reynolds had surprised Miriam again with another appearance at the pub, this time slugging back liquor like the world was coming to an end. She'd appeared genuinely shaken up, which was odd enough. But then the man—Adam—had taken the seat beside her, and she'd been clearly agitated by his presence.

Curious, and feeling protective of her favorite professor, Miriam had done something she rarely did. She lowered her self-imposed mental barriers and tapped into what her grandfather called "the sight." She'd seen something she couldn't begin to explain, something that had put her on the shaken up side of the equation, right along with Dr. Reynolds.

"Miri, what you doing? You look like you seen a ghost."

She looked up, managed a smile for her father, who stood in the doorway. Although he'd come to America in the late 1940s, when he was a young boy, he still had an accent, most likely because his parents and grandparents had continued to speak Romani in their homes.

And although he was well-educated—a chemical engineering degree from Rice University—he sometimes lapsed into old childhood language patterns, especially when he'd been working eighty-hour weeks at his petroleum engineering firm.

"So you okay?" he asked.

She could tell him about it, about how she had used her ability today, and the startling results. She could tell him that Adam's aura was unlike anything she'd ever seen, that it was all white light. No colors, none of the rainbow spectrum of blue, green, red, yellow, orange, violet (varying arrays in most people); no black (usually signifying evil); no gray (usually signifying illness).

Just . . . *pure light*. Not any sort of normal human aura pattern that she had ever seen.

And while her father probably couldn't explain what Adam's aura meant, he wouldn't think what she'd done was strange. He had the sight, too, as had his father before him, and his grandmother before that.

But she didn't want to share this with him tonight. It didn't feel right. She managed a smile. "I'm fine, Papa. Just thinking."

"You think so much, Miri," he said fondly. "Too serious, working too much. You need to get out more, have fun. Maybe even find a nice young man."

Next he'd start going on about her hair and makeup and all the earrings. It was the only thing on which she defied him. She enjoyed being a little wild and different. It made life more interesting—and with her abilities, she really *was* a little weird.

"Ah, Papa, you'd just terrorize any man I bought home," she teased, although that might actually be close to the truth. Anyone she dated would be subjected to her family's intense scrutiny. "Besides, I meet a lot of people at the pub. I'm very happy with work and school."

He looked at her over his glasses. "Bring a nice boy home for Mama and me to meet. Maybe we surprise you."

"You might. Good night, Papa."

"Good night." He went on toward the kitchen, to indulge in his nightly ritual of Blue Bell vanilla ice cream.

Blowing out a breath, Miriam stared at the fifty-dollar bill. Funny thing about all the anecdotal stories regarding Gypsies—there was truth mixed in with the lies and the misinformation and the prejudices. There was actually a reason why one of the marks made by Gypsies, at least in those in Miriam's Romanichal lineage, was that of fortune-telling—and psychic abilities.

Miriam not only saw auras, but she also had psychometric abilities. She could read the history of an object by touching it, or pick up emotions of the person who had possessed the object, sometimes seeing events surrounding that person. She rarely tapped either ability, because she felt that doing so invaded people's privacy, and it fostered volatile situations and subjective conclusions.

Blessed with very high intelligence, she preferred logic and objective reasoning. She was her father's daughter, through and through. While she respected her Romanichal heritage and was also proud of being an American, her real passion was pursuit of knowledge in the sciences. She wanted to be an engineer, not a fortune-teller.

Thank goodness she was able to control her abilities—to shield herself and block them at will. She only resorted to her gifts when she thought it was necessary or would be helpful to someone. Today, not only had Dr. Reynolds been extremely rattled when Adam showed up, but something about the man had reached past Miriam's barriers, setting off her internal radars.

So she'd read his aura, which had been surprising enough. But then he'd handed her the fifty and strode off after Dr. Reynolds. Staring after him, Miriam had made the decision and opened herself to the energies absorbed by the bill.

The rush of images and energy had been startling, overwhelming, alarming, and . . . intriguing. She didn't exactly understand what she'd seen, but one thing was certain: The life force and events surrounding this Adam were beyond anything that was normal. It was as if he was not of this Earth.

She couldn't tell if he was good or evil, although Dr. Reynolds certainly seemed apprehensive about him. Enough so that she'd drawn a gun on him, which had truly shocked Miriam and spurred her to call 9-1-1.

More concern snaked through her. She couldn't ignore what she'd seen. She'd opened the door when she lowered her shields and tapped into the sight.

Now she'd have to do something. At the very least, she could try to warn Dr. Reynolds about Adam, to reinforce the professor's own obvious reactions to the man.

Miriam didn't know if her logical, ultra-intelligent professor would listen to her. It would probably destroy any respect she had for Miriam, any chance at a letter of recommendation for graduate school.

Even so, she had to do *something*. Miriam sighed. She'd speak to Dr. Reynolds tomorrow.

And hope to God it helped somehow, although after what she'd seen . . . She shivered. There were a lot of things out there—unseen things that weren't human, that were astounding and at the same time, utterly terrifying.

Darkness and light, balanced precariously against one another.

She had the unsettling feeling she'd just unveiled the face of a supernatural vortex that could go either way.

THREE

STROKING the long-haired Siamese that had insisted on invading his lap, Adam waited for Julia in a living area that was tastefully decorated, but felt cold and sterile. *She doesn't spend any time here*, he thought, looking around the room, which was done in sage green and gold. The sofa and loveseat had a formal, unused look, with every cushion in military precision formation.

There was none of her personal energy, no clutter, no knickknacks; everything was spotless. The bookcases along the far wall were the only exception to being unused, as they contained books that were obviously well read and carried Julia's vibration.

No, the heart of the house was the office across from the bedroom. He'd seen it after he let himself in through the front door, readily dealing with two dead bolts and then locating and disarming the security system.

He hadn't been inclined to ring the doorbell and have Julia refuse him entry. The urgency of the situation and the inconvenience of having to heal his nose and bruised face, not to mention dealing with bloodstains on his Gucci suit, had, to his way of thinking, negated formalities and good manners.

No one else ever defied him, much less inflicted physical injury. As a Sanctioned, he was one of the most powerful beings on Earth. He was responsible for every Sentinel and conductor in Texas, and for ensuring any Belians in the state were tracked down and removed. His was a disciplined, well-orchestrated operation, and no one had ever questioned his authority.

Until Julia. He had to admit she offered intriguing—if not painful—challenges. But he no longer had time to be indulgent. He had to take action fast.

He heard her coming down the hallway. Despite her handicap, she moved with surprising quietness, but his highly tuned hearing could pick up sounds that human ears couldn't.

She stepped into the living room. She had on a long, navy blue terry cloth robe over flannel pajamas, and wore plain navy slippers. She was well covered, probably a defensive tactic against him. A smile quirked the corners of his mouth. "Nice pajamas."

She looked down at the pattern of frolicking poodles. "They were a gift from Marla. You know she has a thing for poodles."

Adam thought of Bryony, Marla's toy apricot poodle who generally hated Sentinels, yet managed to be highly entertaining. The dog had even been part of the wedding procession when one of Adam's best Sentinels, Luke Paxton, had married Julia's sister. "Yes, I do recall that."

She stared at him, no trace of humor in her eyes. The knuckles on the hand gripping the cane were white with tension. "So talk."

He gestured to the armchair, which he'd left vacant in deference to her leg. "So sit." He saw the protest coming and headed it off. "No, Julia, we will not have this conversation with you standing. And I *will* be here as long as it takes to come to an acceptable outcome."

Her expression hardened. "Meaning until you have your way."

He didn't see any sense in pretending otherwise. "Sit, Julia. Please don't make me force your compliance." He rarely strong-armed humans; it was his sworn duty to protect them. But in crucial situations, or where Julia was concerned, sometimes it was a necessity. Not that she ever appeared intimidated by him.

"You really are a jerk, Adam."

"I won't argue that point." He wasn't a mind reader, but he could clearly pick up her tempestuous emotions, could see the red and orange flashes in her aura. Normally, she was calm and emotionally contained, to the extent that he had trouble reading her. Today was an exception.

She walked to the chair, casting the cat curled in his lap a contemptuous look. "Traitor," she muttered. "No more Fancy Feast for you."

Cats loved Adam; they seemed to sense his uniqueness and responded to the heat and light that was an intrinsic part of his energy. In return, he appreciated their discriminating intelligence and aloofness; their I-don't-care-what-anyone-thinks-go-to-hell-if-you-don't-like-it attitude. His own life was lived much along those lines.

He watched Julia laboriously settle into the chair. He didn't like the pallor of her skin, the pain haunting her eyes, or the fact that now that her anger was abating, her aura had a faint gray tinge. She was mentally and physically exhausted, but he feared they were running out of time and he had to press forward. Since this afternoon, he had a new concern.

"What do you know about the bartender who was at the Red Lion today?" he asked, addressing the latest matter first.

Julia looked confused. "The bartender? Do you mean Miriam?"

"Is that the name of the young woman who served our drinks, then called the police on us?"

"She called the police on *you*. She happens to think very highly of me. And yes, her name is Miriam. Miriam White."

"You know her?"

"She's one of my students. I've had her in several of my classes. She's the one who gave me Luke's name after Marla disappeared, which led me to you—unfortunately."

His concern increased. "Anything else you can tell me about her?"

"Why are you asking?" Julia's eyes narrowed. "Oh, no. Don't tell me she's a conductor. You are *not* going to involve her in your weird schemes, Adam. I mean it. She's a nice girl, and one of my brightest students."

He held up a hand to head off a possible tirade. "She's not a conductor, as far as I can tell. There was just something about her, like she somehow knew I was different." He considered, decided to let the matter go. "Forget it. I'm sure she was just concerned because you were upset."

"You think?" Julia muttered.

"Let's talk about the reason for my visit," he said, addressing the more crucial matter. "I told you earlier today that a Sentinel is missing."

"Do you think he—I assume we're talking about a man—is dead?"

"This is a male Sentinel, his name is Matt Stevens, and he's not dead. But he hasn't contacted me in over five days, and he's not answering his phone or responding to e-mails. I sent someone to his house in San Antonio, but he wasn't there."

"Then how do you know he's still alive?"

"Because I'm picking up intermittent flashes of his life force. Then it will fade out, as if he's losing consciousness, although even then, I should still be able to sense him. Perhaps he's somehow being shielded from me. Then I'll detect his essence again, and then it will wink out. I've never experienced anything like this before."

"Can you sense the life force of every Sentinel in Texas?" she asked, jumping to the obvious conclusion.

"Yes." Adam realized he would have to answer Julia's off-topic questions. She possessed a brilliant intellect, further enhanced by good common sense. Her intelligence was a definite asset. Besides, she would balk if he didn't explain things to her; he knew firsthand how stubborn she could be.

"Think of every Sentinel in the state as a computer in a network, with me as the network server," he explained. "I can sense and track the individual energy patterns for each Sentinel in the network."

"Can you communicate through this so-called network?"

"Not usually. Most Sentinels don't have the ability to send or receive telepathic messages over great distances."

"But *you* can?" she asked, catching the fact he hadn't included himself. Even tired, she didn't miss a beat.

"I can telepathically communicate with other Sanctioned or High Sanctioned." Since the High Sanctioned didn't have physical bodies, telepathy was the *only* way he could commune with them.

She angled her head. "How about conductors? Can you track them as well?"

He knew she wouldn't like the answer, but opted for honesty. "Yes. Once I've met the conductor and familiarized myself with his or her energy pattern, I can keep track of that person." Basically, he internalized the energy and it became part of him. He was a conduit of numerous life energies.

Her mouth thinned. "Oh, that's just great. 'Big Brother is watching' has become a reality. And here I thought your bathroom trick was bad enough."

Adam didn't rise to the bait. The truth was he didn't regret invading Julia's privacy. Letting her know he could, and would, give as good as he got had been justifiable. If he allowed her to get the upper hand, she'd be even more difficult to manage.

Besides, seeing her nude had been an added bonus, one he hadn't expected. He wasn't completely nonhuman, and obviously not immune to the sexual energy engendered by close proximity to Julia. He'd discovered her body was magnificent, full and curvy, not the thin, angled frame of so many contemporary women. Yes, a pleasurable experience, for the brief moments it had lasted. No regrets there.

What did bother him, however, were the tears he'd seen tracking slowly down her face, and the sense of despondency she'd projected, so unlike her. The Julia he knew was both fire and ice, a woman who fought valiantly for her loved ones. A vital, intelligent woman whose quick thinking and decisive action had saved both Marla and Luke's lives in downtown Dallas six months ago.

He felt a flare of fury against William Bennett, for what the man had done to Julia and Marla, and the renewed pain his release in two days would cause. But Bennett would never have the chance to get near Julia again. Adam would see to that.

He exhaled, forced his focus back to the problem at hand. "I'm not Big Brother," he said. "My only concern is the welfare of the Sentinels and conductors in my region."

"And completely under your command," she snapped. "Let's not forget that." At least her ire had brought back some of her color.

"Tell me about your vision today," he said, shifting gears.

"Oh, the vision you forced on me?"

"The same." No apologies on this, either, although it was his general philosophy that conductors should not be coerced.

But Julia had already given her services in Dallas; not only that, she was a matched conductor to him—a Sanctioned—an occurrence that was totally unprecedented, as far as he knew. Sanctioned didn't do conductions and, up until now, did not have synchronized conductors. There had to be a reason for the match.

"What did you see, Julia?" he persisted. He noted the rebellious set of her jaw, and added, "A man's life could hang in the balance."

She sighed, relented. "Not anything I believe would be helpful. I saw some sort of theater, filled with people, who started panicking and screaming and trying to get out. Many of them were trampled. Then everything faded."

"Any idea where this was?"

"No," she said, her frustration evident. "There wasn't anything to identify the place."

"Did you see what started the panic? Was there gunfire or explosions of some sort?"

She shook her head. "All I heard was the screaming."

"Something else, perhaps, like fire?"

"Now that you mention it, there may have been smoke. . . ." Her gaze became unfocused, as if she were turning inward. "Or maybe it was just dust reflected in the light."

"Any idea what type of theater? Movie, live production?"

"No . . . I didn't see the front area, just the graduated elevations of rows of seats. It could have even been an auditorium, like a college classroom." She threw up her hands. "I'm sorry, Adam. It flashed by so quickly."

He considered asking her to try for another vision, but she looked so drained, he opted against it. "Nothing to be sorry about," he said. "I know you can't control the flow of a vision. It's fortunate that you see as much as you do."

"Fortunate for whom? Seeing glimpses of the future is a pain in the rear. It's almost as bad as dealing with you."

"Ah, there's the Julia I know."

"I've given you the information you wanted. Now, are we through?"

He glanced down at the cat, scratched between its ears. "I need you to go to San Antonio with me tomorrow." He felt her shock shoot out like a solar flare.

"I can't do that. I have classes to teach."

"Matt Stevens lost his wife four months ago. They had been married twenty-two years." Adam looked up, locked gazes with Julia. "She was killed by a Belian."

Her expression mirrored horror and sympathy. That was something he admired about both Marla and Julia— they genuinely cared about others, perhaps because of their own painful experience.

"I'm so sorry for him," Julia said. "But I can't go to San Antonio."

He ignored her protest. "I've been extremely worried about him. He's been in a deep depression, and I suspect he's been drinking heavily. To have him suddenly start fading out like this is very alarming. Think about it, Julia."

Adam continued to hold her gaze. "It could be one of two things. He could become open to Belian influence, or he could go off the deep end on his own. Either way, he's far more powerful than normal humans. He could be very dangerous and a real threat."

He could practically see the information processing in her mind. Her eyes widened as she stared back at him. "A Sentinel gone rogue?"

"That's what I fear. Matt is one of my most powerful and experienced Sentinels. I'm not confident another Sentinel could take him down, and I wouldn't ask that. This is something I have to do. You can see why I need your help."

"No, I can't. You're a big boy, Adam. You've being doing this for—what did you tell me—hundreds of years?"

"If Matt has gone rogue, you're probably the only one

who can tell me what he'll do next, where he'll go. We have to find him before he hurts someone. It may already be too late."

"Damn it, I-I can't do this." She rubbed her forehead.

It was obvious she was too exhausted to think clearly. He shooed the cat from his lap, frowning at the long white hairs plastered to his black wool pants. Standing, he offered her his hand. "You need to get some rest."

She ignored the hand and struggled up on her own. "I intend to, as soon as you leave and I finish grading papers for my class on Friday."

He shook his head, his patience gone. She was swaying on her feet, and he was responsible for her welfare. He didn't give a damn about class papers. He raised his hand toward her. She was going down—now.

The burst of energy was so subtle, so swift, she didn't even have time to register it. She sagged forward, and he caught her and swung her up into his arms.

She wasn't a small woman, but his superhuman strength allowed him to carry her with ease. He strode down the hallway to her bedroom. She was soft and warm in his arms, so unlike the prickly woman he normally dealt with. Her scent, a mix of lavender and vanilla, drifted up, teasing his senses.

He couldn't remember the last time he'd held a woman like this. Especially one whose mere nearness sent his body on full alert with a flood of testosterone, and gave him his second hard-on of the day. The last time he'd been affected like this had been six months ago, when he'd first shaken hands with Julia.

The time before that had been about . . . two or three hundred years ago.

Ignoring his newly raging libido, Adam lowered Julia to her bed, slipped off her robe and slippers, and slid her beneath the covers. He sent a powerful mental command, insuring that her sleep would be deep and dreamless.

Staring down at her, he noted that the lines of tension on her face had eased. But they'd be back tomorrow. So would her acerbic personality—as soon as she discovered that she *was* going to San Antonio with him, and that he had manipulated circumstances so that she had no choice in the matter.

Absolutely no choice at all.

JULIA fumed as she drove her white Honda to the university. Adam Masters was . . . he was—oh damnation, there weren't enough uncomplimentary adjectives in the known Universe to describe the man. Although *sneaky* and *devious* certainly topped the list.

She had awakened this morning with no recollection of going to bed the night before. Her groggy state and the stack of ungraded papers on her desk, along with the memory of Adam demanding she accompany him to San Antonio and then ordering her to get some rest, enabled her to draw a conclusion that had high odds of being accurate.

It was infuriating, and also disconcerting, to know she'd been manipulated by him, and totally at his mercy. And that he'd most likely put her to bed, as if she were a child. Well, she could be just as determined and obstinate as he could. She wasn't going to become involved with any more Sentinel crap, and she was not—repeat, *not*—going to San Antonio with him.

For all his forcefulness and the power he wielded, she knew there were lines even Adam couldn't cross. She didn't believe he would do anything illegal, such as kidnap her. She was well aware of the Sentinel code of honor, and while he might stretch the boundaries to the limit, he would never desecrate that code. He could try to wear her down verbally and mentally, but she was stronger than he realized, and she was now familiar with his tactics.

He might be used to getting his way with everyone else,

but Julia didn't cower before anyone. The hell she'd faced twelve years ago had irrevocably hardened her. An image of William Bennett flashed though her mind. Tomorrow he'd be free. Fear rose, swift and brutal. Her chest tightened and her heart stuttered.

Another reason why she couldn't help Adam. She had to deal with this new upheaval in her life, come to terms with it, and somehow fortify her defenses. She wasn't giving up her carefully cultivated life, her career at the university, just because a monster had been set free. Bennett wasn't going to win.

But right now, today, she would focus on math and science, on the students she prodded and tried to inspire on a daily basis. She'd concentrate on one of the constants in her life, outside of family—the joy of sharing knowledge, of teaching.

She parked in her handicapped space, got her briefcase and cane, and entered Hoffman Hall, the hub of the mathematics department. Her main office was here, although she also taught physics and had a small cubicle at the Science & Research building.

As she got off the elevator at the sixth floor and walked down the corridor past various offices, she was soothed by the textures of academia: the photos of distinguished alumni and staff lining the walls; the scent of coffee mingled with the musty flavor of books and paper; the muted sounds of copiers, printers, phones, and voices.

Some of the terrible tension inside her eased. This was her world, her existence, her lifeblood. She was alive and vital here. She could lose herself in the intricacies of university politics, in spirited discussions on various theorems with her colleagues, and in the classroom with her students.

She took a moment to stop at the main reception area, to check her mail slot and say hello to Tami Lang, the office manager and assistant to Dr. Elias Moreno, the head of the mathematics department.

"Hey, Dr. Julia," Tami, an attractive, vibrant woman in her forties, greeted her. Tami was a force in her own right—an energetic whirlwind who was ruthlessly organized yet glowed with true Southern charm. "How are you today?"

"Fine," Julia said, forcing a cheerful front. "Anything new or interesting going on this morning?"

"Well, there's the usual shortage of funds, political backstabbing, and staff grumblings," Tami replied. "And then . . . we have this really hot guy who is meeting with Dr. Moreno right now." She gave Julia a knowing smile. "Is there something you haven't told us?"

Julia stared at her, confused. "What are you talking about? And who is the man meeting with Dr. Moreno?"

"Mr. Masters. I assume you know him. When he came in this morning, he said it was urgent that he speak with Dr. M. Then I heard him mention your name before Dr. M. closed the office door." Tami fanned herself with a periodical. "Mr. Masters is *very* impressive."

Oh, no. The heart palpitations returned. This was bad—very bad. "How long has he been in there?" Julia turned and started toward Dr. Moreno's office.

"About thirty minutes. Where are you going? Wait—"

But Julia wasn't about to stand on ceremony, not with Adam loose in the math department. She strode to Dr. Moreno's door, bracing herself for major damage control. Before she reached it, it swung open, and Adam stepped out, followed by Dr. Moreno, who was positively beaming. Since the diminutive Spanish man rarely even smiled, this was a very bad sign indeed.

Adam, looking his usual *GQ* self, was wearing a charcoal gray suit, set off by an elegant gray and red striped tie. "Good morning, Julia," he said, showing no surprise at seeing her.

She gripped her cane, too stunned to react. Dr. Moreno stepped around Adam, his expression turning sober. "Dr.

Reynolds, you should have phoned. You did not have to come in today, not under the circumstances."

"Circumstances?" For a crazy, jumbled moment, Julia thought Adam must have told the department head about William Bennett. She'd never discussed that part of her past with anyone at the university, had kept her career separate from her personal life.

"I am so sorry about the death of your Aunt Willie." Dr. Moreno patted her shoulder awkwardly. "I understand you were very close to her. Please accept my condolences. Certainly you will want to attend the funeral in San Antonio."

"My Aunt Willie?" Julia shot a scathing glare at Adam. "Funeral in San Antonio?"

"I felt I needed to tell your boss," Adam said smoothly. "Considering how upset you were, and how concerned about taking time from work."

Julia's blood pressure shot up. "You told him *that*?"

"It is good your cousin did so," Dr. Moreno interjected. "You take very little personal leave or vacation, Dr. Reynolds. You must certainly attend your aunt's funeral!"

Julia's gaze shot back to Dr. Moreno, another shock piling up on the first. Her boss was very strict about leave and discouraged employees from taking personal days. He'd been somewhat difficult when she'd taken off suddenly six months ago.

Her eyes narrowed and she turned back to Adam. "You did something to him," she hissed. "You took control of his mind—"

"I knew if I explained the situation, he would fully understand your need to take off a week or two to bury poor Aunt Willie and settle her affairs," Adam said, with a warning look.

"A week or two!"

"Take all the time you need," Dr. Moreno said. "I have already spoken with Dr. Richards, and he has agreed to take your math classes. I'll speak with Dr. Bruce about your physics courses, and I am sure he will be able to get them covered."

Julia swayed, suddenly light-headed. "But—"

"It is fine. Fine!" Dr. Moreno said brightly. He nodded at Adam and waved what looked like a check. It appeared to have quite a few zeros in the amount. "Thank you again, Mr. Masters, for your most generous donation to the department's expansion fund."

Adam inclined his head. "It's the least I could do, especially since one of your best professors will be on hiatus for an indeterminate amount of time."

Generous donation? Indeterminate amount of time? Julia lifted her cane, trying to decide where to hit Adam first.

She was abruptly smothered by two arms going around her, followed by the warm press of a soft body and the scent of Organza perfume. "Oh, Dr. Julia, I am so sorry about your aunt," Tami said against her ear, and hugged her tighter. "I didn't know you had family in San Antonio."

"Surprise, surprise," Julia muttered.

Tami released her, and she drew a deep, shuddering breath, considered her options. She could tell Dr. Moreno and Tami that she'd never seen Adam before in her life— that he was delusional, and they needed to call security. But that was risky, and Adam might be able to override her, either by freezing her vocal chords—again—or using some sort of brain control over her coworkers.

She desperately tried to think of another solution, but nothing came to mind. Adam had so neatly boxed her in, she didn't see a way out. Of course, once she left the office, she could simply refuse to go anywhere with him.

Dr. Moreno cleared his throat. "I hope the interview while you are in San Antonio won't be an imposition. Your cousin—Mr. Masters—assured me that you would be glad to do it, that it would be a welcome distraction from your grief."

Feeling like she'd stepped into *The Twilight Zone*, Julia

could only stare at her boss. "Interview?" Add sounding like a parrot to the mix.

"Yes. You are aware we have been evaluating candidates for two open teaching positions?"

And where was this going? "Of course."

"Well, one of the top candidates is Dr. Melissa Curtis, and she is currently in San Antonio. Mr. Masters suggested you could speak with her while you're there, and offer an evaluation on her suitability for the mathematics department." Dr. Moreno's gaze darted to the check in his hand, then back to Julia. "I would be most interested in your input. I've already spoken with Dr. Curtis, and she said she will await your call. Tami has her phone number."

The sharpest box cutter wouldn't get Julia out of this, unless she wanted create a major scene, which she had already ruled out, and risk her position at the university, a position she'd worked extremely hard to attain.

She shot a venomous look at Adam, wishing a thousand agonies on him. He stared back blandly, apparently smart enough not to display a victorious smirk. She'd find some way to make him pay for this.

"I'll write down Dr. Curtis' phone number for you." Tami went behind her desk and pulled out a file. "Oh, and do you have the name of the funeral home for your aunt?"

"The arrangements haven't been finalized yet," Adam told her. "We'll have to let you know later."

Julia was furious and so upset, she was shaking. Clenching her free hand, she drew a deep breath, tried to calm down. She felt trapped, much like she'd felt when William Bennett had pinned her to the ground, and it was an awful feeling. Adam had a lot to answer for.

"I need a few minutes in my office," she said, amazed at how steady her voice was. She bared her teeth in a feral smile at Adam. "You can go on—*cousin*. I'll catch up with you later."

"Oh, I don't mind, waiting for you—*cousin*. When you're done here, I'll follow you back to your house, and we can load your things into my car for the trip."

The bastard had thought of everything. Seething, she started for her office. Adam wisely stepped out of her reach as she marched past him. He was also astute enough not to follow her. She entered her office, barely resisting the urge to slam the door. Sinking into her chair, she grabbed her head in utter frustration and thought about screaming. Of course she couldn't do that either, so she settled for gritting her teeth until her jaw ached.

Damn, damn, damn!

She didn't see a good way out of going to San Antonio, but she'd let Adam Masters know he had no true power over her. Never again would she give away her personal power. He could force her to go with him, but he couldn't force her cooperation.

If she decided to help him, it would be her decision— not his. Assuming he lived long enough, which didn't have a high probability.

HE woke up groggy and disoriented. Through blurry, gritty eyes, he scanned his surroundings, which were unfamiliar. He was in a cheap hotel room, sprawled on a polyester bedspread, an empty whiskey bottle near his pounding head. Where was he?

He tried to get up, groaning as his head throbbed even more, and the room seemed to spin. Where . . . Susan . . . The realization hit him, as it did every time he gained consciousness. Susan was dead. The knowledge cramped his gut, clamped a relentless vise around his heart.

He wanted that vise to squeeze harder, harder. To destroy his heart and end this eviscerating pain. But it never did. His cursed heart kept beating, forcing him to go on.

He managed to sit up. He had no recollection of how he'd gotten here. Ignoring his aching head, he tried to concentrate, getting visual flashes of explosions, smoke, screaming people. What the—?

You don't know what you did, do you? a voice hissed in his mind. *You would be shocked to know what you're capable of. Of the violence that lurks inside you.*

"Stop!" he gasped, grabbing his head. "Who the hell are you?"

Remember the fear emanating from the people? The screams? The blood? Beautiful, beautiful blood. Feel it calling to you.

"No . . ." But he felt a dark stirring inside. He dragged his shaking hands in front of him. Stared at the filth and blood crusting them. God, what had he done?

Susan is dead. Rotting in the ground. You will never see her again.

"Shut up! Don't talk about her!"

Your grief is dragging you down. You're a drunk and you're weak.

"Get the hell away from me!" He tried to scramble off the bed, staggered and fell to his knees.

You're far too weak. You're no match for me.

He felt the insidious undertow, tried to fight it. But it sucked him under, into the beckoning allure of the Darkness.

Where the pain faded, replaced by rage and bloodlust.

And power surged.

FOUR

MIRIAM knew Dr. Reynolds was usually in her office before her first class each day, so she decided to look for her there. She was nervous, and had absolutely no idea what she was going to say to her brilliant, practical professor.

Well you see, Dr. Reynolds, I have psychic abilities, which I inherited from my Gypsy ancestors. Yeah, that should go over well in the logical, scientific camp.

Miriam got off the elevator and hesitated, again asking herself why she should do this, risking a relationship with a professor she admired and respected, as well as a possible shot at a scholarship. *Oh, right*—her mental checklist reminded her.

Point one: The Adam guy who approached Dr. Reynolds yesterday had a very strange aura that was all light.

Point two: Reading the energies from Adam guy's fifty-dollar bill indicated good battling great evil (and Miriam really needed to stop watching the Sci Fi Channel so much).

Point three: She'd had disturbing dreams all night, with distorted images of Dr. Reynolds and Adam and some other guy Miriam had never seen before, and a dark, threatening presence that had scared the hell out of her.

And most important was point four: Miriam's every instinct was on full alert, and the inner voice that she listened to and trusted absolutely was telling her she had to do this. Whenever she ignored that voice, she regretted it. So . . .

Squaring her shoulders, she strode toward Dr. Reynolds' office. She glanced idly at the reception area as she passed it, did a double take. Adam guy was right there, with Tami.

Oh, shit. Nearly stumbling, Miriam righted herself and scooted past the arched opening. Once on the other side, she leaned against the wall, her heart pounding. Catching her breath, she sidled back to risk a peek. Animated as usual, Tami was talking nonstop, and Adam's dark, intense gaze was fixed on her. He didn't appear to have seen Miriam.

Even without using her sight, she could see he radiated power. The dark suit looked good on him, emphasizing his tall form and black hair and eyes. The diamond stud in his ear gave him a piratical air. She dropped her mental shields slightly, took in the glaring white light around him, and then hastily raised them again. How could he be surrounded by glowing light and yet feel so shadowy and dangerous?

His presence here was further proof that he was involved with Dr. Reynolds in some way. Which meant Miriam's inner voice was right, as usual. Edging backward, she hiked her backpack over her shoulder and quickly walked to Dr. Reynolds' office.

Outside the partly closed door, she took another deep breath and knocked. Nothing. The door was cracked and the lights were on. She knocked again.

"If that's you, Adam, go the hell away."

Very strange. Miriam opened the door a little farther. "Dr. Reynolds, it's Miriam White."

"Oh, sorry. Please come in."

Dr. Reynolds sat in her chair, her face flushed, and her hair completely mussed. Her normally neat desk had books and papers stacked on it, and a large, flat-bottom briefcase was open by her chair.

She waved Miriam in. "Sorry for the mess. What can I do for you?"

Miriam looked around, sensing agitated energy scattered through the physical disorder. She'd never seen the professor or her office like this. "Are you okay, Dr. Reynolds?"

"Oh, I'm just great," Dr. Reynolds said, her voice strained. "I'm getting ready to go on a trip. What do you need?"

Miriam sank into the visitor's chair, swallowed hard. "I don't know how to tell you this, but I'm—uh—I'm somewhat . . . intuitive."

"Oh. Really?" Dr. Reynolds leaned back in her chair. "Must be a full moon or something causing all this woo-woo crap."

"Excuse me?"

She waved her hand again. "Don't mind me. This day has just been full of surprises. What about you being intuitive?"

"Well, I am somewhat . . . psychic, although I know that probably sounds strange to you. But I can sense things sometimes. I've, uh, got some concerns about that Adam guy you were with yesterday."

"You and me both," Dr. Reynolds muttered. "Actually, I don't think you're strange at all, Miriam. If anything, this is a good indication of your intelligence. Anyone in their right mind would have concerns about that 'Adam guy.'"

Oh, man, this was too weird. "You know he's in the reception area?" Miriam asked.

"Unfortunately, yes. Was he alive when you saw him?"

"Uh, yes, he was."

"Damn. I knew it was too much to hope for a lightning bolt to strike him dead, especially inside Hoffman Hall."

"Dr. Reynolds, are you *sure* you're okay?"

She gave a mirthless laugh. "That's relative, don't you think? I'm alive. I'm healthy. Why let little things like early release programs, overbearing Sentinels, Aunt Willie's funeral, and a psychic sightseeing tour of San Antonio bother me?"

Miriam tried to sort through the hodgepodge of odd things just thrown out. She settled on what seemed the safest—albeit unhappy—subject. "Your aunt died? I'm so sorry."

"Oh, don't be. I didn't know her at all."

Nor did the professor look grief stricken. She looked . . . angry. Miriam was even more confused. "I'm sorry, all the same. Like I said, I'm here because I felt I needed to warn you about Adam. I know this is even weirder, but I can see auras and—" She paused to see how her professor was taking this.

"And his is black, right? Probably the same shade as his heart—assuming he has one."

Okay, so maybe Dr. Reynolds was having some sort of psychotic episode. Brilliant people were often known to have erratic mental health.

"Actually, his aura is white. Pure white light. It's not a normal aura. Most people have a variety of colors around them."

Dr. Reynolds stared at her. "Fascinating. I've never given much thought to auras and what they might mean. So Adam's aura is abnormal. That figures."

"It's definitely unusual. And there's more."

"There always is, where he's concerned. What else?"

"I think he might be involved with some sort of . . ."

Miriam inhaled, then plunged in. "Dark forces. I know that sounds wacky."

"No, actually it doesn't. While this discussion may not be scientifically based, I know exactly what you're talking about."

"You do?"

"Afraid so." She started putting papers in the briefcase. "As a matter of fact, that's why I'm going to San Antonio. That, and for a pretend funeral."

A pretend funeral? "I don't understand."

Dr. Reynolds sighed. "Trust me, it's best that you don't know. I'll be gone for a week, maybe more. Dr. Richards will be covering my math classes."

Oh, great. Richards was such a dork. Miriam could teach the class better than he could. But that wasn't the issue right now. She mentally backtracked over the conversation. "Does your trip to San Antonio have anything to do with Adam?"

"We're going together. He thinks I can help him with a situation there. We'll see about that."

"But what about you pulling a gun on him, and the dark images I'm sensing, and his strange aura?"

Dr. Reynolds was silent a moment, then she leaned forward. "Listen, I must apologize. I'm not quite myself today, and I'm talking off the top of my head. Don't worry about Adam, or whatever dark images you might be picking up. It's just a little problem he's having, and he wants me to accompany him. Nothing you need to worry about."

She slid some books into the briefcase. "I do appreciate you sharing your concerns with me, and your willingness to disclose your abilities. Not everyone understands that sort of thing, so it took courage for you to do that."

"But, Dr. Reynolds—"

"We'll have to discuss it more when I get back," she interjected firmly. "Until then, feel free to contact me if you have any problems with your courses. You do have my e-mail address, don't you?"

That information was on every class syllabus. Miriam nodded. "Yes."

"Let me give you my cell phone number as well, just in case." The professor rattled it off as Miriam scribbled it on her backpack. Then Dr. Reynolds said, "I'm really sorry, but I've got to finish gathering what I need to take with me. Perhaps we can schedule a meeting after I return."

"Sure." Effectively dismissed, Miriam stood, still not reassured. "Be careful. Have a safe trip."

"I'll be fine, but thank you for your concern. Good-bye."

Miriam left reluctantly, opting to take the back stairs rather than go back by the reception area. Well . . . that whole thing with Dr. Reynolds had been very odd. Extremely out of character for the professor. Miriam didn't feel very good about the outcome, either.

Something was terribly wrong. And although her internal alarms were clamoring full force, she had no idea what to do about it.

JULIA pulled into her garage, the door already lowering behind her car. Adam parked in the driveway and got out, taking his umbrella with him.

He inhaled deeply. The local weather bureaus had given only a 20 percent chance of rain, but he was attuned to the natural forces, especially any form of water, and he could feel the moisture gathering. It would be raining shortly.

He walked up the sidewalk to the front door. The beds fronting either side of the porch were immaculately maintained, with small, trimmed shrubs and pine bark covering the dirt.

But there were no plants or flowers—no color to brighten up the yard or neat brick house. Much like Julia dressing plainly and not wearing makeup, as if she'd declared a moratorium on living life to the fullest twelve years ago. Adam was of the opinion she'd done just that.

He rang the doorbell, heard it chime through the house. He waited, rang again. There was no sense of inside movement toward the door. Since he'd been behind Julia the entire way from the university, she knew very well who was ringing her doorbell. She simply wasn't going to respond.

Not that he blamed her—he'd definitely pulled a fast one on her today. He'd gone over that fine line he'd always insisted the Sentinels under him respect. But he also knew that in real life, situations weren't always black or white. This particular scenario had a lot of gray—and a lot of potential to become extremely serious, with far-reaching consequences.

Still, Julia wasn't exactly a willing participant, and she was being dragged into the thick of it, with her life being disrupted in the process. William Bennett's release would have created a certain amount of upheaval, however, without Adam's presence.

Concluding she wasn't coming to the door, Adam held his palm toward the double dead bolts, willed them to turn. He gestured the door open. He stepped into the neat tiled foyer, closed the door behind him, and hooked his umbrella over the knob. The long-haired Siamese was lolling in the hallway, but when he saw Adam, he sprang up and trotted toward him with a welcoming meow.

At least someone was happy to see him. He leaned down to give the cat a few strokes, then used a mental command to send him on his way. Flaring out his senses, Adam located Julia in her bedroom. He strode to her room, pausing in the open doorway.

She was in the walk-in closet, struggling to heave a suitcase off a high shelf. He noted that her purse was on the bed, hopefully with her gun still inside it, reducing the chances of him being used for target practice.

He moved to the closet. "Let me get that," he offered, getting an elbow shoved into his midriff for his trouble.

"Get out," she snapped.

Ignoring the discomfort—she'd used a surprising amount of force—he took down the suitcase. "Where do you want this?"

She yanked it away from him, a murderous glint in her eyes. "I don't think it's anatomically possible to put it where I want it."

He accepted her anger, as well as the fact that he was the cause. Opted to work around it—for now. "Anything I can do to help?"

"You can go to the kitchen, get my sharpest knife, and impale yourself upon it."

Avoidance didn't seem to be working. "I think I'll pass on that. Perhaps we should have it out now and clear the air. It appears you need to vent."

"What I need is my life back. For you to go away, and leave me the hell alone!" She pushed past him and limped toward the bed, dragging the suitcase behind her.

He followed, keeping a watchful eye on her purse. "Julia, you know that's not going to happen. At least not until we've had a chance to find Matt."

"Then by all means, let's get to San Antonio as quickly as possible. The sooner I can get you out of my life, the better." She heaved the suitcase on the bed, raked him with the crystal-sharp gaze that he felt certain could put the fear of God in her students. "You can wait in the living room while I pack."

"I'll do that." In the interest of keeping things manageable, he weighed confiscating the purse against enduring her ire. But if he couldn't hold his own against one very angry math professor and her purse and gun, he might as well leave his physical body and return to the ethereal plane. Julia would certainly like that, but he wasn't close to calling it quits on this lifetime. Besides, he enjoyed the challenge she presented.

So he left her to packing and settled into the wingback chair in the living room. The cat immediately jumped into his lap and began purring. Stroking him absently, Adam took out his cell phone and made some calls. The first was to his secretary—actually she preferred to be called an administrative assistant—but old habits died hard.

Although they inhabited mortal bodies, Sentinels lived longer than regular humans, assuming they didn't get killed, and Sanctioned lived even longer than Sentinels did. Adam was considerably older than he looked, and through the years and changing times, he had had to readjust his vocabulary.

He told Cheryl he would be handling some business in San Antonio, and asked her to make reservations for him and Julia. After leaving her with instructions for dealing with various projects and possibilities, he called Luke Paxton. Luke was one of his best Sentinels, and just happened to be married to Julia's sister.

Both Marla and Julia were strong conductors, a discovery that had alerted Adam to the startling possibility that there could be hereditary links between conductors.

Up until then, the birth of human conductors had appeared to be a purely random phenomenon. Conductors were able to psychically link with Sentinels and enhance their tracking abilities, so they provided crucial assistance in hunting down Belians. Since there were only a small number of known conductors, even less of conductors who were precise matches to individual Sentinels, any knowledge that could help Sanctioned and Sentinels locate conductors was vital.

It was becoming even more important in light of the fact that the Belian population appeared to be increasing, while less Sentinels were being born. They needed every possible advantage in the ongoing war against the Darkness.

"Hey, Adam," Luke answered.

"Hello, Luke. How is Marla?"

"She's pretty shaken up about Bennett's release."

"That's understandable. It would be extremely unsettling to have your attacker set free."

"You're telling me." Luke blew out a breath, and Adam could picture him running his fingers through his long blond hair. "Man, I'd like to personally escort that lower-than-a-Belian scum to the fires of Saturn."

Adam felt the same way, but unfortunately, terminating human lowlifes didn't fall under the Sentinel directive. "I trust you're aware you're not to approach or harm Bennett in any way, unless he threatens innocents."

"I know, damn it." Luke's voice vibrated with anger. "But I don't have to like it."

"The reason I'm calling is I'm going to be tied up for a while and I need you to keep surveillance on Bennett while I'm out of pocket."

"That's fine by me. I'd prefer to know where that bastard is at all times. What's going on?"

"We've got a problem in San Antonio. I'm heading there to deal with it."

There was a pause on the other end. "It's Matt, isn't it?"

"What makes you say that?"

"He didn't sound like himself the last time I talked with him. Seemed off."

"And you didn't inform me?" Steel edged Adam's voice. All his Sentinels knew he wanted to be informed if anything, no matter how trivial, seemed wrong or out of place.

"I just assumed it was because he was grieving over Susan. But it's more than that, isn't it?"

"I'm afraid it might be. I haven't been able to get in touch with him."

"Ah, shit. I guess I screwed that up. I'm sorry, Adam."

"Just keep me informed whenever anything appears odd to you."

"Do you think Matt might be dead?"

"No, he's alive, but I can only sense him intermittently."

"That's not possible, is it?"

Adam decided to keep his suspicions to himself for now. He trusted Luke implicitly, but he didn't want his Sentinels to feel they had to provide backup in possibly taking down one of their own. That was his responsibility alone.

"Apparently it is possible," he said, "although I've never come across this before. So I'm going to check on Matt, and I want you to keep track of Bennett while I'm gone. Get Davis and Stamos and any other initiates not on assignment to tail him. I want him covered 24/7."

"Will do. I'm assuming we don't need to worry about Julia. She talked with Marla a little while ago. I understand she's going to San Antonio with you, and that's she's not too happy about it."

"That would be an understatement." Adam looked up as the lady wheeled her suitcase into the foyer. She was talking into her cell phone.

"No, Mom, it's just a business trip for the university. I'll leave out plenty of food and water for Ike. You just need to check on him every few days and scoop the litter. Marla can't do that, because of the pregnancy." She shoved the suitcase upright, using so much force, it pitched forward before rocking back. "I couldn't tell you before now. The trip was arranged without my prior knowledge."

She gave Adam a look that would wither the sexual organs of a mortal man—not that his appeared to be entirely immune—and stomped off toward the kitchen, holding her cane in a death grip. It was going to be an interesting trip.

He returned his attention to Luke. "Julia's safety will be my responsibility."

"I guess you tracked her down at the Red Lion Pub yesterday because of Matt. This must be really serious if you're pulling her in."

Knowing how close Julia and Marla were, Adam wasn't surprised Luke knew about the pub. "I don't know yet how serious the situation might be. But I think Julia's assistance will be crucial. She's going along with it . . . for now."

Luke had the nerve to laugh. "I wish I could be there to witness the fireworks. Good luck, boss."

"A little respect for your superior would be appreciated."

Luke was unrepentant. "Yeah, well, you have *my* respect. But Julia's is another matter entirely."

"I'll handle her." He hoped. "You keep track of Bennett and let me know immediately if anything comes up. I want daily reports, either e-mail or phone."

"I'll take care of everything here, and contact you every day."

"Good. My best to Marla." Adam snapped his phone shut, slid it into his coat pocket, and headed to the kitchen. He stepped in, saw Julia pouring dried cat food into two large bowls. She still had the phone against her ear, and with his enhanced hearing, he heard a line ringing, then a man's voice answer.

"Hello, Jeff?" She shifted, set the cat food down. "It's Julia Reynolds. I'm sorry, but I have to cancel on you."

Cancel? Who was this man? Adam hadn't found any evidence of a boyfriend when he'd thoroughly investigated Julia six months ago. But he hadn't checked since then. He felt a startling surge of possessiveness that shocked the hell out of him.

"I have to go out of town," Julia was saying. "We'll have

to reschedule." She listened a moment. "No, it's nothing serious, just a business trip. I don't know when I'll be back, so I'll have to call you. . . . Oh, thank you. Sorry this is such short notice. . . . You, too. Good-bye."

She disconnected, glared at Adam. "I can't believe I had to do that. I've been waiting weeks for him."

He stiffened, experiencing a totally alien emotion. Surely that wasn't jealousy. "Waiting weeks?"

"Yes, weeks. And I've had to deal with this damn leak all that time."

Now confusion rolled through Adam. "Leak?"

"Yes, leak." She raked him with another testicle-curdling gaze. She certainly had the look perfected. "You know, a hole in a pipe—that's a metal cylinder used to carry water—and water leaking through the hole and causing damage. I have one in my bathroom. Jeff Delozier is the best plumber in Houston, maybe all of Texas. It's difficult to get him. I've been waiting three weeks for him to come fix it. And now I have to reschedule."

Adam felt an inordinate sense of relief that this Jeff was nothing more than a professional contact for Julia. Then, disconcerted by his feelings, he sternly ordered himself to put aside his odd reaction. Despite the fact that Julia was a perfectly matched conductor to him—and that it was un-heard of for a Sanctioned to match with a conductor, much less participate in a conduction—he couldn't allow emotions to cloud his judgment. Too many people depended upon him.

Still, his reaction was fascinating, something he'd ponder at a later time. He didn't intend to ignore the match with Julia, not that he could, after the visions he'd seen. There were very few coincidences in the Universe, so there was a reason for the link between Julia and him. He would open himself to guidance, and make use of the match as necessary.

He'd have to learn to deal with the emotions that apparently went with such a bond. Along the way, he'd enjoy the unusual and intriguing challenges that were certain to occur in dealing with Julia Reynolds.

FIVE

IT started raining as they exited the loop onto Interstate 10, big fat drops that fell sporadically at first then picked up in intensity and velocity. Adam switched on the wipers and turned up the radio, which was set to a local station playing an eclectic mix of blues, jazz, and light rock. Julia was surprised he hadn't chosen a classical music station. He seemed the type.

The rain and decreased visibility didn't seem to bother him—not that she'd ever seen him perturbed about anything. But then she suspected he was a cold-blooded species, or possibly an android, disguised as a human.

She wasn't normally affected by rain herself, but the gloomy aura of the day only served to drag her deeper into a rare funk. Unfortunately, she wasn't an automaton like Adam. Despite her best efforts, her emotions surged in tumultuous waves, pounding through her in random, nonlinear patterns. Dark memories of William Bennett and the ensuing gut-twisting fears mingled with indignation and fury aimed at Adam Masters. The added sense of loss of control over her life flowed into the already unstable mix of emotions.

She clenched her hands in her lap, battling to regain her normal ironclad self-control. Over the past twelve years, she'd become a master at ruthlessly steamrolling her emotions into a smooth, manageable pavement. She'd created a life cocoon of logic, discipline, order, and, most importantly, predictability. Perhaps it was a dull existence, but it helped her feel safe—and in control of her life, which was vitally important to her.

Now both William Bennett and Adam Masters were destroying the cocoon, which had been her lifeline to sanity and functionality. Bennett was the reason she'd had to burrow behind walls in the first place, and damn him for breaching them now. The same went for Adam.

Right now, every time she glanced at him, sitting there so utterly contained and smug, she felt more agitated. She was glad she'd broken his nose, not that he'd suffered for long. Yet her vehemence bothered her. She wasn't a violent person, had never wished harm on anyone—except when it came to Bennett or Adam.

Funny how the two men created similar upheavals in her life.

She looked out the window. The rain had slowed to a fine mist. The sudden, increased volume of the radio drew her attention. She looked over to see Adam adjusting the sound, his expression intent.

In what sounded like a newscast, a female voice was saying, "Don't yet know the cause of the fire at the IMAX Theater in downtown San Antonio around eight last night. Investigators are saying flames started in several different parts of the theater, setting off mass hysteria. At least three people are dead, and an undisclosed number were treated at area hospitals for injuries and smoke inhalation. There is speculation that it was arson and police are saying . . ."

The woman droned on, but the shock ricocheting through

Julia blocked out the rest of the words. *Fire? In a San Antonio theater?* Flashes from her vision yesterday replayed in her mind. Smoke, screams, terrified stampeding.

"You knew about this?" she asked.

His gaze flashed to her. "Yes." Keeping one hand on the wheel, he reached between the seats, pulled a soft leather briefcase from the back, and handed it to her. "There's an article in the morning paper, if you want to see it."

She was having trouble assimilating the data. She managed to get the satchel open, slid out the newspaper. The story about the fire was on the front page. She stared at it, her thoughts a kaleidoscopic jumble. "How long have you known this?"

He glanced back at her. "It just happened last night."

Which was his evasive way of admitting he'd known about it since then, probably as soon as he left her house. She looked at the article again, disbelief and anger blurring her vision. "You knew about this, and you suspected it's what I saw yesterday. But you didn't bother to tell me."

"There's nothing you could have done. We'll sort it out once we get to San Antonio."

Rage simmered inside her. "You kept me in the dark this morning. Rather than tell me what my vision was, and instigate a rational discussion about how this might provide a concrete reason for me to go to San Antonio, instead you resorted to lies and subterfuge to force my compliance. You—Oh!"

Fury exploded like a nuclear blast. "You son of a bitch!" Blindly, she struck out at him with the newspaper. "You sneaky, lying bastard!"

She felt the car swerve before Adam righted it. "Julia! Stop!" She didn't care if he wrecked the damn Mercedes. She wanted to pound some of her own pain into him.

Realizing the briefcase was a much more substantial weapon, she smacked him in the head with it. "You Neanderthal! You arrogant, overbearing jackass!"

"Damn it, Julia!" He pulled over to the shoulder of the highway, began slowing.

Pure emotion driving her, she had her seat belt off and the door open before the car stopped. As it lurched to a standstill, she swung her legs out, grabbed her cane, and took off. She didn't know where she was going—not that she could see past the red haze wallpapering her vision.

She only knew that if she didn't get as far away as possible from Adam Masters, she would explode from the rage. There would be nothing but raw, bleeding bits of her scattered like debris from a plane crash.

"Julia! What are you doing?"

She ignored him, her focus on navigating the downward slope from the road. But with her bad leg, she couldn't maneuver the wet grass and uneven surface. She felt her leg slipping out from beneath her and tried to catch herself by digging in her cane. The next moment, she was on her rear, bumping down the incline. She ended up sprawled out like a rag doll, her backside throbbing from the fall.

Adam was there in an instant, kneeling beside her. "Are you all right?"

Gasping, she tried to sit up, but he pushed her back down. "Be still until I'm sure you didn't break anything." He started running his hands along her legs.

She smacked his arm. "Get the hell away from me!"

Lightning quick, he grabbed her shoulders and pinned her to the ground as he leaned over her. His black-as-sin eyes glowed with preternatural power. His expression was fierce with anger. "You'd better damn well accept the fact that I'm not going anywhere. And I *will* check you for injuries, with or without your cooperation. I'll keep you in place by force, if necessary. This can be easy or hard. Your choice, Julia."

Knowing he wouldn't hesitate to immobilize her, she sagged back and closed her eyes, trying to still the trembling that wracked her body. She also tried to ignore the feel of his hands sweeping over her legs, arms, and beneath her.

His touch was firm but also surprisingly gentle. It sent a tingling rush of heat through her body, setting off that damned chain reaction of sexual need. It certainly wasn't calming.

"Would you hurry up?" she snapped, opening her eyes to glare at him. "I want your hands off me."

"You're lucky they're not thoroughly warming your backside. What the Darkness were you doing?"

For the first time, she noticed the redness and swelling on the side of his face, compliments of her hitting him with the briefcase. He was still angry, if his glowing eyes were any indication. Her own anger surged. "Trying to get away from you and your power games."

His lips firmed. "So we're back to that. I've already told you I am *not* going away. The sooner you accept that, the better. Can you sit up?"

He slid his arm around her and she struggled upright. "How do you feel?" he asked.

She was stiff and cold, but that appeared to be the worst of it. "I'm fine. Just let me get up."

He helped her, grasping her upper arms and steadying her as she made it to her feet, feeling about as graceful as a drunken elephant. She looked down at her wet, muddy, grass-stained suit and felt chilled to the bone.

"You're shivering. Here." He slipped off his expensively tailored suit coat and wrapped it around her.

Heavenly warmth and his unique scent surrounded her. She took a deep breath, felt her aching muscles protest. "Thank you," she murmured.

His expression closed, he retrieved her cane from the ground and handed it to her. Then he took her arm, turning her toward the car. As she struggled up the incline, he put his arm around her again, easily propelling her up the slope.

When they reached the car, she saw the engine was off, although her door was still flung open. Adam stopped by the door, blocking it. "Before we get back in the car, and I remove all possible weapons from your reach, I think we need to deal with your anger. Tell me what set you off."

"Why? It doesn't seem to matter what I say. You won't listen."

"Funny, but I believe I've said that about you." His gaze was steady and serious. "I'm listening now. Talk to me, Julia."

Just like that, the resentment and outrage rushed back in a torrent. "All right." Her voice shook, and she took a shuddering breath. "I'll tell you. You charge into my life, disrupting it and forcing a horrifying vision on me. Then you invade my privacy—my bathroom, for God's sake. You . . . you—"

Her voice broke, and hot tears flooded her eyes. Oh, great, she was going to cry. She *never* cried—hadn't given in to self-pity for a long time. She blinked furiously to hold the tears at bay. "You're no better than Bennett."

Genuine shock flashed across his rapidly bruising face. "By the Light, how can you say that?"

Of course he couldn't understand. He was a pompous ass. "You took away my choices. You forced me against my will. Whether it's physical or mental, it's still a personal assault."

And to her, it was. After Bennett, she'd promised herself no one would force her to do *anything* ever again.

"You took away my personal power," she whispered, her throat constricted. "But I refuse to be a victim ever again." Her tenuous control cracked, and the tears spilled over. "And you made me lose control. *Damn it!* I hate when that happens!" She turned, took a step away, mortified that he should see this moment of weakness.

He grasped her arm. "You are *not* going anywhere."

She tried to jerk free, like that was going to happen,

with his super-Sanctioned grip. She settled for keeping her back to him while she struggled to pull herself together.

"I don't suppose you'd allow me to hold you and offer comfort," he said quietly.

She was surprised by this oddly nurturing gesture from him. How long had it been since anyone had held her, to give comfort, or anything else for that matter? How long since she'd felt safe and cherished? Oh, it was tempting. But this was Adam, she reminded herself—demanding, controlling and threatening on far too many levels. "Don't even think about it," she retorted.

"Then at least look at me."

She sniffed, scrubbed at her face with her free hand. "Why?"

He made an exasperated sound, grabbed her other arm, and turned her toward him. Determined to regain her composure, she lifted her chin and glared up at him. The compassion in his eyes unsettled her even more.

"Julia, you are not—will never again be—a victim. You are a brave, resourceful woman, and you have my utmost respect."

He must be up to something—he was being far too nice. "Like I believe that."

"It's the truth, but you'll just have to take my word for it."

She tried to hold on to her anger, but it was edged out by a growing physical awareness of Adam, of the feel of his hands on her arms, of his scent and heat and vitality. Of a growing sexual need permeating the emotional fog. Back to that again. She supposed it was better than the pain. Marginally.

She pushed against him and he loosened his hold, but didn't relinquish it. "Are you all right now?" he asked.

"Oh sure, I'm just grand. I think it's safe to conclude the meltdown is over."

"Then you should feel better."

Despite her personal mantra of logic and control, his neutral reaction annoyed her. "Do you always have to be so freaking calm?"

"One of us has to be," he pointed out.

The rest of the fight went out of her. "It's usually me," she said wearily. "I'm always the voice of objectivity and reason."

His tugged her closer, one hand sliding to her shoulder. "I think you're a brilliant woman. Quite capable of logic, when your focus isn't disrupted."

"And I think you're an overbearing jackass."

"You've already said that. You might try for something new and original." His hand moved to skillfully massage the knot of tension between her shoulder blades.

It felt so good she almost moaned. *Great.* Her control was still in shreds. She shoved against him again. "Let me go, Adam."

He did, but she noticed he shifted so that she was hemmed in between the car, the open door, and him. He obviously wasn't taking any chances. "It's cold and wet. Why don't we get back in the car to finish this discussion?" he suggested, still in his annoying reasonable mode.

But he was right. Shivering despite the protection of his coat, she got into the car. He waited until she was settled, then closed the door. He came around and slid behind the wheel, closed his own door. After tossing his briefcase, her purse, and her cane onto the backseat where she couldn't readily reach them, he turned toward her, one hand resting on the steering wheel.

Despite the fact his once-crisp shirt was now filthy, he was cool and composed, while she was a mess, inside and out. She felt oddly compelled to defend herself, although she had no reason to impress this man. "I'm normally not weak like this."

"I never thought you were. That's why I resorted to

strong-arm tactics. I assumed it was the only way to gain your cooperation."

"You know what they say about people who 'assume.'"

The corners of his sensual mouth kicked up. "Ah, there's that acerbic wit. Yes, I know what they say." He leaned over, reached inside his coat she was wearing, and produced a handkerchief. "Here."

She took it, her gaze sweeping over his bruised face. First his nose, now this. "I'm not a violent person, either."

One ebony eyebrow arched. "Really?"

"Yes, really." She slipped off her glasses, blotted her eyes with the handkerchief.

"Julia, I owe you an apology."

She lowered the handkerchief. "That's the understatement of the year." Okay, so maybe that was the pot calling the kettle black, since she probably owed him a few apologies, but still. "I just can't believe you're admitting it."

"Why not? You're right. I didn't stop to think that my actions put me in the same league with Bennett, perish the thought. Free will is a tenant of humanity, and of the Sentinel code of honor. I should have respected your choices. I assumed that since you had assisted us once, you'd do so again, and that the situation warranted desperate measures. I'm truly sorry my actions stirred memories of Bennett."

He sounded so sincere, she felt the tightness in her chest easing. "Bennett's release from prison had already resurrected the memories. But an apology from you is very . . . unique." She cocked her head, studied the swelling along the right side of his face. "I think I hit you too hard. Maybe you have a concussion."

"What I have is a conscience. And the Sentinel code of honor I'm sworn to uphold. In my concern over the situation in San Antonio, and my refusal to ask my Sentinels to hunt one of their own, I overstepped the boundaries." He leaned back, stared out the windshield. "I'm taking you home."

Surprise jolted through her. "Back to Houston?"

"Yes. I should never have forced you to come with me."

"But . . . what about Matt Stevens? The fire at the IMAX?"

"I will deal with them as soon as I reach San Antonio."

"What about the fact I'm supposed to interview Dr. Curtis for a position with the math department?"

He shrugged. "As I said, you're very resourceful. You'll think of something." He started the car, adjusted the heat to a higher level.

She considered this, righteous indignation building. He was telling her what to do again. He'd jerked her around, created upheaval in both her personal and professional lives. And after everything, he was going to toss her back into the melee of her personal life, a mess that he'd created? Like hell he was.

"Wait just a damn minute. You can't make this decision for me. I get a vote here." She shifted toward him, poked his arm hard. "Who died and made you God?"

He started to speak, but she held up her hand. "Don't answer that. You're definitely not God, although you think you are. Let's get something straight. You've made it very clear that I have free will. Therefore, I'm choosing to exercise my right to make my own decision. I'm going to San Antonio with you."

"Julia—"

"Adam!" she mimicked him. "For once, you're not calling all the shots here. You dragged me into this. You're not getting rid of me so easily."

"I'm beginning to see that. What exactly has convinced you to help me?"

She wasn't even sure herself. She picked up the crumbled newspaper, smoothed it out to study the article. "A lot of people were there for me after . . ." She shook her head, shutting off the memories. "For some reason, the attack left me with this ability to see future events. If it can assist you in helping that poor tormented Sentinel and preventing more people from being hurt, then I can only assume I'm supposed to go with you."

He did a passable job of keeping the smugness out of his expression. "So you're accompanying me of your own free will?"

She gave him her narrow-eyed professor look. "I just said that. But let me clarify something else. I won't jump just because you tell me to."

"Really? There's another surprise. Now let me tell *you* something. You *will* agree to defer to my knowledge and experience in these matters. To listen when I give you crucial directives."

"I'll concede you're the expert here. I do actually have enough good sense to listen when necessary. But I also want your word that you won't do any of that pseudo magic crap to me. No paralyzing stuff."

"I will not give my word on that. If I think you're in danger, or for that matter, if I'm in imminent peril of losing a body part because of your temper, I won't hesitate to do what I think necessary."

"I don't have a temper. I'm very rational and calm."

"You're quite capable of becoming a loose cannon."

She gave an unladylike snort of denial.

He raised an arrogant *I'm-right-and-*you*-know-it* eyebrow.

They glared at each other a moment.

He finally inclined his head. "Shall we call a truce?"

She considered. "For now."

A quick smile flitted across his lips. "Oh, I certainly wouldn't expect the peace to be permanent." He stared at her another long, unsettling moment. "You know, Professor," he continued, "since you have made the decision to work with me, there is one other thing you need to keep in mind."

"What's that?" she asked warily, suspicious of the sudden glow in his eyes.

He lifted his hand to the side of her face. "This."

Just that one touch sent tingling frissons of sensation down into her body. "Not going there," she said firmly, trying to shove his arm away.

He didn't move. His fingers were warm against her chilled skin, generating combustible sparks at points due south. He leaned closer. "There's this perfect, precise conductor/Sanctioned match between us. Not to mention what I've seen in my visions."

Her body went on full red alert, alarms blaring at every key nerve junction. And he was merely touching her. "I don't want to know what you've seen." She pressed back against the seat, tried to squirm sideways and create more distance between them. But there was nowhere to go.

He slid his other hand along the opposite side of her face, effectively trapping her head. Starbursts of light flared in his eyes, and the air around him glowed brighter, like a halo.

Her heart started racing faster than sound, constricting her chest and making it impossible to say anything else. Worse, she found herself leaning toward him, as if being pushed by an invisible force. This was so *not* good.

"There's no need to tell you what I've seen, because your body already knows," he said, his harsh voice mesmerizing. "It recognizes a bond that goes back thousands of years. A bond that is both highly spiritual and"—he leaned in, brushed his lips against hers, sending a bolt of pure electricity through said body—"physical. Very physical," he murmured.

Erotic need rushed through her veins like molten lava. *Not good, not good, not good*, her mind chanted, even as her body voted to take this further and instigate a deeper kiss. *No, damn it!* It took every ounce of will she possessed to turn her face away, and give a hard shove against Adam's chest. He released her, sank back into his seat.

"I already told you in Dallas that there would be nothing

physical between us. Absolutely *no* conductions, no sex," she said, as soon as she could muster enough air. And why the hell wasn't he breathing as hard as she was?

"Denial doesn't change the truth, Julia. It won't stop what's already been set in motion. But don't worry. Whatever happens between us will be completely of your own free will."

She didn't like the sound of that. She wanted to argue, to fiercely debate and vehemently insist that hell would freeze over before she'd become involved in any way with Adam. But he was a master at verbal sparring, and right now, she wasn't up to stepping into the ring with him.

She needed to regroup and reorder her thoughts and what was left of her decimated routine—not to mention corral her unruly body. She had to get her balance and find some center of calm in the storm that swirled around Adam Masters, and the turbulence from William Bennett's release.

"Nothing to say?" Adam asked coolly. When she just glared at him, he gave her that smug smile she detested. "Good. Then we understand one another. Fasten your seat belt." He put the car in gear, shot her another look. "The ride could get very rough."

Crap, she thought, as she reached for her seat belt with shaking hands. *No, make that* crap *to the tenth power.*

SITTING on her bed, Miriam stared in dismay at the three Tarot cards she'd just turned up. The first was the Magician—manifesting power and fire. Miriam felt certain it represented Adam. The second card was Death—transformation, change, letting go. The third was the High Priestess—wisdom, mystery, and the divine feminine. That had to be Dr. Reynolds. Then there was the Knight of Swords, which represented a man who was courageous and active, a warrior who could also be very domineering.

But it didn't feel like Adam, so it was someone else, but who?

Miriam blew out a breath. This was her third attempt to convince herself she shouldn't get involved in whatever was happening between Dr. Reynolds and Adam. The first attempt had also involved drawing three Tarot cards and getting the Devil—entrapment, tyranny, and obsession; the Emperor—authority, protection, discipline (Adam again); and the Tower of Destruction—shattering structures and disruption.

Attempt two had been using a pendulum to determine if she should stay in Houston or go to San Antonio. The pendulum had done nothing over Houston, but gyrated insistently over San Antonio.

She really didn't want to leave her comfort zone and get involved with possible dark forces and a man with an inhuman aura, but she didn't want the Universe metaphorically hitting her in the head for not listening, either.

"One more time," she muttered, picking up the crystal quartz stone and silver chain, and going back to the Texas map spread over one end of her desk.

She took a deep breath and centered and grounded herself, then prayed to the Father/Mother/God for purity, protection, and guidance. She held her hand over the map and let the chain slide down, with the crystal dangling above the paper.

When the chain was completely still, she asked her question. "Please show me where I need to be now. Should I stay here in Houston and go about my usual activities, or travel to San Antonio to help Dr. Reynolds?"

She slowly moved the pendulum over the Houston area of the map. Nothing. She edged the pendulum toward San Antonio. The chain started vibrating as she neared the mapped city; when it was above San Antonio, the pendulum began swinging in small but steady clockwise circles.

Damn. With another sigh, Miriam stilled the pendulum and slipped the chain over her head, sliding the stone beneath her shirt. It looked like she was taking a trip. She wondered how she would explain this to her parents. Or to anyone she knew who was of sound mind.

She got her traveling backpack and began putting in clothing and toiletries. There was a tap on her door, and she paused. "Who is it?"

"It's Papa. May I come in?"

"Of course." Realizing she'd locked the door—unusual for her—she went to open it.

Her father stood there, wearing his beloved Houston Astros T-shirt over baggy sweatpants and holding a ceramic mug in his hand. He wasn't much taller than Miriam, but his thick, luxurious hair had very little gray, and he was a vigorous man for his age. Tonight, however, he looked tired and worried.

"What's wrong, Papa?"

He held up the mug. "Trouble in the leaves."

She felt a sinking sensation. Her father drank hot tea after breakfast and dinner, and always read the tea leaf dregs, a method of divination called tasseomancy, and a family tradition that dated back generations.

"What about the leaves?" she asked.

"They indicate challenges ahead—for you, Miri."

Surprise, surprise. "Good or bad challenges, Papa?"

He shook his head. "I'm not sure. I also consulted the cards."

Instead of Tarot, he read a deck of regular playing cards, another family tradition that was very old—and eerily accurate. Miriam took a deep breath. "What did the cards tell you, Papa?"

"Strange things. I got the heart queen—that's you, Miri. I also got the queen and king of clubs—two people you maybe know? And the six of hearts, a trip. Jack of diamonds—trouble ahead." He stared at her, too perceptive as always. "You've been acting thoughtful lately. Something going on?"

Well, at least she knew she'd chosen a destined course of action. "Yes, Papa, there's definitely something going on. And I'm leaving for San Antonio in the morning. Why don't we go scoop some Blue Bell ice cream and I'll tell you about it."

SIX

SURREAL images came into focus then blurred, except for one vivid image of the Devil, sporting midnight hair and glowing eyes. He didn't have the traditional horns, but she knew who—what—he was. He beckoned to her; she shook her head, refusing to go to him. He reached toward her, his arm contorting and stretching grotesquely. . . .

Julia awoke with a start, confused. The motion of a moving car jolted her back to reality. She looked over and there was the Devil incarnate—Adam Masters, calm and in full control—behind the wheel. Oh, yes, now she remembered. Unfortunately.

She must have dozed off after they got back on the road after her meltdown, which hadn't accomplished a darned thing. And which she felt certain, although she couldn't exactly pinpoint how, had given Adam another point on the scoreboard.

He glanced over, his dark gaze assessing. She noticed his face looked completely normal, the bruising and swelling gone. "Feeling any better?" he asked.

She shifted, winced as her bruised backside protested. He obviously hadn't done any healing on her. "Where are we?"

"Coming into San Antonio. Looks like we're just ahead of rush hour."

She realized they'd already exited off the interstate onto Commerce Street. She hadn't been to San Antonio in years. The downtown area looked older and smaller than she remembered, possibly because of the newer, larger buildings looming over old churches and government buildings. There was a lot of construction in the area as well; an indication that San Antonio, like most Texas cities, was growing.

They passed Alamo Plaza, the street that went to the Alamo, the famous historical landmark that squatted incongruously within the San Antonio downtown. Then they turned on Navarro Street and again on College Street, and pulled in front of the Omni La Mansión del Rio, one of the most elegant hotels along the Riverwalk.

I should have known, Julia thought, trying to finger-comb her hair into some semblance of order. Adam had a penchant for the highest quality, which seemed incongruous in view of the fact that Sentinels and Sanctioned were reincarnated Atlantian priests and claimed their mission on Earth was spiritual.

The valet attendant came around to open Adam's door, while a bellhop came to assist Julia from the car. She managed to hastily divest herself of Adam's coat before her door was opened. But her leg had stiffened and it was a struggle to get out of the car. The bellhop offered his hand, and she reluctantly took it, managing to slide out and stand.

She grabbed the top of the door, not trusting her screaming leg muscles, and cursing the fact that her cane was out of reach. Then Adam was beside her, pressing her cane into her hand. "Take it slow," he murmured.

She started for the hotel entry, stumbling as her leg gave out. Adam moved against her left side, his arm slipping around her lower back and creating a steel band of support. He kept her upright and moving forward. She squelched the protest that rose to her lips. Her aversion to him so freely touching her didn't trump the embarrassment of falling flat on her face.

They entered the elegant lobby, with its large terra-cotta tiles polished to a high gloss, recessed lighting, dark paneled wood, Southwestern rugs, and the hushed murmur of voices that intimated money and prestige. Adam led her to an upholstered bench seat across from the check-in desk. "You'd probably be more comfortable waiting here," he said.

She sank down, rubbed her throbbing leg. She didn't even want to think about what a mess she was, with her filthy pantsuit. She probably stood out like rough homespun in the midst of this Spanish Colonial elegance.

Adam strode to the desk and spoke with the clerk in low tones. No matter that he was in shirtsleeves, and a muddy, rumpled shirt at that. He radiated authority and power, and a smooth sophistication that garnered him deferential treatment. He also radiated something else, something Julia had been trying to ignore since she first met him—a raw magnetism and an aura of sensuality. Several of the female clerks and guests gave him appreciative glances. He appeared oblivious to them.

But he didn't seem indifferent to Julia, and unfortunately, she was becoming increasingly aware of him as a man, even at a distance. *Damn.* She did not need her libido coming to life after a dozen years, most especially not with Adam. Telling herself that didn't seem to stop her heart rate from accelerating as he walked back to her.

Just a physical response to the conductor/Sanctioned energies, she told herself—*physical* being the key word here. She had a powerful intellect, and she believed in mind over matter. She could—and would—control her reactions.

Adam offered a hand and helped her up. They walked to

the gilded elevators in silence. He didn't speak unless he had something to say, a trait Julia appreciated, since she was the same way. Outside of her classes and her family, she lived a solitary existence.

He pushed a floor button, and the doors whispered shut. "We have a parlor suite," he said, as the elevator started up. "I believe you'll find it's very nice."

Julia remembered the two adjoining suites they'd had when they'd been in Dallas hunting the Belian bomber. "There's no plural in that phrase. Don't you mean suites?"

"No. We have one suite with two bedrooms. Because of the situation, I felt it would be best to keep you close."

Bad enough to have to put up with Adam for several days; to be in the same rooms with him would be maddening. Plus he probably had some ulterior motive for sharing a suite; he didn't do anything without a reason.

"I don't think that's necessary," she protested. "Surely this can't be more dangerous than tracking a crazed bomber was."

"I don't know how dangerous it might be. I've got a missing Sentinel who may be possessed by a Belian."

"Possessed?"

The elevator stopped and the doors opened.

"Let's discuss this after we're settled."

Julia's thoughts were whirling. *Possessed?* This was beginning to sound like a B horror movie.

"I know the past two days have been stressful for you," Adam said. That was a definite understatement. He stopped before a door, didn't bother with the electronic card key. Instead he made a quick motion with his hand, and the red light blinked to green.

"Show-off," Julia muttered, still thoroughly irritated over the single suite. She knew arguing would be futile. Her only option was to march downstairs and get her own room. That should only cost about, oh, four or five hundred dollars a night. She could afford it for a few nights, but still—

"Unfortunately, we don't have the luxury of much downtime." Adam ushered her inside with another of his smooth moves.

They were in a small foyer area, with a richly carved, marble-topped dark wood commode with a matching mirror above it. Wrought iron light sconces flanked the mirror, and a large bouquet of fresh flowers sat atop the commode. Julia looked around the sumptuous room.

The upholstered sofa and love seat, both with a bank of matching pillows, looked surprisingly comfortable, and a soft brown throw was draped over the love seat arm. The lush beige carpeting and creamy walls balanced the massive furniture and dark colors. Across from the sofa, two sets of glass-paned doors obviously opened onto a balcony overlooking the Riverwalk. Everything about the room screamed "expensive," yet it looked inviting and functional.

Impressed despite herself, Julia said, "Not too bad."

"I'm sure you would have preferred a Days Inn. I'm glad you're not disappointed."

He was a smart-ass as well as devious and controlling. "I'll make do."

He gestured toward a door at the end of the room. "I'd prefer you'd take that bedroom, and let me have the one closest to the entry."

She understood he was taking the role of protector, placing her farther from possible danger, and she accepted that. He was much stronger and a very powerful being, and she would be foolish to deny it. She had enough battles to pick with him. "Fine," she said.

"Our luggage should be here shortly. I'm sure you want to clean up and change." His gaze swept down her. "And I know your leg is hurting. Perhaps a soak in the tub would help."

"Thank you, Doctor Masters. Do you think you can manage to stay out of my bathroom this time?"

Humor gleamed in his eyes. "I'll try to avoid the temptation."

"Try very hard," she suggested. Turning, she made her way to the end of the large room, stepped into the bedroom, and closed the door. She didn't lock it. Why bother? There was no stopping Adam if he wanted in.

She looked around the bedroom. It was just as impressive as the front room, with a king-sized bed, a massive wood armoire, and small accent tables with Spanish-style lamps. There was a desk with an upholstered leather chair and an ornately framed mirror above it.

Julia went to the bathroom door and sighed with appreciation. Marble countertops were lined with luxury products, and the marble sunken tub looked heavenly. She had to admit Adam had good taste in hotels.

She noticed the thick white robe hanging on the back of the bathroom door, and decided she didn't need a change of clothing before she bathed. She stripped, tossing her bedraggled suit on the leather desk chair, and indulged in the luxury of a long soak.

When she came out of the bathroom, feeling semihuman again, she saw her suitcase sitting on a luggage stand, and her business case and computer placed by the desk. The discarded pantsuit was gone. Making a mental note to add her bedroom to Adam's off-limits list—obviously mentioning only the bathroom had been a tactical error on her part—she got dressed.

As she ran a comb through her damp hair, she smelled fresh coffee. While she rarely allowed herself more than two cups a day, she suddenly craved some. She'd missed lunch and felt the need for something to take the edge off her unusual fatigue and sharpen her wits—a definite necessity around Adam Masters.

Grabbing her cane, she went to the door. She could hear

Adam talking and assumed he was on the phone. She opened the door, started out, then stopped in surprise. He wasn't alone. A young, dark-haired man stood before the French doors, glaring at Adam, who sat on the sofa, seemingly relaxed.

"Why won't you tell me where Matt is?" the young man demanded. "I'm certain you know."

"No, I don't." Adam's voice was low and calm.

"You have to know something," the man insisted, vibrating with tension. "You're Sanctioned. You're intentionally keeping me in the dark, and I want to know what's going on. Just because you're over me doesn't mean you have the right to lie to me."

"That's enough." Steel edged Adam's voice. "You're out of line."

The young man's jaw clenched and his hands fisted. He opened his mouth to speak, but Adam held up a warning hand. "Stop right now. Get control of yourself. You don't want to go against me on this." He turned his head to look at her. "Julia. Please join us."

She hadn't been in his line of vision, but she wasn't surprised he'd sensed her presence. "I think I should give you two some privacy to talk," she hedged, easing backward.

"No. This involves you, too." He gestured her forward.

Reluctantly, she came into the room, aware of the young man's gaze on her cane. She stopped beside the couch, feeling the animosity he radiated.

"Julia, this is Sean Stevens," Adam said. "Sean, this is Dr. Julia Reynolds. She's—"

"I know what she is," Sean hissed. "She's a fucking conductor. We don't need her involved in this. She has no business being here."

He started toward her, but Adam came to his feet in a superhuman blur. "Enough!" Stepping in front of Julia, he held up his hand. Peeking around his broad frame, she saw light flare from his palm. Sean stumbled a few steps back.

"You'd better calm down before I'm forced to take disciplinary action," he told Sean.

Sean stood there, his chest heaving. "Think carefully about what you say and do next," Adam warned him. The young man stared at him with a smoldering gaze, but remained silent.

Trepidation coiled through Julia. She didn't want this to escalate further, didn't want to see what Adam could—and would—do to this obviously distraught young man, who was also a Sentinel. She could sense the faint connection now that she focused on it. Not the startling jolt she experienced with Adam, but a resonating thread of energy.

"When you're ready to sit down and discuss this in a rational manner, then I'll tell you what I can," Adam said.

She felt the power humming below his utterly calm exterior, had to admire his control. Apparently Sean realized he was on shaky ground and managed to reign himself in. "Fine." He sat on the love seat, slouching back carelessly, although his hands remained clenched.

"Have a seat, Julia." Adam moved out the heavy coffee table and took the middle of the couch, closer to Sean.

Resigned, she sat on his right. Sean glowered at her. Interesting, since she'd assumed that conductors—not that she was accepting that assignment—were in demand and valued by Sentinels.

"Dr. Reynolds is a conductor," Adam said. "But that's not why I've brought her here."

Sean's dark eyes narrowed. "Oh, so she's just your piece of ass on the side? And I thought the Sanctioned were celibate bastards—" His voice ended on a gurgle and he raised a hand to his throat.

"Since you won't shut up, I'll do it for you. I'll also restrain you, if necessary. Your decision." Adam's voice was low, unemotional, despite the tension in the room.

"Maybe I should leave you two alone," Julia said. "I'm obviously making things worse."

"No. I want you here." Adam looked at her. "Matt is Sean's mentor, and has been since Sean was thirteen. Sean is understandably upset about Matt's disappearance, but Sean has no excuse for his behavior and lack of control." He looked back at Sean. "Matt trained him better than that."

Julia saw the flash of emotion on Sean's face and her heart went out to the young man. "He's just worried about his mentor," she said softly, then went into professor mode. "Why don't we all settle down and start over?"

Adam asked Sean, "Are you willing to hear me out now?"

Sean gave a stiff nod and dropped his hand. Tried to speak, his voice returning, but cracking. "Y-yes."

"All right, then." Adam leaned back. "As I was saying, Dr. Reynolds is not here to assist in conductions"—he glanced at her—"at least not at this time."

Oh, not at any time, she thought.

"She is here," Adam continued, "because she is a high-level precognitive. If she can access Matt's energy pattern, she might be able to tell us what he'll do next, or where he might go."

"In other words, to track him like some animal," Sean snapped.

Adam gave him a long, level look. "No, not to track him, but definitely to help us locate him."

"We don't need her to do that. I'm sure there's some reason for Matt to be gone." Desperation hitched Sean's voice up.

"You know he would never disappear without letting us know his plans. Or go a week without contacting me," Adam replied. "Something *is* wrong, Sean, but I'm not yet certain what it is."

"He's not dead. He's not! He can't . . . be." Panic leached the color from the young man's face.

"No, he is not dead. I can tell you that much."

Relief swept Sean's face, followed by determination. "I want to help you find him."

"Until I know the situation, I'm not going to risk any of my Sentinels. You need to let me take care of this."

"He's my mentor, and my father, damn it!"

"You will either step back, or I'll send you away until this is resolved." The steel returned to Adam's voice, and Julia knew full well he'd back up his ultimatum.

Sean apparently realized that. He muttered, "Fine." He stood, grabbed a leather jacket slung over the love seat back. "I'm out of here." He strode to the door.

"Wait," Adam ordered, rising.

Sean stopped, shooting a resentful glance his way. Adam walked over to him. "That includes you staying away from the house. Don't go back there again."

"Fuck that! It's my home, too."

"But you also have an apartment now. I don't want you at Matt's."

Sean looked away, his jaw clenched. "That house is still home to me."

Adam reached out, clasped his shoulder. "I understand that you're upset," he said. "That you're worried about Matt. I give you my word that finding him is my top priority."

Sean swung back around, his eyes glittering. "And *then* what are you going to do?"

"Everything I can for him. You have to trust me on this."

"I don't have any choice, do I?"

"No, you don't. But I still need you to do your job. I want you to monitor all possible Belian activities in San Antonio, and check in with me every day."

Sean shrugged. "Yeah, sure. Whatever."

"Then I'll talk to you tomorrow." Adam dropped his hand and stepped back. "Walk in Light."

Sean jerked open the door and left without another word. Adam closed the door, stood there a moment.

"I feel for him," Julia said. "He's just a kid."

"He's twenty-four years old, and he's also a Sentinel. He knows his duty, and he knows he must maintain control in every situation. I refuse to accept less from him." He looked at her. "You may think I'm a coldhearted bastard, but my chief concern is always the welfare of my Sentinels and conductors."

"I know that." And she did. Adam certainly had a ruthless side, but he did have a conscience—of sorts—and apparently, a heart. She remembered how he'd crouched over a critically injured Luke in Dallas, his expression fierce as he channeled energy into Luke's wounds, his harsh voice raw as he ordered the Sentinel to stay with him. He had literally willed Luke to live.

"You handled Sean well," she added. "You could have busted him. I'm glad you didn't. He's acting out under duress."

"He's always been a tough case," Adam said. "His Sentinel father was killed when he was just a few months old. His mother was a drug addict, and he grew up on the streets of Los Angeles. It took a while for the Sanctioned there to track him down and get him away from his mother."

She felt a new wave of compassion. "That's awful. How did he get to Texas?"

"We felt it was best to get him away from the bad influences in Los Angeles. Matt wasn't mentoring anyone, and he and Susan had no children. They were delighted to take in Sean. He rebelled a lot at first, but came around eventually, and became devoted to them. They legally adopted him when he was fifteen. Susan's death shook him up almost as much as it did Matt. And now Matt is missing."

"Leaving Sean upended," Julia said. "No wonder he's so hostile. There's a lot of fear and grief beneath that anger."

"I understand that, but I can't allow him to forget his purpose or training." Adam walked over to an alcove that had a dining-sized table with six chairs. Good grief, just how big was this suite? Going to the coffeemaker on a sideboard, he poured two mugs of coffee.

"Sean is too powerful to let his emotions dominate his actions. Self-control and discipline are crucial traits for Sentinels." He returned to the sofa, offered her one of the mugs. "There's no room for emotional reactions, or questioning my orders."

"Of course not, Mr. Macho Sanctioned. That would be too difficult on your ego."

Adam sat beside her. "You're the only one who truly challenges me."

She sipped the excellent coffee, sighed. "How did you know this was what I wanted?"

"Just a guess. You still look tired."

"Gee, thanks. And you look—" She eyed him, noting the black trousers and charcoal gray cashmere pullover sweater, which showed off a very nice physique. *Not going there.* "A little casual. And here I thought you even slept in a coat and tie."

He shook his head. "Acerbic wit must run in the family."

Julia wrapped her hands around the warm mug. "Why was Sean so upset that I might be a conductor? Can't a conduction help track Sentinels?"

"Not in theory, no. Sentinels operate out of the upper three spiritual chakras, which vibrate at a higher level than the four Earth-based chakra energies of Belians. That's why Belians can't readily track Sentinels—they can't access the upper-level resonance. During a conduction, a conductor amplifies the Belian's energy signature that the Sentinel has already absorbed, and helps create a psychic lock on the Belian. But it doesn't work the other way."

"Then why would my presence threaten Sean?"

"Because he already suspects the same thing I do—that Matt has been possessed by a Belian."

"You said that before, but there's no scientific evidence that possession actually exists."

"Nor is there evidence of Sentinels, Sanctioned, or Belians. Yet you're well aware of our existence."

"That's bad enough," she muttered. "I didn't need to add possession to the equation. Next you'll be telling me that vampires and werewolves really do exist."

"Oh, you wouldn't believe what's out there."

"And I don't want to know," she said firmly. "Let's get back to the possession issue. How does it happen?"

"There are two basic ways a Belian can enter the Earth plane," Adam explained. "By being born into a human body—and yes, reincarnation is an integral part of the universal plan."

"I told you I didn't want to hear anything else."

A small smile flirted with his mouth. "Little coward."

"Just overwhelmed." Now, why had she ever admitted that to him? Adam was the kind of man—supernatural being?—who would exploit any weakness, if it served his purpose. "Make that sensory overload," she corrected. "Just stick to the pertinent facts, please. No more data than necessary."

"All right. As I was saying, a Belian can be born into a human body, or it can enter this plane by taking possession of a body. Coming in by birth is the most common way, but there are a fair number of possessions."

She tried to get her mind around the idea of a person being possessed, while the theme from *The Exorcist* played eerily in her head. "Isn't it almost impossible for someone to become possessed?" she asked. "And if they are, what happens to the person who's already in the body?"

"It's complicated. It is difficult to take possession of a body unless the person is weak or ill in some way. When it does happen, it's possible that the original soul in the body can remain there, repressed by the invading soul."

"Wait. Are you saying that Belians have souls?"

"All living things, animals included, have souls."

"So Belians have evil souls?"

"All souls come from one source—the Creator. All are loved and cherished by The One. But some of them have wandered away from the Light."

"Looks like quite a ways."

Adam did smile this time. *Damn, the man is sexy when he smiles. Stop thinking that!* she told herself.

"You could say that," he said. "In the case of a possession, the original soul could remain, overshadowed by the Belian soul. Or it might leave the body, in which case, when the Belian is cast out, the body dies. That's the common scenario."

Meaning very poor odds for a person possessed by a Belian. "I assume Sean knows this."

"He does, which is why he's reacting so strongly. Matt is the only family he has."

Julia considered. "But you believe Matt is still alive. Assuming a Belian has possessed him, that means both Sentinel and Belian souls are inhabiting the same body."

Adam nodded. "That's exactly what I think. It appears Matt is holding on and fighting back. The times he's in control of the body are when I can sense him."

"When there's a void, the Belian must be in control," Julia surmised. "And since a conductor can help track a Belian, then I might do just that. Theoretically, of course, since I'm not here in the role of a conductor." And she planned to keep it that way.

"Of course."

She ignored the sardonic tone in his voice. "So what happens when you find Matt? Will you be able to force the Belian out of him?"

"I don't know. I've never dealt with a situation like this. I can exorcise the Belian and send its sorry soul to burn on Saturn. But I don't know if I can save Matt. That's why I can't—won't—allow any of my other Sentinels to handle this."

He paused, his expression grim. "There's a very good chance I'll end up destroying Matt's physical body, casting his soul from the Earth plane."

In other words, he might have to kill Matt. And she might be the one facilitating it.

SEVEN

THEY went to the IMAX Theater, which was at Rivercenter Mall. Adam wanted to investigate to confirm whether or not a Belian was behind last night's carnage, and if it was a link to Matt. He asked Julia to wait inside the mall. *Probably just as well*, she thought, sitting on a bench seat, flanked by huge pots of frond-type trees. She didn't have any breaking and entering skills, or the ability to redirect minds should she be seen and questioned. But she had no doubt Adam would be able to gain entry to the closed theater without difficulty or being noticed.

She sighed and tried to stretch her stiff body. Behind her, a bank of glass panels soared several stories high. They overlooked the waterway, which was illuminated by hundreds of nighttime lights. Way above her, brightly colored contemporary tapestries hung quietly, despite the hustle and bustle of people through the thoroughfare.

Although the mall was warm from all the bodies and movement, Julia was chilled. She felt like she had just taken a step on an irrevocable and terrifying path. She had no idea what horrors lay ahead, but if they were even a tenth of what had happened in Dallas, it would be very bad. And there would be no turning back.

Not that she would. She'd told Adam she'd stick it out. Even if that meant dealing with the fierce and unsettling sexual attraction between them. Not to mention the violence and mayhem and high body count that Belians generated. And all of it was nonlogical and inexplicable in her scientifically based world.

She saw Adam striding toward her, tall and imposing in his black trench coat. Against the more casual shoppers and sightseers, he stood out like a prime number among a string of transcendental numbers. But he appeared oblivious to the stares, his focus solely on her. He stopped beside her. "We need to go."

She allowed his assistance to stand, having resigned herself to the fact that it was both easier on her leg and more expedient than fighting him every time he offered. However, she sidestepped his subtle attempt to take her arm as she started walking. "Where are we going?"

"To Matt's house." Ignoring her warning glare, he grasped her left arm anyway, giving her unobtrusive support and moving her toward the nearby exit. "I need to see it, to read the energy patterns and get any information I can. I'd like you to be there, to see if you can pick up anything."

"And I'd like you to let go of me."

"I suggest you pick your battles, Julia." He tugged her through the doors. "And there will be a battle. There was a Belian at the IMAX last night."

She hated hearing that. She gave up trying to extricate herself as a renewed feeling of dread swept through her. Now it was certain they were about to step into the Sentinel otherworld.

They were silent on the drive to Matt's house. He lived in an older residential section of the city, where the houses were modest but well tended. Adam parked in front of a white brick and frame house with a double garage. The bank of tall windows between the garage and the front porch were dark, and there didn't appear to be any lights on elsewhere in the house.

Adam stared at the house a long moment. "I can't sense him anywhere." He looked at Julia. "I want you to stay in the car while I check things out. Have you got your gun?"

"It's right here in my purse."

"Get it out, have it ready. If anyone or anything approaches the car in a threatening manner, shoot first, and ask questions later."

Oh, great. Now she could add shooting someone to the possibilities. But she understood the seriousness of the situation, the potential danger of a Belian—one Adam thought might be in the general vicinity. She pulled out her Tomcat, rested it against her leg.

"Do not hesitate to shoot if you feel you are in danger," Adam reiterated.

"Don't worry. If it comes down to a Belian or me, there's no contest."

"If the house is clear, I'll come get you."

"I can hardly wait."

He gave her a look—she couldn't tell if it was amusement or exasperation—and got out of the car. As he strode away, the car doors locked on their own. Julia scanned the area, but all she saw was a young couple walking a massive dog. She tried to relax, but her nerves were on edge. She imagined a dark form coming out of nowhere and ripping off the car door. So many monsters in the world . . .

The man moved toward her, the glare of the kitchen light behind him shadowing his face. "Where have you been, Julia? I warned you about seeing other men, but you didn't listen. Now I have to punish you." Shock and terror swept through her as he lunged forward, grabbing her with one meaty hand, the other one balling into a fist and raising to strike. . . .

She jolted at the tapping on the car window, her heart leaping and going into a frenzied pounding. It took a moment for her to realize it was Adam, not William Bennett. *God.*

Adam opened the door. "The house is clear, so you can—" His gaze focused on her face, his eyes narrowing. "What happened? Did you see something?"

Only a demonic ghost. "No, it's nothing."

He rested his hand on her shoulder. "And *nothing* is why you're pale and shaking, and your heart is racing?"

"I'm just tense. You might track down monsters on a regular basis, but this is new territory for me."

"I would say you've had some experience in that area," he said quietly.

Why did the man have to be so damned perceptive? "I'm fine," she insisted, swinging her legs out of the car. But she was still shaking, a reaction to the sick rush pummeling her body. Who needed caffeine when adrenaline was only a memory away?

She got to her feet and took an unsteady step toward the house. "Let's get this over with."

But he blocked her, sliding his hands down her arms. Even through her jacket, she could feel their heat. "Take a minute and settle down." He pulled her lightly against him.

"Adam—"

"Hush." He splayed one hand over her upper back. She felt a subtle flow of energy radiating into her, soothing, calming.

Some of her tension dissipated. Of its own volition, her head eased against his chest. His trench coat smelled fresh and clean, and from beneath it came an entirely too enticing scent of expensive cologne and primal male.

If he could bottle that scent, she thought inanely, *he could make a fortune and there would be a lot of turned-on women and sexually satisfied men in its wake. No, no, no!* What was wrong with her? Oh, right—the Sentinel/conductor attraction, and her awakening libido. Nothing a little—or maybe a lot of—self-control couldn't handle.

She pushed away from him. "Enough of the woo-woo stuff. Let's get this done."

"All right." He steered her toward the house. "The place is a mess," he said as they went up the sidewalk. "Obviously, Matt hasn't been functioning well at all. I should have kept a closer watch on him."

Her nerves tauter than violin strings, she went for levity. "Like you don't have a fleet of Sentinels and a horde of Belians and the vast state of Texas to rule over."

"That's no excuse. Every individual in my care is of vital importance."

"I hate to break it to you at a time like this, Adam, but as I've already pointed out, you are *not* God. Despite your delusions to the contrary."

"I'm not the one with delusions, Julia, nor am I in denial. I know exactly what's happening here."

She opted to ignore his implication that she was avoiding the reality between them, and remained silent while he opened the door and went ahead of her. She smelled the stench as she entered the house—rotting food and stale air and sweat. Layered over that was another foul odor she couldn't identify. It was nasty, like putrid eggs and decaying vegetation.

She placed a hand over her nose as she looked around. The front room was a jumble of tossed clothing and mail, plates of old food, and liquor bottles. Couch cushions and garbage littered the floor, and the pictures on the walls were askew, the glass broken in some of them.

"I see what you mean about the mess," she said. "What is that awful smell?"

"Do you smell more than old food and filth?"

"I don't know . . ." She lowered her hand, risked another sniff. *Ugh.* "It's like there's something dead and rotting."

"There is, in a way. Can you sense or feel anything?"

She looked around the room, could imagine the despair and emotional upheaval that had created the mess, but couldn't really feel it. "No."

"So you don't have empathic abilities, like Marla does."

"No. After Bennett—" She paused, took a breath through her mouth. "After that night, I could suddenly see flashes of future events. And Marla started picking up emotions from people. I don't know which is worse."

"These abilities don't have to be curses." Adam glanced around. "The overriding stink in this room is from a Belian."

"Belians stink?"

"Many demons leave a stench."

"Demons? Oh, please, that sounds like a melodramatic horror novel."

"We don't have time for detailed explanations of the complexities of the Universe. Suffice it to say that the byproduct of some tainted souls reflects the nature of those souls."

"Then why can't you just track Belians by their bad smell?"

"Because corporeal Belians look and smell like any other human. The incorporeal ones are what you would term *demons*. They can be very dangerous, despite their lack of a body. Many of them move in and out of dark realms and absorb the essences and odors of those realms."

She didn't even want to think about other realms. "Why do you keep telling me things I don't want to hear?"

"Would you rather go into a situation ignorant and unprepared?"

"I'd rather go back to Houston and forget any of this ever happened."

"There's a surprise. Why don't we focus on the current scene? There are other indications that a Belian was here." Adam took Julia's hand.

Her heart kicked up again. "I assume it's time to trigger one of my visions?"

"Not yet. I want to show you something through a third-eye link."

"I'm confused. Aren't we doing a third-eye link whenever I tap into Belian energy patterns through you and have visions, like I did in Dallas and then again last night?"

"Yes, but in that situation I was deliberately 'downloading,' if you will, the Belian psychic signature. The third eye can be used for various scenarios, and there are a number of ways a third-eye link between two people can work. For now, I'm just going to show you the energies in this room. You'll be seeing what I see when I investigate a BCS."

She was intrigued, despite the circumstances. "Anything for the team."

"I'll hold you to that." He entwined his fingers with hers. Heat and desire rolled through her.

She braced herself against the sensual onslaught. "Can't you turn that off?"

"Turn what off?" Feigned innocence tinged his voice.

"You know damned well what I'm talking about. Can't you block the sexual energy stuff? It's really annoying."

"It affects me, too, Julia. Since I've never had this experience before I met you, I'm not an expert on diverting the energies. But I have some ideas on how it can be dispersed."

She snapped her teeth in frustration. "Do you have to be such a guy?"

"Apparently." He looked genuinely disconcerted. "I seem to be learning the ins and outs of testosterone."

She laughed, despite herself. Adam surprised her with a smile, and she felt the strain between them easing. "How can we be acting like this in such an awful situation?" she asked.

"Humor is good. It's not one of my strong points, but I think we're going to need it, because things appear to be pretty grim. Let's take a look at the patterns. Ready?"

"I guess."

"Just close your eyes, and try to blank your thoughts."

She did, and almost immediately, she saw the room in her mind, but it was surreal and distorted. Wavy lines moved from ceiling to floor, and she assumed they were energy waves. She saw dark swirls moving around the room, coming together to form a large, grotesque shape, then shifting back into random swirls.

They moved around the room, sporadically coming together and separating in ominous patterns. Occasional sparks of light flashed in and out of the main shape. It was like watching a hokey ghost film, except the swirls were black instead of white. The awful smell intensified, almost gagging her. She heard a low hum of some sort. It sounded mechanical rather than human.

"What is this?" she asked.

"You're seeing the energy patterns left by the Belian."

"It's that dark shape?"

"In a manner of speaking. We're seeing it in its discarnate form."

"Is that strange sound from the Belian?"

"Yes, it's an echo of the residual energy. I think you've seen enough. I'm going to break the link now."

He let go of her hand, and the images winked off. She opened her eyes to the room in current reality. "I don't know what to make of that."

"It gives me a lot of information. I'm just sorry Sean had to experience this. He was here a few days ago—against my orders. He told me a Belian had been here, but insisted Matt must have left before that. He's in denial." He shook his head. "Come on. We're done here."

Julia was only too glad to get out of the house. She stepped off the porch and drew in a deep breath of untainted air. "So if the Belian is in a discarnate form, then it hasn't possessed Matt."

Adam took her arm and started walking toward the car. "I said it *was* in discarnate form, not that it still *is*. The fact that it was here, in Matt's house, and that I can only sense Matt intermittently, leads me to believe the Belian has possessed him.

"Not only that, but the Belian that was at the IMAX last night was in a human body, although its image was blurred, so I couldn't see what it looked like. Since you had a vision about the IMAX fire after I transmitted Matt's energy pattern to you, it can't be a coincidence."

"So Matt is possessed by a Belian?"

"I believe so."

Which meant they would indeed be tracking Matt down. *Damn.* Julia started to say just that, but a sudden flash of mental images sent her reeling. Caught in the throes of a precognitive vision, she stumbled and fell against Adam. Then she lost all awareness of everything but the unfolding vision.

ADAM rose early the next day, did his prayer and meditation rituals, and then spent an hour on his laptop, reading reports from his Sentinels and sending directives. He'd spent three hours the previous evening doing the same. Belian activity was extremely high in Texas right now. The only positive aspect of that was that the Sentinels working for him were too busy to speculate about his presence in San Antonio.

He'd never faced having to take out one of his Sentinels, and it didn't sit well with him. Unfortunately, and especially in view of Julia's latest vision, which had occurred spontaneously, without any push from him, there was a good possibility that he might have to kill Matt.

Troubled, he shut down the computer and got ready for a workout in the hotel exercise facility. He might be a Sanctioned, but he had to keep his human body in shape. He looked in on Julia before he left the suite. She was sound asleep, burrowed under the covers.

Her face and one arm were uncovered, giving him a glimpse of the poodle-print pajamas. She was one of the quietest sleepers he'd ever known. If he hadn't been able to see her aura, he'd have been tempted to make sure she was breathing.

In sleep, her relaxed expression lent her a youthful and innocent appearance. But awake, her face was animated and challenging. He liked that Julia the best. He also enjoyed the surprising aspects to her normally predictable personality.

In truth, he found her absolutely fascinating and—under certain circumstances—delightful. He knew she was disciplined and could be pedantic, but then she'd show that caustic wit and do something unexpected. Like drinking the better part of a bottle of merlot last night, after they'd returned to the hotel and discussed her vision. She'd also indulged in the chocolates left during the turndown service—both hers and his.

Making a mental reminder to get more chocolate and wine, he left a note for Julia by the coffeemaker, and went to work out.

When he returned an hour and a half later, she wasn't in the suite. Her bed was neatly made, and her laptop and briefcase were gone. But there was no note. He checked with the lobby desk to see if she'd left a message, but there was none. Concern and irritation snaked through him. Where would she have gone?

Closing his eyes, he focused on her, reaching for her unique energy pattern. He could call forth the energy signature of every Sentinel and conductor in Texas, all of which he initially absorbed and then stored in a spiritual "cache," for lack of a better word. Sanctioned could tap and manipulate otherworld dimensions that transcended Earth's limited parameters. It was the only way they could handle all the energies they had to absorb and manage.

He readily found Julia's signature, felt her vibration,

clear and strong. But that didn't tell him where she was. Keeping his focus on her energy, he quickly changed from his workout clothes and headed for the lobby. She wasn't there, and he decided to take the Riverwalk exit, although he couldn't believe she'd be foolish enough to go there after what she'd seen last night.

But she had. Her vibration grew stronger as he came outside, and it was easy enough to track her to the Riverwalk level of the hotel's elegant Las Canarias restaurant. She sat at one of the linen-draped tables, working on her laptop. A plate of fresh fruit and a croissant and cup of coffee were set off to one side. It was a clear, cool morning, and the sunlight reflected gold and red shades in her hair.

Adam strode over to her. "Good morning, Julia."

She glanced up, an annoyed expression on her face. "Adam."

"Mind if I join you?"

"Do you really care if I mind?"

"No." He pulled out the chair to her right and sat. "What are you doing here?"

She gave him her professor look. "I'm eating breakfast. Lots of normal humans do it. By the way, I put it on your tab."

So she was in *testy* mode this morning. He leaned back in the chair. "Why did you leave the suite without telling me?"

"First off, you weren't there. Secondly, I wasn't aware you were my social secretary."

"I am responsible for your safety. You're certainly aware that, according to your vision last night, the Belian could be attacking somewhere along the Riverwalk."

"I am responsible for my own safety, Mr. Macho. I'm a big girl, and I've been taking care of myself for a long time."

One disadvantage of the challenging aspect of her personality that often intrigued him was that it could also be annoying as hell. "A rampaging Belian with a gun trumps a stubborn female, even one with an attitude. You're smart enough to know that."

"I know I saw a man shooting into a crowd, and I know it was on the Riverwalk." She gestured toward a group of elderly tourists taking photos of the water. "But there were a lot more people than there are right now, and it wasn't *here*. The Riverwalk winds all over the place. There's no telling where the shooting will actually occur, unless we can walk or boat the entire area and see if I can spot it."

She had a point there. In Dallas, her precognitive ability had given her extremely detailed and accurate visions of events before they happened. She'd been able to visually identify one of the bomber's targets and give Adam enough information for them to locate a second target. But this was a different scenario.

"We're possibly dealing with a being more powerful than your garden-variety Belian," he said. "Although this is a first for me, I can only assume that if a Sentinel and Belian are sharing a body, then the powers of both come into play. If the Belian is in control and can harness the Sentinel's powers, then the danger increases exponentially. A healthy dose of fear and caution would be appropriate here."

Julia's lips firmed. "I've got experience with monsters. I've faced terror and pain. I've also faced death. I refuse to let fear paralyze me, or keep me hiding behind locked doors. I—God." She clenched her hand into a fist. "Today is Friday. It's Friday, and he's being turned loose."

Closing her eyes, she drew a shuddering breath. "I won't let it undo me. I won't."

That's why she was so reactive today. It wasn't anger, but fear. The man who'd enacted her worst nightmare—only it had been real—was once again free in the world. A powerful surge of protectiveness flowed through Adam. She shouldn't have to endure this.

"Julia." He reached out and clasped her clenched hand. "Bennett won't get anywhere near you. He'll have to go through me first, and that will never happen."

She looked at him, her eyes anguished. "You can't be with me forever, Adam. I can't count on anyone besides myself. I'm the only one who can face my demons and defeat them." She pulled her hand free, and struggled to compose herself.

We'll see about that, he thought. She was not facing Bennett alone.

A waiter approached the table. "What can I get you, sir?"

"Just coffee, black." Adam looked back at Julia. Some of her color had returned.

"Besides," she continued as the waiter left, "if I had to put up with you all the time, I'd go stark raving mad. I haven't done anything to deserve that much punishment."

"I think you've got it backward. I would be the reward."

"Talk about arrogant," she muttered, picking up her coffee.

"Why don't we talk about a game plan instead?"

"Gee, I don't know if I have time. I have to attend Aunt Willie's funeral. You *do* remember that?" She set her cup down. "I also scheduled lunch with Dr. Curtis on Wednesday, assuming we're here that long. That's the earliest date she's free. And I have you to thank for this fun event."

"The credit really should go to the Belian."

She rolled her eyes. "*So* not buying that one. All right then, what do we do now?"

"What you mentioned earlier is probably the best plan. We need to cover the Riverwalk and see if we can locate the area you saw in your vision. We could start by—" A thrashing sound from the manicured shrubs behind them interrupted him.

"Let go of me, you creep!" shrieked a female voice.

"Goddamn it! That burns like hell!" came a familiar male voice.

"I told you to let me go! I'll spray you again, I swe—ouch!"

Adam came to his feet, turning to see Sean dragging a struggling young woman out of the lush landscape. Sean's face was red, his eyes watering. The woman, who had spiked hair dyed several shocking shades and looked very familiar, managed to twist and knee him in the crotch. Adam winced as Sean doubled over, but the young man didn't release his hold.

Instead he shook her like a rag doll. "Bitch!" he yelled.

"Bastard!" she yelled back, slinging her backpack at him.

"Sean! What the Darkness is going on?" Adam demanded.

"Miriam!" Julia gasped.

Adam sensed Julia coming to her feet, felt her coming to his side.

The young woman's head whipped around, and he realized why she looked familiar. She was the woman from the bar—also Julia's student, and someone he'd recognized as a potential complication.

Miriam White had just become a real problem—and a big one.

EIGHT

Friday morning, Miriam hitched her backpack purse over her shoulder and left the hotel. The air was crisp and clear, the sun was shining, and it promised to be a nice day. She'd driven to San Antonio last night, figuring it was best to do whatever it was she was meant to do, and be done with it.

She'd been lucky to find a room at an older Comfort Inn close to the Riverwalk. San Antonio enjoyed a healthy tourist trade year-round, although the busiest part of the season had pretty much wound down. However, the upcoming weekend was the San Antonio Oktoberfest celebration, and a lot of people would be in the city for that. But she had a room and was set to go.

Now, to locate Dr. Reynolds. Miriam had a general idea of where to look, because she'd used her pendulum over a map of San Antonio this morning. It had gyrated most strongly over a section of the Riverwalk between St. Mary's and Navarro. That made sense, as the strongest concentration of San Antonio hotels were clustered on or near the Riverwalk.

She figured she could walk the area and continue to use the pendulum. If that failed, she'd call Dr. Reynolds' cell phone. Not ideal, as she preferred the *"Oh Dr. Reynolds, what a surprise. I never thought I'd run into you here"* approach. But she'd do whatever it took.

She walked to Commerce and turned east. Then she turned on St. Mary's Street and walked the short distance to the Riverwalk. As always, it was like entering a different world, a cocoon of stately trees sheltering the gently lapping waterway: the old-world ambience of the hotel and restaurant patios, huge umbrellas, and potted plants, intermingled with the energy of people, music, and mouthwatering scents. She had always loved the Riverwalk, despite the masses of tourists.

Now to find Dr. Reynolds. Miriam strolled along, scouting a good spot to pull out the pendulum. As she slowed, eyeing a vacant bench, she happened to look up toward the multilevel terrace of a hotel restaurant just ahead on the right. There was Dr. Reynolds, sitting at a table and working on a laptop. Miriam stumbled and nearly fell. What incredible evidence of the Universe orchestrating events. Serendipity in full force.

A little stunned, despite her conviction she was meant to be here, she debated what she would say to her professor. She started toward the table, turning phrases over in her mind. Then Adam appeared in her peripheral vision, striding toward Dr. Reynolds. *Shit!* She did not want to tangle with him before she had a chance to talk to Dr. Reynolds.

Dr. Reynolds gave Adam a look that was far from welcoming; he pulled out a chair and sat down. Miriam edged closer, hoping to hear their discussion. A waiter approached the table, and she turned around, in case Adam looked her way.

Peeking around a few moments later, she saw the waiter was gone. She picked out a large palmetto tree closer to the table for a cover. It wasn't very broad, but it was her best option. She sped to the palmetto and hunkered down. Setting her backpack on one side, she slid her legs out, as if she were just resting there, and hoped they didn't notice her. She could hear them clearly from here.

"I have you to thank for this fun event," Dr. Reynolds was saying.

"The credit really should go to the Belian," Adam replied in that odd, rasping voice.

Miriam leaned around, saw Dr. Reynolds roll her eyes. "*So* not buying that one. All right then—"

"What the hell do you think you're doing?" came a harsh male voice near Miriam.

She looked up to see a dark-haired man bearing down on her, his expression fierce.

"What?" she managed, before he grabbed her arm, jerked her up. "Hey!"

His dark eyes blazed. "I saw you sneaking around the tree, spying on Adam. What are you up to?"

"I'm not doing anything. Let me go!" She tried to shake free, but he had an iron grip. So she kicked his leg instead.

He merely grunted and tightened his grip. "Who are you? Why are you watching Adam?"

She didn't care if he knew Adam. No one manhandled her. She slid her hand inside the front pocket of her backpack, wrapped her fingers around her pepper foam. "Let me go, or you'll be sorry." She thumbed the canister safety off, just in case.

"Like that's going to happen." He yanked her away from the tree. "We'll just see why you're lurking and spying."

"Let go of me, you creep!" She pulled out the foam and let him have it in the face.

He reeled back, but kept his hold on her arm. "Goddamn it! That burns like hell!"

"I told you to let me go! I'll spray you again, I swe— ouch!" She hissed as he practically jerked her arm from its socket and began dragging her toward the terrace. Furious, she twisted and slammed her knee into his crotch.

He gasped and doubled over, digging his fingers even more painfully into her arm. He shook her hard. "Bitch!" he yelled.

"Bastard!" she yelled back, slinging her backpack at him. She couldn't believe he was still on his feet and still had hold of her.

"Sean! What the Darkness is going on?" came another male voice.

"Miriam!"

Crap. That was Dr. Reynolds.

Gasping, she looked around. Both Adam and Dr. Reynolds were on their feet, staring at her. The game was up.

"Miriam White, I believe?" Adam asked.

She nodded, glared at the man still painfully squeezing her arm. "You're hurting me."

"Sean, let her go," said Adam.

The younger man, apparently Sean, shook her again. "But we don't know what she's up to."

Dr. Reynolds strode forward, and rapped her cane sharply against his back. "Let her go immediately."

With a frustrated gesture, he released Miriam. His face was bright red and swollen from the pepper foam and his eyes were watering. She couldn't believe he wasn't howling in pain.

"I'm trying to protect you, and I get hit from all quarters," he muttered.

"Step away from the girl," Adam ordered.

"Fuck it, then." Sean strode a few steps away, emanating fury.

"That's enough." Adam told him. He turned around, his gaze sweeping the startled diners on the terrace. Several of them had cell phones out. "Everything's fine," he called out. "Just a lovers' quarrel. Sorry for the disturbance." His attention shifted to Miriam.

She sidled toward Dr. Reynolds, who put a comforting arm around her. She sighed in relief. She knew her professor wouldn't let those two lunatic guys near her, realized on an intuitive level that Dr. Reynolds could hold her own with Adam. And he was definitely the one in charge, the one with the power. Today Miriam didn't even have to concentrate to see the light blazing around him.

"So, Ms. White, what are you doing here?" he asked.

"I told you already," Sean snapped. "She was spying on you. Hiding behind that tree there and watching you."

The game was definitely up. "Yes, I was observing you," Miriam admitted, meeting her professor's questioning gaze. "Not spying, really, but watching. I wanted to talk to you, Dr. Reynolds. But I didn't want to interrupt with *him* there." She gestured toward Adam.

Adam's eyes narrowed. "And why is that, Ms. White?"

"Oh, stop with the interrogation routine." Dr. Reynolds hugged Miriam against her. "The girl is trembling. She's been manhandled by one of your testosterone-laden lackeys. Look at the bruises on her arm." She swept her free hand along Miriam's exposed lower arm, and Miriam winced. She could see the dark splotches already forming.

Dr. Reynolds turned her toward the table she and Adam had been at. "We're going to sit and let this poor girl settle." She gave Sean her most intimidating professor stare. "And you, young man, are going to calm down and start acting like a responsible and rational Sentinel. You owe Miriam an apology for your behavior."

"Me? She's the one who sprayed me and kicked me in the balls. All I did was shake her a little."

"You're far more powerful than she is, and if you have the usual Sentinel abilities, you could have just immobilized her with your mind."

Sentinel? Powerful? Mental immobilization? Miriam

sank gratefully into a chair at the table and wondered what she'd gotten herself into.

"I agree with Julia," Adam told Sean. "You overreacted— again. I expect better from you."

Sean looked chagrined. "I guess I went overboard when she sprayed me with the pepper. But I didn't hurt her." He cut his gaze to Miriam. "Sorry."

"That's a start," Adam said. "Have a seat at the table. We're going to sort this out."

The waiter hurried toward the table, a carafe of coffee and a cup and saucer on a tray. "Is everything all right here?"

"Yes," Adam told him. "It's all resolved. Ms. White, would you like something to eat or drink?"

A bowl of Blue Bell vanilla ice cream drowning in hot fudge sauce would be a balm to her nerves, but she opted against it. "Uh, hot tea, please."

Sean refused anything, and the waiter left.

Adam went to Dr. Reynolds' chair, waited for her to sit and helped her slide it in. *At least he has good manners*, Miriam thought. But there was more to it than that—it was a protective, possessive gesture, if she was reading the energy right.

He took the remaining chair. "I'd like to know why both of you are here this morning."

"I happen to live in San Antonio," Sean said. "And I'm worried about Matt. I know what you said last night, but, damn it, I deserve to be in on this."

Adam held up his hand. "We'll get to that." His dark, piercing gaze settled on Miriam. "Ms. White, I'd like you to answer the question."

She wished she could consult her Tarot or have time to meditate on the matter, but she was in the hot seat. She honestly wasn't sure what to say.

"Ms. White, we're waiting."

"Just call me Miriam." She hesitated. "I'm here partly because of Dr. Reynolds, partly because of you, and because . . ." *Oh, hell, just get it over with.* "Because I've seen some things about you and had some dreams, and both my intuition and the Tarot cards guided me here."

There. She'd said it. Miriam looked around the table. Dr. Reynolds looked startled and Adam looked thoughtful. Sean scoffed, "She's here because of some wild dreams and some cards? I find that hard to believe. Just look at her. She's a freak."

He really was a jerk, one with serious anger issues.

"Be quiet, Sean," Adam growled.

"Why would you think dreams and cards would have no credibility?" Dr. Reynolds asked Sean. "No one questioned my ability, or Marla's, or Kara Cantrell's. From everything I've seen, you guys employ all sorts of unexplainable phenomenon in your work."

Miriam blinked in surprise. This was an unusual statement, coming from her highly intelligent and ultralogical professor. Of course, she still had no idea what was going on here.

"You're absolutely right," Adam said, with another warning look at Miriam's new nemesis. "Sean knows that. So, Miriam, visions and other signs have guided you here?"

She nodded. "It started when you came into the Red Lion Pub on Wednesday. I could see that you were upsetting Dr. Reynolds, so I looked at your aura, and it wasn't normal. Then I read the vibrations off the money you gave me and picked up some really strange stuff. That night, I started having weird dreams that involved you and Dr. Reynolds and . . ." She looked at Sean, realized he'd been the other person in her dreams. "Him."

Ignoring his derisive snort, she went on. "I wasn't sure what any of it meant, except that I was somehow involved and needed to do something. So I went to see Dr. Reynolds yesterday to try to talk to her about it."

"She told me she had concerns about you, and that you weren't normal," Dr. Reynolds said to Adam. "That was a shocker."

His attention remained on Miriam. "So you can read auras, and have psychometric abilities?"

"Yes."

"And you've had precognitive dreams?"

"Not precognitive, really, just flashes of things. To be honest, nothing very clear or specific. I'm not sure I can even explain what I saw. But I think the purpose of the dreams was spiritual guidance, to bring me here."

Adam kept staring at her, and she clasped her hands together in her lap. "You have the sight," he said. "Gypsy heritage, I presume."

She wasn't surprised he was so perceptive. "I am from a Romanichal lineage. I have the sight with the cards and auras and sensing energies from items, but my abilities don't generally show me future events."

"Oh yeah, she looks like a Gypsy," Sean sneered. "She has all those hair colors. The multiple earrings add flair. Must be the latest punk Gypsy look."

"Be quiet, or I'll use my cane on you again," Dr. Reynolds told him.

"Miriam, how did you find Julia?" Adam asked. "She didn't know where we were going to stay, so unless you had contact after we arrived, you couldn't have known our location."

Figuring she might as well go for full disclosure, Miriam tugged the chain from beneath her sweater, held up the quartz crystal. "I used this."

Again, he showed no surprise or skepticism. "So you have dowsing abilities as well. Anything else?"

"That's pretty much it."

"Fascinating." He sat back, drumming elegant fingers on the table. "What does my aura look like?"

So bright she almost needed sunglasses when she focused on it. "Mostly white light, without the other colors."

"I expected it to be black," Dr. Reynolds muttered.

Ignoring her, he nodded as if he already knew his aura was all light. "This adds a new slant to the situation. I believe Miriam is supposed to help us with our . . . problem."

"Wait just a minute," Dr. Reynolds interjected. "What do you mean? Are you telling me now that Miriam is a conductor? Back in Houston, you said she wasn't."

"Hell no, she's not," Sean said before Adam could reply. "Thank The One."

Adam sent him an annoyed look. "No, she's not a conductor. But there are many people in the world who have psychic gifts that can be useful. There's a reason Miriam is here, and I have to trust that it's providence. We need to utilize her abilities."

"Yeah, to track down Matt. I know that's what you're planning," Sean said. "I need to be part of it!"

"Perhaps you do," Adam said. "Miriam, you're certain you saw Sean in your dreams?"

She already knew the answer, but she studied the young man anyway. He had the same thick black hair, a little unkempt and down to his shoulders; the same dark, flashing eyes as the man in her dreams. His face was currently burned and swollen, but the strong, chiseled features were there, as well as the firm lips. When his skin healed, he'd be ruggedly attractive, if not for his arrogant and rude personality. Not to mention the anger.

"Yes, he's the one." *Unfortunately.*

"All right, then." Adam looked around the table. "Let's go up to the suite, where we'll have privacy. We'll explain the situation to Miriam."

"Oh, no," Dr. Reynolds said. "No. If she's not a conductor, there's no need for her to be here. Miriam, you should return to Houston. Forget all this weird stuff, and resume your normal life. Or as normal as it can be, considering your abilities."

"I can't." Miriam stared helplessly at her professor. How could she explain that she'd learned the hard way it wasn't wise to ignore very specific and direct guidance from the Universe? "I know I need to be here."

"Miriam is astute enough to recognize a spiritual directive when she receives it," Adam said. "And she's conscientious enough to act on it. Would you ask her to go against her beliefs?"

"I would ask her to remove herself from a dangerous situation and let the so-called experts handle it," Dr. Reynolds replied.

"Has it occurred to you that she *is* one of the so-called experts? She certainly has unusual gifts that lend themselves to this situation," Adam countered.

"Hey! I'm right here," Miriam interjected. "And I am a responsible adult, capable of making my own decisions. Dr. Reynolds, I appreciate your concern, but I'm here for the exact reasons Adam stated. I've been directed here, and although my spiritual philosophy may be unorthodox, it is one I believe in. I've learned to pay attention and go with the flow—which brought me to San Antonio."

Dr. Reynolds looked unhappy, but she raised her hands in a gesture of surrender. "I can't fight the two of you." She leveled a threatening gaze on Adam. "But I'm holding you responsible for her safety, Adam. I mean it."

"Of course. I'm responsible for everyone here," he said. "Now that we have that settled, let's go up to the suite and explain everything to Miriam. She needs to know the facts. Then we'll come up with a plan."

Miriam guessed she was glad to hear that, because she sure didn't know what was going on here, or who Adam and Sean were. All she knew was that she'd been hurled down the rabbit hole, and it was sink or swim.

They damn sure weren't in Kansas, or anywhere approaching science and logic, anymore.

MIRIAM looked pale and shell-shocked—not surprising after everything Adam had just told her. Remembering how staggered and incredulous she'd felt when Adam had unloaded the we-are-supernatural-beings bit, along with some show-and-tell demonstrations, Julia could certainly relate to her best student.

"Let me get this straight," Miriam said. "Atlantis really did exist, and there were the good Atlantians and the bad Atlantians, who were called Belians. The Belians were responsible for the destruction of Atlantis. Now they're reincarnating on Earth in human bodies, as serial killers, mafia types, dictators—really bad people. The Sentinels are the good Atlantians, who are reincarnating on Earth to track and remove the Belians. Both groups have superhuman powers."

"That's right," Adam said. "But despite those powers, we all have mortal bodies and can be killed."

"So how do you track the Belians?" Miriam asked.

"It's difficult, because they can shield their presence, which we can also do," Adam explained. "Because of this, we sometimes bring in certain humans who are born to be conductors and enhance the Sentinel abilities. These conductors are always the opposite sex of the Sentinel, and often have their own psychic abilities."

Sean shot Julia a glance and then walked over to stare out the French doors. She could just guess what he was thinking—about the hot, steamy sex that usually occurred between Sentinels and conductors. And the fact that she and Adam were precisely matched.

Knowing Sean probably thought they were engaging in wild conduction sex sent a flush of heat to her face, even though she and Adam would never come close to that. She felt a surprising regret about it, and mentally shook herself. Time to get back to reality.

"Actually, Adam and I are not doing any conductions," she said. "My part in this is to allow Adam to feed me energy from Belian crime scenes, and try to get a precognitive vision from that."

"Wow," Miriam said. "Are you telling me you're a precog?"

"Afraid so. But I don't see future events on a regular basis. Just when something—or someone"—Julia glanced at Adam—"triggers a vision."

"That's really cool. No wonder you didn't hold up a cross when I told you I was intuitive."

"One other thing," Julia added. "Adam isn't just a regular Sentinel. He's a Sanctioned, a higher level than Sentinels. He's more powerful, and usually just oversees and coordinates Sentinel and conductor activities. He normally doesn't stoop to our level."

"We can go into more detail on that later," Adam said. "Miriam, does your arm hurt?"

She had been absently rubbing the bruised arm, and she dropped her hand to her side. "It hurts a little. If I could get some ice and ibuprofen, I'm sure it will be better."

"It will get much better," Adam said. "Immediately. Sean, you did the damage, so you can fix it." He gestured toward Miriam.

Lips firmed, Sean turned from the French doors and walked to her. "I didn't mean to hurt you. Give me your arm."

She took a step back, cradling the injured limb protectively against her chest. "I don't want you touching me again."

"Cut the drama." He pried her arm free and straightened it. "Just be still." He ran his hand over it.

She watched, even more wide-eyed. "I can feel heat. And there's light around your hand. And—" She closed her mouth, staring at her arm as he released it. "The pain is almost gone, and the bruises are lighter. How did you do that?"

"Sentinels can manipulate energy," Adam explained. "Sean can't completely heal your arm, but he was able to draw healing energy from the Earth and channel it into the arm. It's enough to reduce swelling and speed up the healing process. The arm should be completely fine by tomorrow."

"Oh . . . Wow . . . Okay, then." Miriam looked at Sean. "Thanks for doing that."

He shrugged and returned to staring out at the River-walk.

Miriam looked shaken up. Who could blame her? She'd just had a lot of unbelievable information dumped on her. Even with her metaphysical background, it had to be hard to take in.

Julia felt a resurge of protectiveness toward her student. "Adam, I think we've done enough this morning. Maybe Miriam would like some time to herself, to assimilate everything. Then she'll probably have some questions."

"I agree. I'm booking another suite here at the hotel. Sean, I want you and Miriam to stay there."

"*What*?" Sean and Miriam both screeched at the same time.

"I have a place to stay—my apartment." Sean shot Miriam a disgusted look. "Even if I didn't, I don't want to be babysitting *her*."

She glared back at him. "I sure as hell don't need you around, either, jerk."

"That's enough," Adam said. "Both of you are acting like children. Sean, if you want in on this, you'll follow my orders without hesitation, or I'll ship you out of here. I understand we've got some Belian activity in Alaska.

"And, Miriam, please cooperate on this. Later today, we'll fill you in on the details of our situation. Trust me when I tell you it might become very dangerous. I suspect we're going up against a very powerful Belian, and one of my best Sentinels is missing. I'm not taking any chances with you or Julia. From now on, we're using a buddy system. Neither of you is to go anywhere alone. You might not like Sean, but he can—and will—keep you safe. I also want all of us in close proximity, so that we can access data and act quickly, if necessary. Is that clear?"

Miriam hesitated, looking as if she might bolt at any moment. "Say yes," Julia advised her. "Adam may be a macho, overbearing jackass, but if anyone can manage a dangerous situation with minimal casualties, he can. Besides, his suggestion is logical."

"Okay, I guess."

Adam looked at Sean. "Are you onboard?"

Sean nodded, but it was obvious he didn't like any of it.

"It's settled, then," Adam said. "Sean, take Miriam back to her hotel to get her things, then get what you need from your apartment. Be sure to scan thoroughly before you go in. Keep your weapons close and ready."

"Will do."

"After you leave your apartment, I want the two of you to return to the hotel," Adam continued. "I'll have a suite waiting, and the key cards will be at the desk. Take some downtime, get some lunch, and let Miriam get her bearings. Answer any questions she might have. And be civilized about it, or you'll be headed for Alaska. Miriam, do whatever you need to center and recharge yourself.

"In the meantime, Julia and I are going to do some reconnaissance, and it might take a while. I want you to meet us back here around five. I'm hoping we can tap Miriam's abilities to help us create a working plan. Any questions?"

Still sporting a deer-in-the-headlights expression, Miriam shook her head, and Sean muttered, "No."

"Good. For once, we're in agreement. Let's get going."

Julia watched the two walk stiffly to the door, keeping an icy gap between them. When the door closed behind them, she said, "I don't like this. I hate involving Miriam. She has a brilliant future ahead of her—in science, not Belian hunting. And to pair her with Sean, after the way he treated her, is totally illogical."

"We need all the help we can get. And I'm not one to ignore guidance from a higher source. It makes perfect sense to put Sean and Miriam together. He will be able to protect her."

"I'm trusting you on this one, Adam. You know Sean better than I do. But if he does anything to traumatize or hurt Miriam, she and I will be on the first flight back to Houston."

"He won't hurt her, at least not physically. But he is somewhat volatile right now and, as you've seen, tends to shoot off his mouth." Adam shook his head. "Being born a Sentinel doesn't guarantee full emotional control or maturity. Sean has a long way to go in that arena. But his powers are well developed and he has solid control over them. He also has a good spirit, but he's still working through the emotional trauma of his childhood. However, something tells me Miriam can hold her own."

"I hope so." Julia limped to the couch, lowered herself down, trying not to wince. Her backside was bruised and sore from her tumble yesterday. "I'm still shaken up over Miriam showing up here, and her psychic abilities. She's never given any indication of them in the two years she's been taking my classes."

"Why would she? Have you ever discussed your ability with anyone other than Marla?"

"Point taken. I guess Miriam doesn't like to broadcast the fact that she's different." Julia shifted to get more comfortable.

"Still sore?"

"Not too bad."

"Liar. Want me to rub it and make it better?"

Even the man's harsh voice was sexy as hell, not to

mention the erotic images his loaded suggestion triggered. *Mind over matter*, Julia told herself firmly. "No, I don't."

"Pity. You have a very nice backside."

Was he trying to bait her? She honestly didn't know, as she was extremely rusty in the flirtation/sexual innuendo department, and had never been a femme fatale to begin with. She decided the best course was to bring the focus back around.

"Why did you change your mind about Sean being involved with the search for Matt and/or the Belian? I guess they're one and the same, if they're inhabiting the same body."

"It is an odd juxtaposition, and one I've never come across." Adam sat on the love seat, stretching his long legs to the outside of the coffee table. "I wasn't going to involve Sean, but there are two reasons I've changed my mind. The first is that it would be a major battle to keep him out of it. It's one I would ultimately win, but at what cost? The second is Miriam's sudden presence here. We've already established there has to be a reason for her involvement, and if she saw Sean in her dreams, then he's meant to be a part of this."

"So it's back to the woo-woo factor."

"I never said this was an exact science."

"Tell me about it."

He chuckled, the harsh sound of his voice and his rare humor oddly endearing. "Poor Dr. Reynolds. You've shaped your reality with logic and math theorems, only to find there are things that go bump in the night and that don't give a damn about known science. It's got to be disconcerting."

The warmth in his gaze sent more heat skittering through her. God help her, she was determined to keep her emotional distance. "What sort of reconnaissance are we going to do?"

"Exactly what we discussed earlier: Check out the River-walk, looking for the spot you saw in your vision."

She remembered how grueling the process had been when they'd looked for the next target of the Dallas bomber, and how they'd been too late on two occasions. "What if that doesn't work?"

"Then we'll see what Miriam has in her bag of tricks, and take it from there. I have the feeling we're about to run out of time. Unfortunately, for the moment, there's not a damned thing we can do about it."

Julia had the same feeling herself. And she'd already seen firsthand what monsters could do.

WILLIAM Bennett stepped off the Greyhound bus and walked outside the terminal. Damn, he'd forgotten how intense the Houston traffic could be, even during the early afternoon. Funny how certain things slipped your memory when you were locked away in the bowels of hell. He sure didn't remember which Metro bus he needed to find his way to his brother's apartment. Then he'd have to check in with his parole officer. Yeah, like that was something to look forward to.

Before his release, he'd had to commit to living with Donald for a while and going to work at the sheet metal plant. His brother was a supervisor there and had gotten William a job on the assembly line. Manual labor—after he'd owned a successful business. But that business was gone now, along with his house. It burned in William's gut.

He looked down at the ill-fitting khaki slacks and oxford shirt he was wearing—the one set of civilian clothing given him for his release. He had fifty dollars in his pocket and would receive another fifty after he reported to his parole officer. *A hundred fucking dollars and an assembly-line job.* Definitely scraping the bottom of the barrel.

He could lay the blame for his ruined life squarely on one lying, cheating bitch. Just the thought of Julia Reynolds raised his already high blood pressure even more. She'd betrayed him—first by ignoring his orders and dating other men. Then, when he'd punished her, she'd called the police on him, testified against him in court. She'd been such an actress on the stand, playing the abused victim, lying, saying she'd never come on to him, even denying they had a relationship. *The whore.*

Still, thinking of her made him horny. She'd had a lush, curvy body, and he could still remember how good it had felt, fucking her and finding release inside her. It had been his right to discipline her, but he'd been punished for it. She would pay. They all would.

He would play the game, would tell the parole officer whatever he wanted to hear. Even though he wasn't supposed to go anywhere near Julia, he would find her. He would make it clear, once and for all, that he was not to be thwarted.

She would be very sorry she'd ever challenged him.

NINE

DRIVING a dark green Ford Mustang GT that had seen better days, Sean shifted gears and gunned it. *Nothing wrong with the engine*, Miriam thought, clutching her backpack against her. She tried not to gasp as he swung around a slower-moving car, missing it by what looked like a few atoms.

"Would you slow down?"

His ebony gaze flashed to her. "Scaring you, punk girl?"

What a bastard. "Uh, *yeah*. I'd like to live a little longer, like another sixty or seventy years or so."

"Oh, that's right. You're just an ordinary, fragile human." His tone implied that ordinary humans were scum. He took a turn way too fast, and she slid toward him.

Grabbing the door armrest, she fought the urge to close her eyes. "News alert, *jerk boy*. You're human, too, if I understood Adam correctly. So be sure to crash on your side."

He swung into the Comfort Inn parking lot, screeched to a neck-jolting halt. "Yeah, but I'm a lot stronger, and a hell of a lot smarter. I heal a lot faster, too."

He was right about the last statement. Already, Miriam could see the red on his face was fading, the burns less intense. "So you can heal yourself, like you did my arm?"

He leaned back in his seat. "I can repair certain things completely, given time. Gunshot wounds, broken bones, heavy blood loss, things like that, are more of a problem."

"Which means you're mortal. You can bite it, just like any of us." She opened the car door, got out. "But unlike you, I don't have a death wish. So let's take the rest of this pleasant jaunt a little slower, okay? I have no qualms about asking Adam to send you to Alaska. Might cool you off a little."

He scowled at her implication she'd be all too glad to rat him out to Adam. She offered a feral smile, pleased to have this one hold over him. "I'll be right back."

But as she walked to her room, she had to push away the edges of utter panic. What had she gotten herself into? She'd seen a lot of things in her psychic forays, knew there were a lot of bump-in-the-night things that the average person had no clue existed.

But this—superpower beings from Atlantis battling on Earth in the ever-popular good versus evil theme—took the prize. *And both Sentinels and Belians look like ordinary humans.* She thought of Adam and Sean's striking looks, and the magnetism both exuded. *Okay, maybe not totally ordinary, but still.* If Dr. Reynolds hadn't been so upset around Adam, Miriam would never have taken a closer look, would never have guessed he wasn't a normal human.

She grabbed her larger backpack, stuffed her things into it, her attention still on this morning's events. She'd also been more than a little shocked to discover Dr. Reynolds had precognitive abilities. Who would have guessed? Plus the professor was a conductor—a matched human conduit for a Sentinel.

She found it very interesting that conductors were always the opposite sex of a matched Sentinel and wondered if that created some sort of sexual attraction between them. It sure seemed like Dr. Reynolds and Adam had a chemistry thing going, especially given the way he had looked at Dr. R., his gaze heated and devouring.

More than I want to know, Miriam decided as she went into the bathroom and collected her toiletries—the various hair and makeup products she used when she wanted to flaunt convention and project an image totally at odds with whom she really was. She smiled, thinking how her unconventional style had set Sean off. She'd have to play it up even more.

She would stay and see this through. She'd already decided that when Sean called her a freak and a punk Gypsy. If nothing else, she'd hang around just to annoy the hell out of him. But she had a feeling this wasn't going to be fun and games. She couldn't shake the gut feeling that something really bad was coming.

She left her room to find Sean slouching in the hallway. "I told you'd I'd be right back," she said.

"Yeah, and Adam told us to play buddy. If anything happens to you, my ass will be in the grinder." He wrenched the backpack away from her and took off for the parking lot. She had to run to keep up with him.

"What about my car?" she asked. "I don't think we should leave it here."

"We'll swing back by to pick it up after I get my stuff. Then I'll follow you to the hotel."

"That will work." She got into the Mustang.

They didn't speak as they drove to his apartment, in an older complex in a rundown neighborhood, at what seemed to be at a slightly lower speed, although the driver's surly attitude didn't improve. Nor did his manners when he ordered her to stay put and keep her pepper foam handy.

She watched him get out of the car, aware of the large gun he wore in a holster beneath his leather jacket. She'd seen the flash of the weapon when he'd dragged her along the Riverwalk. Now she could see the subtle shift of his coat, his right hand ready to reach toward the holster as he walked up the chipped cement steps to a battered metal door and paused. It was stuff like that, along with Adam's grim vibes, which further convinced her that this Belian situation was very serious business. Sean stood there a few moments, then unlocked the door and went in.

He returned a short time later with a small duffle and slung it into the back seat. Next they stopped at Taco Cabana, where Sean got two large bags of to-go food. Then they retrieved her car and drove to the hotel.

The room keys were waiting for them at the desk, as promised. Their suite was two doors down from Dr. Reynolds and Adam. As they entered, Miriam looked around the elegant, inviting living area with appreciation. She wasn't overly materialistic, but she could enjoy luxury as well as anybody.

"Must be nicer than you're used to," Sean commented. "Taking a break from slumming."

Actually, her father made a very good living, and her mother was a psychologist with a private practice, so they lived a very comfortable lifestyle, in a modest but lovely home. Miriam also had a full scholarship to the University of Houston, and earned her own spending money and paid for her course books with her job at the Red Lion Pub, so money was not a problem for her family. Not that she would explain any of that to jerk boy.

"Oh, you know what bums we Gypsies are. Thieves and liars, too, according to popular bullshit. So, yeah, this place is pretty cushy. Probably lots of small items that will fit easily in my backpack."

He almost smiled, but he made a snorting noise instead and turned away. *Good thing*, Miriam thought, because with his face returning to normal and his great build, he was entirely too attractive. Probably knew it, and had a trail of broken hearts behind him.

Bad boys were entirely too appealing to a lot of women. Not her. She was waiting for a guy who was smart enough to count to twenty-one without being naked, and who would respect her mind and treat her as an equal. A relationship like her parents had.

They ate the food Sean had bought, and it was really good for takeout, solid Tex-Mex with some great salsas and homemade tortillas. Miriam ate one taco and one burrito, watching in amazement as Sean tackled a huge pile of enchiladas, burritos, and nachos. She couldn't eat that much in a day. The guy must have an amazing metabolism.

"So," she said as he paused eating to drink his Coke, "who is the missing Sentinel?"

She could see right away she'd hit a nerve from the flash of pain in his eyes. "His name's Matt Stevens." He snatched up another burrito, bit into it.

"And you know him well?" she pressed, curious about his reaction.

"Damn it, do you have to talk all the time?"

No one had ever called her a chatterbox and she'd spoken to him as little as possible. "Sorry," she said. "It's just that I'm trying to understand what's going on here, and from what Adam said, this Sentinel—Matt—appears to be involved in whatever situation you're so concerned about."

"So Adam thinks. But Matt's just missing, that's all. There's got to be some explanation, got to be some reason— Ah, hell." Sean tossed down the unfinished burrito and rose to pace. "What does Adam know? He's always so smug, thinks he's so smart."

"According to Dr. Reynolds, Adam is a higher level than regular Sentinels, and more powerful. Maybe he *is* as smart as he thinks, and knows what he's talking about. Care to fill me in?"

"Shit." Sean ran his hand through his thick black hair. With his dark complexion, he likely had a Hispanic heritage, which might explain some of the fiery temperament. "Matt's been missing for over two weeks. Adam says he hasn't been able to get in touch with him, but knows he's still alive."

"And he knows this how?"

"He can sense the life energies of all the Sentinels and conductors he works with. It's a Sanctioned thing."

Just one more overwhelming bit of information for Miriam to absorb. "Boy, that gives new meaning to the saying 'reach out and touch someone.'"

That got another almost-smile, but no other information. "So Adam thinks Matt's disappearance is somehow linked to the Belian," she theorized. "And if you find one, you'll find the other? Like the Belian has kidnapped Matt, or something?"

"Yeah, something like that." Sean started gathering up the trash and leftover food. "I don't want to talk about it any more. I don't like nosy females, anyway."

Miriam could tell he was upset, but he didn't have to be such a jerk. "I don't like assholes, either."

She gathered her stuff and took it to one of the bedrooms. Tossing it on the bed, she turned to close her door. But she hesitated when she glanced in the living room and saw Sean pulling a photo frame from his duffle. He handled it gently, his expression almost reverent as he looked at it.

She should have left him alone, but she felt compelled to go to him. "What is that?"

"It's personal," he said without looking up.

"A family picture?" she guessed, coming closer. "Could I see it?"

He radiated reluctance, but she really wanted to see his family. So maybe she was nosy. "Please? I'd like to see."

He turned the frame toward her. It was battered, the wood cracked on two sides, the glass broken. Inside was a photo of a man and woman and a younger version of Sean.

"What happened to this?" she asked, studying the picture.

He shrugged, but she sensed sadness rather than indifference. "I guess Matt got upset and broke it. I took it from his house two days ago. The place was a wreck, stuff everywhere." He seemed to draw in on himself. "No big deal."

Like she believed that. The light was beginning to dawn. "So this is Matt. Is he your father?"

"Not biologically, but he and his wife, Susan, basically raised me. They adopted me nine years ago."

Now she understood why he was so upset about Matt's disappearance. She looked at the vibrant brunette standing next to a man with dark blond hair. "They're very attractive. Did Susan disappear with Matt?"

"She's dead," he said bluntly.

Just step right in it, Miri. "I'm so sorry." Impulsively, she reached over to cover his hand with hers. Her fingers brushed along the wood.

She didn't mean to open herself to the energies of the picture; it just seemed to happen spontaneously. A blast of energy exploded around her, followed by a series of terrible, violent images.

She jolted back like she'd been burned, and stared at Sean, horrified. "Oh, my God."

SITTING on the sofa in their suite, Julia longed for a nice soak, and tried not to rub her aching leg too blatantly. She was exhausted and discouraged. Four long hours on the Riverwalk, some on foot, and some via the water taxi service. The water taxi had stopped at numerous places, but unfortunately, many of the umbrella-shaded restaurant terraces and the shops looked so similar, it was hard to differentiate.

She'd been certain she'd recognize the area she'd seen in her vision, but hadn't counted on how everything flowed into the next, how different things looked today than they had in her vision. Last night, she'd seen the River-walk packed with people, and today it had been less populated.

Her failure could mean loss of life. She thought of the bomber in Dallas, how much damage he'd inflicted, even when she had been able to pinpoint his targets. She felt sick inside.

Adam had been nonjudgmental, but she knew he was disappointed and concerned. He was currently bringing Miriam, who was sitting on the love seat, up to speed on the situation. "So we have a Belian who has possibly possessed the body of a Sentinel—Matt Stevens, who is Sean's father and mentor."

Miriam didn't look surprised. "Yes, I—Sean told me about Matt."

She glanced at Sean, who stood stiffly just inside the entry. His expression was blank, but Julia knew he had to be upset. Adam hadn't soft-pedaled anything; any hope Sean might have harbored about Matt had just been destroyed. He was too smart to miss the implications.

"Did he?" Adam sent a speculative glance Sean's way. "Well. To continue, we know from Julia's vision there will be some sort of altercation somewhere on the Riverwalk, but we don't know exactly what, or when, or the precise location. We weren't able to pinpoint it today."

And it was Julia's fault. Damn it, her presence here was worthless at this point.

"What type of altercation?" Miriam asked.

"That's probably too mild a word. I'm expecting a physical attack or explosion or something that will injure people," Adam replied. "Belians are adrenaline junkies, and their payback is the rush they get from terror, chaos, and pain. They thrive on those things. That's why they typically go for a high body count, like the bomber we tracked down last year.

"The other element is blood, which is how they show honor to Belial, who was their leader on Atlantis, and who demanded the blood of human sacrifices."

"Blood." The color leeched from Miriam's face. "Belial. Oh, man." She looked at Sean. "That explains what I saw this afternoon."

Adam came to full attention. "Tell me what happened." His voice was utterly calm, but Julia sensed his intensity.

Miriam's shell-shocked expression had returned. "It happened when I touched Sean's family picture. He said he got it from Matt's house two days ago, so maybe what I saw came from Matt."

"Two days ago." Adam looked at Sean, then back to her. "You're probably picking up on recent energy. What did you see?"

Miriam closed her eyes, as if seeing it again. "Blood. There was a large group of people, and blood was spurting from them. I heard gunshots and screaming, and then the words, 'All for Belial,' spoken by a man. I felt intense hatred and anger." Deathly pale, she looked at Adam. "I hadn't even heard of Belial until you told me about him just now."

His expression grim, he asked, "Did you see anything specific? A face or a place? Any details that might help us locate a potential attack?"

She shook her head. "No. It happened too quickly. I'm sorry."

"It actually ties in with Julia's vision. Let's consider the possibilities." Adam sat on the sofa near Julia.

She felt the warmth emanating from him, along with the tug of arousal that was a given. He was so dynamic, so completely in control, she found herself wanting to burrow against him, to draw on his strength. She hated her sudden neediness. For years, she'd done just fine on her own.

"We believe there will be an attack on the Riverwalk,"

Adam continued. "It was daytime in Julia's vision, and there were a lot of people. It will probably occur on a weekend, when it's more crowded. What Miriam saw confirms the weapon of attack will be a gun. Since we suspect the Belian has possessed Matt, we know what it will look like."

Sean's jaw worked, but he nodded. He could no longer deny Matt was possessed. "Okay. So we know a lot of stuff, but what do we do about it?"

"This is where I think Miriam's particular talents might be helpful."

She squared her shoulders. "I'll do what I can. What did you have in mind?"

"I want you to use your crystal to try to divine the exact area of the attack." Adam pushed the coffee table closer to Miriam and unfolded a detailed map of the Riverwalk.

She slipped the crystal and chain over her head. "I hope I can tap into the right energies. I'd do better if I could hold something the Belian had touched, like the photograph."

"That won't be necessary," Adam told her. "I'll feed you a little of the energy I've picked up from it."

Concern skittered through Julia. She knew how nasty Belian vibrations could be. "Adam, don't you think that will be too much for her?"

"She can handle it. I'm only going to channel a small amount. And Sean and I will shield."

"Shield?" Miriam asked. "Is that like calling for protection?"

"That's exactly what it is," Adam said. He pulled a pendant from beneath his cashmere sweater. Julia had seen Marla's husband, Luke, wearing something similar, but this was more ornate. Entwined gold and silver wire framed the pink stone, and it appeared there were inscriptions ringing the edges of the stone itself.

"Wow," Miriam said. "That's pink quartz, right?"

"Yes, similar to your scrying stone, but this one is attuned to the vibration of the Tuaoi stone, also known as the Great Crystal, which was on Atlantis."

"It wasn't destroyed with Atlantis?"

"No, but that's another story. Do you do any sort of centering or protections?"

"Always," Miriam said. "There's a lot of bad stuff out there, and I don't want to attract it to me."

"Smart girl." Adam looked at Sean, who had slipped out his own crystal pendant. "Then let's get to it."

He wrapped his fingers around his pendant, closed his eyes. Miriam and Sean followed suit. Julia could feel the surge of air and heat and power. The hairs on her arms stood on end, and the room practically crackled with energy. It reminded her of college physics experiments with electrostatic machines—except this was being done without any machine.

"Oh, man," Miriam breathed, opening her eyes. "I've never felt anything quite like this. It's awesome."

"And hopefully, it will offer sufficient protection from discarnate entities, and keep the Belian from sensing us." Adam tucked his pendant beneath his sweater, sat beside her on the love seat. "Are you ready?"

She swallowed, nodded. Holding the chain in her right thumb and index finger, she positioned it a few inches above the map, over the Drury Inn, where the buildup began at the north end of the Riverwalk.

"Turn your left palm up," Adam requested. He placed his right hand over her upturned palm. "Now proceed as you normally would."

Miriam bit her lip, her gaze moving to Adam's hand, then back to the map. "Will the Belian attack be near this area?" she asked in a low voice. The pendulum moved slightly back and forth. "That's a no," she explained.

She moved the pendulum farther east, near the Omni La Mansión del Río. "Will the Belian attack be here?"

Again, a slight back and forth motion. She drew a deep breath, shuddered.

"What's wrong?" Julia asked.

"Just a little nausea." Miriam's eyes were a little glassy, and she was still very pale. "Like I've eaten something rotten."

"It's the Belian energy," Adam said. "It won't cause any permanent damage. We'll clear any residual from your system when we're done. Can you hang on?"

"Yeah, sure." Miriam's voice was shaky, but her hand was steady enough. She continued to move the pendulum a little bit at a time, getting steady "nos"—until she reached the Hyatt Regency area of the Riverwalk. Then the pendulum began swinging in a circle. "That's a yes."

"Can you pinpoint it more?" Adam asked.

She tried, but from the Hyatt Regency south through the heaviest concentration of restaurants, the pendulum kept circling. "I don't know why it's picking such a large area," she said, frustration in her voice.

"Because nothing is set in stone," Adam said. "The Belian has chosen a general area, and will strike when the opportunity presents itself." He pulled his hand back. "You can stop now, Miriam. Thank you."

She lowered the chain. "We can try for a date and the time of the attack."

Adam nodded. "Good idea. How do we do that?"

Per Miriam's instructions, Julia got a piece of paper and drew lines dividing it into quadrants, putting the dates for the current day, Saturday, Sunday, and Monday, one in each quadrant.

"We're screwed if it attacks today," Sean said.

"I don't think it will," Adam said. "It will wait for larger crowds. With all the people coming in for Oktoberfest, the Riverwalk will be very crowded this weekend. My money is on Saturday or Sunday. But like I said, nothing is set in stone. It probably hasn't planned all the details yet."

Miriam used the pendant over the dates, and it circled over both Saturday and Sunday. It did the same thing with all the times they wrote on another piece of paper.

"Great," Julia said. "He's going to attack sometime on Saturday or Sunday, anywhere from the Hyatt Regency to the Hilton Palacio del Rio. Piece of cake."

"Not 'he,' 'it.' The Belian might be in a human body, but it has no true humanity," Adam reminded her. He studied the map. "The information gives us a place to start."

Not commenting, Sean turned and walked toward the dining area, his body tense.

"Miriam, I'm wondering if you could use the pendulum to locate the Belian," Adam said. "It's not staying at Matt's, but it's got to be somewhere around San Antonio."

"I can try."

Adam went to his briefcase on the table and returned with a map of the entire city. They spent another thirty minutes with Miriam going painstakingly over every inch of the map, without any positive sign from the pendulum. Finally Adam curtailed the exercise.

"We're not doing any good here," he said. "The Belian obviously has control of Matt, and is well shielded. It's a powerful son of a bitch. It's most certainly drawing some of that power from Matt."

Miriam looked despondent. "I haven't been much help. What else can I do?"

"Believe me, any information is useful," Adam told her. "Do your psychometric abilities ever show future events?"

"Very rarely. When I hold an object, it usually shows me things about the last owner—emotions, current events, or events in the past. I'm generally not precognitive. What happened this afternoon was very unusual."

Adam considered. "Then I don't think there would be any benefit in retrieving anything else from Matt's house for you to read."

"We don't have many answers on the particulars of an

attack on a huge number of people on the Riverwalk," Julia pointed out. "But you can't just let this go, Adam. You have to contact the authorities."

"And tell them what? That they have to close one of the largest and busiest sections of the Riverwalk for the entire weekend, and maybe beyond that—all without any proof of eminent danger? Should I call Homeland Security and tell them there will be a terrorist attack?"

He shook his head in frustration. "We face this dilemma with every Belian we track. We have to be careful about raising too many alarms and risking exposure. Not only that, but warning people doesn't stop the Belian. It just goes somewhere else to wreck havoc."

He rose and went to stare out over the Riverwalk. "I'm responsible for every innocent who becomes a victim. *Damn it!*"

When Julia had first met Adam, she'd been convinced he had ice water in his veins and a stone heart. But now she knew better. The more time she spent with him, the more she realized the weight of the burden he carried every day of his existence, and how capably he handled it. Sure made it hard to stay mad over his arrogant and dominating behavior.

Compassion drove her off the couch and over to him. She placed her hand on his arm, felt the strength of tensed muscles, along with the usual jolt of sexual awareness. "I'm not suggesting you're mishandling this, Adam. But surely there's something we can do."

"Believe me, I'll continue to look for something."

She dropped her hand. "I wish I could do more."

"You can," he said softly. "And very soon."

A chill went through her, but she wasn't backing away from this fight. "All right."

He looked over her at Sean and Miriam. "I want you two to go to your suite, and stay there until I contact you. Order room service if you get hungry.

"Sean, do a cleansing on Miriam to get rid of any residual Belian energy. Also, I've got an extra police scanner, and I want you to set it up and monitor it constantly. Miriam, do any meditation, dowsing, Tarot reading, whatever you think might give you more insights."

He looked back at Julia. "You're with me, professor." The dark magic in his voice sent waves of heat curling through her.

They spent a few minutes entering everyone's mobile number into each cell phone. Then Sean got the scanner, and he and Miriam left. Adam closed the door behind them, stood there a minute. "Something has to break soon, or we're going to have a large number of casualties."

"I would say the probabilities of your assumption being correct are high." Julia's leg began trembling, so she made her way to the couch.

Adam followed, settling down next to her. The air around them charged with heated energy. "Let me work on that leg for you."

He was too damned perceptive. "No, it's not necessary. You don't need to—Adam, stop!"

But he already had her leg lifted onto his lap, and her shoe slipped off. He slid his hands beneath her pants to massage her cramping muscles.

"Damn it, Adam!" She reached for her cane to smack him, but it slid out of her reach and pitched a few feet away. "Whatever happened to 'no means no'?" she fumed, trying to free her leg.

"And whatever happened to your claim that you're not a violent person? That's a theory that needs revisited."

"The violent tendencies only come out when I'm around you," she muttered. "When you're forcing me into untenable situations."

"I'm not forcing you into anything right now. I'm just trying to ease your pain." His fingers pressed into her calf and her abused muscles practically moaned in relief.

All right, so it felt wonderful. The man had great hands,

not that she would admit it to him. He didn't need any encouragement. She leaned her head against the sofa back, her thoughts blurring.

"I have an interesting theory about you," Adam said, his fingers tracing heated patterns on her calf.

She shook away the mental fog. "It's more likely a conjecture. Theories don't mean anything without proofs to back them up."

"I believe your basic nature is fiery. That up until twelve years ago, you probably were an extroverted personality, with razor-sharp wit and brilliant repartees."

He was closer than she'd like to admit. But she wasn't that person anymore. The outgoing, vivacious woman she'd been had died, a casualty of Bennett's brutality. And it was none of Adam's damned business.

"That's just abduction methodology," she told him. "You're assigning an explanation to your observations. It's guessing, which has no scientific value."

"For whatever reasons—perhaps this sexual chemistry between us—it appears I bring out your edgy side," he said, ignoring her statement. "Somehow I'm able to trigger all that marvelous fire and passion, and the latent violence behind it. I find it very . . . stimulating."

"I am *not* violent!"

He slid his fingers a little higher to the sensitive area behind her knee, and she shivered. Primal sensations surged up her leg, settling in her belly and elsewhere. *Damned sexual energy.*

"Great. Here we go again," she muttered. "This is why you shouldn't be touching me. Enough, Adam." She tried to retrieve her leg.

"Why do you keep fighting the inevitability of the attraction between us?" His voice dropped to a dark-magic rumble that sent a new wave of heat curling through her. "Am I so abhorrent to you that you can't accept the fact that we *will* come together sexually?"

Oh, man. This would be so much easier if he wasn't so gorgeous and sexy. "Why are you so determined to force a nonexistent issue?" she demanded, trying to ignore the tension pounding through her head. Worse than the tension, than the relentless pull of desire, was the taunting, underlying fear of intimacy with any man.

She wasn't a coward, damn it. Besides, this attraction wasn't the real thing. "You're a Sanctioned. You've been celibate for centuries, and you're not supposed to be affected by so-called matters of the flesh."

"Tell my body that." His gaze dropped to her tingling breasts. "While you're at it, maybe you should consider your own physical responses."

"Let go of me." She jerked her leg down, scooted to the end of the couch. "You know I can't control my physical responses to you. That's purely a chemical reaction, and has nothing to do with what I really want."

He stared at her a long moment, those disturbing star-bursts of light flashing in his eyes. "I think you're in denial about what you really want. You need to accept the attraction between us, Julia. It's not going away. We're going to have to work in close proximity, so this will happen a lot. Especially considering what we need to do next."

Uh-oh. "And what's going to happen next?"

"I've worked and reworked the Belian energy from the IMAX crime scene and from Matt's house. I've fed some of it to both you and Miriam, and gotten inconclusive results."

He rubbed the bridge of his nose. "I've got to have more information and a stronger psychic signature to work with. That leaves only one option."

His burning gaze locked with hers. "We need to do a conduction. Tonight."

TEN

MIRIAM entered the suite still feeling nauseated, and she had a nasty headache brewing as well. The floral scents in the living area that had been refreshing earlier were now cloying, souring her stomach even more. Sean came in behind her and closed the door as she started toward her bedroom.

"Where are you going?" he asked. "We have unfinished business. I have to debug you."

The last sentence made her think of the bugging scene in *The Matrix. Ewww.* "Don't worry about it. Half a bottle each of Tums and ibuprofen should do the trick."

He grabbed her arm, pulled her back. "Nope. Sorry. I've got my orders." He tossed the scanner onto the armchair.

She figured it wouldn't do any good to struggle; she couldn't win in a physical match with him. If she had her pepper foam handy, that might even the odds.

"And I'm sure you do *everything* Adam tells you," she

taunted. It might be childish, but she felt like hell, and wasn't on her best behavior right now.

"You may not believe this, but I generally follow orders. Adam and I might not agree on how to handle the current situation, but he is my boss, for lack of a better word. So I am duty bound to get rid of any Belian energy still inside you."

She hoped the "debugging" wasn't as unsettling as the feeling when Adam buzzed her with a little Belian energy. That had been nasty and foul, burning inside her like alcohol on a wound. "Fine. Could we make this as painless as possible?"

He made clucking noises—very mature and appealing. "It won't hurt for more than a few minutes."

"Great," she muttered, trepidation coiling inside her. She'd had enough unpleasantness for one day. Had it really been less than eight hours since she left the Comfort Inn this morning, in search of Dr. Reynolds? It seemed more like days.

Sean placed his large hands on either side of her face. They were warm and surprisingly gentle for such a tough, angry guy. "Close your eyes," he told her, "And try not to scream too loud."

"Very funny," she muttered. But she found herself bracing, until she saw the laughter in his eyes. "Oh, don't tell me you have a sense of humor. That's too many shocks for one day."

"Sorry about that." He grinned, and she saw he had dimples. Add that to the bad-boy persona and the dark good looks, and the guy was killer. She was off balance and not thinking clearly. No way would she allow herself to be attracted to him.

"Okay, do your thing," she told him, and closed her eyes.

His fingers tingled against her skin. Slow, hypnotic warmth rolled through her body. With her inner eye, she sensed more than saw bright, cleansing light flowing in the heated wake, chasing all vestiges of darkness from her body. Her stomach calmed and her muscles relaxed.

But a new sensation tensed her muscles. A new type of heat caressed her skin. Desire sparked and flared; sexual energy rolled through her veins, turning her body on like a light switch. Need sizzled in several key spots. Startled, it took her a moment to figure out what was happening. Damn it! The guy really was a class A bastard.

"Cut it out!" She slapped Sean's arms away and stepped back. "You're a lowlife slime, you know that?"

His eyes narrowed. "What the hell are you talking about? I just did you a favor."

Some favor. No way could he not know, especially since she had no doubt he'd used some of his special powers to turn her on. Both Adam and Sean had said she wasn't a conductor, and therefore she assumed she wasn't in the sexual attraction loop that apparently occurred between Sentinels and conductors. But that didn't mean Sean couldn't zap her with some sexual mojo and try to take advantage of her. *What a jerk.*

"You know what? Just keep your distance."

Anger flared in his eyes. "Gladly. I don't like hanging with freaks anyway—especially when they're crazy."

So he was just yanking the sexual chain for grins? At least she could respect the basic lust a young, healthy guy might feel, even for a woman who wasn't his type. In her experience, most twenty-something guys didn't require much to get turned on. But she believed Sean was playing with her, and found it infuriating. Damned if she'd show it, though.

"I wouldn't point too many fingers, Mr. Supernatural." She scooped up her backpack and headed to her bedroom.

"Hey, a 'Thank you for getting rid of the evil Belian sludge inside me' would be nice."

"Oh, go burn on Saturn." Sean had told her about Belian expulsions to Saturn earlier, and it gave her supreme satisfaction to throw that back at him before she closed the door.

Then she locked it very deliberately, although she didn't know if a mere lock would be effective against a Sentinel. She wondered if there was some sort of metal or alloy that disabled them. For all she knew, they might even be repelled by garlic.

Not that any was necessary, because she and Sean seemed to naturally repel each other. On the other hand, if it worked on Belians, that would be helpful. Apparently, Belians were the epitome of true evil.

And she had a very bad feeling about the one they were hunting.

A conduction. Julia stared at Adam, feeling as if the wind had been knocked out of her. Shock fired through her, the kind that made it impossible to think clearly, much less assimilate accurate data. But then Adam had the ability to reduce her to both bumbling idiot and raving lunatic status.

"You led me to believe that you needed me for my precognitive visions. And I made it clear that we wouldn't do any conductions. I can't—"

Coward. She'd been wrong—she *was* a coward. She should be willing to do *anything* to stop this Belian. But old demons were raising ugly heads, spurring painful memories that overrode rationality. She felt like she was on a roller coaster, going from a physical bombardment of sexual energy to an emotional bombardment—all of it a highly unstable mixture.

"I did not mislead you about needing your visions," Adam said. "And I've referred several times to the spiritual and physical bonds between us, and what I've seen in my own visions. We just discussed all of this."

"If your visions are so damned powerful, why the hell do you need me?" She struggled to her feet.

"Julia." He stood, moving forward as she tried to back away. He reached out and grasped her arm. "Listen to me. We will *not* have sex, unless it is by mutual agreement."

"What about the conduction? What kind of game are you playing, Adam?"

"Sit down. Give me a chance to explain."

"I can't. Not right now." She whirled, looking for her cane. She desperately needed to put some distance between them, needed time to regain her self-control.

She hated that her thoughts were in a tumult. That she had panicked like a wounded animal and overreacted. That Adam had the power to shake up her hard-won control—and that he had to see her like this. He was a powerful adversary—one who would ruthlessly take advantage of her weakness if it suited his purposes.

But worst of all was the brutal reminder she might never get over what Bennett had done to her. That he might win.

"Julia. You're going to hear me out." Determination edged Adam's voice. In one swift move, he sat on the couch, pulling her down beside him. His arm circled her shoulders, effectively pinning her against him.

She tried to get free, found her limbs going rubbery, while a strange lethargy flowed through her. She managed to raise her fist and hit his shoulder, but it was like moving slow motion through quicksand and carried no force. "How dare you take advantage of me with your freaky abilities!" At least her vocal chords were working.

"Believe me, you'd know if I was taking advantage. I'm just helping you to calm down, so we can discuss this rationally—something that's supposedly one of your strong points. And so I can explain that a conduction doesn't necessarily include sex."

Surprise stilled her struggles. "*What?* I thought sexual surges and intercourse were part of the deal."

"All conductions involve a sexual surge as the energy

initiates and flows up through the four lower chakras. But the actual sex is optional. It makes the conduction more effective, but it's not necessary. In this case, as a Sanctioned, I can pull in more energy, so we'll still have a very clear conduction without joining physically."

"Oh." She was definitely in the bumbling idiot category now. "I didn't know. Nobody told me that."

"Marla never mentioned it?"

"We've never discussed her sex life. I guess she's reluctant because of . . . damn it." She tried to push against him, getting the quicksand effect again. "Let me go."

"In a minute, after I'm certain you won't try to mutilate me." He slid his hand along her shoulder, kneaded the knots there. "You're so tense. Take a deep breath, and try to relax."

She felt like a fool, but she did what he requested, so he'd release her. Being this close to Adam was wreaking havoc on her libido again, almost like a sensual overdose. She might be psychologically crippled when it came to sex, but her hormones were alive and well and currently clamoring, given the fact he was such a primo male. Not to mention the Sentinel/Sanctioned/whatever/conductor bond.

Her utter embarrassment at her behavior helped quench some of the hormonal fire. For the second time in as many days, she'd lost all sense and self-control, her emotional meltdowns going way beyond sane actions.

"I'm sorry. I don't know what got into me," she murmured. "The panic was a gut-level reaction. I keep telling myself that I'm over the ra—" Even now, she couldn't bring herself to say *rape*. It was just a word. Why couldn't she say it?

"What happened twelve years ago," she continued. "I won't give Bennett any victory over me—at least, that's what I keep telling myself. But the thought of being with any man still throws me. I hate this loss of control. I hate my cowardice."

His hand slid over the nape of her neck, an unsettling, possessive gesture. "Listen to me, Julia. You are *not* a coward. Not when you were attacked, or when you testified against that bastard and put him away, and went on with your life. And you're not a coward now. You're just dealing with a lot of unsettling things, including Bennett's release. You're normally so self-contained and controlled that you probably never vent your feelings. Sooner or later, the pressure valve is bound to blow."

Great. Dr. Masters was in session, and worse, he was probably right. But he wasn't her therapist, and she wasn't delving into her psyche with him. She brought the discussion back around to the matter at hand.

"I want to catch this Belian as badly as you do. I want his rotten soul to burn on Saturn for an eternity. And I want to help make that happen. Even if my emotional baggage might put a crimp in a sexual conduction, if we can do one without the sex, I'm completely willing."

"That's the Julia I know and admire."

"And I would like to be able to move now."

He released her, and she felt the strength returning to her limbs. She slid away from him, resettled herself at a safer distance. "I know you told me you had visions, but I never really thought about what that meant. Why do you need me if you're capable of seeing things?"

He stood and went over to the wet bar, produced a bottle of merlot and a corkscrew. She found herself staring at his ultraprimo butt, hastily forced her attention elsewhere.

"Like you, I can't always control what I see," he said. "It's very difficult for me to envision Belian activities, because of their shielding abilities. Why your precognitive ability can get past those shields is one of those universal mysteries. It's also a point in our favor."

He opened the bottle and got out two wineglasses. "A conduction works by amplifying the Belian's psychic signature that's already been gathered, unraveling some of the layers and revealing more of the Belian's essence. It provides deeper insights into the Belian, and often more information."

She considered that. "I remember you telling me that in a conduction, the third-eye energies of both the Sentinel and the conductor merge to create the magnification of the Belian psychic signature."

"That's correct." He brought a glass of wine to her. "I know we haven't eaten yet, but it's probably best to wait until after the conduction. However, there's nothing wrong with a tonic to calm the nerves."

She accepted the wine. "I'm not sure one glass will do the job."

He tapped his glass to hers. "When we're done, you can have the rest of the bottle if you want. I'll even throw in some chocolate."

She had to smile. "You know, you can be really nice when you want to be."

His expression turned serious. "You might not think so when all is said and done."

Just like that, they were back to the reminder that he was a Sanctioned, capable of being utterly ruthless if he deemed it necessary.

Not to mention the fact that they were about to do a conduction.

IT was a constant struggle keeping the cursed Sentinel under control. He had to wage the battle whenever the alcohol began wearing off, whenever the Sentinel had a surge of awareness and fought to regain the upper hand. But he was clever, and he used the Sentinel's foolish grief over a mere human, used his weakness for alcohol, to keep him in an emotional and physical stupor.

By doing so, he was able to maintain control—just barely. He had the disadvantage of trying to function in a physical body that was impaired by booze, of having to deal with constant hangovers. And whenever the Sentinel started regaining cognizance, he had to force more alcohol into the body to keep control.

But Belial's hunger for blood, for vengeance, sustained him. He was more powerful, more cunning than the mourning Sentinel. Hatred was far more potent than weak, nonproductive emotions like love or empathy. And blood was far headier than liquor or drugs. It offered an indescribable euphoria, forged a bond with Belial.

Belial was with him now, giving him strength and purpose. He had planned to make the blood offering over the weekend, when the Riverwalk would be more crowded with humans, to give more glory to Belial. But he sensed he was being hunted. And the Sentinel was stirring again, fighting to get back to the surface, back in control.

He had to strike while he had the upper hand.

So he strolled the Riverwalk, pleased that there were a lot of people out tonight. They were eating, listening to music, shopping, or just walking. All unaware of their destiny to glorify Belial. They thought they were safe, and the many police officers patrolling the Riverwalk added to that sense of false security.

He spotted a policeman ahead of him, and Belial suggested a grand plan. One that he had never considered. It was unexpected, and so devious, so brilliant. It involved tapping into the powers of the subdued Sentinel and adding them to his own impressive abilities. Then he would reach out—just so—and take control of the policeman's mind.

And then . . . There would be blood for Belial. All for Belial.

* * *

HIS name was Tomas Olvera, and he was good at his job. He'd been on the San Antonio police force for six years and genuinely liked people, which made him well suited for patrolling the Riverwalk. He had a low-key, personable way about him that could calm the rowdiest partygoer. But he could also be tough, if the need arose.

He loved his beat, because it wasn't strenuous work and it wasn't particularly dangerous. It enabled him to spend quality time with his family and not worry about leaving them prematurely. He adored his two children, Anna and Daniel; he and his wife, Maria, had a great marriage. Life was good.

Tomas was on duty this balmy Friday night, but he was off tomorrow and planned to take his family to Six Flags for Daniel's fifth birthday. As he patrolled the Riverwalk, he thought about the miniature motorized four-wheeler he'd gotten Daniel, and how his son would love it. Another part of him kept a sharp eye out for any problems.

The headache struck with sudden and debilitating force. It felt like someone had stuck a hot poker in his head. A wave of dizziness swept through him. He stumbled, tried to catch his balance. He reached for his radio to call for help.

But darkness descended, inexorable . . . and final.

JULIA sat on the sofa, her tension palpable. She was pale, despite the wine. Adam had moved the coffee table aside and pulled an armchair across from her. He sat, took her cold right hand in his left. "Do you trust me?"

A spark of humor flared in her eyes. "About as far as I can shove you. Throwing you would be impossible."

He could feel her anxiety, sense the roiling emotions beneath her composed exterior. He wasn't nervous, but low-level adrenaline buzzed through him. "If it makes you feel any better, I've never done this before, either."

"Good. I'd hate to be the only conduction virgin here." She gave him a challenging look. "Are you sure you know what to do?"

"Of course. It's my job to know these things."

"I can count on one constant with you—arrogance."

He knew she was saying that to ease some of her tension. In the past two days, she'd become more relaxed around him, not always on her guard or so prickly. She might not realize it, would probably deny it vehemently, but subtle changes in her body language when they were together told him otherwise. It had surprised him earlier when she put her hand on his arm and offered her support. Progress.

"There are a few things you should know," he said. "Once the conduction starts, don't break our hand connection. Brace yourself, because the energies will rise fast, and they'll be very powerful. You'll feel strong sensations, possibly discomfort, in certain centers of your body as the chakras open. You'll probably see colors and hear sounds. When our third eyes open and engage, you'll see images flashing by at a rapid speed, and they might be disturbing. You don't have to try to decipher them, or do anything but hold on. I'll be able to absorb them and mentally replay them later."

"So I'm basically just a lowly conduit."

"Not lowly—you're an extremely important component of this process. I'm going to shield now. Give me a few moments."

He pulled the pendant from beneath his sweater with his free hand, and going a step further than his earlier shielding, opened his crown chakra without preliminary meditation; something only Sanctioned could do.

Immediately, his soul was sucked from his body, hurtling up, up, up, into the spiritual planes. Looking back, he saw the shining silver cord anchoring him to his physical body; saw the Earth far below, a glistening orb of jewel tones.

Then he saw the shimmering, wavering shapes of the High Sanctioned, felt the jolt of their immense power like an electrical shock. Heard the cacophony of sounds that, with focus and intent, could be translated into comprehensible words—divine messages from demigods.

The mystical veil that separated the current physical life from the akashic records of all existence, past, present, future, dissolved. Adam could see his past lives, flashes of Atlantis and the temple where he had served The One. It was a heady experience, and one in which a weaker being could become enmeshed. For Adam, it was merely an attunement of his power for the conduction.

He dropped back down to Earth, slid into his body with ease. As he settled, he chanted the ancient Atlantian words of supplication: *Being of Light, surround us in your love and protection. Shield us from all that is not of the Light. Guide us to vision and truth, so that we may serve the Light.* He felt the protection of The One wrap around Julia and him. It was time.

"Ready?" he asked, releasing the pendant.

"Is that a rhetorical question?"

"I'll take that as a yes. Hold out your left hand, and turn both hands palm up." He placed his hands over hers, palm down, and then wrapped his fingers around her hands. "Don't let go."

He didn't even have the words out before the energies surged up into the base chakras, exploding like gasoline torched by a match. Sexual need punched through him, bursting open the four chakras almost simultaneously with flashes of red and orange. A burning sensation in his chest competed with the raging demands of his sudden erection.

He'd just thought he could retain control. Now he wasn't so certain.

He felt Julia jolt upright. "God," she gasped.

"Easy now," he murmured. "The base chakras are open. Hold on."

Her fingers gripped his hands like talons. The burning moved to his throat in a burst of vivid blue. "Fifth chakra open," he said, working to keep his focus.

"Don't tell me there's more." Her voice was strained, husky.

He couldn't even answer. He was struggling with the shocking revelation that handling this was pushing him to the limit. And he was a Sanctioned. The clamoring of his physical body almost overrode the spiritual, demanding that he haul Julia down on the couch, strip her naked, and bury himself in her lush body.

It took immense will to resist those base demands, for his intellect to dominate. He held the line—barely—as an arrow point of intense pressure filled his head, showcased by a blanket of indigo. The pressure increased, pulsing toward his forehead. A firework display of violet colors shot in every direction.

"Adam!" came Julia's distressed cry.

"Crown chakra open," he managed. "We're in. Hang on."

Energy rocketed back down through the lower chakras, and back up, back down, back up. It felt like his body was rocking from the force. His third eye linked with Julia's in an audible pop, colors changing from violet to indigo and back again.

Images began flashing at split-second speed. He shoved everything else aside—the pounding sexual need, the shattering g-force of the racing energy, the feeling of his body being tossed around like a leaf in a tornado—and concentrated on locking the images into his brain.

Even as he did, on another level, he was aware of Julia, of her labored breathing and pounding heart, of the sharp edge of panic. "Stay with me, Julia. I need to you to hold on."

"I'm here," she whispered.

"Good." He returned his full attention to processing the images. Gradually they began to slow, then to fade. As they did, the energies ebbed, swirling away like water down a drain, until only a faint tingling remained.

Feeling like he'd run a twenty-mile race, Adam opened his eyes and released Julia's hands. She stared back at him, her chest heaving, her eyes dilated, her skin flushed. The scent of arousal, the heat of excruciating sexual desire, hung between them. He could see her breasts were swollen beneath her suit jacket, could see the imprint of her nipples, and his body responded in a primitive rush that had his dick throbbing.

He wanted to feel the weight of those breasts in his hands, to explore the taste and texture of her skin, to learn how it felt to be inside her. To possess her completely, in the most primal way a man could claim a woman.

Shaken, he had to forcibly derail his thoughts of seducing her, of proving she wanted him as badly as he wanted her, that she could enjoy sex again and Bennett couldn't control her life any further. It stunned him again, how the physical needs of the body could almost overcome even a mind as powerful as his. He had a new respect for his Sentinels as he forced back his body's frantic demands.

"Are you all right?" he asked.

"That's relative," she replied, still breathing hard. "I'm alive—I think."

He could feel the residual energy radiating from her. He had automatically begun channeling the excess in his body back to the elements, something he did routinely after meditation. That didn't apply to the acute horniness inundating his body, but then there weren't many options for dispersing that. "Here, give me your hand again."

"I don't think so. I'm going to take still being alive and cut my losses."

He leaned forward, grabbed the closest hand, which sent another jolt though his system. She was trembling, and his protective instincts kicked in. "I'm just going to release some of the energy still charging your chakras."

She let him channel it off, and he felt some of the tension leaving her body, felt the tremors easing. "That *is* better," she said. "Got anything for a killer headache?"

"As a matter of fact, I do." He moved to sit beside her, placed one hand on her forehead, one on the back of her head. He resisted the urge to lean down and breathe in her natural, intoxicating scent.

"Take some deep breaths." He pulled healing energy into her head, dissipating the pressure and heat built up there. "Is that better?"

"Much, thank you." She shifted, crossed her legs.

He didn't have to look any further than his own lap to guess why. "Unfortunately, there's nothing I can do about the excess hormones, except suggest a cold shower and/or certain battery-operated appliances. Unless you've changed your mind about having mind-blowing sex with me."

"Not going to happen." But her gaze went south, lingered on his straining erection before shifting away. "Oh. Well. I guess we're both in the same boat there."

"As I've already mentioned, it's a new experience for me," he said wryly. "Now we need to shift focus and work on the images we just saw. That's the most crucial aspect of this conduction. Can you remember any of them?"

She shuddered. "Only too well. Some of it was similar to last night's vision, but other things were different."

"The images were surprisingly clear and smooth." He closed his eyes, mentally triggered a flow of the images, like a slide show. "Yes, very clear and more like watching a movie . . . or a vision."

He opened his eyes, looked at her. "From what I understand, this isn't what Sentinels usually see during a conduction. They see disjointed, jerky pictures, which they have to go back and piece together. I think we're looking at one of your visions, which I've never been able to see before now. But apparently the amplified third-eye link of the conduction not only triggered a vision, but allowed both of us to see it."

"That makes sense. This was like my other visions, except it wasn't exactly what I saw last night," Julia said. "This time, it was like I was watching through someone's eyes. Do you think that was the Belian?"

"My guess is yes." Adam closed his eyes again, reengaged the images. "It's moving along the Riverwalk. There are a lot of people. There's a police officer ahead."

"I saw the policeman, too. That was different from the other vision."

"The officer is pulling a gun. Shooting into the crowd." Adam also saw people screaming and running, some jumping into the water to get away from the shots, and blood everywhere. But there was no need to mention that. "That's different from what you saw last night, isn't it?"

"Yes. I didn't see the shooter then, and this time, there was much more blood." Her voice was low, strained.

He opened his eyes. She looked even paler. "Try not to think about that. Focus on little details."

She bit her lip, nodded. "I saw the policeman's hat fall off."

He closed his eyes again. "I'm seeing that now."

"But I never saw his face. Does it help that he had black hair?"

He had just realized the same thing. Alarm snaked through him. "Wait a minute. Wait. Black hair. That can't be right."

"Why not?"

"Matt has dark blond hair. Something's not right here."

"You just said I was probably seeing through the Belian's eyes," she pointed out. "Which means he—it—is looking at the police officer. But the officer was the one shooting. That doesn't make sense . . . does it?"

"No, it doesn't."

"There were a number of differences in this vision. It's hard to identify them, because this one happened so fast, and the lights were so bright."

"The lights," he said. "Yes. There were lights all along the Riverwalk. That can't be right. What you saw last night occurred during the daytime."

"Yes, the sun was shining. But just now was . . ." Her eyes widened. "It was at night, Adam."

He'd already come to that conclusion. A very nasty feeling vibrated in his gut. "It was too clear and vivid . . . like real time." He was on his feet, reaching for his coat and BlackBerry.

Julia pushed herself up. "So the Belian is going to change the time of the attack?"

"I'm afraid it already has."

There was a sudden pounding on the door. Adam whirled, reaching it in three strides and throwing it open. Miriam stood there, her eyes wild. "Sean sent me to tell you there's been a shooting on the Riverwalk. It happened just minutes ago. There's so much on the scanner, it's hard to get the details. He's listening for more information."

"Oh, no," Julia said.

"Damn it!" Adam clenched his hands. "We're too late. Miriam, go tell Sean to get his weapons and meet me in the lobby immediately. After that, come back here, and bring the scanner with you. Think you know how to use it?"

"Yes. I watched Sean operate it."

"I want you ladies to stay together, and to monitor the scanner, in case there's anything else. If there is, call me immediately. Do not leave the hotel, keep the door locked, and wait to hear from me. That clear?"

They both nodded, and Miriam started back to the other

suite. Adam forced the fury and frustration away. He felt himself slipping into full Sanctioned mode, calmness and power descending. He was going to track down this Belian and dispense it from the Earth plane.

He only hoped Matt wouldn't be a casualty.

ELEVEN

HE surfaced slowly, an excruciating headache pounding in his head, and his body feeling battered and weak. He felt like he'd been beaten. Worse, he was confused and disoriented, like . . . before. He looked around the unfamiliar room, vague memories struggling to surface. Why couldn't he think? Was he sick, had he been in an accident?

He got to his feet, swaying as he took in his surroundings, obviously a cheap hotel room. Where the hell was he? He didn't remember this place, yet it looked familiar. A feeling of déjà vu came over him. Buzzing in his ears turned into a harsh whisper.

You don't want to be awake. You don't want to remember. Susan is dead. She was killed, and it's your fault. You're responsible for her death. But you don't want to think about that. You want to drink, to forget. To go back under . . .

The spear of pain was like a shock to his mind, forcing some clarity in its wake.

Drink, you want to drink. There's a bottle by the bed, the voice hissed in his ear. *It will help you forget about Susan.*

Oh God, Susan. Susan! He turned toward the nightstand, saw the bottle there. It was so tempting. He didn't want to remember. To feel. To see the image of her grave. He took a step, but the sudden roiling in his stomach sent him around and to the bathroom. He was wretchedly sick, throwing up until there was nothing but dry heaves. He heard his phone ringing in the other room, but was too weak to get up to answer it.

He stayed on the floor a few more minutes. The purging seemed to make him more alert, but it didn't diminish the throbbing in his head. He pushed himself up and to the sink, stared in the mirror. The image looking back shocked him. A gaunt, pale face, bloodshot eyes, filthy uncombed hair. That wasn't him. Couldn't be him. Hell, did he even know his name?

He had to get a grip. He leaned down, ignoring the sudden dizziness, and splashed cold water on his face. He came up to look in the mirror again, heaved a shuddering breath. *I'm Matt . . . Matt Stevens*, he told himself. *I'm a Sentinel. I*—Jesus, what was going on? He had to call Adam. As if on cue, his phone rang again. He turned and started out of the bathroom.

You don't want to answer that. You don't want to call Adam. Because then you'll have to remember, the voice taunted. *Susan is dead. Susan is dead. Susan is dead.*

A new rush of pain brought memory flashes. But these weren't of Susan. These were . . . a theater, fire, smoke, people screaming. Then more images . . . a policeman shooting into a crowd.

No! He wouldn't . . . he would never do that. Never!

Oh, yes, but you would. You did. You started that fire in the IMAX, killing three people. Belial was very pleased.

No. His head throbbed harder, and he grabbed the

doorframe for support. The phone stopped ringing. He had to get to it. He had to call Adam.

But tonight was even better, the voice said. *Tonight, you helped me control that cop, made him start shooting. All those people, all the blood. Glorious blood.*

He saw it then, the policeman shooting into a crowd of screaming people, blood spurting, the shots and screams going on and on. *No, no, no!* Staggering to the bed, he collapsed, gripped his head with both hands. It felt like an ax was embedded in his head, like it would split in two.

"No!" he screamed. "No!"

Yes. And there will be more killings. More blood for Belial. Drink, fool, drink. Get the bottle and drink.

Of its own accord, his shaking hand reached toward the bottle on the nightstand. *No,* a part of him moaned. He knew he had to stay conscious, had to fight this thing. He tried to focus, tried to hold on.

Yes. You want it. It will help you forget. The voice was relentless, the force on his arm too strong.

He did want it. He wanted oblivion, to be free of the pain. Why should he fight it? Susan was dead. His life was over. He allowed his fingers to be curled around the bottle, for it to be brought to his mouth. Then all resistance was gone as he welcomed the bitter burn down his throat. As he prayed to forget. The phone rang a third time, but he ignored it.

Instead, he sank into unconsciousness.

ADAM and Sean moved through the throngs of people who were all trying to see what was happening. Dozens of police and emergency vehicles were parked on nearby roads, the flashing red, orange, blue, and white lights a visual assault. Voices and radios crackled through the air. The two of them stopped at the police barricades, just behind the hordes of news reporters.

"There's no sense expending energy trying to slip past the police," Adam said. "I just wanted to see what I could of the scene." He glanced behind him. They were south of Crockett and the Hyatt Regency. Ahead of them, the crime scene was along the string of restaurants which had been indicated by Miriam's pendant. "Looks like Miriam nailed the area."

"Son of a bitch. So she did."

Adam forced back his fury at the situation and his inability to stop it. "We'll walk around the exterior area and see if we can pick up any traces of the Belian's energy. Then I'll come back later, when the scene has been cleared, and see if I can get anything else."

"I want to come with you." Sean looked calm, but Adam sensed the emotional upheaval beneath the surface.

"I'll think about it," he said. "But consider that I might be able to do more, if I don't have to work around your fear and concern for Matt."

"But it wasn't Matt." Sean stared beyond the barricades, where police and crime personnel bustled in an intricate ritual of removing the dead and collecting evidence. "You said the shooter had black hair."

"It doesn't appear that Matt did the actual shooting." Adam debated, then decided not to share his suspicions yet, although there was a good possibility that Sean would figure it out. Because it was the only thing that made sense.

A sudden jolt of awareness had him turning, looking in all directions. *Matt.* He was sensing Matt. The thread was faint, and wavering, as if Matt might be sick or injured. But he was conscious, at least for the moment. "Hang in there, Matt," Adam murmured, pulling out his BlackBerry and scrolling down the directory to Matt's number. "Try to fight it."

"What is it?" Sean asked.

"I'm picking up Matt's energy." Adam listened to the phone ring. "Come on, come on, pick up."

But it went into voice mail. He didn't bother with a message. If Matt still had the phone in his possession, he'd see who had called. Adam hit Send again, got voice mail. "Answer, damn it!" He put the call through a third time and it went into voice mail. He was about to send a fourth call, when the light that was Matt's essence flickered out. There was nothing there now but a gaping void, a hole in the Sentinel network. And the faint, oozing stench of Belian energy.

"Lost him." Adam slid the BlackBerry back into his pocket. Emotions rolled through him—frustration, grief, concern, and anger. Frustration that all efforts thus far had resulted in failure. Grief for the innocents who had been killed and injured at the IMAX, and shot down in cold blood tonight. Deep concern for a good man who was one of his best Sentinels and who might not survive this situation.

And anger at himself, because he was ultimately responsible for those destroyed by the Belian. By the Light, he was a Sanctioned. Failure was unacceptable.

"Shit," Sean said.

Adam turned and walked away without another glance at the carnage behind him.

"YOU sure know how to mix a mean margarita." Julia settled back with her second drink and watched Miriam paint her toenails a deep purple. "That's an interesting color."

"I can mix any drink in my sleep. I've been a bartender for three years now." Miriam sat back and studied her toes. "You like that color? I've got a matching shade to put in my hair." She smiled. "That ought to put jerk boy's Jockeys in a twist."

On the end table by the sofa, the scanner crackled with an ongoing stream of voices. The television was also on, with news reports giving the same limited information over and over, because the details of the shooting were still sketchy, and nothing substantial had been officially released. Julia and Miriam already knew more than the newscasters, so they were only half listening. Better to tune it out than dwell on the horror.

Julia pushed her half-eaten hamburger and French fries around on her plate, then set it aside. They'd had the concierge get them the liquor and mixers they needed for margaritas, and they'd ordered dinner from room service. She rarely ate junk food, which might be one reason a burger and fries had been so appealing. But she'd found herself concentrating on the alcohol, hoping it would dull the sharp edges pressing in on her.

And there were several—the specter of William Bennett, both past and present, hanging over her; the horror of a powerful Belian unleashing its bloodthirsty malice on innocent people; and her own awakening libido and attraction to a man who was way out of her league.

She shouldn't even be thinking about herself, or sex in any form, at a time like this. But her body was still tingling from the raging lust generated during the conduction. The conduction itself had been overwhelming, both horrifying and intriguing. She could deal with the chakra energies and the images—she hoped. What she didn't need was for her body to come awake sexually, or to have these carnal thoughts which focused on one man. *Adam.*

It was simply the Sanctioned/conductor link. She knew that on an intellectual level. She and Adam were on two completely different planes of existence, their only commonality a bond that couldn't be explained by any known science. *Logic, reason, and routine* was Julia's life mantra—the only things that had kept her on an even keel the past twelve years. She didn't need—or want—sex to upset the balance of her carefully ordered life.

Sure. Tell that to her body. It was humming to life, sexual need becoming a relentless craving. For the first time in twelve years, she actually began to think she might be able to have a nonplatonic relationship with a man. But not with Adam Masters. He was too far out of her realm. She needed to find a nice, staid professor or engineer. Until then, she needed to exercise her considerable self-control.

She gulped down a generous portion of her margarita. Like that was going to help anything. "Ready for a refill?" Miriam asked.

It was tempting, but Julia shook her head. "No. I guess I'd better stay reasonably sober, in case Adam wants to do a third-eye link tonight." Or another conduction.

She hoped it wouldn't be the latter. She wasn't sure she could control herself if her hormones ramped any higher. She had a sudden mental image of Adam nude, of him sliding over her and inside her, his eyes hot, and that incongruous diamond stud in his ear glittering. *Get a grip*, she told herself. But that didn't stop the heat wave that swept her body.

"Are you okay, Dr. Reynolds? You look flushed."

"It's just the drink." Julia picked up the copy of *Journal of Numerical Mathematics* she'd been flipping through earlier and fanned herself with it. "And please call me Julia. I think our relationship has advanced beyond professor and student."

"Sure . . . Julia." Miriam capped the polish. "It feels strange calling you that. But I guess it's not any stranger than all the stuff you've been telling me."

Over their first margarita and the food, Julia had related the story of the Dallas bomber/Belian. She'd filled in some of the information gaps on Sentinels and Belians and conductors, and answered Miriam's questions. They'd skimmed along the edge of the sexual aspect of conductions. Julia didn't have all the answers there, and Miriam didn't seem anxious to discuss sexual matters with her professor.

Julia had to admit it was a relief to be able to discuss the situation with someone who was a "normal" human—well, normal compared to Adam and Sean. Miriam was open-minded, laid-back, and her brilliant mind quickly assimilated and correctly interpreted the data. Probably because of her own abilities and experiences, she hadn't batted an eyelash at the details, not even at the possibility of possession.

Miriam had a few choice things to say about Sean, and Julia had found herself laughing at Miriam's narrative and her opinion of him. She was relieved to know that Miriam understood some of the demons driving Sean's abrasive behavior, and could hold her own with him. Julia wasn't so sure she could say the same in her dealings with Adam.

"I think I *will* have a third margarita," she decided, when Miriam got up to refill her own glass. To hell with staying sober. Being clearheaded hadn't helped her thus far.

"Good decision, Julia." Miriam brought over the pitcher, poured with a flourish. "It might make this news crap more bearable. Or not. Hey, want me to paint your nails for you?"

Julia wasn't quite ready for purple nail polish—yet. "Maybe after this drink."

"Sounds good." Miriam settled on the love seat, took a healthy swallow of her drink. "So are all Sentinel men hot?"

"Hot, as in good-looking?"

"Yeah. You know—" Miriam waved her hand, with its color coordinated dark green-and-purple-striped fingernails. "Attractive, magnetic, and sexy as hell. I've only met these two Sentinels that I know of—Adam and Sean, but both of them are prime. They've got that ultra-bad-boy vibe that has the attraction factor of a black hole. I don't even like bad boys, and I can feel the pull. I can only guess the draw would be much stronger for a conductor, and very hard to resist."

Tell me about it, Julia thought. She remembered Damien

Morgan, a Sentinel she'd met in Dallas. Yep, he had the sexy-as-sin aura, too. "I think they all have a magnetic appeal," she said. "It's not just looks, but more of an intangible quality. And yes, it seems the attraction is more powerful between Sentinels and conductors, even more so if they're matched."

"You should know," Miriam said. "You and Adam have really heated vibes when you're around each other. He looks at you like he could eat you up in one big bite. It's kind of cool."

So now that they were on a first-name basis—or maybe it was the third margarita—Miriam wasn't as shy about the sexual talk.

"It's not like that with Adam and me," Julia protested, resisting the urge to fan herself again. "Our relationship is strictly platonic."

"If you say so." But Miriam didn't look convinced.

The sound of the front door opening caught their attention. Sean came in, followed by Adam. Both men looked grim, and the air around them practically crackled with negative energy.

"Uh-oh," Miriam said. "The auras don't look so good. Lots of red and orange going on there."

Sean stalked to the wet bar, checked the mini-fridge. Finding nothing there, he grabbed the margarita pitcher and a glass. "I hope this stuff has juice."

"It does," Miriam said. "But probably not enough."

Julia's focus was on Adam. His face set in hard lines, he took off his trench coat, tossed it over a dining room chair. His body was as stiff as his expression.

"Did you find anything helpful?" she asked, although she suspected not. "Or maybe I should say useful?"

"Not a goddamn thing." Sean downed the contents of the glass.

"Too many people there to get a clear reading," Adam

said. "I'll have to go back later for that. But we picked up traces of the Belian. It was definitely there."

"In the vision tonight, we saw a dark-haired man shooting the gun," Julia said. "We thought at the time that wasn't the Belian. Does that still hold?"

"Yes." Adam paced around the table.

"So what does that mean?" Miriam asked.

Sean clutched his glass. "It means Matt wasn't the one pulling the trigger."

"That's not completely true," Adam said. "What happened tonight makes the situation trickier. It appears the Belian has been able to tap into Matt's Sentinel abilities, which combined with its own abilities, makes it very powerful and formidable. I believe that with that combination, it's able to dominate other minds—something a Sentinel or Belian couldn't normally do. And tonight it used mind control to force a police officer to draw his gun and start shooting."

"So that's what happened," Julia said, feeling sick inside. Knowing the Belian had used an innocent person as the instrument of its evil made the situation even worse. "That's why we didn't see Matt in the visions and dreams."

"It wouldn't have been Matt you were seeing," Sean said. "It was the fucking Belian."

"In Matt's physical body," Adam pointed out. "But yes, we all need to remember that. We might come face-to-face with someone who looks like Matt, but it might not be Matt who's in control."

Julia watched Sean turn away, his shoulders slumping. He was facing the possible destruction of a man who was the only father he'd ever known. "What a mess," she said.

"One positive thing is that Matt is fighting back," Adam said. "I felt his energy again tonight, tried to phone him. He didn't answer, but he was conscious longer this time. We have to hope he gains the strength to overcome the Belian."

Miriam sent Sean a sympathetic glance. "What do we do now?"

"We need to keep our focus on the Belian," Adam said. "There will be more attacks, and they will probably escalate. Belial's thirst for blood is never sated, and as a result, Belians constantly crave the thrill of disaster and human suffering. We have to figure out where this one will hit next."

He paced the dining area, apparently deep in thought. Halting, he said, "We can't do much more tonight. We picked up only a trace of the Belian's energy, not enough to amplify the psychic signature we already have."

It was pure cowardice, but Julia felt a surge of relief that they probably wouldn't do another conduction tonight.

"Sean, I want you to feed what little Belian energy you absorbed to Miriam," Adam said, and then looked at Miriam. "I'm sorry to do that to you, but I'm hoping it might generate some information through the cards or the pendulum."

"I can handle it," she said, "but we might want to hit a drugstore first and stock up on some Pepto-Bismol. That Belian stuff makes me nauseous."

"Sean can help you with the nausea. And, Miriam, thank you. Your abilities and your cooperation are appreciated."

"You're welcome. I know I was sent here for a purpose, and I hope I can help."

"You already have," Adam said. "Sean, I also want you to monitor the police scanner through the night, and contact me if you hear anything that's the least bit suspicious. I'm going to shift my attentions elsewhere."

"Okay," Sean said. "But I still want to go with you when you return to the BCS."

"I'll think about it and let you know. For now, let's call it a night."

Sean opened the door and waited while Miriam gathered up her stuff. "Hey, how do you like my nails?" she asked as they walked out.

"You really don't want to know," he said.

Adam closed the door and sighed. Julia suppressed a laugh. "She's learning how to yank his chain."

"It's probably good for him. He's too closed-minded in some ways, and in others, mature beyond his years." Adam sat on the couch and rubbed the bridge of his nose. "This is a hell of a mess, and it's my fault. I've got to get a handle on it."

He'd never sounded this shaken before, or at least, he'd never allowed her to see it.

She sat next to him. "You're blaming yourself?"

"I'm responsible for everything that happens in Texas, and for this current situation. I should have kept a closer eye on Matt, should have taken action faster when he started fading out."

"Someone always has to be responsible. Someone has to be in charge and make the executive decisions. But that doesn't mean this is your fault," she pointed out. "Texas is a big place, and you've told me there's a lot of Belian activity, and you have numerous Sentinels and conductors to coordinate, keep track of, and generally meddle in their lives. Don't force me to remind you yet again that you're not God."

"I'm well aware of that fact. But it's good to know you won't let me forget." Despite the light tone of his words, he still radiated tension, and his eyes were shadowed.

She had the absurd urge to comfort him, to rub the tension from his shoulders, and ease the weight of his responsibilities. Not a good impulse, and one she would avoid. "So now what?"

"I don't know yet." He tapped his fingers on his thigh. "I need to work with the energy I picked up tonight. It's not much, just enough to tell me that the Belian was on the Riverwalk during the shooting. But it might be enough to trigger one of your visions." He held out his hand. "If you would."

"Oh, you know I live to see images of carnage and terror." She drew a deep breath and steeling herself, took his hand.

She waited for the disoriented sensation, for the gray fog preceding her visions, but it didn't come. She felt the usual tingling sexual energy, but that was all. After several moments, she opened her eyes, looked at Adam. "There's nothing. I'm not seeing anything."

"I was afraid of that." He released her hand. "There's nothing to see yet. The Belian hasn't decided its next move. When I can get closer to the actual crime scene on the Riverwalk, I'll pick up more energy, and then perhaps we'll be able to glean more information. Right now, I've got to check in with my Sentinels and check on Belian activity in the rest of the state. Later, I'll probably go for a swim."

"A swim? It's October."

"So it is. The Omni La Mansión has a heated pool, and I always use it when I'm here. Water is our element. It centers Sentinels and Sanctioned, energizes them, fosters mental clarity. At this point, I need all the help I can get. You know what really worries me?"

Somewhat surprised he'd reveal his concerns to her, she asked, "What?"

His expression turned deadly serious. "That the combined abilities of Matt and the Belian makes this Belian more powerful than a Sanctioned."

Her breath hitched as she considered the ramifications. "Are you saying it would have more power than you?"

"That's exactly what I'm saying. And it means I might not be able to defeat it."

TWELVE

HOURS later, Julia found herself unable to sleep. The absence of her normal routine, along with a jumble of thoughts about Bennett and tonight's shooting, made sleep impossible. Giving up on tossing and turning, she slipped on her robe and went into the living area to get her magazine.

The room was empty, but the light was still on. She saw Adam's bedroom door was open and a light was also on in there. Curious—okay, maybe nosy—she walked over. But he wasn't in his room, and the bathroom was dark.

On the bedroom desk, his laptop was closed, and his papers put away. He'd been on his third hour of reading e-mails and making phone calls when she'd told him good night. And that had been almost two hours ago.

He must be swimming—at one thirty in the morning. Wondering if he was related to the Energizer Bunny, she sat on the sofa and tried to read. But she was restless and couldn't concentrate. Her thoughts wandered to Adam again. Maybe if she went down to the pool, walked around, and took in some fresh air, it would help relax her. It was better than sitting here.

She changed out of her pajamas, got her jacket and key card. She also pocketed her gun and the permit to carry it. At this point, she wasn't going anywhere unarmed, and she fiercely resented the necessity.

The hotel pool was outside, in a lovely enclosed courtyard that was beautifully landscaped with a terra-cotta and sculpture fountain against one wall, and palmettos and huge pots of flowers around the perimeter. It had wrought iron tables and chairs and a row of chaise lounges, and was well lit.

Adam was doing laps in the illuminated pool. It was like watching a sleek dolphin—or perhaps a shark would be a more apt description—in motion. He moved through the water as if it was his natural environment, strong and sure and smooth. For a few moments, she just stood there and enjoyed the flowing grace and power of his body.

Finally she stirred herself and decided he didn't need to catch her gawking. She drew in a breath of the night air. It was fairly balmy, winter not yet encroaching on San Antonio. Although watching Adam swim was more appealing, she started walking the perimeter, hoping to work off her insomnia.

The sound of laps stopped. "I see you decided to join me."

She turned, saw Adam at the ladder. "I couldn't sleep. I thought maybe some fresh air might help."

"Why don't you come in? The water is heated."

Julia hadn't brought a bathing suit, which was just as well, since she always felt self-conscious wearing one. She liked the water, though, and had been an avid swimmer when she was younger. She'd used aquatic exercises to regain her strength after Bennett's attack.

"I don't have a suit."

His dark eyes glinted. "You could strip down."

Her heart stuttered. "I don't think that's a good idea."

"I just meant down to the bare essentials, although I have no objection to nudity." He flashed a pirate's smile. "Besides I've already seen *all* of you."

Her heart went from stasis to a fast trot. She was playing with fire, but found the bantering invigorating. "Reminding me of that fact won't win you any points on the final exam."

"Then come over to the steps. You can at least dip your feet in. Being near the water should calm you."

"Do I look like I'm not calm?"

"One never knows with you, Professor."

She scowled at that, but made her way to the end of the pool. Adam swam the pool length and rose from the water and up the steps like an ebony-haired Adonis. The water sluiced down his body, and what a body—beautifully sculpted muscles and smooth golden skin, with the perfect amount of dark chest hair, tapering down his flat abs and disappearing suggestively beneath his bathing suit.

Oh, man. Suddenly warm, she stopped to take off her jacket and drape it over a wrought iron chair. She kicked off her shoes. "I'll probably regret leaving this here," she said as she leaned her cane against the table.

"I know I'll feel better with it out of your reach." Adam stepped out and offered his hand. "I'll keep you steady."

Steady wasn't the word she'd use for what she was feeling at the moment, as she took in his muscular legs and the way the wet suit clung to the front of him, highlighting the bulge there. She didn't need to see him naked to know he was on the positive side of well endowed.

She told herself that it was a *good* thing she was becoming sexually aware of men. Sure it was. It meant she was getting over the attack. That sounded like good reasoning.

Wondering what the hell she was doing, she bent down and rolled up her pants legs to her knees. Then she straightened and put her hand in Adam's, bracing for the inevitable jolt of sexual energy. It sizzled through her, stronger than usual. *Great.* Water appeared to be a conductor of Sentinal—or Sanctioned—energy. And wasn't science a wonderful thing.

Trying to keep her gaze above his chest, she walked to the steps, let him help her sit on the edge of the pool. She put her feet two steps down and sighed in appreciation. The water was just warm enough to offset any chill in the air, and felt heavenly to her sore feet.

"This does feel good," she said, propping her hands behind her and leaning back a little.

Adam slipped back into the pool, settled on the step beside her feet. "Water is life, and has healing properties. It also enhances Sentinel abilities."

He leaned an elbow on the step behind him, looked up at her. "I don't think it's a coincidence the Belian attacked along the Riverwalk."

"Do you mean that aside from the fact there were a lot of people there, the water itself played a part in his plans?"

"*Its* plans," he corrected. "And, yes, that's exactly what I mean. The Belian is struggling to maintain its hold on Matt's physical body, as well as keep the upper hand mentally. Then it had to tap into Matt's powers and exert a lot of effort to control the policeman and make him start shooting."

Julia knew from the barrage of news coverage they'd listened to all evening that Officer Olvera had killed himself after the bloody spree. He'd been a model cop, and everyone who knew him was shocked by what he'd done. He'd also left behind a wife and two small children. It was terrible and sad.

"So the water along the Riverwalk helped the Belian carry out his—its—plan," she said.

Adam nodded. "That's what I think."

"Then it would be logical for the Belian's next attack to be near water."

"That's a very strong possibility," he agreed.

"That should narrow our search."

"It's still a big arena. There's Six Flags, and its water park, although I don't know if that part is open right now. There are several state parks and SeaWorld, and the Belian could hit the Riverwalk again.

"Plus we have to consider that we don't know who it will use to do its dirty work. We're not just looking for Matt, but anyone the Belian can control." Adam ran his hand through his wet hair. "I've got to get a handle on this thing, and fast."

"Have you reconsidered calling in reinforcements?"

"Not unless it becomes absolutely necessary. I don't want my Sentinels to have to hunt one of their own. I'm already allowing Sean in on this, against my better judgment." He considered a moment. "Even if I bring in other Sentinels, there's no guarantee they could go up against this Belian, not with it tapping Matt's powers."

"So it's basically you against this thing."

"Yes. As I've already said, it's my responsibility. Failure is unthinkable."

"Failure is a relative thing," Julia said. "Let me ask you something. Can you fly?"

"Of course not."

"Outside of a few woo-woo abilities—some devious and underhanded, I might add—you're basically in a physical body, and subject to the physical laws of Earth. Is that right?"

"To a large extent, yes."

"Then let me point out—again—that you're just one man, despite any superpowers you might have. You can't foresee everything that's going to happen, and for the most part, you can't second-guess this Belian. The tools at your disposal are two mere human females who are dependent on visions, Tarot cards, and a piece of crystal on a chain, to come up with clues that indicate *possible* events. And those can change with the whim of this Belian."

She leaned forward, resisting the urge to touch Adam. "It's really not any different than the situation we faced with the bomber in Dallas. Taking him down involved luck as well as divine intervention. I would say that all you can do now is keep chipping away at it, and trust in God. She's the one who's actually in charge here."

"She?" His lips quirked into a smile. "Your feminist streak is showing. One thing I like about you, Julia— you're smart. Quite brilliant, as a matter of fact. You're good at helping me clarify the issues, and breaking them down to their most basic components."

He ran his hand through the water. "Somehow, you always manage to balance me. Before I met you, I thought I was completely grounded." He looked back up at her. "But you upend me, and then jerk me back to reality. You help me focus on the issues, and you usually manage to keep me in my place."

"I don't believe that for a moment," she told him. "But I *wish* someone would keep you in your place."

His eyes darkened, taking on a predatory glint. He slid his hand slowly up her leg, stroked. Shock slowed her reaction for a moment, then she tried to kick her leg free. "What are you doing?"

His fingers wrapped around her calf. "You also make me feel things I haven't experienced in hundreds of years," he said, his harsh voice softening. He resumed the sensual strokes. "You remind me, as you did just a moment ago, that I'm a man, in a physical body, with physical needs."

Any so-called brilliance she might have dissipated like a mist. Her brain turned to mush as lightning bolts of sensation streaked up her leg and to her groin. She could only stare as Adam pushed up to sit on the ledge beside her; couldn't even react when he palmed her shoulders and pulled her toward him. Those odd, mesmerizing starbursts were in his eyes again.

"I've been wanting to do this since I saw you again at

the Red Lion Pub," he murmured, leaning closer until his lips were hovering over hers.

Her brain finally registered the fact that she was facing a red alert situation. "Oh, no." She put a hand on his wet chest, tried to shove him away. He moved maybe a millimeter. "You are *not* kissing me. I mean it, Adam."

"It's been a very long time since I've done this," he continued, as if she hadn't spoken. "Let's see if I remember how it's done."

"Adam—"

His mouth came down on hers, insistent, melding into a perfect fit. She stiffened under a new layer of shock, tried to protest, to push him away—do *something*—but her traitorous body had other ideas. Such as her lips opening under the demand of his. Like her tongue sliding against his, in a mating dance as old as Atlantis. And her hands sliding up his water-slicked chest to grasp his shoulders.

He hadn't forgotten a damned thing in however many hundreds of years he'd been celibate. He kissed her with a shattering intensity that bound every molecule of oxygen in her body. Except for that one brief time at the Dallas/ Fort Worth airport—again with Adam—she hadn't been kissed in over twelve years. Even then, she'd never been kissed like *this*.

Heat and need flooded her body, and she felt herself melting against him. *Not doing this*, her mind shrilled, even as she realized that little hum of pleasure was coming from her. She arched her body, the only thoughts in her clouded mind that she was wearing way too much, and that she wanted him to touch her more intimately.

As if reading her mind, he slid his fingers over her midriff, leaving a sizzling trail. They closed over her breast, squeezing gently, then teased the nipple through her bra. Tension gathered and coiled inside her, and she knew a climax was building, that if he would just move his hand down between her legs . . . God, what was she doing?

Somehow she found the will to wrench her mouth free, grab his arm, and shove him away. "Adam," she gasped. "Stop this now! Why the hell did you do that?"

His eyes gleaming, he slid his hand behind her neck, tried to tug her back. "Because I wanted to. And so did you."

With stunned disbelief, she resisted. "Why are you playing this game?"

He dropped his hand to rest possessively on her thigh, a little too close to ground zero. "I'm not playing a game."

She knocked the hand away. "Oh, please. You could have anyone—someone beautiful and sophisticated. Every woman in the hotel lobby yesterday wanted to throw herself at you."

"You're the one I want, Julia. My perfect match. And you have your own special beauty."

He was full of it. "This is crazy. It's totally illogical and makes no sense and—" Then why did it have so much appeal? Why was her body feeling vital and alive—and so desperately needy? And why the hell wasn't he breathing as hard as she was?

She felt like screaming in frustration—at both herself and Adam. *It's just the Sanctioned/conductor link*, she again reminded herself. That needed to become her mantra: *It's just the link. Just the link. Just the link.* Nothing more.

"This is a really bad idea," she said firmly, scooting farther along the pool edge.

"Why? My body thinks it's a grand idea."

Of her own volition, her gaze dropped to his lap, to the erection beautifully showcased by his wet bathing trunks. So he was affected, and had been on several occasions, which made her feel minimally better.

"Try to pay attention here." He slid close enough to

grasp her chin and turn her face back to his. "You liked it, too, Julia. Admit it. You kissed me back—very well, I might add. You liked me touching you. I could sense your need. I wasn't forcing you. You were right there with me. So why shouldn't we take this further?"

"Because I'm—" She closed her eyes against the rush of painful memories. Another argument to add to the pile. "I'm not whole. I'm getting better."

At least, she fervently hoped that was true. "I think I'm getting better. And because of you—or maybe I should say, because of the nonscientific pull between conductors and Sentinels, or Sanctioned—" She waved her hand. "Whatever. Due to that link, at least I'm feeling things again. But this—us—isn't real. It's just a physical attraction."

"It's more than that, and you know it. But we are in physical bodies, have physical needs," Adam pointed out. "I believe we just discussed that fact a few moments ago."

"I was talking about the physical limitations of Earth, not—" She waved her hand again, not quite willing to say "screwing like minks," which she strongly suspected would be the case with Adam. "You know."

"I'm not sure I do. Maybe you should use scientific terms, Professor."

Abject frustration stabbed at her. "I'm not sure even hand puppets would get the message through your thick skull." She paused, wondered how she could make him see reason. "We're from two different worlds, Adam. We have nothing in common. I don't think I'm ready for a sexual relationship with anyone, but if—or when—I am, it will be someone on my level, someone in my world. Not some god from Atlantis."

She felt very real regret that she wasn't bold or brave enough to indulge in such a possibility. But she was a practical, intelligent woman. Most of the time, anyway.

"I'm not a god," Adam muttered.

"Close enough. I'm calling it a night." She lurched to

her feet, knowing it was best to put some distance between them. It was obvious she couldn't think clearly when he was within a ten-yard radius. But her leg had stiffened, and she lost her balance when she tried to pivot and climb out. The next thing she knew, she was falling backward into the water. She came up sputtering and drenched.

"Are you all right?" Adam took her arm.

She jerked back. "Damn it! I'm all wet!"

He kept his grip on her, his gaze sweeping her chest. "You certainly are."

She didn't have to look down to know that her wet top clearly revealed her state of arousal. "I didn't peg you for a wet T-shirt type of guy, but I guess you're a Neanderthal, like the rest of the male population."

"I'm a man. We've established that fact several times now."

She wouldn't be reminding him of that again. "Let me go, Adam. Playtime is over."

He released her. "I guess it's safe to say you didn't find the water calming."

Despite the situation, she had to laugh. For such an intense man, he had a surprising streak of humor. "I don't think being around you is ever calming."

She turned and plowed through the water toward the steps, determined to get out and to her cane without embarrassing herself a second time. He beat her to the steps, and offered his arm to help her out. She let him, and held on until her cane was firmly in her hand.

He got them both the thick, luxurious white towels the hotel provided its guests. She did the best she could to wipe off the excess water, but she still left a wet trail as she got her coat and started toward the hotel.

"Julia."

His husky voice halted her steps and she turned. He had dried off and wrapped a towel around himself. Naturally, he wasn't a dripping, drowned-rat mess like she was. She tried to ignore the fact that in that towel and with his hair slicked back, he could give the Sean Connery version of James Bond a run for his money. "What?"

He stepped close enough for her libido to hum. "This isn't over between us. As a matter of fact, it hasn't really started. I'm not going to walk away from destiny. I'm betting you won't, either."

She shivered, despite the heat radiating from his body. "I know who I am, Adam. I'm a plain, ordinary professor who is happiest working at the university and living an uncomplicated life. That's my destiny. I can't be anything else."

"There you're wrong. You are a complex woman, and so much more than you realize. When you have sex with me—and make no mistake, we *will* end up in bed—it will be completely of your own free will."

"Nice fantasy—and that's what it is." She turned away and went inside.

Adam followed her into the elevator and pushed the button for their floor. The doors whispered shut. "I'm going to change and go investigate the Riverwalk murder scene," he said coolly, as if they hadn't just been discussing sex.

"It should be calm enough by now for me to slip in undetected. I've decided to take Sean with me. He's already in the middle of this, and he's holding up so far, so I'll allow him in on the investigation—as long as he can handle it. Keep your gun close and call me if you have any concerns."

At the reminder of what they were facing, she felt exhaustion seeping through her. "All right."

"This also means we'll try to trigger a vision first thing in the morning. We might have to resort to a conduction."

Oh, joy. "You know I'll do whatever is needed, Adam."

He nodded, his gaze serious. "Yes, I know, and I appreciate it. You're a woman of valor, Julia."

Shaking her head at his misconception of her, she preceded him into the suite. "Get some rest," he told her. "I'll see you in the morning." He turned toward his room.

"Adam," she called out impulsively, then felt foolish when he turned back.

"Yes?"

"Stay safe, okay? Walk in Light."

His gaze was warm and intimate. "I will, Professor."

She shut her door, leaned against it, and cursed herself for being a fool. She couldn't allow herself to get too close to Adam, to mistake pure unadulterated lust for anything other than a mystical attraction. He was light-years out of her league, and nothing could ever come of their . . . association, for lack of a better word.

Absolutely nothing at all.

BATTLING the cursed Sentinel was draining him. It was taking more and more effort to keep the Sentinel subjugated. The Sent was growing more aware, trying to struggle and surface more often. It didn't help that others of his kind were looking for him.

He'd felt the ripple of awareness, the energy of a conduction, even as he was taking control of the cop last night, but he hadn't been able to focus on it. The Sentinel must also be aware of the others, must be responding to them.

He couldn't let that happen. He'd have to keep the physical body weak, even though it then became his weakness as well. But Belial was giving him strength and purpose. Last night, the blood—all that glorious blood—had bolstered him, energized him. Belial was very pleased, but it wasn't enough. It was never enough.

As the early-morning light seeped through the threadbare hotel curtains, he poured the cheap whisky into a plastic cup. He downed it, savored the burn in his throat.

He'd drink enough to feel tipsy, but not enough to impair his superior reflexes.

It didn't matter that he was damaging this body. As he made more kills and grew in strength, he'd be able to take over a better body, one with a soul that wouldn't resist. He'd miss being able to tap the Sentinel's abilities, but he couldn't wholly serve Belial if he had to fight to maintain control all the time.

He poured another round of whisky. And set his plan for the next kills into motion.

JULIA woke feeling groggy, with gritty eyes and an aching body. She squinted at the blurry clock, gave up, and reached for her eyeglasses. Eight o'clock. It had been three in the morning before she fell into bed, which explained why she felt so crappy.

A new day, she thought. Another day of conductions, tracking evil, chaos, terror—and Adam. Groaning, she rolled stiffly from the bed and went to shower.

She dried her hair, dressed, and went to join in the fun. As she entered the living room, she smelled coffee and food. Adam, Sean, and Miriam were seated at the dining table, which was loaded with silver-domed serving dishes and plates of eggs, various breakfast meats, fruit, and breads. It all looked delicious, but her focus was on the coffeemaker.

"Coffee," she said. "Give me coffee."

"Good morning, Julia." Adam rose and went to pour her a cup.

"It's not good until I get some caffeine in me. Thank you." She took the mug from him and eased into an empty chair. She looked around as she sipped.

Adam, still standing, looked fresh and alert, and damned good in jeans and a black turtleneck sweater—wait a minute. The man was in jeans. Of course they were designer and looked expensive, but still. That was a first.

Sean didn't look tired, either, although he'd been out on the Riverwalk with Adam in the middle of the night. He wasn't fashion-plate clothed, but had his own appeal in faded Levis and a long-sleeved olive henley shirt, with the sleeves pushed up his masculine forearms. Miriam was right—he certainly had the bad-boy air about him. From the looks of his heaped plate, his Sentinel appetite was alive and well.

On the other hand, Miriam was pale, with shadows beneath her eyes. Her hair wasn't spiked quite as high today, and she wore only two rings in each ear. She was drinking hot tea, and had a small amount of eggs and fruit on her plate. It seemed the Sentinel and Sanctioned were weathering the lack of sleep better than the regular humans.

All three of them looked grim, and no one was chatty, so Julia guessed no good news had come their way. She took a few more sips, decided the caffeine would just have to catch up with whatever jolt she was sure to receive when she asked for a report. "Did you get any information from the Riverwalk?"

Adam refilled his coffee and sat down. "We got what we expected."

Sean pushed his plate away.

"Don't talk all at once," Julia said, getting a small smile from Miriam, but no other reaction. "I'm assuming you were able to visualize the crime, to see the Belian in some form."

She already knew from prior experience that when Sentinels visited a Belian crime scene, they could usually "see" the crime. But although Belians couldn't totally block their energies from a BCS, they could distort it enough to make their images blurry, so they didn't show up clearly.

"Yeah, we saw it," Sean said.

"Actually, the energies weren't distorted," Adam said. "I can only surmise that the Belian didn't bother to blur the images, because we already know what Matt looks like.

We saw Matt walking behind Officer Olvera and raising his hand toward the officer. Olvera fired into the crowds and then . . ." Adam shook his head. "Yes, we know exactly what happened."

"Son of a bitch Belian," Sean said. "It wasn't Matt directing the shooting."

"We know that," Julia said, her heart going out to Sean. "I understand Matt is a wonderful person, and a strong Sentinel."

Sean looked at her, his dark eyes shadowed. "He is. He's a great guy."

"But the Belian is a bastard." Miriam set her tea down with a clink. "Pardon my language, Dr. Reynolds—I mean Julia—but it's true. And he's going to strike again soon."

"Did you pick up something last night?" Julia asked.

"Yes and no. Sean did the nauseating energy sharing, but the pendulum didn't hit on anything. I worked with the Tarot, and they seemed to be firing, because I got cards that represented each of us. Those were followed by some really bad cards: Death, The Devil, both reversed. Then for the grand finale, I turned up the Ten of Swords, also reversed. Reversed cards indicate the most negative outcome."

"So what does the Ten of Swords mean?" Julia asked.

"Oh, death, violence, continuing suffering without end," Miriam told her. "Like I said, really bad stuff. But there's no new information."

"Miriam didn't get solid results because we had minimal energy to work with," Adam said.

"This morning I woke up with that sick feeling in the pit of my stomach again." Miriam looked at her plate with distaste. "Guess I'm living on antacids for the time being."

And Julia was ready to make merlot and chocolate her main form of nutrition. Hanging out with Sentinels and Sanctioned and hunting the spawn of Satan tended to change your priorities.

"We picked up substantially more Belian energy at the crime scene a few hours ago," Adam said. "If we work that energy, we might get more solid information."

And I so look forward to being exposed to Belian energy, Julia thought.

"So are you going to try to induce a vision or do a conduction?" Sean asked, his narrow-eyed gaze focused on Julia.

Miriam looked at her speculatively. Julia felt heat flushing her cheeks. She busied herself with her coffee. She wasn't about to admit they'd already done one conduction, or to explain that the one yesterday and any future conductions she and Adam might do would be nonsexual.

In any case, it wouldn't be entirely true. All close contact with Adam was becoming sexually charged.

"We're going to do whatever is necessary to close in on this," Adam said. "I'm concerned that the Belian will strike again today or tomorrow. It will certainly go for a high body count, and since this is October, most of the theme parks and major tourist attractions are only open on the weekends. So it will have to strike today or tomorrow, or wait another week—which it won't do."

Unfortunately, his logic was sound. Looking at Sean and Miriam's faces, Julia could see they agreed. "What do you want me to do?" Sean asked.

"Work with the newest Belian energy," Adam replied. "Feed some of the psychic signature to Miriam. Miriam, I want you to take the map of San Antonio and use your pendulum to see if you can find the location of the next attack. Or maybe it will show us the Belian's current location. If those attempts are inconclusive, try the Tarot cards again."

"Great," Miriam said. "Good thing I got two bottles of Pepto last night."

Adam looked at Sean. "I expect you to make sure she

doesn't suffer from contact with Belian energy. Continue monitoring the scanner. Touch base—by phone—if either of you gets anything, but give us at least thirty minutes."

As Sean and Miriam left, Julia felt her heart rate kick up. When Adam closed the door and turned to face her, her entire body went on red alert. *This is ridiculous*, she told herself. Just chemistry, pure and simple.

And yet, that chemistry might be the key to tracking down a monstrous killer. *All right, then. Time to get started.*

THIRTEEN

DAVID Gains lived alone in an efficiency apartment on the southwest side of the city. He was a casualty of military service, having lost part of his right leg during a foray in Desert Storm. He'd suffered more than the injury. They had called it post-traumatic stress syndrome; he called it hell.

Since then, he'd scraped along. His marriage to his wife, Missy, hadn't survived his demons, but his daughter, Emily, was the light of his life. He'd buried himself in the one thing he'd excelled in most of his life: sharpshooting. He wasn't a violent man; he simply found solace in his weapons.

Today was no exception, as he settled down to clean his newest acquisition, a SIG SG 550 rifle with a flip-up front sight and a collapsible rear stock. The knock on the door surprised him, because he rarely had visitors. He looked through the peephole, felt a rare sense of pleasure. Undoing the dead bolts, he opened the door.

"Hey, man. This is a surprise. What brings you by?" He slapped his old military buddy on the shoulder. "Come on in."

He studied the man who stepped through the door, noticing he looked thinner, and appeared stressed. "Are you doing okay?"

The other man nodded. "Yeah, I am."

"Have a seat. Let me get you a beer." David headed to the kitchen, somewhat worried about his friend—really the only one he had. Matt had suffered a terrible tragedy a few months ago, and hadn't been by recently. He didn't look so good today.

David grabbed two beers, popped off the tops, and took them back to the living room. He handed one to Matt, sat down opposite him. "So what's up? Is Sean okay?"

Matt lifted his gaze from the SIG on the coffee table, smiled. But his eyes looked funny, unfocused. "I need someone to do a job for me, David. And I think you're the man to do it."

"What kind of job?" David's confusion increased as a wave of dizziness hit him.

"Yeah, I think you'll be perfect," Matt said, from a long distance away.

And everything faded to gray and then to black.

INFUSED with a new dose of Belian juju, compliments of Sean, Miriam tried to focus on the pendulum over the map, but her stomach was roiling. Man, that Belian energy from the Riverwalk was bad stuff. She'd always had an iron stomach and rarely got sick, but this was nasty. She glanced at the couch, where Sean was seated, setting up the scanner on the coffee table. He didn't seem affected by the energy, and she wondered how he did it.

She drew a deep breath, hoping to calm her system. It only made her feel worse. *Oh, no.* She bolted to her feet and ran to her room, praying she'd make it in time.

"Miriam! What's going on?" Sean called after her.

"Back . . . minute," she managed before she slammed

her door and dashed into the bathroom, where she was violently ill.

Good grief. She hadn't thrown up since she was a child, for which she was grateful, as it was a highly unpleasant experience. She sagged back on her heels, closed the lid, and flushed. Her stomach felt better, but now she had a vicious headache brewing. Maybe she'd find the strength to get up in, oh, a few hours or so.

"Did that help any?" Sean said from behind her.

Oh, crap. This was mortifying. There were just some things a girl didn't want a guy—or anyone, for that matter—to see. She so did not need him here. "Go away. I can deal with this."

"Yeah, right," he said, and then she heard water running. A moment later, he put a cool, wet cloth into her hand. "Here."

She pressed the cloth to her face, and it seemed to help. "Thanks. Now please leave. I can take it from here."

"Do you think you can stand?" He took her arm and pulled her up.

She made it upright, but was a little shaky on her feet, although she refused to admit it. "Okay, you can go now. I'm fine." She attempted to step away and stumbled.

His arm went around her, and he steadied her against his side. "Sure you are. Why don't I just hang around a little longer?"

"Better idea—why don't you just go away?" She turned to glare at him and cringed when a sharp pain spiked in her head.

"I can tell you have a headache," he said. "And I'm not leaving."

She'd really like to learn how he knew so much, but was too puny to ask right now. She shoved at him. "Do you mind? I'd like to rinse my face."

He moved back, and she went to the sink. She splashed cool water over her face, grateful that her eye makeup was waterproof, and then rinsed out her mouth. As she got a towel to wipe her face, she saw he was staring at her array of cosmetics and hair products.

"Why the hell do you need all this shit?"

She knew where this was going. "Maybe I like being unique and not looking like everyone else."

He gestured toward the vanity. "But most of this stuff makes you look like . . . a freak."

Even though there was some truth to his statement, hurt twined through her. She knew what she looked like with the crazy hair and heavy makeup and wild jewelry.

"Well maybe that's because I *am* a freak, which you've pointed out yourself," she said. "Admit it, Sean, I am different. Your average person doesn't read objects and auras and Tarot cards and have weird dreams."

"Having unusual abilities doesn't make you a freak. Hell, if that was the case, I'd have to point the finger at myself and a lot of other people. But the spiked hair in those weird colors, and the makeup and other shit makes you seem like one."

"You know, you're awfully conservative for being, what, twenty years old?"

He scowled. "I'm twenty-four."

Miriam smiled to herself. She'd figured he was around twenty-four or twenty-five—just wanted to needle him. "Oh, you're really that old? I guess that makes sense, considering how uptight you are."

"Hell. I just"—he ran his hand through his thick dark hair—"I just grew up in an insane environment, okay? I like things to be normal."

She suspected he hadn't meant to reveal that much. "Then let's just back off the judgment routines and call a truce for now. We might get more done that way."

"I'm willing to give it a shot." He stared at her a moment, his dark eyes serious. She found herself looking at his well-shaped mouth, the solid chin, the one-day beard growth, felt a tingle of warmth. Told her hormones to settle down. She was not a bad-boy kind of girl.

"Okay, then." She picked up the Pepto-Bismol and turned toward the door. "A dose of pink stuff, then back to the pendulum."

He grasped her arm. "Not yet. Let me work on the stomach and the headache first."

"I don't know. . . . Is it anything like the debugging?"

He grinned, showing those dimples. "Oh, it's *much* worse. Close your eyes."

"Why? Does it keep the sacred healing energies from working?"

He rolled his eyes. "No, it doesn't. But I need to concentrate, and don't want to be distracted by you watching me."

"All right." She closed her eyes and waited.

He placed his hands on each side of her face, like before. She felt the heat and tingling sensations flowing from his hands, felt the calming warmth spread through her head. The throbbing eased, and she "saw" small starbursts of light behind her eyes. Then he pulled his hands away and placed them lower, just below her left breast and over her stomach. More soothing warmth bathed that part of her body, and she could almost feel her stomach unclenching and settling.

Then it happened again—that slow, seductive slide of desire through her body. Her unruly hormones again sparked to life and sent urgent messages to her breasts and points due south. Every system in her body surged to green light, go. As she struggled to assimilate the sensual assault, surprise turned to anger.

"Hey!" She stepped back, shoved Sean. "Why are you doing that?"

His brows shot up. "Doing what?"

"You know what."

He threw up his hands. "I don't know what the hell you're talking about."

Did he think she was stupid? "Stop trying to turn me on whenever you touch me." She started around him.

"*What?*"

She swung back around. "Oh, quit playing games, Sean. And quit messing with me. I don't appreciate it."

His eyes narrowed. "I am not messing with you. And I'm certainly not coming on to you. Believe me, you're not my type."

Dual prongs of embarrassment and anger speared through her. If he found her such a turnoff, then he needed to keep his distance. "The same goes here. From now on, keep your hands and your roving energies to yourself." She turned and stalked back to the dining table and the map and pendulum.

She focused on releasing the disruptive emotions. Sean was such a . . . a guy. He was arrogant, obnoxious, angry, and a jerk. And . . . She felt a flare of lust. To be honest, he was sexy as hell. Unfortunately.

Mind over matter, she told herself. She had a strong intellect and had always been able to focus on, and achieve, her goals. She wasn't going to let some hotshot bad boy throw her off balance. She was here for a reason, and although she didn't fully understand why, she knew it wasn't about Sean Stevens. He was just a distraction—maybe an obstacle thrown out by the sometimes capricious Universe. It was time to get to work on issues that really mattered.

She took a few moments to center and protect herself. Then she raised the pendulum over the map, and began a slow sweep. "Is this the site of the next Belian attack?" she asked several times, getting negative reactions.

Sean slouched on the couch, listening to the scanner. They were back to a wall of tension hovering between them. She did her best to ignore it and focus on the pendulum.

She asked the question again—and nearly jolted out of the chair when the pendulum began circling wildly. "Sean—"

But he had already seen the pendulum's movements and was at the table. "Son of a bitch. Look at that thing go." Still staring, he pulled out his cell phone and hit Speed Dial.

"WELL, that was informative," Julia said sarcastically. "Why aren't my visions more detailed and helpful? They worked well in Dallas."

Adam released her hand. "The Belian in Dallas had already chosen its targets and carefully planned each bombing. This Belian is far less organized, and is probably being distracted and weakened by Matt. Besides, you saw a few things."

"Oh, sure, I saw the sun shining down. But I saw that in the vision about the Riverwalk, and it turned out to be dead wrong. And I saw lines of people waiting to go through some sort of gate ahead, but no distinct landmarks. Since we're already expecting the Belian to attack where there are a lot of people, that's a shocker."

"You expect too much," Adam said. "Among the lines of people, you saw a lot of teenagers and children. That tells me it's probably at a theme park."

"Well, that narrows it down to two or three places, all of them huge."

"I agree it's still too big an area. We need to do a conduction and see if we can get more information."

Julia had suspected it would come to that, and she sighed inwardly. She was tired, mentally and physically, and wasn't looking forward to a sexual bombardment that was equivalent to sticking a piece of metal into an electric socket. Adam's insistence that sooner or later, they *would* engage sexually put her on edge.

Not to mention those moments of insanity at the pool last night—what had she been thinking? That would also make matters worse. Now she knew how seductive Adam's lips were, how good he tasted, how she responded to him, to his touch, despite her determination to keep her distance.

And—for whatever illogical reasons—he'd made it clear he wanted her. She knew better than to believe that he could find her sexy and attractive, so he must have an ulterior motive, which she wouldn't put past him. Maybe he was hoping to seduce her into a sexual conduction, just so they'd get better results. That was as mortifying as a pity fuck, and made the argument for resisting even stronger.

"A conduction it is, then. Nonsexual, of course," she said, feeling to need to restate her stance. "Let's get to it."

Adam stood and moved the coffee table, then pulled the armchair over to face her. "This might be more intense than the first one," he warned, settling into the chair. "The energies tend to accumulate and build over time."

Just what she wanted to hear. "I'm putting you in charge of damage control," she said. "Or maybe that should be energy control."

"I'll handle it. You know I won't allow anything to happen to you, Julia." That intense, predatory look was in his eyes again, making her very uncomfortable.

Despite the fact she knew he could be devious and manipulative, could yank any number of chains with her, she did trust him. He would protect her, with his life if necessary. It was a sobering reality.

"I know," she said. "So do your shielding and let's get this done."

He pulled out the pendant, wrapped his fingers around it. His harsh voice rumbled out words in a beautiful and compelling language. Strange, but she could swear she felt her body moving like the rise and fall of waves. She also thought she could see the air around him growing brighter, could feel the currents around both of them warming like a caress.

He held out his hands, palm up. She placed hers palm

down over his. His fingers entwined with hers, and immediately she felt the first energy surge. Assault was a more accurate description. It felt like molten lava was pouring into her vagina and spewing upward through her abdomen and midriff. Burning sexual need inundated her body.

"Easy now," Adam soothed. "The initial surge is always the hardest. The four lower chakras are open."

Like being blasted by dynamite, Julia thought, her body throbbing with need. She could only hold on as the burning sensation spread to her chest, her throat, and her head. Colors began flashing behind her eyelids, a rainbow spectrum far more intense than last time.

Excruciating pressure built behind her forehead, then exploded in a vivid indigo color that bled slowly down her line of vision. She wondered that her head didn't explode at the same time.

"We're in," Adam said. "All the chakras are open."

The color shifted to a deep blue; she felt some sort of click in her head.

"Third eye engaged," he said. "Ah, here come the images."

She tightened her grip as pictures began flashing by. *Two men, waiting in a line of people. One had chin-length wavy blond hair. He looked like he hadn't shaved in a week. His eyes were strange, kind of glittering. The second man had brown hair and was ordinary looking. He was taller and thinner, wearing a trench coat, and walked stiffly, like something was wrong with his body.*

"This is interesting," Adam murmured. "So clear."

She couldn't respond; her throat was too constricted as the images filled her mind. *The brown-haired man in the trench coat was climbing a ladder up the side of some sort of structure. Then he was taking out a gun from beneath the coat and unfolding the stock . . .*

A tsunami wave of desire rushed through her, derailing her focus. She found it necessary to let go of all mental control, to just let the images rip past and not try to decipher them. But that didn't ease the clawing sexual need. She was wet between her legs, and her breasts felt full and achy. Her skin felt too tight, as if it would split open if she didn't find a physical release.

"Hang on," Adam murmured. "Just a little more."

Water, way down below . . . a beautiful expanse of blue in a man-made pool of some sort. Silver flashes in the air above the water. The barrel of a gun pointing downward, the view through the gunsight . . .

The image winked off into darkness. Gone so suddenly, she jolted. The gray clouding her vision swirled away like a windblown mist.

"Don't let go yet," Adam told her. "I'm going to channel off as much energy as I can."

She felt the psychic energy ebbing away, felt the odd after-tingling in her muscles. Its departure didn't do a thing for the lust still raging through her body. She rubbed her forehead, where a nasty headache was gathering.

"I think I had a vision during the conduction, like last time," she said.

Adam moved to sit beside her, placed his hands on each side of her face, and she felt the pain in her head easing. "Yes, you did. And again, I saw it with you."

"Dolphins," she said, as her mind cleared and refocused. "I saw dolphins."

"Yes. We know where he's going next." Dropping his hands, he pulled out his phone.

It rang before he could dial. He put it to his ear. "Sean. I was about to call you. We think we know where the next attack will be . . . Yes, that's what we're guessing. How did you know? I see. Let's move out then. Meet us in the hallway."

He clicked off and looked at Julia. "Miriam's pendulum just gave a positive response on the location for the next Belian attack. It correlates with what we saw. Let's get going."

* * *

HE felt as if he were watching himself from a distance. Nothing seemed real. He was walking at a right angle from the entrance, and along the side of a stadium. He felt the weight beneath his trench coat, marveled at the technology that could create a weapon that could be collapsed into such a short length and still be so deadly.

"Hurry," Matt's voice urged him. "Your job is very important, and there's not much time."

He couldn't really feel his body. It was like he was floating a few inches off the ground. Maybe he was dreaming . . .

"Here," Matt told him. "See the ladder built into the wall? You have to go up there. You have to do your job."

His body seemed to move of its own volition, and he went to the ladder, started up steadily. Yeah. This was it. He had a job to do.

OFF-SEASON didn't appear to have affected the attendance at SeaWorld. At eleven thirty in the morning, the lines were long. With Sean beside him, and Julia and Miriam right behind, Adam pushed through the people waiting for tickets.

"This is an emergency. Let us through," he called out, also using mental compulsion to make people step aside. Sean was doing the same.

But some people were slow to react, and some simply refused to move. There were a lot of children around, which required more cautious movement. *Damn!* He didn't know how much time they had, but feared it wasn't much.

He'd called his contact at the San Antonio Police Department, and they'd decided to go with an anonymous tip that there might be an attack at SeaWorld. After the Riverwalk shooting last night, the police should be quick to respond.

Adam hoped it would be soon enough.

* * *

*H*E *reached the top of the ladder, with the incessant voice
in his head. He had a job to do—vital and important. The
roof fanned out into a wedge shape and angled up slightly.
He found himself on a concrete catwalk that had a pipe
railing along the outer sides.*

*He lay down and bellied his way forward until the cat-
walk intersected in the vee of two other catwalks coming
in from either side. He scooted to the very end of the vee,
looked down. He was about fifty feet up, in what was obviously a maintenance area of the stadium. Below, directly
across from him, dozens of people were settling into
seats.*

*"They are the enemy," the voice insisted. "They must
be executed."*

*He scrabbled back out of sight, picked up the gun, and
unfolded the stock and popped out the sights and the tripod.*

ADAM looked around. Which way to go? The park was
huge, and the Belian could be anywhere. He stopped by
the magnificent fountain near the Clydesdale Hamlet,
turned to Sean. "See if you can pick up anything."

He flared out his own senses, felt the faintest trace of
energy. The Belian had come through here. But when, and
which direction had it gone? *Matt*, he thought, *now would
be a good time to help me out here.*

But it was wishful thinking and nonproductive. As was
his concern about how Sean would handle things if they
came face-to-face with the Belian and/or Matt. But at this
point, he needed all the help he could get.

He turned to the others. "If Julia's vision was accurate,
we have to assume that the crime scene will be higher up,
requiring a climb up a ladder. So we'll split up and check the
highest structures here. Leave the rides for now, and focus

on buildings. Sean, if you come across Matt, let me know immediately through the radio phone. I don't expect you to confront him, unless you have to take crucial countermeasures. Are we clear on that?"

His expression tight and solemn, Sean nodded. "Yes."

Adam consulted the SeaWorld map he'd picked up. "Then you and Miriam go to the left and toward the stadium where they have the *Cannery Row Caper*. Julia and I will go right, toward the dolphin and whale shows."

He glanced over his shoulder, saw police officers coming through the entrance. "Looks like we have reinforcements. Let's move quickly and see if we can handle this without them."

Julia made no comment as he took her arm and moved her rapidly toward the closest stadium. He could feel her pulse pounding beneath his hand, knew she had to be apprehensive. As well she should be.

"I want you to tell me if you see any landmarks or signs from your vision," he told her. "That's the only reason you and Miriam are with us—to ensure we locate the Belian. But once we do—"

"Yes, yes, I know. You've already told me at least two other times now. Get away, remove myself from all possible danger, let you do your job, yadda, yadda, yadda."

She might be nervous, but she was vintage Julia—which meant she might be obstinate. "Exactly right," he said. "And exactly what I expect you to do, Julia. I mean it. Your presence would not only endanger your life, but it could distract me. It will require my full attention to take down this Belian."

"Is that why you sent Sean in the other direction?" She gave him a sober look. "The odds are high that we've pinpointed the most likely site for a Belian attack. I can only assume you've sent Sean to check elsewhere to protect him."

She was too astute at times, but there was no reason to

lie to her. "Not to protect him, exactly. He's very capable of taking care of himself. But I don't know if he'd be able to fight Matt—or a Belian that looks like Matt. He could become a liability, which would make my job even harder."

She nodded. "I tend to agree with you."

So now he'd set the stage and done all he could to protect those in his charge and give himself a clear shot at the Belian. He was prepared to give it his all.

He just didn't know if he or anyone else could stop this thing.

THE show had started, with blaring music and swirls of color as the human performers exploded into action. Then the dolphins burst out of the water in graceful, amazingly high arcs, and the audience went wild.

"Do your job!" the voice said inside his mind.

But snatches of clarity made him pause, and he stared over the gunsights at all the people below. Emily liked the dolphins. Hadn't he brought her here?

"They are the enemy!" the voice screamed in his head. "Execute them!"

His thoughts blurred and once again, he felt like he was dreaming. Of its own volition, his finger slid over the trigger. Squeezed.

And squeezed again and again.

ADAM heard the shots coming from the stadium, knew that they were already too late. "Find a safe place to take cover," he yelled at Julia. Then he took off, ramping up to superhuman speed.

Thinking of her vision, he raced to the rear of the stadium, looking for a ladder. He saw Matt, standing by the rungs attached to the building. Matt was looking up the structure with a glittering gaze. Adam had no doubt the Belian was in control and had some sort of mental lock on the shooter at the top.

"Matt!" he yelled, hoping to distract him. He felt a faint surge of Matt's consciousness as the man turned toward him and blinked.

But it was the Belian that quickly rebounded and drew a gun from inside its leather jacket. Lightning quick, Adam dropped and rolled, pulling his own weapon. A bullet hit the ground inches from his head. He raised his weapon to return fire. His arm jolted suddenly to the side, his shot going wild. The gun was wrenched from his hand. Stunned, he realized the Belian had mentally manipulated his arm and the gun, a feat which should have been impossible on a Sanctioned.

Adam rolled the other way as another shot barely missed him. Leaping to his feet in a blur, he charged Matt, taking him down. They grappled, Adam trying to keep its gun turned away. But the Belian was incredibly strong, matching Adam's strength.

Adam managed to get his left arm free, smashed the Belian's nose. It screamed and he used the distraction to pound its gun hand against the ground, forcing the weapon loose. It wrenched its other arm free and punched him in the jaw. He gritted through the pain, plowed his fist into its gut.

They struggled, deadlocked, slipping in the blood pouring from the Belian's nose. Its strength was alarming. They pounded at each other, the blows hard and brutal. Rolling, the Belian managed to pin Adam. He stared up into eyes that glowed with madness. "Matt," he gasped. "Get control."

The eyes flickered, and for a moment there was sanity there. Then hatred and fury flashed in them. Pain exploded in Adam's head as something smashed against it. For a moment he was totally disoriented and at the mercy of the Belian.

"You bastard!" Julia shrieked from somewhere nearby.

What the hell was she doing there? A loud *whap* indicated she'd hit something with her cane. Most likely the Belian.

It roared like the animal it was. Taking advantage of the distraction, Adam landed several punches to its face, hitting the smashed nose again. It twisted away and he kicked free. He tried to roll up and defend Julia, knowing it would go after her. But waves of agony and dizziness knocked him back.

"Julia!" He forced himself upright, scrambled for his gun a few feet away. Tried to clear his vision. Saw two Julias looking back at him.

"You're bleeding," she said. "Lie back down."

"It's mainly the Belian's blood," he managed. "Where did it go?"

She gestured to a blurry group of police coming their way. "He saw them and took off. Are you all right?"

"Sure," he said, as his legs gave out, and he slid to the ground.

FOURTEEN

"I really don't have time for this," Adam told the ER doctor as she picked up a syringe with a local anesthetic. "I have to speak with the police. Besides, there are a lot of people more seriously injured than I am."

"There weren't many survivors of the shooting," Dr. Meyers said. "And they've been taken to the trauma units at University Hospital and Brooke Army Medical Center. You got the Baptists."

She rubbed antiseptic on the gash, ignoring his wince. "You need stitches before you go anywhere," she added firmly. "And although your CT scan came back normal, I'm fairly certain you have a concussion. You were unconscious for several minutes."

Adam scowled at Julia, who had readily provided this information, despite his warning glares at her. She smiled back sweetly, her own anger simmering beneath the surface. It was preferable to the fear. The fight itself, and then the Belian grabbing a nearby pipe and smashing it into Adam's skull, had scared ten years off her life. She'd hit the Belian in the head with her cane as hard as she could. Then she'd felt new terror as the Belian started toward her, until it saw the police and took off. Adam had indeed passed out for several minutes.

But he'd been his usual arrogant self when he regained consciousness. He'd been furious with her for not taking cover, instead staying close and risking her life. She'd been just as furious at him for being a general idiot. And at herself for caring so damned much. She didn't need to have feelings for Adam. Emotional involvement with him was a dead end.

Yet focusing on him instead of the grisly scenario inside the stadium had helped her keep her sanity. She couldn't do anything—not a damned thing—for the latest victims of a twisted monster, and it made her sick inside. But she could throw her energy into seeing that Adam was all right.

He'd been forced to go the emergency room, or raise unwanted questions. Given a little time and a chance to go into a meditative trance, he could have healed himself, but not with police, SeaWorld security, and emergency personnel all witnesses to his injuries.

Since he couldn't get out of treatment, she'd felt justified telling the doctor he'd been unconscious. He might be able to self-heal, but she was more comfortable with a scientifically based form of medicine and wanted to ensure he made a full recovery.

"You're lucky your other injuries aren't serious," the doctor continued, starting the sutures. "Your orbital socket is still intact, although you're going to have a heck of a shiner. Those cracked ribs aren't going to feel so good, either."

Julia felt a little guilty that Adam was probably experiencing a lot of pain, because Sentinels had such fast metabolisms that anesthetics and painkillers broke down in their bodies too quickly to offer much relief. Fortunately, it appeared he had enough control over his body to block the pain of being stitched up.

He continued glaring at Julia as the doctor pulled the thread through the gash. "You're really enjoying this, aren't you?"

"Seeing you get what you deserve is a rare and entertaining occurrence," she said, then sobered. "However, knowing that so many people are dead because of the shooting today makes this an awful day."

His expression turned even grimmer. She wondered if the Belian knew its life expectancy was now markedly shorter, because she'd certainly put her money on Adam. He might be a pain in the rear, but he took his responsibilities very seriously and had the tenacity of a pit bull.

Just then, two detectives came into the curtained alcove, showed their badges to Adam and Dr. Meyers. "Almost done here? We need to ask you some questions about today," one of them, a tall, beefy man with graying hair, told Adam. Julia sighed and leaned against the wall to ease her leg. It was going to be a *very* long day.

She was right. When they finally got back to the hotel around eight that night, she was utterly exhausted. Adam had been able to convince the police that he had nothing to do with the shootings. He'd told them he'd seen a man from his PI agency standing behind the stadium and acting suspiciously; had approached him and been attacked. Julia didn't know if Adam used mind powers on the police, but they had accepted his story.

Still, it had taken hours for them to check Adam's background, and for him to answer an interminable amount of questions. She'd had to answer her share of questions as well, but Adam had briefed her while he waited for treatment in the ER, and so her story matched his.

She didn't like police procedures. No matter how low-key the detectives who had questioned her, no matter the courtesies they had extended her, it was a so-called blast from the past, and not a good one. She'd spent plenty of time answering police questions, both in the hospital shortly after Bennett's horrendous attack, and later, when she was recovered enough to answer questions in the Harris County prosecuting attorney's office.

Today had raised more ugly memories of the events twelve years ago—just nasty icing on the horrendous events at SeaWorld. She was drained, emotionally and physically. Adam must have sensed it, because his lecture about her disobeying his orders at SeaWorld had been short and not as blistering as it might have been.

And for once, she welcomed his supporting arm as they entered the hotel lobby and walked to the elevator, although she'd been careful to avoid leaning against his cracked ribs.

Sean and Miriam were waiting for them in the suite. Miriam's eyes widened when she saw Adam. "Oh, man, you don't look very good. Are you all right?"

"I will be." Adam closed the door.

Sean was on him when he turned around. "Did you have to tell the police that Matt was the man you were fighting with?" he demanded. "God damn it, Adam, you just signed his death certificate."

Adam stepped around Sean and took off his ruined coat. His face was battered and he looked exhausted, which concerned Julia. She'd never seen him appear the least bit tired, even when he manned the Belian bomber hunt in Dallas, going three days with virtually no sleep.

"I had no choice in the matter," he said. "I planned to tell them I didn't know Matt, but then they confiscated the pipe he used on me, and got several clear fingerprints. He left his gun behind, too. Since he works for my private investigation agency—as do you—and has an investigator's license and a gun permit, his prints are on file with the state. What would you have me do? Tell a lie that would immediately be discovered, and bring suspicion down on me?"

Sean's expression turned bleak. "Shit," he muttered. "This is a disaster."

"Tell me about it." Adam went to the bar and got out the scotch. "There's a lot of damage to our cover, not to mention the loss of life."

"We've been listening to the scanner and watching the TV since we got back," Miriam said. "It's awful." She looked pale and tired, too. *Poor girl*, Julia thought. She'd seen a lot of disturbing things over the past few days.

"The police killed the shooter. They've identified him as David Gains, Matt's old military buddy." Sean sank onto the love seat, placed his head in his hands. "I really liked him. He was a decent guy. He had a little girl."

"I know. I'm sorry." Adam came over and sat carefully on the couch. "It's going to get tougher before it's over."

Sean raised his head, his eyes blazing. "I want to be in on it every step of the way."

"I have to know you'll be objective," Adam said quietly. "There's a good possibility Matt won't survive this."

Sean's jaw tensed. "I know. I've been thinking about it a lot. That's not Matt doing these horrible things. I know he would want us to stop this monster, even if it meant sacrificing him. He's always lived by the Sentinel code. It means more to him than his life."

"Matt has always honored our purpose here." Adam said.

Her heart aching for Sean, as well as all the people who'd lost loved ones today, Julia sat on the couch by Adam. "I'm sorry about this, too, Sean. I know it's hard on you."

Miriam, who was standing behind the love seat, briefly rubbed Sean's shoulder. "We're all sorry. Adam, do you want me to get you some ice for your eye?"

"No, I'm fine. I'll work on my injuries shortly. Let's discuss our game plan." Adam sipped his scotch, contemplated. "I know I broke the Belian's nose, and I inflicted other damage."

He shifted, winced a little. "It's got at least as many injuries as I do, so it's got to be in a fair amount of pain, enough to slow it down. I've been feeling Matt on and off since then, so I know the physical injuries have weakened the Belian's hold. Since it has to heal itself and continue to control Matt, it has to work that much harder. I believe that will buy us some time, maybe a day or two, before the Belian strikes again."

"The police will probably show Matt's picture on television, which will make it harder for the Belian to move around freely," Julia pointed out.

"And will probably get him arrested," Sean said.

"That's not necessarily a bad thing," Adam replied. "It's to our advantage to have Matt detained. If he's in jail, the Belian can't launch any more attacks. We'll be able to get to it, and maybe deal with it without harming Matt.

"Later tonight, we'll go back to SeaWorld and work the BCS. We'll also check Matt's house. Then we'll see if we can trigger Julia's visions and Miriam's abilities. Miriam, in the meantime, work with your pendulum and Tarot and see if you can locate Matt. Anything you can pick up might help us. In other words, we're going to keep doing the same things we've been doing. I know the process must seem monotonous."

Miriam arched a brow with a silver ring through it. "Oh, yeah. Atlantians, Belians, people with superpowers, shootings on the Riverwalk and at SeaWorld. Very monotonous."

That got a slight smile from Adam. Then he became serious again. "If we don't sense an attack coming tomorrow, Sean and I will check the hotels in the area, showing Matt's picture to see if he's at one of them. Of course, if his face gets plastered on TV, someone may remember seeing him and call the police. But that's out of our hands." He glanced at each of them. "Thoughts, questions?"

Julia wanted to point out that Adam looked like he'd

collapse if he didn't get some rest, but refrained. Instead, she said, "We should all take a little downtime. I don't see how we can be effective if we're all running on empty." She desperately needed some rest herself—she was mentally and physically worn-out.

Adam nodded. "I agree. I think we have a little time before another strike, and we can't go back to SeaWorld for several hours. We'll rest, eat, meditate, pray, do whatever we can to stay focused and in the Light. I've got to do some healing work on myself. Sean, be back here at midnight."

"Sure." Sean stood, and Miriam followed suit. "Later."

He went out the door. Miriam hesitated, looked at Adam. "I'll do my best to find the Belian's location."

"I know you will. We're very fortunate to have your assistance."

She raised her bejeweled hands. "Yeah, well, I haven't contributed much to the cause yet."

"You've done plenty." Adam glanced at the doorway. Sean was already gone. "It occurs to me that one of your contributions might be to keep Sean grounded. I need him calm and clearheaded."

She made a wry face. "I haven't had much luck there, either, but I'll try. I hope you feel better. I guess we'll see you later." She left, closing the door behind her.

"She's a good kid." Adam sank back.

"Yes, she is. And she's got a brilliant mind." Julia was alarmed by his appearance. Maybe he looked worse because of the stitches on the side of his face, the black eye swollen nearly shut, and the blooming blue and purple colors over his face—not to mention his wrinkled, stained clothing—but he appeared washed-out and ill. "Adam, you look awful."

"Thank you for pointing that out. I just haven't had a chance to recharge, which I need to do when I'm not sleeping. I'm also not used to being in pain this long. I normally have the chance to heal myself soon after any injuries." He looked at her. "A necessary ability when I'm with you."

"Oh, please," she scoffed, although she wanted to reach out and smooth away his pain. "You can hold your own with powerful Belians. A human female should be no challenge."

"You'd think so. But it appears you're a deviation on the bell curve, Professor." He held out his hand. "I could use some of your vitality right now."

She stared at him suspiciously. "Just what does that entail?"

"A simple third-eye link. No visions or anything like that."

She kept her hand back. "No weird brain drain or energy dumps?"

"What, you don't trust me?"

"Why would I trust a man dumb enough to take on a crazed Belian bare-handed?"

"I had a gun."

"A lot of good it did you," she muttered. "Shades of Dallas."

Today had been a brutal reminder of that. In Dallas, she'd watched a madman hold her sister hostage with a knife to her throat. She'd used her cane then, as well, to save her sister. Seeing the Belian on top of Adam, whacking him with a pipe, had brought back the horror.

"While I should probably thank you for coming to my aid today, I don't want you to ever risk yourself like that again," Adam said. "If the police hadn't been there, the Belian would have come after you. And I might not have been able to protect you."

Like she would have stood by and watched him get killed. "We've already had this discussion. Not doing it a second time."

He reached over and took her hand. Immediately, she felt the tingle of sexual awareness. But she also felt that sensation of waves rising and falling and a soothing warmth. There was a low-level hum, like an electrical flow. She felt the tension easing from her body.

She leaned her head back. "You're not sucking out my soul or anything like that, are you?"

"Of course not. I have my own soul."

"You probably got it from the Devil."

"Now I'm offended."

She smiled at that, and turned her head to look at him. "I am sorry that you were hurt today. Is this helping any?"

Warmth glowed in his good eye. "More than you know. I wasn't lying when I told you that you ground me, Julia. Your life energy complements mine."

Disconcerted, she tried to think of a snazzy comeback, but her thoughts were scattering like autumn leaves in the wind. Her body was sinking, and she was incredibly sleepy. A sudden realization jolted her to a more alert state. "Are you doing something to me?"

"What do you think?"

"That you're underhanded and devious, even when you're injured. And that you're probably up to something. Oh hell, I don't know." She was too frazzled to know much of anything right now. "This had better be helping you, Adam."

"Just rest for a few moments. Let yourself drift. Let go of today's events. There's nothing we can do about them, or about the Belian right now. Instead, we need to focus on healing and recharging ourselves."

He threaded his fingers with hers, lowered their hands to the sofa between them. She closed her eyes with a sigh. She was so tired. . . . And he was right about letting go. If she held on to the memory of the past few days, she wouldn't be able to function. She was definitely drifting. . . .

"Let go, Julia. Trust me, and let go." There was command in his voice, and a mental push.

She slipped into a warm cocoon of darkness.

* * *

THE alcohol had been a mistake. Even with the fast Senti-nel metabolism, his reflexes had still been slow at Sea-World. It had also made it very difficult to focus on David Gains and control him.

Then he'd been attacked by that man who had to be a Sentinel, only his energy felt different. The cursed Sentinel inside him had responded to the man, and tried to come to the surface. If it hadn't been for the effects of the booze and the internal battle with the Sentinel, he'd have beaten that man. He'd have shot him, and bathed in the blood. He'd have killed the stupid bitch with the cane, too. He should have been victorious.

As it was, he'd had his nose broken, sustained fractures and contusions, been whacked with a cane, and forced to flee the police. They shouldn't have been there. How had they known?

Cursing, he pressed the folded cloth to his nose. The bleeding had almost stopped, but the blood loss had weak-ened him. His body was a mass of aches and pains, and his head throbbed where that bitch had hit him. And the strug-gle with the damned Sentinel inside him had become in-cessant.

He called to Belial for the strength to overcome these challenges. He would heal, he knew, but it might take a day or two. Then he would create a new plan of action.

Until then, he'd revel in the lives taken today, all the blood offered to Belial. The glory and honor of that would uphold him, sustain him. Belial was very pleased.

And there would be more . . . much more.

JULIA awoke to a slow, rhythmic sound. She was still tired, exhausted. Keeping her eyes closed, she stretched, her sore body protesting the movement. The surface beneath her cheek felt odd—hard, rather than the down-filled softness of the hotel pillows. And that sound . . . that steady, lulling thud . . . A heartbeat. Her eyes opened.

She was sprawled across Adam, both of them lengthways on the couch. And she was fitted against him like metal to a magnet, her head on his chest, her right leg resting between his. Confused, she saw that the room lamps were on, and it was dark outside. Then she remembered what had happened at SeaWorld and Adam's injuries. And she was putting considerable weight on his cracked ribs.

She shifted, feeling the weight of his arm across her back, and something else pressing against her abdomen. *Oh, man, how had this happened?* She tried to lift enough to slide off him, was halted by his arm tightening around her. She glanced at him, saw his eyes were closed.

"Adam, wake up."

"I am awake," he said, his raspy voice languorous. "But I couldn't get up without disturbing you."

Too late on the getting up part, she thought, trying to figure out how to move from this position without inflaming things more. Soft-pedaling probably wouldn't work. "Let me move," she said. "Your ribs have got to be hurting. And your—" She looked at him again, saw his eyes were open and glowing. "Your . . . face. Well. It's much better, and most of the swelling is gone. Couldn't you heal it completely?"

"I could. But if the police decide they have more questions, I need to appear relatively normal, which in this case would mean slower healing and some residual bruising."

She couldn't resist reaching out to gently touch his cheek. "Does it still hurt?"

"Not at all. I took care of that. And the ribs are back to normal."

"That's good." She smoothed her fingers over his face, feeling the roughness of a day-old beard that cast a very masculine shadow on his face. "You do need to shave."

He smiled. God, the man had a sexy mouth. "Tell me about it. I can command the Earth's energy. I can heal myself and others, travel outside my body, and move things at will. But I can't stop my facial hair from growing. Or control other . . . things."

That was patently obvious. "Must be tough being a semihuman guy." *But he does such a bang-up job of it*, she thought. And she had to be honest—having a sexy male like Adam get an erection when he was in close contact to her was a real turn-on. Which was a bad thing.

Reluctantly, she dropped her hand. Pressed against him as she was, she felt more than his erection. He radiated heat, and his phenomenal prime-male scent teased her senses. She wanted to stay there, wrapped in the comfort of his warmth and strength, to soak up his amazing energy that was both calming and stimulating at the same time.

It wasn't just sexual. She wanted to forget about the horror of the past two days, to forget that there were two monsters she personally knew of out there—William Bennett and a Belian. And she wanted to return to her normal, uneventful life, and put all this behind her.

Except then Adam would be gone, back to his own life. It was inevitable. Even so, she was slow to move away. The energy flowed around the two of them, as predictable as the tides. She was very aware of the sensual tension spreading through her body, like the inexorable flow of lava down the banks of an erupting volcano. This was a dangerous game, one which could—and would—leave her bleeding, at least emotionally.

Preservation finally kicked in. "Adam—" She had to stop and clear her throat. "Let me get up."

He released her, and she slid away from him, pushed awkwardly to her feet. Certain her hair must be sticking straight up, she tried to smooth it down, while she studiously avoided looking at his crotch. "What time is it?"

Sitting up, he swung his feet to the floor and looked at

his Rolex, which had miraculously survived the fight with the Belian. "Eleven twenty five." He stood, and she realized he was still in his torn and bloodstained clothes. "Sean should be here around midnight. I need to take a quick shower and change."

Then they'd return to the Belian crime scene, and pick up more of its energy. A shiver went through her.

"Are you all right?" Adam asked.

What was she supposed to say to that? *Hell, no. But thanks for asking.* "I'm fine. Go do what you have to."

His expression said he didn't believe her, but he turned and went to his room. Feeling strangely bereft and restless, Julia knew she wouldn't be able to sleep yet. So she went to the bar and poured herself a large glass of merlot.

And wondered how much she'd have to drink to find oblivion.

•

FIFTEEN

JULIA had a headache the next morning—her punishment for drinking three glasses of merlot before finally stumbling off to bed. She was, however, spared the stress of a conduction, because Adam and Sean hadn't been able to get close to the BCS at SeaWorld. The area was still crowded with police and reporters and lots of people with morbid curiosity. They'd try again after midnight.

So they were in wait mode, because there wasn't much else they could do. Sean and Miriam decided to check out the Riverwalk, the Alamo, and Market Square. None of those were far away, so they could return at a moment's notice, if necessary.

Adam used the day to take care of his PI agency business, touch base with his Sentinels, and read the numerous reports and e-mails he received on a daily basis. He did that at the desk in his room.

Julia graded the papers she'd brought with her, worked on some lesson plans, and tried to read her *Journal of Numerical Mathematics*. But she was too unsettled to concentrate. Normally, she had formidable focus—like Energizer Bunny Adam, working away in the other room. But she knew this was just the calm before the storm, that there would probably be more death and destruction before this was over. She tossed the magazine on the dining table, and sat back with a sigh.

She wondered how Adam could handle all this. How he remained so cool and calm, even among the horrifying loss of innocent lives, through the chaos and pain Belians were so adept at bestowing.

Yet she knew how much he cared. Beneath that arrogant *GQ* facade were a heart and soul that were attuned to every Sentinel and conductor in his domain, and that felt a keen sense of loss whenever a life was snuffed out—be it his own people or innocent victims. She sure wouldn't want his job.

The ringing of her cell phone jarred her from her macabre thoughts. She pulled her purse toward her and got the phone. The readout told her it was Marla. It was Sunday, she realized, the day she always talked to her sister and her parents, although they often chatted through the week. But she'd been so far off any schedule or normal routine, the days had blurred together in a surreal mishmash of events.

She clicked the answer button. "Marla! How are you?"

"Oh, I'm great. Getting as big as a house. Good thing Luke is such a tank. I'd hate to outweigh my husband."

Hearing her sister's voice, experiencing her flip wit, was a welcome diversion from the current scenario. Julia found herself smiling. "Isn't that's a woman's prerogative when she's pregnant?"

"That's what I keep telling myself while I'm shoveling in the ice cream and chocolate. And it's really strange, but I'm craving pickles, just like the old wives' tales about pregnant women. I'm going for those big, extra-salty kosher dills, so I guess the stories aren't just tales."

Julia chuckled. "Maybe you're just making up for being constantly sick the first four months."

"I don't even want to think about those months. This baby owes me big-time. So, how are you? I've been thinking about you and worrying—just a little. Oh hell, I've been worrying a *lot*. Hanging out with Sentinels can become dangerous in a hurry."

"Tell me about it. I have vivid memories from Dallas to remind me."

"You didn't call me Friday, or yesterday, even though I left you messages. Of course, I know how bad you are about checking them. Gotta give you an F there, big sister."

"Sorry. I haven't even looked at my phone. I'm fine, really."

"Why did Adam drag you off to San Antonio? It seemed awfully sudden and secretive, although stealth is one of his specialties."

"You got that right." Julia hesitated, not sure what to tell Marla. She was fairly certain Adam hadn't told any of his Sentinels the reason for his trip to San Antonio. Although she usually shared everything with her sister, she knew Marla couldn't keep things from Luke. "I'm helping Adam with a project here. He's trying to trigger my visions to resolve a situation. No big deal." And Marla buying that had very low odds.

"Oh, please. Everything Adam does is a big deal. Actually, that applies to Sentinels as well. If a Belian is involved, it's always a major problem. Are you sure you're okay?"

"I am, really. I can't talk about this project, except to tell you Adam is on top of things."

"You'd better not be lying to me," Marla said. "I currently outweigh you by a significant amount. If I find out you're holding out on me, I'll come down there and sit on you."

Julia decided to divert her sister's attention and bring up the topic she knew was on both their minds. "That would probably be over Luke's dead body, especially under the current circumstances. Have you heard anything about Bennett?"

"Not a thing, although I've been thinking a lot about that bastard. But you know, Jules, he's going to have trouble finding us. Since he went to jail, we've all changed jobs, moved, and taken unlisted phone numbers. Mom and Dad live in the town house now, and since they've both retired, they travel a lot. You finished your doctorates and joined the university staff and I've only been at this job six years. We don't go to any of the old places, or hang with many of our old friends. There's no easy way Bennett can find us. Besides, he'll be in violation of his parole if he comes anywhere near us."

Julia wasn't so sure about their anonymity, especially with the all-seeing eyes of the Internet. "I hope you're right."

"You and me both. I also hope Luke will lighten up. He won't let me out of his sight. I can't even go to the bathroom without him knowing about it—and believe me, right now, I have to pee a *lot.*"

Julia laughed. "You always cheer me up, no matter what."

"And just why would you need cheering up? Beside the fact that you're stuck down there with uptight Adam."

Julia glanced up and realized the object of discussion was standing in his doorway, watching her. He was in his usual black silk shirt and cashmere slacks, but the top two buttons of his shirt were undone, and he'd rolled the sleeves halfway up his forearms. Even with the bruising and stitches on his face, he was so alluring, it should be illegal. Her throat went dry, and her heart went into a trip beat.

Good grief, she was like Pavlov's dog, her body now responding to the mere sight of him. He raised a questioning eyebrow. *Marla*, she mouthed, and he nodded and walked to the coffeepot.

"Julia! Are you still there?"

Dragging her gaze from Adam's butt, Julia said, "I'm sorry. A little distraction." And a whole lot of hormones totally out of control. Either that, or she was going into menopause twenty years ahead of schedule. "I'd better go. If you talk to Mom any time soon, tell her I'll call later this afternoon."

"Sure. You're really okay?"

"Yes. I'm fine. And, Marla, don't discount Bennett. We both know he's not sane. Unless they pumped him full of antipsychotic drugs while he was in prison—and we know how flush the Texas Department of Criminal Justice budget is—he's likely to do anything. This is a good time to actually listen to Luke."

"I know you're right. When you get back, we'll discuss this more. Don't let Adam get too overbearing."

"Too late, but I'm working on it. I love you."

"I love you, too. Stay in touch, okay?"

"I will. Good-bye." Julia clicked off, put her phone back in her purse. She looked up to meet Adam's cold gaze.

"You don't need to worry about Bennett," he said. "After we handle the situation here, I will deal with him."

But she knew Sentinels weren't allowed to instigate vigilante justice on anyone—or maybe that should be anything—other than a Belian. At some point, she was going to be back on her own. She only hoped Bennett didn't find either Marla or herself. Because then she'd have to do something that had been on her mind for twelve years.

She'd have to kill him.

WITH the cursed Sentinel subdued for the time being, he had some time to look back over his accomplishments of the past few days. He had liked being able to take over and control someone to be his puppet, almost as much as he'd liked the blood. It was a heady feeling to be able to issue a mental command and watch it carried out.

He was well aware he couldn't do it without tapping into the Sentinel's powers, but he also liked knowing the Sentinel had a part in creating the destruction. It was interesting that he could also tap the Sentinel's memory, which is how he'd found the soldier puppet. And that had been extremely successful.

Now he wanted to try something different—as soon as he got the Sent bastard permanently under control. Currently, it was still an in and out battle. But for the most part, he was maintaining the upper hand. As soon as he felt confident in his control, he'd put his new plan into action.

He wanted to see if he could dominate a mind that was more primitive and instinctive. And nonhuman.

ADAM hated having to wait for something to happen, rather than being in a proactive position to stop the Belian before it struck again. Sunday's inactivity chafed on him, yet he had no choice in the matter. Neither Julia nor Miriam had gleaned any new information. They were all forced to play the waiting game, hoping the Belian wouldn't do anything for another day or so.

He was heartened by the fact that he felt frequent flashes of Matt's essence, which told him the Belian was expending huge amounts of energy just to control Matt, and to complete self-healing. Adam had tried Matt's phone several times, but now it went straight into voice mail, so it was either turned off or the battery was dead.

So they waited. Julia had been on edge most of the day, which for her, translated to testy. He understood why, having heard the last part of her conversation with Marla. He agreed with Julia's assessment—William Bennett *was* a major concern, not to be taken lightly.

She didn't believe Adam would be around long term to ensure her safety. He was well aware she planned for them

to go their separate ways when this Belian was sent to
Saturn, but she would learn differently. He expected that
to be a major battle, but had no doubt as to the outcome.
Arrogant? Perhaps. But then he had the power of divine
destiny on his side.

He also knew the murders in San Antonio were weigh-
ing heavy on Julia, and there wasn't anything he could do
about that. She was strong, resilient, her soul a bright light
in the Universe. She was entitled to her attitude.

Besides, he enjoyed her sarcastic comebacks and caustic
wit. He found her formidable intelligence more than a match
for his. Damned if she didn't keep him on his toes, a rarity for him. If he hadn't been so focused on the Belian, he
would have found her company entertaining, even relaxing—
another rarity. He didn't know anyone else to whom he responded like that.

Now he hated to ruin their growing rapport with dese-
crated Belian energy. But it was necessary when working
with a conductor, especially one as precisely matched as
Julia was to him.

He looked at his watch as he entered the hotel suite. It
was shortly after three AM, Monday morning. He and Sean
had finally been able to access the BCS. It had been a
mess, a mishmash of energies—from the shooter, Matt,
the Belian, the police, SeaWorld employees, and all the
others who had trampled the crime scene.

When they'd gotten away from the area, Adam had
worked with Sean on culling out extraneous energies, fine-
tuning the process of distilling the Belian's energy. Sean
was holding up fairly well, considering the circumstances.
It was a good thing; Adam feared he might need additional
help to bring down the Belian.

He told Sean to get a few hours of sleep before they
woke Julia and Miriam. He planned to do the same. Even
he needed some sleep, especially since he was expending

energy to gradually heal his face. Plus he needed to be fully recharged when he came face-to-face with the Belian.

Which would be very soon. Adam knew the son of a bitch wouldn't wait much longer before striking again.

JULIA blinked bleary eyes at Adam as she practically inhaled her coffee. She'd never been this caffeine dependent in her life, but hanging out on the dark side was exhausting. That, and two seriously sleep-deprived nights, just zapped the energy right out of a girl.

Not so for Adam. He looked rested and sophisticated in one of his trademark dark Italian suits. Must be what all the coolest Sanctioned wore when going into battle against Belians. She had to admit it was easier for him to pack his Glock beneath a suit coat and not draw notice. He wore that gun in a waist holster, and carried a second gun in an ankle holster. She suspected he had other weapons at his disposal, but she hadn't seen them. His Rolex probably had secret spy gizmos, à la James Bond.

"The detectives from Saturday insisted on meeting me this morning in the lobby," Adam said, obviously not happy about it. "They had more questions and took up almost an hour. Now it's almost eight thirty."

Julia could practically feel the concern and impatience radiating from him. Funny, but when she'd first met him, he'd seemed so cool and reserved, she hadn't sensed anything. She'd assumed he was cold-blooded and unemotional.

Now she knew better. Now she was somehow attuned to him and could read his emotions. She wasn't at all sure she liked it, but that didn't negate the reality. She watched him settle beside her on the sofa.

"We need to get a line on the Belian as quickly as possible." He held out his hand. "Let's try for a vision first."

Her visions had been pretty sketchy lately, unless fueled by a conduction, but she hoped it would be different this time. She placed her hand in his, thinking how familiar and normal this was becoming.

The Belian energy was potent this time. She immediately felt a psychic punch that knocked the breath out of her and created the sensation of her body being tossed in a tempest of waves. The gray mist didn't just descend; it exploded on her visual screen, an instant blackout.

Then it disappeared just as quickly, and bright sunshine almost blinded her. A quick cinematic visual swept over large blocks of color in cement, then again the sunshine obliterated the view. When her eyes adjusted, she saw she was at a juncture of walkways. She heard the sound of children, then ahead of her she saw a profusion of brightly colored birds inside an enclosure. A sign above them said *Lory Landing.* Where was she? Turning, she saw a large sign in the shape of an elephant's head, some distance back.

The children's voices drew her attention again, and she saw several groups of them on the pathways. Obviously they were on some sort of field trip, but she still didn't recognize the place. The unmistakable roar of a lion cut through the voices, and then she realized the location. It had been years since she'd been there, and it had changed a lot, but she knew it.

The lion roared again—an ominous harbinger of death and destruction.

THE Belian energy had made Miriam throw up her toenails—again. And Sean had insisted on playing nice and taking care of her—again. And when he touched her to dissipate the negative results of the energy, she'd gotten turned on—again. Well, at least things, as crazy as they seemed, were following a predictable pattern. Unfortunately, the only thing *un*predictable was where the Belian would strike next.

Feeling shaky, and not just from nausea, she picked up her backpack and carried it to the dining room table. Sean went to the mini-fridge while she dug out her Tarot cards. He walked to the table, offered her a cold Coke. "Here. This should help your stomach."

"Thanks." For a short-fused, supernatural bad-boy type, he could be really considerate. And sexy. *Nope. No sexy allowed.*

Popping the can tab, she settled at the table. She was surprised when Sean took the chair next to hers. So far, he'd spent his time on the sofa, either using his laptop or watching news reports and listening to the scanner, which he ran nonstop. She'd gotten so used to the static and voices, she hardly noticed them anymore.

He watched as she shuffled the cards. "Why these instead of the pendulum?"

"I use the cards more than anything else. They're not as invasive, yet they can be more detailed."

"What do you mean, 'not as invasive'?"

She paused the shuffling. "If I make the decision to look at someone's aura, or open myself to the energies of an object, then I receive very personal, specific information about the person involved. It might be information I have no business knowing. If I use the pendulum, it's limited to my questions—and I might not know which question I need to ask. But the Tarot cards have numerous answers and nuances and guidance. With them, I trust that I'm being shown the exact information I need at that moment."

Sean nodded, approval in his gaze. "That shows your spiritual integrity."

"I don't know about that." Miriam set the cards on the table. She cut them three times with her left hand, flipped the top card.

"Which card is that?"

"Strength, upright." She stared at it. "Courage, energy, inner will."

"I guess that fits, since it shows a lion."

"Maybe. I'm just not sure what it means in this instance. It's obvious we need those things to get the Belian, but we already know that." She put the card back, started reshuffling. Cut three times again, pulled the top card. Strength, upright, again.

"That's interesting," Sean said. "It came up again. Any other meanings?"

"Well . . . the underlying message is that we are humans, not beasts, and we can channel our energy and our will. We can control our baser nature, can rise above weakness. It's also the astrological card for Leo."

She put the card back, reshuffled. She felt funny doing this in front of Sean, especially since he'd been so antagonistic toward her at the beginning. "So you don't think this is too weird?" she asked.

"No. Actually, I think it's kind of cool. I don't really have anything against Gypsies. Especially since I met you."

It was nice to find such easy acceptance. She put the deck down, cut into three piles. Turned up Strength again.

"What are the odds of that?" Sean murmured.

"One in seventy-eight. The mathematical odds are the same with every shuffle and redraw." Miriam stared at the card, a chill going through her. She had no doubt this was a very intentional, specific message. She just wasn't sure what it meant. "It's reversed this time. That gives it a more negative connotation. Power wrongly used. Defeat, surrender to evil."

Sean's expression hardened. "Not going to happen." He pulled out his cell phone. "I think it's time to check in with Adam."

SIXTEEN

"MATT and Susan loved the zoo. They've been support-
ers for years and used to go every few months." Sean said.
"I wonder if that influenced the Belian."

"Possibly. It obviously tapped into Matt's personal
psyche to find out about David Gains and bring him in to
do its dirty work," Adam said. "So it might have gotten
ideas about the zoo from Matt."

They were all in Adam's Mercedes and pulling up at
the San Antonio Zoo. Julia's vision and Miriam's Tarot
card depicting a lion had clinched the next location. Adam
had again called his police contact. After the shooting
at SeaWorld, he expected the police would react very
quickly.

Situated along the San Antonio River and next to Brack-
enridge Park, the highly acclaimed zoo covered fifty-six
acres, and housed more than thirty-five hundred animals.
It was a big place, with a lot of exhibits. The huge parking
lot was quite a distance from the entrance, so Adam dropped

the others off, parked, and with no one in sight, super-speeded it back to the entrance.

Since it was a weekday, it wasn't terribly crowded, but as he joined the others, Adam was concerned to see several groups of school-age children. He still wasn't sure why the Belian would pick the zoo, where the people were more scattered and a higher body count not as likely. But it was a place Matt had frequented, and there were a lot of trees, restaurants, educational centers, and numerous other places in which to hide.

Once again, he decided they should split up and cover more territory. And although he was fairly certain of the general area where the Belian would attack, he still hoped he could take Matt down without Sean being there.

"Sean, you and Miriam cover the right side of the zoo." He consulted the map. "It looks like there are a lot of curving paths, and I want you to check them all. Radio me if you see anything the least bit suspicious. Julia and I will take the left side."

The big cats were on the left side of the zoo, and that's were Adam expected the Belian to go. The roaring lion in Julia's vision and Miriam's Leo/lion Tarot card were strong indicators. As Sean and Miriam walked briskly away, Adam looked at the distinct split in the path. "Which way?" he asked Julia.

She studied the area. "That way. I saw those colored blocks in the cement."

The blocks turned out to be a huge snake that had been cleverly embedded in the cement path. Adam took Julia's arm as they started toward the Reptile House.

"We will not have a repeat of what happened at Sea-World," he said firmly. "Once you verify the area you saw in your vision, you will retreat to a safe distance and stay there. No heroics."

"Believe me, I'm not planning on getting in the middle of the fight. But I hope you'll be more careful this time."

"I know what to expect now. I'm definitely more prepared." And he was. The Belian wouldn't escape him this time.

"Good." She looked at him, her brown eyes deadly serious. "You might be a pain in the rear, but I'm going to be really angry if you get your arrogant self killed."

"Why, Professor, I didn't know you cared."

"Tell me about it. It's a surprise to me, too." She turned and walked on.

Adam found himself smiling, despite the situation. He would deal with this Belian. Then he and Dr. Julia Reynolds had a date with destiny.

SOME of the other big cat enclosures weren't as secure as the lions. It would be easier for a leopard or a jaguar to get out, if it were mentally driven enough. But he wanted a lion. After all, the lion was the king of beasts, wasn't it? It was the most impressive of the big cats—and a bigger challenge.

He'd prove to these cursed Sentinels that he was superior. That Belial couldn't be defeated.

THE lion compound was quite a way from the zoo entrance, basically at the far end of the park. Adam hadn't confirmed they were heading for the lions, but Julia suspected that was the destination, as it was the logical conclusion. She had to push to keep her leg moving the distance, and the upward slant of the black asphalt path didn't help. She kept a lookout for anything familiar.

The first thing was the sign for Africa Live—a huge elephant's head. "Adam, that's one of the signs I saw in my vision."

He slowed. "Do we need to go in?"

She stared, saw no other markers. "I don't think so. Let's go farther."

They passed one pathway to the left, but the second left path resonated for Julia. There was the sign for Lory Landing, and inside a massive enclosure, flocks of brightly colored lorikeets congregated in a rain forest setting.

"Here's Lory Landing and the birds. We're close."

"Which way?"

"I'm not sure. It got a little blurry here." She took another look around. "Left, I think."

"Toward the lions," he said, not a surprise to either of them.

HER name was Samantha Green, but everyone called her Sam. She was blonde and petite and cute as a bug. But underneath the spritelike appearance was a very intelligent and ambitious young woman. She was finishing up a degree in zoology and loved her job at the zoo. She didn't make much as a zookeeper, but she considered it a stepping-stone to greater things. She enjoyed working with the big cats, and she was very good at it. She had a way about her, with her soft, sweet voice, that the animals responded to.

She was headed to the lion compound to clean out their night enclosures, observe their interactions, and ensure there were no behavioral problems. She took the route past the hyenas and the tigers, then turned into the walkway that went between the tigers and lions, to the back entrances.

She didn't think much about the blond-haired man standing near the employee walkway. Lots of people wanted to see the inner workings of the zoo, often stopped to watch zookeepers at work. She offered a polite hello as she went by, continued toward her destination, a metal door with a sign that said Employees Only.

A sudden wave of dizziness washed over her. Startled, she braced herself against a cement wall. She drew a deep breath to slow the spinning sensation. But her vision began to go gray. She gasped and reached for her radio phone, but darkness descended swiftly. Then there was nothing but an empty void.

IT was ridiculously easy for him to slip into the female zookeeper's mind and take control. To urge her on to the employee entrance of the lion compound and enter the codes required to give her access. He followed at a discreet distance, keeping the mind lock. She was very receptive to his suggestion that she leave the outside door open, and that she open the steel door between the lion's night area and the outdoor compound.

The lion he linked with was a different matter. Its mind was an unfamiliar haze of energy and blurry thought forms. But he sent it waves of pain and hate and anger. He showed it mental images of the open doors. Jabbed at it with images and pain until it roared with confused fury and bolted for the open doorway.

The blonde zookeeper, standing there so submissively, eyes blank like a zombie's, was its first victim.

There would be more.

THEY turned left on the pathway and went a few more yards. Tension knotted Julia's muscles, and she had a sick feeling in the pit of her stomach. Something was about to happen. She could feel the hairs standing up on her arms. She saw a man up ahead, moving backward in their direction, his focus on something around the path bending to the left. She'd seen the messy dark blond hair before, knew who he was.

Adam tensed. "There's Matt. Get out of here. Now." He pulled out his gun and took off with a superhuman burst of speed.

Her heart pounding so hard she could hardly breathe, Julia started to back away. Then she saw a huge golden flash barreling from the walkway farther ahead and to the left of Matt and Adam. A lion, loose and running hard.

She moved quickly to the side, pressing herself against a railing. Laughter caught her attention; she turned her head and saw the group of children who were lined up to enter Lory Landing to see the birds. They were directly in the lion's path. "Oh, God, no." Without hesitation, she stepped in front of the animal and swung her cane at it.

The cane smacked across its chest. With a roar, it pivoted and charged her. "Adam!" she managed to scream. She stumbled back, just as it leaped.

ADAM wasn't going to give the Belian a chance to run or fight back. He raised his gun, aiming to maim, but not kill. He wanted a chance at saving Matt. He saw a flash of movement in his left peripheral, but kept his focus on his target. He pulled the trigger, saw Matt stagger, as red blossomed and spread across the top of his left shoulder. The man whirled around, jamming his hand into his leather jacket.

Adam aimed for another shot.

"Adam!" Julia's panicked scream caught him. He looked around and saw a lion loping toward her. Saw the children behind her screaming and scattering.

Shock ripped through him. "No!" he yelled. A bullet grazed his arm. His attention jerked back to the Belian for a split second. He shot it in the lower leg, and then whirled and raced toward Julia.

There wasn't a damned thing he could do about the Belian right now, not with Julia and innocent children in harm's way. And, God, the lion was on her. *Julia!*

He acted instinctively, raising his arm toward the animal and discharging a blast of energy. The lion flew through the air like a giant stuffed toy, and crashed against the hyena enclosure. Adam sent another burst of energy at the creature to sedate it as he ran to Julia.

She lay faceup like a broken rag doll, pale as death, with blood spurting from deep slashes across her chest. "Julia!" He dropped beside her, raising his hands over her wounds and directing a burst of healing energy. "Somebody call 9-1-1!"

He fumbled with one hand at his pocket for his radio phone, the blood running down his wounded arm making it slippery and hard to grasp. He managed to grip the phone and press the Talk button. "Sean! Get over to Lory Landing! Julia's been hurt."

"I'm right here," came Sean's voice behind him. "Miriam and I doubled back. We knew it would go down near the lions."

Thank The One. He dropped the phone and momentarily pulled his attention from Julia. "Do you see Matt anywhere?"

"I just saw him running down one of the pathways. I figured you needed me here worse."

"Try to stop the bleeding, then." Adam returned his full attention to Julia, channeling energy with both hands, his blood dripping down to mingle with hers. "Julia, stay with me."

But her eyes were turning glassy, and he knew she didn't see him. She was in shock, and losing blood fast. Her breathing was labored. He was barely aware of Miriam kneeling and pressing her jacket against Julia's chest wounds; or Sean ripping off his shirt and pressing it over Julia's abdomen, where there was more bleeding; or of the people crowding around them.

All he could see was her light fading. Terror roared through him. He couldn't lose her, *he couldn't.*

"Her aura is turning gray," Miriam gasped.

"Julia! Stay with me!" he commanded, his voice breaking. "Don't you leave me. You stay right here. Do you hear me? Julia!"

As she continued to fade, he prayed, harder than he ever had in his many lifetimes.

SHE was rising upward. There were blurred images below her—people kneeling beside someone's sprawled body, with more people standing behind them. Obviously something was wrong, but she felt a sense of elation rather than sadness.

A brilliant starburst of light drew her attention from the scene below. She was on the threshold of a pathway, and the light shimmered at the other end, beckoning. What, again? She'd already been there, done that, twelve years ago, when she'd technically died from the injuries inflicted by Bennett. But it was a pathway this time, not a tunnel. Interesting . . .

Analytical thoughts scattered then, as more ethereal ones drifted through her mind. The light curled toward her, promising warmth and peace and freedom from the pain. A low humming voice filled her, telling her she was loved and cherished.

She started toward that wondrous light, without a limp. Her leg was perfect again. She was pain free and glorious, ready to merge with the light. Ready to go on to the next level—

"Julia!" Another voice—one she knew well—shattered the aura of peace and well-being. "I command you to stay here!"

Command? What arrogance! And yet . . . she didn't want to leave Adam. They had somehow forged a bond that she felt even now. She started to turn back, but the light pulled at her. She drifted around and toward it. She was floating now. . . .

"Julia, stay with me!"

The anguished plea faltered her movement. She was torn, so torn. The light made the decision for her, drawing her closer. She flowed toward it, her physical body lying down below, now just a shell. She didn't need it where she was going.

"Don't leave me. I need you."

The utter desolation of those words vibrated across the path, sent out ripples of energy like a stone thrown in water. The air around her changed, heating and creating a suction that tried to pull her back. But she was almost to the blindingly bright doorway.

"*Julia!*"

She shot backward with g-force pressure. Then everything went dark.

SHE heard the voices first—a brisk female voice she didn't recognize, then a raspy male voice she'd know anywhere.

"If she wakes up in pain, she can hit the dispenser pad on the Demerol drip," the woman said. "But you shouldn't push it for her."

"I understand."

Where was she? Julia tried to open her eyes, but it was too much effort. She felt surreal, yet at the same time, her body felt heavy and weighed down.

"Use the Call button if you need anything," the woman said.

"Thank you."

She tried to rouse herself, to move. Agony burst through her chest, sent claws of pain lower. She moaned.

A hand slid over her arm, rubbed soothingly. "Julia, be still. Your injuries aren't completely healed yet. But you're safe, and all will be well."

She needed to open her eyes, but she hurt so badly. Tried to speak, only managed guttural sounds.

"Shhhh. Be still, my love. I'll take care of the pain."

A soothing warmth spread through her chest and down into her abdomen, and the agony faded.

"There now. You're fine, Julia. I'll take care of you. We'll get through this together. Go back to sleep."

His voice was soothing, lulling. The waves returned, gently rocking her body. She managed to draw a full breath, and felt her frantic heart rate slowing. It was all right. Adam was with her. She was confused and disoriented, not sure where she was, or why she was in this state. But Adam was there. He wouldn't let anything hurt her.

Reassured, she let herself sink into oblivion.

HOUSTON had over thirty public library branches throughout the city and a huge-ass main library on McKinney Street. Who'd have thought? It just so happened there was a bus line going to the branch nearest to his brother's dump of an apartment. And wasn't Bitch Fate lining things up just so.

William Bennett got off the bus and sauntered to his friendly neighborhood library. He had plenty of time—his parole officer couldn't see him until Thursday. Too busy, or some bullshit like that. Probably overworked and underpaid, which really made William's heart bleed. Not that he gave a fuck. He couldn't report to work or do much of anything until his PO approved his game plan and signed off on his work application.

That was just fine with William. He had other plans, ones that didn't require any goddamned approval. He walked into the library, took in the scent of books and paper and metal and wood. Was hit with a gut-punch reaction of how similar the smell was to his office supply store. The one he no longer owned, all because of that lying bitch.

Yeah, well, he'd have the last word over her. Before he beat and choked the breath out of her traitorous body.

Not too many people were using the computers on a

Tuesday morning, and he picked one as far away as possible from the information desk. He'd had very little access to computers at the prison, and things had changed a lot in the past twelve years. But he was a smart man, and it didn't take him long to get the hang of the fucking new and improved Internet.

Or to do a search for Julia Reynolds in Houston, Texas. And wouldn't you know—she was now a professor at the University of Houston. Taught both math and physics. He remembered she'd always been a smart one. Had been working on a doctorate when she first sashayed into his store, pretending to look at binders and presentation folders and asking oh-so-innocently about the latest TI scientific calculators. But he'd known why she was really there.

When he'd given her his full attention, just as she'd demanded, she'd thrown it back at him, the cheating, lying whore. He'd lost twelve years of his life, not to mention his livelihood and his home, because of her.

Payback was going to be hell—for her. As for him, he was really looking forward to it.

Revising his search options, he looked up Houston's Metro bus system, and then found the closest route going to the main campus of the University of Houston.

ADAM sat by Julia's hospital bed. He had the adjustable bed tray set up as a temporary office—laptop, BlackBerry, police scanner set at low volume. Despite the many matters demanding his attention, his focus kept shifting to Julia.

He looked at her, saw her breathing was deep and even and her face relaxed. She wasn't in any pain right now, and he intended to keep it that way. He was also healing her wounds—and they'd been substantial—but very gradually. He didn't want to raise any suspicions while they were still in the hospital, so he'd wait to do a full healing until after she was discharged.

Every time he thought about the lion attacking her, saw the horrific image that was indelibly imprinted on his mind for all time, he felt himself aging another lifetime. No doubt her quick intervention had saved lives. No doubt there were a lot of grateful parents standing in line to thank her for protecting their children.

But he had told her no heroics, had expected her to remain out of harm's way. She was incredibly courageous, stubborn and hardheaded beyond belief, and utterly infuriating. He was both immensely proud of her and furious with her. Thank The One she would make a full recovery. And when she did . . . he was torn between turning her over his knee and paddling some sense into her, or kissing her senseless—or both.

But for now, while she was injured and helpless, he would take care of her and protect her. He had hired private security to keep the press and nonmedical personnel away from her room. He was letting Sean monitor San Antonio for signs of Matt or the Belian, although he was sensing Matt quite a lot, which meant the Belian had been weakened by the two bullet wounds Adam had inflicted. Hopefully that had bought some time before the next Belian attack.

His BlackBerry rang, and he saw it was Luke. Adam had felt it necessary to tell Luke and Marla what had happened with Julia, as there was a strong possibility they'd hear about it on the news, even though he'd managed to keep Julia anonymous—for now. Fortunately, her parents had left yesterday morning for a trip to the Smoky Mountains, so they weren't in the loop.

"Hello, Luke."

"Hello, Adam. How's Julia?"

"She's doing well. Should be discharged tomorrow. Did you have to tie Marla up to keep her in Houston?"

"I thought I might have to, but then she had some abnormal contractions, and the doctor ordered her on bed rest for a few days. I've reassured her that Julia is fine, just sleeping a lot, and you're keeping her pain free. But if she doesn't hear from Julia tomorrow, I can't guarantee anything."

"I'm sure both the baby and Marla will be fine. Julia will call her tomorrow."

Luke was quiet a moment. "A lot of shit has gone down in San Antonio the past few days. Those shootings on the Riverwalk and at SeaWorld. Then that business at the zoo. Sounds an awful lot like Belian activity to me. It all has something to do with Matt, doesn't it?"

Adam rubbed the bridge of his nose. The Sentinel code demanded honesty. "Yes, it does."

"Oh, man, I hate to hear that. If you need any help, you could call in Damien. He's not too far away. Or I'll come, if you want me to."

"No, I don't want either of you here right now. I can't give you any details. I have a special situation that I need to handle."

"Damn. That can't be good."

That was Luke Paxton—master of the understatement. Adam suspected Luke had pieced most of the puzzle pieces together. "It's problematic," he said, "but I hope to have everything under control in the next few days."

"You know I'm here if you need me. But I'm calling for another reason. I think we might have a problem with Bennett."

"What's going on?"

"I've kept a continual tail on him, and up until now, he stayed close to his brother's apartment. But today he took a bus to the library. Spent an hour there, then caught another bus. Davis was tailing him, and is following the bus right now. He just called and told me the bus is headed for the University of Houston."

That could only mean one thing. "Julia must be named in the university staff listing."

"Yeah, that's what I'm thinking. And the son of a bitch has found her. What do you want me to do?"

"Just have Davis stay on Bennett. Its obvious Bennett knows where Julia works, so the damage is already done. I'll call Tami Lang in the math department and warn her about Bennett. I'm sure she'd refuse to give him any information on Julia, but I'll also advise her to call security when he shows up. I'll ask her to call the physics department and warn them as well."

"I don't like this," Luke growled. "Bennett might come after Marla next."

"It's very possible. But he'll have to get past you first."

"Yeah, like that's going to happen."

"I have full confidence in your ability to protect your wife. For now, continue to keep track of Bennett. When things are cleared up here, I'll be back in Houston and we'll come up with a permanent solution." Although that was going to be tricky. Adam wasn't allowed to dispense souls to Saturn just because they were vicious, lowlife scum. He only had jurisdiction over Belians. But he *would* find some way to deal with Bennett.

He ended the call with Luke, retrieved the university math department number from his BlackBerry directory, and called Tami. He kept it brief, told Tami that Bennett was a disgruntled graduate student who had been annoying Julia, and advised her to call security, and also forewarn the physics office.

"The funeral was very tasteful," he replied when Tami asked about that. "No, I don't think Julia was very close to her aunt. Dr. Curtis? Let me see . . . I think Julia has an appointment with her tomorrow." One that would have to be rescheduled. "Why don't you give me that phone number again, in case Julia misplaced it?"

He took the number and told Tami good-bye. Then he closed his eyes and sat there, simply letting all the bits and pieces and various details drift through his thoughts. He found that situations often clarified and settled if he did that—in effect turning them over to a higher consciousness. Next to trance-state communications with the High Sanctioned, it was the most effective way to process information.

"Adam?"

The voice was hoarse and barely audible. He snapped to attention and saw Julia's eyes were open and watching him. For the first time in twenty-four hours, they were clear and aware. She was returning to the conscious world—and back to him. The darkness that had been swirling in his thoughts dissipated like smoke into air.

He had the oddest sensation of being touched by light.

SEVENTEEN

WHO'D have thought a hotel suite would ever have looked so wonderful? Or that she would feel so good two days after being mauled chest to abdomen by a lion? Fortunately, the lion had been several feet back when it clawed her, and the wounds had been fairly shallow. But she was still stitched and stapled down the front of her body, although thanks to Adam, she was pain free and almost healed. Ah, the miracles of modern Sentinels. Too bad she couldn't share that pun with the scientific community.

She sank onto the sofa and patted it fondly. "How do you feel?" Adam asked, sitting next to her. "Any pain or discomfort?"

"No, none at all." She rolled her shoulders and arched her back to stretch her chest. "It's amazing. You're a good healer."

"Fortunately for you." His expression hardened and she could guess what was coming next.

She held up a hand. "Please don't start with the lectures. Have some mercy."

His dark eyes glittered dangerously. "You don't know how lenient I've been with you. If anyone else had so blatantly disobeyed my orders, they'd have found their rebellious soul on Mars, learning how to resist impulsive urges and let go of stubbornness."

"Mars, huh? Sounds like quite an experience." She studied his face, taking in the sharp angles and the beard stubble, those midnight eyes, and that sensuous mouth. Sometime during the past two days, he'd lost his stitches, and didn't have a scar. All signs of his Saturday injuries were gone. He was stunning. But he was so much more than a gorgeous male.

Emotion swelled inside her. He'd been with her the entire time at the hospital, her anchor in a physical and emotional storm. He'd kept her calm and comfortable, had explained and reassured, dealt with the doctors, nurses, and all the mind-boggling details involved in a serious injury and subsequent hospitalization. Somehow, her emotional barrier had slipped these past two days. Of course, nearly dying again tended to make a girl reevaluate things, to tap into the well of brutal honesty.

She felt so much for this man, no matter how hard she'd resisted her feelings. She knew nothing could come of it. Lowly mortals and gods didn't mix well, if mythology was any indication. Adam had a higher calling, and was responsible for hundreds—maybe thousands—of souls, if you counted the innocents he protected. She was a very plain, lowly professor whose greatest joy was teaching. They were oil and water. But that didn't stop her feelings.

She forced her thoughts away from that dangerous direction, changed the subject. "What's the latest on the Belian search? Since you've been with me for two days, I'm assuming there hasn't been another incident."

"Nothing on the radar. Matt has been in and out, and I can only assume the gunshot wounds weakened the Belian, and slowed it down. Sean and Miriam have been on the search."

She shifted toward him, cocked her head. "You're giving Sean free reign on this?"

"I had to. I wasn't going to leave you alone in the hospital, and Sean has held up well. He and Miriam have been checking hotels and rentals, showing Matt's picture around. She's also been working with the cards and the pendulum. Nothing's clicked yet."

"Damn it." Julia clenched her hands in her lap. She felt sick inside, assaulted by a jumble of emotions that went beyond her complicated feelings for Adam. Bad enough that events in her life had cost her so much, and had hurt her family and friends as well. Bad enough that her demons were alive and well and kicking, and William Bennett was a free man. The fact that she was leaching resources that should be used to help other potential victims made it that much worse.

Waking up in the hospital again had been a resurrected nightmare. Adam's presence had been the only thing to make it bearable, but that didn't assuage her guilt. "I hate it that my injuries pulled you off the hunt," she said. "My needs should never have superseded those of the innocents in the path of this Belian."

"You are just as important to me as anyone else."

She didn't agree, but that didn't discount her gratitude. "I'm not sorry you were there with me, and I thank you for that. I was terrified when I woke up and realized where I was. It was too much like . . . before. I might have lost it if you hadn't been there."

"I'm glad I could keep you from going wild and whacking people with your cane."

"Very funny. And you telling the doctors and staff that you were my fiancé was hilarious. *Not*."

He didn't look the least bit repentant. "It was expedient. And I find it has a certain appeal."

"Get real, Adam."

"I am deadly serious."

O-kaay. Time to move away from the personal discussion. Some distance from the man himself might be a good idea. She shifted forward, again marveling at the lack of pain. "I'm going to bathe. Those nice little moist towelettes at the hospital just aren't as good as the real thing."

He stood and helped her up. "Make it a shower for now. You can soak after I get the bandages off and the staples out."

Whoa. "I'm supposed to go to the doctor next week for that."

"That's not a good idea, especially since you'll be completely healed in one more session. Plus your scars will disappear. There's no good way to explain that."

"Thank you, Dr. Masters, but I'll take it from here. There's a great product on the market called Scargo for those pesky scars." She got her cane and started for her bedroom.

"Why not let me take care of your injuries, since we both know I can do more than conventional doctors. And why the false modesty? I've seen you nude, Julia, more than once."

She thought of him securing the back of that stupid hospital gown as he had helped her hobble to the bathroom. Of the doctor's utter lack of concern for her modesty when he'd pulled her gown up to look at her staples and then had the nurse rebandage them.

Of course, Adam, being her "fiancé," had remained in the room the entire time. She'd been loopy on Demerol (he had suggested she use some to avoid suspicion) and lacked the wits to protest. And wasn't that great stuff for the memory book.

She glared at him. "Thank you so much for the reminder. That's another letter grade off your paper."

He shrugged, a hint of a smile lurking around his mouth.

"I've been doomed to a failing grade since the beginning. You always did like Luke and Damien better."

When had the man developed this startling sense of humor? He'd been such an arrogant hard-ass when she first met him. In a way, she missed those "good old days." It had been a lot easier to dislike him when he'd been demanding and abrasive. It had certainly been easier to maintain an emotional distance, despite the electrifying chemistry that had been present from the beginning.

She escaped to her bedroom, then indulged herself with a long shower. With the detachable showerhead, she was able to wash her body without soaking the expanse of bandages covering her from just above her breasts to several inches below her belly button. She stepped out of the shower feeling human again.

Dried off and enfolded in a soft hotel robe, she was combing her damp hair when she heard her cell phone ring. It sounded muffled and distant, and she looked around for her purse. She knew Miriam and Sean had brought her things back to the hotel after the mauling, so it was here somewhere.

She went to the bedroom door and opened it. Adam held her purse and was retrieving her phone. He handed it to her. "Thanks." She flipped it open, didn't recognize the number. "Hello."

"Julia? Is this *Dr.* Julia Reynolds?" asked an unfamiliar male voice.

"Yes. Who is this?"

"You know who it is."

Great. She was horrible at recognizing voices over the phone. Why couldn't people just introduce themselves up front and save everyone embarrassment? "I'm sorry, but I don't know. Who are you?"

"Ah, Julia, I'm so disappointed you don't recognize me. After all we've been through. I haven't heard your voice in over twelve years, but I remember every little detail about you."

Everything inside her froze. "Bennett."

"See, you do recognize me. Although you used to call me William. I really am disappointed."

Shock set in, numbing her mind. She saw Adam reach for the phone, but turned away and raised her hand to hold him off. "What do you want?"

"You should never have crossed me, Julia. You cheated on me, then you betrayed me. Did you really think you'd get away with it?"

She couldn't think. This couldn't be real. "How did you get this number?"

"One of your students gave it to me. Apparently you gave it to him when he needed help, so he figured it was pretty much public record. By the way, I think he has a crush on you. He doesn't realize you're a whore."

Oh, God. Her heart pummeled her chest. She couldn't breathe. "You're not supposed to contact me in any way." She heard the fear in her voice, knew he heard it, too.

"I was impressed to learn that you have two doctorates now; that you teach at UH. I went by to visit you, but you weren't there. They said you'd gone out of town. Running from me, Julia? It won't do any good."

"I'm reporting this. I'm contacting the police. You stay away from me."

"No way in hell, bitch." His voice changed, pitching up and vibrating with the rage just under the surface. "I don't know where you are, but you'll have to come back sooner or later, and then you'll pay. I promise you. *You will pay.* I can't wait to see you again—and very soon."

Then he was gone. Stunned, she lowered the phone. Adam wrenched it from her numb fingers, put it to his ear. Obviously realizing the connection had been broken, he looked at Julia, his eyes burning. "Sit down, before you fall." He took her arm and led her to the couch, easing her down. "Give me a minute."

He took her phone and strode to the dining table, where his laptop was set up. She watched him as he made a call on his BlackBerry. She felt detached and surreal, too shocked to react.

"Luke, Adam here. Julia just got a phone call from Bennett. The bastard tracked down one of her students at the university, got her cell phone number from him . . . Yeah, that's not a surprise, given what happened yesterday. We could report this to the police, but Bennett will only deny he called Julia, so we need more before we do that. I want you to check with the tail and find out exactly where Bennett is right now. And trace this number."

He pressed a pad on Julia's phone and rattled off the last incoming phone number. "That's where Bennett called from. It looks like he called several times before this, but Julia's phone was at the hotel instead of the hospital. Yes. Get back to me when you know something. And keep that scum in your sights."

He tossed his phone on the table, came back to her. She started shaking then, an uncontrollable shivering that swept through her body like a trapped scream. The memories rushed back. . . .

Bennett turned from Marla's battered, prone body. Insanity and cruelty glittered in his eyes as he stepped toward Julia. "I told you that you belong to me, Julia. I told you not to see anyone else. That you would be sorry if you did. But you didn't listen. I saw you with those other men, saw you acting like a whore. Now I have to punish you. . . ."

"No." She rocked herself, battling the terror that filled her. "I can't go through that again."

"You won't." Adam pulled her into his arms. "He won't get near you, Julia. I told you that you wouldn't have to face him alone and I meant it."

She drew a deep breath, forcing back the fear. Although she wanted to scream and cry and hold on to Adam, let him protect her, she knew that would accomplish nothing. The real world didn't guarantee happy endings.

"It's not your battle." She tried to stop shaking. "We've already had this discussion." She dug deep for the resolve that had gotten her through the past twelve years. "I'm not giving up my life because of Bennett. And I know you damn well can't give up yours."

He moved back to look at her. Determination burned in his eyes. "I'm not letting you turn away from this—from us."

At least this was a battle she could fight. She pushed away. "There is no 'us.' You don't own me, Adam. Just because we have this connection between us doesn't mean you can control me or my life."

"We can discuss our relationship and what it means ad infinitum, but I'm telling you this, Julia: I will not allow anything else to happen to you." His possessive gaze roamed her face. "You don't know what went through me when I saw the lion on you. I thought I'd lost you. I went as crazy as that lion. I wasn't even aware of using my power to hurl it off you. I barely remember working over you. All I could think was that I couldn't lose you. And just now, knowing Bennett was on that phone, taunting you, terrifying you, I felt that way again. You will not shut me out."

The force of his feelings was like a shock wave shattering through her. No one had ever made such a declaration to her, or stood for her like this. But this wasn't a fairy tale, and she had to rescue herself. "Adam—"

His mouth came down on hers, hot and hard. He kissed her with a desperation that was as shocking as Bennett's phone call. Light and electricity sizzled through her. God help her, she didn't want to face the rest of her life—or Bennett—without a taste of this kind of passion. Without a taste of Adam.

She found herself kissing him back, matching his desperation. Desire erupted like a geyser, a scalding force of nature. She curled her fingers through his hair as her tongue tangled with his. He slid his hand inside her robe, splayed his fingers over her bandaged breast. She could feel the warmth of his touch, even through the bandages, could feel her breast swell against his hand. She heard herself moan, and moved her own hand down for a reciprocal caress of his chest.

He lifted his head, and she almost cried out from the loss of his mouth. He stared down at her, his gaze burning, his chest heaving. "If you want me to stop, then you'd better say so *now*," he gasped, his voice guttural. "If we go any further, I can't guarantee my control."

She had almost died two days ago. Would have, if Adam's sheer will hadn't kept her Earthbound. Now, Bennett was after her. There were no guarantees in life. She needed some good memories to get her through what was to come.

"To hell with control," she said, and pulled his head back down.

HE knew she wasn't surrendering; Julia would never surrender to anything. She was coming to him as his equal, giving as much as she took. She kissed him with an abandon that sizzled his blood. The result was that he was rock hard, painfully so. He hoped he could last longer than thirty seconds after he got inside her.

A part of him was terrified. He hadn't done this in at least two hundred years. He sure as hell hoped it was like riding a bicycle, that it would come back to him. He would focus on giving her pleasure, and pray the rest would come, so to speak.

He wouldn't give her a chance to reconsider. There were times Julia thought too damned much. He scooped her into his arms, keeping his mouth on hers as he made his way to his bedroom. It was primitive male instinct that had him choosing his bed over hers. *His.* She was his, although she might argue that point.

But the Universe had created a perfect conductor match for him, and her name was Julia Elaine Reynolds.

He used his mind to yank back the bedspread and top sheet. Laying her on the bed, he settled beside her. He slid off her glasses and put them on the nightstand, then continued the sensual assault on her mouth. He pressed her back enough to open her robe, and ran his hand down her body. Beneath those damned bandages, she was curvy and all woman. He wanted to feast on her, but the bandages were covering some of the best parts. He mentally peeled back the right corner, revealing one perfect breast. The pink nipple was puckered and begging for his attention.

He gave it, leaning down to tease and suck. She moaned, and he started to pull back, concerned he'd been too rough. Her hand clamped against his head, pushed him back. Well, then, she must like it. He kissed the nipple, drew it back into his mouth. Her heat and scent rose up around him— hotel soap and her unique smell, mixed with the feminine musk of arousal. His body was throbbing and screaming for release, but he exerted an iron self-control. *Not yet.*

He skimmed one hand down along the bandages until he found smooth flesh and another best part. She was hot and wet, more than ready. He slipped a finger inside her. She arched against his hand, spreading her legs farther apart. He took that as an invitation and slipped in a second finger. Wanting her mindless and embroiled in pleasure, he stroked in and out.

"Oh, God," she moaned. "Adam! It's . . . too fast."

He had a feeling neither one of them was going to last very long this first time. And that was just the way of things. "Look at me, Julia."

She turned her head, her eyes glazed with passion, her lips swollen from his kisses. He pushed his fingers deep inside her, withdrew and stroked again. "Come for me, love. I want to watch you come."

He started up a rhythm, knowing she was beyond modesty or resistance. He watched her face, savoring the beauty of her passion, the tension of her body, her hands knotting the sheets. As she cried out, he felt the orgasm rolling through her, felt the clamp of her inner muscles around his fingers. It was a heady feeling, knowing he could give her this, and that no other man had touched her in over twelve years.

He held her through the last shudder. She curled into him, hid her face against his shoulder, her breathing ragged. "I can't even think straight," she managed.

"Good. Let's keep it that way." He moved her back and kissed her, tender this time, while he mentally unbuttoned his shirt and unzipped his slacks. He kicked off his shoes, then rose and quickly dispensed with the rest of his clothing.

Julia lay there, her lush, curvy body flushed and her hair wild. She looked like a warrior goddess from ancient times. Her eyes were wide as she watched his ultrafast disrobing. They widened even more when her gaze went lower. "Oh, my."

He was pretty sure that wasn't disappointment in her tone. She looked back at his face, her brown eyes dark and mysterious. "You are so beautiful," she murmured. "I must be dreaming."

"I hope not. That would be such a disappointment." He returned to the bed and took her in his arms. "Now, where were we?"

Her hand slid down between them and her fingers wrapped around his throbbing penis. "I think we were here." Her voice was husky, her touch maddening.

And his control was tenuous, at best. "I promise you can play more later. But, before I embarrass myself—" He stroked down her body, between her legs. Savored her small gasp, the fact that she was more than ready for him. "Let's get to the main event."

Even with his body's raging need, he thought of what Julia had gone through twelve years ago. Her body might be ready for sex, but she was bound to harbor emotional scars. He tilted her chin up, looked into her eyes. "Are you all right with this?"

"I think so."

"You let me know if anything bothers you."

"I'm not fragile, Adam. I won't break."

No, Julia would never break, but past demons could torment her. "Turn on your side," he urged. He helped her to face him, with her damaged leg straight beneath her. He raised her good leg over his hip, pulled her close. For now, he didn't want to be on top of her, didn't want her to feel pinned down.

Pressing against her core, he felt some resistance, despite her aroused state. Not surprising, given her lengthy abstinence. He mentally slipped into her mind, clouding her thoughts, instructing her muscles to relax. He felt the give, as her body accepted his.

He slid into her like a hot knife into soft butter. There was some friction—she had been celibate a long time, and he was so huge and hard, he thought he might burst. But it was an exquisite sensation, like a sword fitting perfectly into a sheath.

He released her mind, and she blinked, looked at him suspiciously. "What did you just—"

"Not now." He pressed all the way in. She moaned, and he pulled back. "Am I hurting you?"

"No," she whispered. "It feels amazing."

He slid in again, watched her eyes go opaque. "Oh, God," she gasped.

"Just Adam will do."

She punched his shoulder. But then he started thrusting,

and she gripped his shoulder instead, her fingers digging in. He tried to focus on her, but his body took over, his mind becoming mush in the onslaught of physical sensation. His skin felt like it would burst. He felt his balls tighten, felt anticipation in every cell. Instinct was dominating now—the urge to mate and find release. And he did, very quickly, in an explosion that sent a shower of colors through his mind.

The hot spurting of his seed triggered wave after wave of sensation, of pure pleasure, through him. All he could do was ride the waves. There was no logic, no control, just feeling. It seemed to go on and on. Finally his climax ran out of steam. He sagged against Julia. "I'm sorry," he managed. "Usually Sentinels have a lot of stamina in . . . this area."

"Really? Maybe Sanctioned fall short there. You can't be perfect in everything." Her voice hitched.

"Smart-ass. Give me a few moments to recover and we'll see about that." He raised his head. "Are you all right?"

The tears overflowing her eyes upended him. "I hurt you!" he said, concerned.

She shook her head, swiped at her eyes. Remorse swept through him. How could he have given in to his baser urges without consideration for the traumas she had endured? "Julia, you should have said something. You should have stopped me."

She shook her head again, managed to speak. "You didn't hurt me. I'm—damn it! Just having a meltdown here." She pressed her face to his chest and sobbed.

Now he felt panic. He could stand before the High Sanctioned, battle powerful Belians, and command dozens of Sentinels. But a woman's tears were out of his realm. Still, he steeled himself and slipped his arms around her. "What can I do?"

"N-nothing. It's just everything. The Belian, all the deaths . . ." She drew a shuddering breath. "The lion, being in the hospital again." Another sob. "Then hearing Bennett's voice. Sex with you. It's overwhelming."

He was starting to understand. "Emotional overload?"

She nodded against his chest. "Yes."

Julia was an incredibly strong woman. But she had endured a lot, and even she had a breaking point. Everyone did. But he hated being the trigger. "We shouldn't have done this."

That got another vigorous head shake. "No. You're wrong." She looked at him then, her face red and puffy—and beautiful in its strength. "This was clean and good and . . . amazing. It was nothing—*nothing*—like it was with . . . then. There's no comparison." She managed a weak smile. "Even if it didn't last very long."

He knew she was teasing, and he was glad to see her smile. It pleased him that she thought their joining was amazing, because it had certainly blown him away. "I guess I'll never live that down—or up."

She sniffled, and he reached over her for the tissues by the bed. He handed her a few. She wiped her face and blew her nose. "One thing, though," she said. "We should have used some form of protection. I'm not on anything."

"It wouldn't prevent pregnancy. If a Sentinel soul is meant to come into the Earth plane and is fated for a particular couple, pregnancy will occur, even it they use multiple methods of protection each time."

Her eyes flared. "What? Are you telling me there's absolutely no way to ensure birth control when a Sentinel and a conductor have sex?"

"That's exactly what I'm telling you. But there is a methodology. Pregnancies don't occur unless the couple is meant to stay together, and the incoming soul is ready. You have to have faith that the Universe knows best."

"Screw that."

He raised his eyebrows suggestively and she scowled. "I'm serious, Adam. I don't want a baby, at least not now."

"Then it won't happen until you're ready."

"Damn straight it won't." She struggled to sit up. "There aren't any immaculate conceptions, are there?"

"Not that I'm aware of." He pressed her back and kissed her thoroughly, feeling her resistance ebb. As far as he was concerned, there was no going back for either of them.

"How did you get so good at that?" she asked, when they came up for air. "You should be out of practice after two hundred years."

"You inspire me." He skimmed his hand over her hair, then down her body. "You look like a mummy, with all those bandages."

"Tell me about it. Do they make me look thinner?"

She was being flippant, as she wasn't at all vain. "You are perfect, just the way you are." He meant it. He wouldn't change a thing about her, except maybe her stubbornness and a propensity for violence where he was involved. Actually, those things were challenges he rather enjoyed navigating. "Let's get these bandages off, and I'll make sure everything is healed."

He didn't bother to add that Sean and Miriam should be back soon from checking hotels and new rentals.

Then the hunt for the Belian would be on again.

IN her own bathroom, Julia soaked in the generous tub. The hot water felt heavenly. Those two days in the hospital, and the stitches and staples and bandages, had left her stiff and sore. She looked down at her bare chest and abdomen, marveling at the faint lines that shouldn't even be close to healed, and should have been vivid scars.

Adam had removed the staples and channeled more energy to the area. He told her the internal stitches should be dissolved and the healing virtually complete. It was nothing short of miraculous—if not completely unscientific.

She leaned back and closed her eyes. Unfortunately,

there was no magic cure for emotional trauma. Oh, she'd get over the lion mauling—she'd done the only thing she could with those children in its path. Adam being with her in the hospital had helped ease her though that trauma.

But she still had the original attack and Bennett to deal with, and the current spree of bloodshed. Not to mention sex with Adam, which had created a whole new set of emotional issues. Not a particularly smart move on her part.

Stupid or not, the memory of going to bed with him sent a heated rush through her body. Seeing him nude had reinforced the Adam-is-actually-a-god-in-disguise theory. He was magnificent, and he'd looked at her—*her!*—like he could eat her up.

When he'd touched her, spoken to her in that harsh, sexy voice, then joined his body with hers, it had been stunning . . . amazing . . . profound . . . and totally upending.

Sex with him had healed her on one level, and ripped her open on another. At least she'd proven to herself that Bennett hadn't been able to ruin her as a woman. Adam, however, had the power to leave her bleeding when all was said and done. She had no one but herself to blame. She'd known any involvement with him was a very bad idea, that nothing good could come of it.

Besides, he might not want to have sex with her again, and she wasn't inclined to risk her emotional well-being, much less a pregnancy, any further. But it was one memory she wanted to keep. Good to know she wasn't dead in the sex department.

A frisson of energy skittered over her skin, jolting her out of her reverie. The hairs on her arms came to attention.

"You look like you're thinking too much, Professor."

She came upright with a gasp. Adam sat on the edge of the tub, cool and gorgeous in black slacks and a charcoal sweater, and holding a glass of wine. He had showered and shaved and looked ready for a *GQ* photo shoot.

She quashed the urge to cover herself. It was pointless,

given what had passed between them. She settled for a glare. "I don't remember lifting the bathroom ban for you."

"I think that's been negated by . . ." His gaze drifted over her. "Certain activities." He took a sip of the wine, handed her the glass. He radiated a satiated possessiveness, like a cat that had just consumed a mouse. Not good.

"I would still appreciate the common courtesy of a knock." And to not be naked every time he sneaked up on her. She took a healthy gulp of wine. What did one say to a god who had just ended her twelve-year celibacy? *"Thanks for my sexual revival. We'll have to do it again some time."* That just didn't have the right ring to it.

"I hope you got several bottles of this stuff." She took another sip.

"Why, Julia, I believe you're becoming a lush."

She finished the wine, handed the glass back to him. "I only drink like this when I'm under duress. That should tell you something, Masters."

He ignored that, instead running a finger down one of the faint jagged lines on her chest. "These look good."

His touch ignited an ember of sexual energy that quickly turned into a major brush fire. Her breasts swelled and the nipples hardened. She shoved his hand away. "Yes, everything is almost healed. And yes, I'm very grateful for your curative abilities. Is there a purpose for you breaking the bathroom ban?"

"Actually, there is." His gaze returned to her face. "I just spoke with Sean. They found a hotel where Matt stayed. He's apparently moved elsewhere, but there's strong Belian energy in the room. Miriam tried to get a reading off the furniture and used towels, but all she picked up was rage and confusion—no images or concrete information. Sean and I will have to work the energy, then link with you and Miriam and see what we get."

Both trepidation and anticipation swept through her. And wasn't that a good thing—*not*. "I can hardly wait."

His lips quirked. "Liar. However, I know you'll do what needs to be done." He leaned down, dipping his fingers beneath the water and trailing them up her calf. Fiery sparks followed in their wake, and wet heat pooled between her legs. "Whatever it takes."

Her breath escaped her lungs and her mind fogged, but her body went on full steam ahead. Fortunately, Adam broke contact and stood. "I have to go, but I won't be long." He strode gracefully to the door, turned, and gave her a heated look. "Stay safe while I'm gone."

After he left, it took several moments for coherent thought to return. She hadn't even considered the possibility of another conduction—most likely sexual, since they'd broken that barrier. Wasn't she the sharp one today?

As for staying safe, safety was a relative thing. She wasn't worried about personal threat from the Belian. Adam Masters posed far more danger, to her mental well-being and to her heart.

"Well, damn!" she muttered, rising and reaching for a towel. "I wonder where the hell he put the rest of that wine."

EIGHTEEN

———

JULIA stared at the clock in her room: five ten in the afternoon. It seemed much later than that, but then a lot had happened today. She'd been discharged from the hospital, received a threatening phone call from William Bennett, and made love with a god—that after twelve years of abstinence. Plus she'd had a staple removal and healing session. She'd taken a two-hour nap—she'd fallen asleep as soon as she'd settled on the sofa to wait for Adam's return—but she still felt drained.

Now she was about to engage in a sexual conduction with said god. Adam hadn't pressured her to do it. He'd simply said, "It's your decision, Julia."

Damn him. He knew she wouldn't refuse to help, not at the cost of more lives. She wasn't a coward; nor was she one to back down from challenges. Since they'd already done the horizontal mamba, what was the use in doing a chaste conduction, especially when a sexual one apparently got much stronger results? Adam seemed to think pregnancy wouldn't become an issue, and she'd just have to trust him on that.

Just what did one wear to a sexual conduction with a Sanctioned? Not that it mattered—she didn't have any sexy lingerie or sleepwear. She settled for her navy blue robe— a kind of comfort clothing. No sense wearing anything under it. Part B couldn't very well go into Slot A if clothes were in the way.

Enough procrastinating. She wiped her damp hands on her robe, got her cane, and went into the living room. It was empty, but Adam's bedroom door was open. She walked over, hesitating just out of sight.

"Come in, Julia."

She stepped into his room. The afternoon light filtered through the window sheers. And wasn't that great—full disclosure two times in one day. She looked at the large bed where she'd lain with Adam a few hours before. The sheets had been smoothed and turned down to the foot.

He was beside the bed, wearing only a pair of black silk boxers. He was a world-class work of art—tall, broad-shouldered, lean and muscled, a perfect male package. Definitely in the god category. She didn't even want to think how she—a plain, plump professor with glasses and short brown hair—would be classified. And yet, here she was.

"How did you know I was outside your room?" she asked. "You couldn't possibly hear me walking on the carpet in this place. It's at least two or three inches thick."

He gave her a slow, sexy smile. "I could sense you— your energy, your special scent."

Her heart took on an irregular beat; heat began coiling in her belly. Even with a separation of ten feet, the attraction between them was lethal. He turned to the nightstand and lit a large, deep purple pillar candle. Enticing, aromatic scents drifted through the air.

"Is that to set the mood?" she asked.

"In a way." He faced her, and she savored the sight of his magnificent chest and abs. "The scents are frankincense and ginger, and the indigo color represents the sixth chakra and the third eye. The candle will help create a stronger sexual surge and enhance the conduction. Although I don't think we'll need it." He stepped closer as he palmed his medallion.

Oh, man, she didn't think they needed any help, either, as long as they were in close range of each other. She felt the energy swirling around her, warming the air, increasing in intensity, as he chanted in that beautiful language. The light radiated from him, like he was the sun. It seemed to reach for her, surrounding her in power and enchantment.

He finished chanting and released the pendant. "Hold your arms out to the side and down a little," he said in a black-magic voice.

Although it seemed like a strange request, she did it. He gestured with his hand, and her robe tie slithered out of its knot, allowing the robe to fall open. *Talk about black magic.* He gestured again, and the robe slipped off her shoulders, dropping halfway down her arms. The breath froze in her chest; her heart's frantic beat continued. Another gesture and the sleeves slid off, the robe falling down her body, pooling on the floor.

Leaving her bare to the world—or in this case, to Adam. His heated gaze moved over her like a caress, a tingling following in its wake. "Show-off," she said, her voice low and shaky. She gestured as he had. "Your turn."

He had to switch to manual mode to get his boxers off, as they were hung up on a very large object. Then he was nude, and she stopped breathing again. He walked to her and held out his hand. She felt like she was standing on a fault line, with an earthquake of seismic proportions about to occur. That fate was a speeding train that couldn't be stopped. Or maybe—as she placed her hand in his—she was going off a thousand-foot cliff in free fall.

He tugged her against him. Then he framed her face with those elegant hands, kissed her deep and hard. Her legs gave out; good thing she was leaning against him. He swung her into his arms and carried her to the bed. He laid her down and settled beside her.

"The sexual surge will come fast, and things might get a little wild, maybe a little rough," he told her. "There's not much foreplay in a conduction. But I won't hurt you, Julia."

She wet her lips. "I know."

"Tell me if it's too much."

She didn't feel any fear. Trust had been one of her issues since the attack, but she trusted Adam implicitly. "I will."

"Expect a powerful surge as soon as our hands link. And don't break the contact, unless it's more than you can handle."

"I won't let you down."

The starbursts glowed in his eyes. "I know you won't. Give me your hands."

Tension throbbing through her, she raised her palms to his. Their fingers linked and her world exploded. Molten heat flooded her vagina and abdomen. Red and orange colors burst behind her eyelids. Intense sexual need overwhelmed all her senses. "Adam," she gasped, twisting against him. "Now!"

"Hold on, love. Get on your side and—"

"No!" she practically screamed as the heat scalded upward to her midriff, and yellow flashed in her mind. She scrambled up and straddled him. He tightened his grip on her hands, but gave her free reign. "Now, now, now!" she gasped. She slid over him, took him deep. She was wet, more than ready, but he filled her almost to the point of pain.

Mindless need spurring her, she moved on him as green

and blue colors filled her mind. The burn moved into her chest and throat. Adam groaned and arched his body to meet her movements. "We're in the upper chakras now," he managed. "Hold on."

There was a flare of indigo, a sharp pain in her head, and then the images started flashing. She was only vaguely cognizant of them. Her body had seized control, moving in perfect sync with his, both of them reaching for the physical flash point. It came just as the final chakra opened and violet blanketed everything.

She cried out as waves of sensation ricocheted through her, the climax so intense, she couldn't do anything but ride it. She felt Adam tense, heard his long groan of release. Gradually, the incredible pleasure receded, along with the images, leaving her utterly drained. She collapsed on him, feeling like a melted, burned-out candle.

As her breath returned, so did sanity, and the realization she'd been like a wild woman, totally out of control. She'd never, ever, done anything like this, not even in the carefree days before Bennett. Mortified, she buried her head against Adam's shoulder.

"I'm so sorry I lost control like that." That was an understatement. More accurate would be "*Staid math professor loses her mind and plays ride-'em-cowboy with a god formerly from Atlantis.*" She cringed. "Please tell me I didn't hurt you."

He wrapped one arm around her and stroked her hair. "You didn't hurt me in the least. It was fast and it was rather wild, but there was absolutely no pain. Quite the opposite."

"I still can't believe I just did that." She shuddered.

"Sweetheart, look at me."

She burrowed closer. "I might be able to face you in, oh, a year or so."

He slid his hand beneath her chin, forced her to look at him. His eyes glowed like molten pools. "First off, you were under the influence of the linked chakra energies. Second, that was the best sex I've ever had. Bar none."

"You're just saying that because it's been over two hundred years since you got any."

He shook his head. "I'm saying it because it's true." He flashed a sexy grin. "You're even better than Cleopatra was."

"Cleopatra? Oh, come on, Adam—"

He kissed her, and her thoughts scattered. Come to think of it, once they formed the handhold, they hadn't kissed or done any sort of foreplay. Hadn't needed it. They'd just screwed their brains out. At least she had. Adam had more or less gone along for the ride—and what a ride it had been.

"Right now, we need to talk about the images," he said.

She sobered instantly at the reminder of why she was naked and tangled with him. "You're right, of course." She shifted off him, gritting her teeth as pain shot through her bad leg. It didn't bend easily, and had taken a beating during her insanity.

He sat up. "Leg hurting?" She nodded, and he pulled the leg toward him and started massaging it. It was painful, and she kept her teeth clenched. Then, as the cramps receded and the muscles unknotted, pleasure replaced pain. The man definitely knew how to give a massage. She could also feel the tingling that indicated he was doing some healing mojo as well.

"Thank you. It feels much better," she said.

Now that she was pain free and thinking straight, she felt uncomfortable, sitting naked on the bed. She slid off and limped over to pick up her robe. She put it on and tied it before turning back to face Adam. She saw he'd put on his boxers, probably in deference to her need to cover herself—although she wouldn't have minded if he'd remained gloriously naked.

He sat on the edge of the bed, and she joined him, turning her focus to the images that had flashed through her fevered mind. "I think I had another vision during the conduction."

"I'm certain you did. It was too clear and precise to be anything else."

"If you saw the same things I did, then you have a good idea where the Belian will go next."

"I think we might have picked up on Matt," Adam said, "although it's unheard of to track a Sentinel through a conduction. But it would be Matt, and not the Belian, who would be driven to this place."

Julia thought about the sadness she'd sensed from the images and nodded. "That's the most logical explanation. But I didn't see any signs specifically naming the place, or any landmarks that would indicate its location."

"I've been there, so I know it. It's very possible Miriam was able to pinpoint this location as well." Adam nodded toward the phone vibrating on the nightstand. "Let's see if I'm right."

He reached over and picked up the phone. "Yes, Sean. Did you get anything? . . . Julia and I saw a cemetery. I'm assuming it's the one where Susan is buried." He listened a minute. "That's the same area Miriam's pendulum indicated? Then I'd say we know where to go. I'll meet you in the lobby in ten minutes."

He clicked off and stood. "Sean and I will handle this. I want you and Miriam to stay here."

"Why? We've gone with you the last two times."

"That was because we needed you to identify the landmarks you'd seen in your visions, and also because we were covering such large areas. We have an exact location this time. We don't need you."

"I think I should have a say in this." She gave him her most intimidating professor stare. "I've already put my life on the line for the cause." Not to mention her body. "I've been involved in three Belian confrontations, and each time I played a pivotal role. One of those times, I saved your very nice rear from possible serious injury. I also spared some children from being attacked by a lion."

"Both times, you disobeyed orders."

"News flash—I don't take orders from you, Adam."

Anger heated his eyes. "I could make you," he said softly, dangerously.

That pissed her off even more. "Then you'd have to keep me under control for the rest of my natural life— while your own life would be hell."

He shook his head. "You are so damned obstinate. Has it occurred to you that I can do my job more efficiently if I don't have to worry about your, or Miriam's, safety? That if we don't need you there, you're better off staying away? Can you not understand that I don't want anything to happen to you?"

Some of her anger dissipated at the frustrated sincerity in his voice. She could relate. "Has it occurred to you that I might be upset if something happened to *you*?"

"Are you saying, once again, that you care about me, Professor?"

Crap. Why had she said that? He didn't need to know how she felt. "Of course not. I just meant I would have to find a new verbal sparring partner. They're so hard to come by."

"You are such a liar, Julia."

"Besides," she said, ignoring him. "If you want me to accept your nonscientific theory that I'm fated to be here and helping you, then you have to let me see this out."

"You would throw that back at me." He rubbed the bridge of his nose, considered. "All right. But only if you agree to follow orders—for once in your life—and do exactly what I say while we're at the cemetery."

"I'll try. But if there are any rampaging lions, all bets are off."

He gave her a stern look, but his lips twitched. "Go get dressed. And bring your gun."

* * *

SAN Fernando Cemetery was located in southwest San Antonio, near Kelly Air Force Base. High, black wrought iron gates marked the entrance, along with a massive granite sign engraved with a simple cross and the cemetery name. Two high flagpoles flanked the split roadway. It was still light outside, although the sun had faded, giving the sky a stark, pale appearance, when Adam drove the Mercedes through the entrance.

"Is there a back way to Susan's grave?" he asked Sean. "We need to get there without being seen. We'll park a reasonable distance away and walk in behind it."

"Oh, yeah," Sean said. "This place is huge, well over a hundred acres. There are numerous driving paths. Take this road to the left."

Adam followed Sean's directions. He felt Sean's tension and hoped bringing him here wasn't a mistake. But he wasn't willing to risk the Belian getting away again. He cast a glance in the rearview mirror at Julia and Miriam. He wasn't at all happy they were along, but hadn't wanted to take the time to battle Julia, or be forced to subdue her in some way. Besides, her arguments had merit. He would have to be matched with a woman who equaled him in intellect and logic. Sure made it difficult—if not impossible—to control her.

She did care for him, he was certain of it. Getting her to admit it was another matter. But they would settle that once this Belian was sent to Saturn. For now, he turned his attention to the hunt. He parked the car where Sean indicated, and the four of them got out.

"Where is the grave from here?" Adam asked.

Sean pointed to his right, to a large expanse of grounds, dotted with graves. "On the other side of that small chapel."

Adam placed his hand on Sean's shoulder, held his gaze.

"My goal is keep Matt alive, but I don't know if that will be possible. I have to know you're going into this as a Sentinel. That you'll do your sworn duty, whatever that requires."

Determination glowed in Sean's eyes. "If I let this abomination continue to exist on Earth, and to use Matt's body for evil, then I dishonor everything Matt has fought for, everything he taught me. I won't let him, or you, down."

Seeing Sean's resolve, Adam nodded, dropped his hand. "The chapel will provide cover for us. We'll move to it together. Then Sean and I will go around and check the grave. Ladies, arm yourselves, Julia with your gun and Miriam with your pepper foam. Have them ready and don't hesitate to use them if you're threatened in any way. Stay by the chapel. I don't want a possible hostage situation, or either of you being injured." He gave Julia a look. "Again."

"Sure," Miriam said, slipping out her pepper foam canister. "Believe me, I don't want to get too near that guy. But what if he's not here? We don't know when he's coming— assuming he does."

"No, we don't," Adam agreed. "What Julia and I saw wasn't nighttime, but it wasn't bright daylight, either. The light is fading now, so this could be the time. I'm feeling Matt off and on, which tells me he's in partial control. He comes here often, so we have to hope our indicators are accurate. If we don't see him, you two will take the car and go back to the hotel. Sean and I will stake out the gravesite." He gestured to Sean. "Let's go. Move quietly and no talking."

They left the road and walked across the expanse of burial plots, being careful to skirt the graves. The headstones jutted from the ground in a profusion of shapes and sizes, and many had brightly colored flowers placed near them. Huge old live oaks and tall topiary shrubs were spaced among the sites.

The cool air was eerily still. As they approached the

small white chapel with its simple wooden cross in front, Adam felt Matt's life force flare and hold, and it was close. "He's here," Adam murmured in a low voice. He pulled his gun and motioned Sean to do the same. As they slipped to the side of the structure, he gestured for the women to stay there.

Julia thumbed her gun safety off, clenched her cane in the other hand. Leaning against the wall, she looked at him, her gaze steady and clear. "Stay safe, you two," she said, very softly.

"Ditto," Miriam said, looking solemn and worried.

Adam felt the energy around him surge as he moved into full Santioned mode. He and Sean stepped around the chapel. He followed Sean's lead, straight ahead, through two trees standing like guards, then toward a group of gravesites.

He saw Matt before they reached Susan's grave. His back was to them, his head bowed toward her grave marker. A faded, dried-up bouquet of flowers sat in the bronzed flower stand, obviously placed there at an earlier date. Adam gestured to Sean to flank right as he moved left.

"I know you're there, Adam," Matt said. He turned, his arm hanging down, a gun in his hand.

Adam tensed, raised his own gun. Stood ready for whatever he had to do.

Matt looked terrible. His hair was matted, his clothing filthy. He had at least a week's beard growth, and his face was gaunt and gray. His eyes were too bright, his motions jittery. He turned his head and looked at Sean, who had also raised his gun. "Hello, son." His voice was ragged.

"Matt," Sean said. "You're in control now, right?" Adam could hear the hope in his voice.

Matt's eyes rolled, flashed, and then glittered with hatred. His face hardened, his mouth twisted cruelly. "Fucking Sentinel," he hissed, raising the gun toward Adam. He moved back, stepping on Susan's grave. "I'm stronger than him, thanks to Belial. He can never hold on for long. I'm in charge here."

Adam tightened his finger on the trigger. "Matt, you have to fight this thing. Gain control of it."

Matt's eyes flickered, but they still mirrored insanity. "That won't work, Sanctioned. And in case you're thinking of shooting me"—he swung the gun toward Sean—"it will be a two for one. Me and a cursed Sentinel."

Adam hesitated, and the Belian laughed. "Fucking idiots, always trying to preserve life. I've got news for you—blood *is* life. Blood is power, and eternity. The ultimate offering to Belial."

"Who is a petty, powerless being playing at being God," Adam said.

The Belian hissed in fury, pulled the trigger. Adam sent a mental jolt just as it fired, forcing its arm to jerk upward, and the shot went wild. Anticipating, Sean had dropped to the ground and rolled. He came up as Adam deliberately shot the Belian in the right arm. It howled, dropping the gun. Blood flowed from the wound. Adam hoped the pain would weaken it.

"Matt, come back to us," Sean said. "I've already lost Susan. I can't lose you, too."

"Susan." Matt shook his head, sanity returning to his eyes. His face twisting with grief, he looked back at the marker. "Susan . . . she's gone. Dead." His shoulders shook. "It's time for me to join her."

"Sean needs you," Adam said. "*We* need you. You're one of our best Sentinels."

"I can't control this-this thing very long." Matt turned back, tears making streaks on his ravaged face. In a super-fast blur, he swept the gun off the ground with his left hand. He pointed it at his head. "I have to end it now, while I can."

"No!" Sean gasped.

Adam forced himself to remain utterly calm and impassive. He couldn't let emotion cloud his mind at this crucial time. "Don't do it, Matt. There might be another way."

Matt's eyes flickered again, and he staggered backward, into the marker. He gasped and started shaking. His arm sagged partway down.

"Matt! Stay with us," Adam said, taking a step closer. "That's an order."

"No!" Matt jolted forward, bringing the gun back up. "You don't know what I've done. Don't know . . . the awful things." He shuddered, more tears slipping down his face. "I'll burn on Saturn for eternity for those horrible things, for all those innocent souls."

"You didn't kill those people," Adam told him. "The Belian did. It's not your fault."

"Yes it is." Matt's expression was tormented. "I got weak, let it in. I didn't stop it, even though I knew . . . By The One, I knew what it was doing." He put the gun against his temple.

"Matt, no!" Sean pleaded.

Matt sent him an anguished look. "Good-bye, son." He closed his eyes, fingered the trigger.

Adam gave another mental shove, jerking Matt's arm downward just as the gun discharged. The bullet tore into his upper chest. Red bloomed though his soiled jacket. He stood there a moment, swaying, a stunned look on his face. Then he collapsed on Susan's grave.

Sean started forward, but Adam moved to stop him. "Wait."

Sean tried to shake off his hand. "Let me go, man. He's injured!"

"We have to cast out the Belian. You know that."

"But if the body dies, Matt dies with it," Sean said fiercely.

"Then we have to move fast. Don't forget that Matt

would want this," Adam reminded him. Hearing footsteps behind him, he turned to see Julia and Miriam rushing toward them.

"Why are you just standing there?" Julia demanded as she came up. She started past him toward Matt. "Aren't we going to help him?"

Adam stopped her with his other hand. "I'm going to do everything I can for him," he said, hoping it would be enough. "But we have to let the body start shutting down, or we won't be able to shake loose the Belian soul. I want you to call 9-1-1 and tell them there's been a shooting and we need an ambulance."

He turned to Miriam. "Help me watch the aura around Matt." He could see auras, but he needed to give all his attention to the Belian expulsion and hopefully, healing Matt.

She nodded, glanced at Matt. "Right now, his aura still has some color, but it's turning gray."

He'd seen that, knew the body was declining. "Good. Keep watching." He looked at Sean, who was staring at Matt with a devastated expression. "Let me do my job," he said. "Then be ready to apply first aid."

He stepped closer to Matt. Closing his eyes, he held out his hands, palms up. He began the intonation to put a psychic barrier around the body and summon the High Sanctioned. The air around him began vibrating.

"The aura is almost completely gray now," Miriam said. "I see some black."

The body was shutting down. *Hang on, Matt*, Adam thought, continuing the chant. He drew energy from the Earth to form a brilliant circle of light.

"Oh, wow," Miriam said. "There's a very bright light around the body."

Adam didn't need to open his eyes; he could see everything that was happening in his mind. Four starbursts appeared in the light circle—High Sanctioned beings, there to take the Belian soul to Saturn.

"More light," Miriam said. "Like four stars, or something. I've never seen anything like it."

Adam continued chanting to hold the light circle. Hissing, the Belian burst from the body, a black distorted form.

"What the hell is that black thing?" Miriam gasped.

Sean said something to her, but Adam tuned them out. The Belian was evading the High Sanctioned, was pummeling the light circle that contained it. The circle wavered, something that had never happened to Adam. He mentally dug in harder, kept chanting.

The black form screamed and slithered away from the High Sanctioned. It pounded the circle again, creating a crack. It was obviously still tapping into Matt's power, and was pushing the limits of Adam's power. He felt the energy weakening, and knew he was about to lose the circle—and the Belian.

He needed help. *Julia.* Her energy had boosted his when he'd been injured. He reached his left hand behind him. "Julia, I need you, *now.* Give me your right hand."

She didn't hesitate or question. He felt her fingers curl around his, mentally saw the flash of indigo and sensed the third-eye link clicking into place. Then her energy was flowing through him. It was like a current had been turned on, as new power surged into the circle and strengthened it.

He started the last part of the intonation in the ancient Atlantian language: *Be thou removed from this plane of existence. Be thou restricted to Saturn, to be purified by the flame of the Karmic Initiator. Be thou to remain there until thou recognizes The Light, The Truth, The One. Then shalt thou return to do penance.*

The reinforced circle held. The Belian howled as the four luminous beings pinned it. Then it was gone, transported to Saturn, the High Sanctioned vanishing with it. Adam let the circle dissipate.

"All the light is gone, and so is that black thing," Miriam reported. "The aura is gray again, but the black edges are getting more pronounced."

"Sean, start working on him now!" Adam dropped down beside Matt, started channeling energy into him. "Stay with me, Matt," he said, sending his will into Matt's mind. "Don't leave us. *Stay.*"

Across from him, both Sean and Miriam were applying pressure to the arm and chest wounds, using Sean's shirt and her sweater. Adam felt a movement beside him, glanced over to see Julia kneeling awkwardly by Matt's head. She leaned close to his ear and spoke to him.

"Matt, Sean needs you. He's still young, and he respects and loves you. You have to stay here, for him. *He. Needs. You.* You can't leave, do you hear me?" She reached out and stroked his matted hair. "I know you're in pain, and you're grieving. But Susan would want you to remain here. Your work isn't done yet. Stay, Matt. Stay, and I'll help you annoy the hell out of Adam."

Matt suddenly stirred and groaned.

"The black is leaving his aura," Miriam said. "Some of the color is returning. I think he's better."

Adam heard sirens in the distance and knew help was coming. He kept channeling the energy. It appeared Matt was going to make it.

IT was over—in more ways than one. The Belian soul had been sent to Saturn, a phenomenon she'd been able to see once she linked with Adam. That was something she wouldn't soon forget, like a scene from a supernatural movie, one that was both creepy and mind-boggling.

Matt had survived. He would be all right. And so would she, Julia thought, as she let herself into the hotel suite. She and Matt had a lot in common, both survivors with more than their fair share of emotional baggage.

They'd spent hours at the hospital, waiting for Matt to get through surgery and answering questions for the police.

Adam had been able to convince authorities that Matt had been looking for the individual responsible for his wife's murder and had followed leads that took him to Sea-World, but that he hadn't been involved in the mass shootings there. However, he had become distraught when he believed Adam was trying to interfere and had fought with Adam by the stadium. Tonight, when he attempted suicide at his wife's grave, Adam shot him in the arm to stop him, causing the self-inflicted chest wound.

Since the evidence bore out Adam's information, and since he did a little "mind-bending" while he was talking to the officers, they accepted the story. Another one of those creepy/boggling scenarios.

After the police left, the four of them continued waiting while Matt was in recovery; then Sean and Adam saw him briefly. He was finally moved to a room, and the men were going to remain with him for a while, so Julia and Miriam called it a night and returned to the hotel.

It was past three thirty on Thursday morning when Julia entered the suite. Utterly exhausted, she crawled into bed without bothering to change. She was up at ten. Adam hadn't returned yet, which was fine with her. She took a quick shower and got dressed.

Then she turned on her laptop and sent Adam an e-mail, telling him she was returning to Houston. It was impersonal and cowardly, but it was the cleanest way to say good-bye. It was time for her to deal with reality and get on with her life—one that couldn't possibly include him. If she thought otherwise, she was either stupid or delusional, and she was neither.

She also sent an e-mail to Tami Lang in the university math department, informing her she would be in tomorrow to teach her numbers theory course. Then she called a sleepy Miriam and told her she was leaving. Since Miriam had her car in San Antonio, she was driving back later.

That done, Julia packed her things and called the desk for a bellhop. Downstairs, she got a taxi to take her to the rescheduled lunch meeting with Dr. Curtis. She'd have to carry her luggage into the restaurant with her, because as soon as the meeting was over, she was going directly to the airport and taking a flight to Houston.

Then, at some point, she'd have to deal with William Bennett. Maybe that would distract her from missing Adam so damned much.

NINETEEN

MIRIAM didn't wake up until almost three in the afternoon on Thursday. She felt sore and groggy, but became more alert when she remembered the Belian had been vanquished. That had been rather cool, actually—another weird quirk in the fabric known as reality. If ordinary people knew how much strange stuff went on in the Universe, they'd probably never leave their homes.

A shower eased her aching muscles. She decided to forego the makeup and hair products and go au natural until she went back to the hospital. In comfortable jeans and a sweater, she padded barefoot into the living area. Sean's leather jacket was thrown on the couch; his wallet and key card were on the coffee table, so he'd obviously returned while she'd been asleep. His bedroom door was closed.

Stifling a yawn, Miriam went to the dining area and made herself a cup of tea. Figuring Sean would be up soon, she started a pot of coffee. She powered up her laptop on the table and checked her e-mail while the coffeemaker hissed and sizzled and the aroma of fresh coffee filled the air.

She'd just made herself a second cup of tea and returned to the table when Sean's door opened. He ambled out, holding his cell phone to his ear. His hair was damp and combed back, and he wore only a pair of faded, low-riding jeans. A gold cross and chain glinted on his muscular chest. Oh, my. She was a sucker for crosses and sexy male chests, especially when they tapered down to ripped abs and a trim waist.

"You're sure he's doing okay?" Sean asked. "Not in any pain?" He went to the coffeemaker, displaying some very impressive biceps as he poured a cup. "All right. I'll be there in a while. Do I need to bring anything, some clothes for him?" He listened a minute, nodded. "Will do."

He closed the phone, looked at Miriam. "Hey."

She forced her gaze away from his body. "Uh . . . hey. How's Matt?"

"He's okay. Adam said he's awake and alert, has minimal pain." He pulled out the chair beside her and sat down. "The collapsed lung slowed down the recovery, but he should be able to come home this weekend."

"I'm so glad to hear it." She sipped her tea, realized he was staring at her. She lowered her cup. "What? Is something else wrong?"

"Nothing, but . . . you. Your hair isn't spiked. You don't have on any makeup."

Self-consciously, she raised a hand to her face. "I'll fix it before we go to the hospital."

"No, I like it." He reached out, touched her head. "Your hair is so soft. Your eyes look larger, and very green." He dropped his hand. "You look . . . really pretty."

A shiver went through her. Wasn't this a kick? He liked the way she looked without enhancements, and she liked—*really* liked—the way he looked without a shirt.

"Uh, thank you." She took another sip of tea. "So, how are *you* doing? This had to be tough on you."

His face took on a shuttered expression. "I'm fine." He

wrapped his hands around his mug, stared down at it. "I'm handling it."

"I'm sorry. I'm not trying to pry into your psyche or anything like that." She placed her hand on his arm. His skin was warm. "It's just that I'm really close to my folks, and I can't imagine how it would feel to lose one, and then face losing the other. I guess you think of Matt and Susan as your parents."

He nodded and looked at her, and she saw the raw emotions in his eyes. "Yeah, they were the parents I never had. My biological mother—well, let's just say her next fix was a hell of a lot more important than feeding me. But Matt and Susan took me in, showed me what a real family is like. Susan—God, I miss her." His face crumbled with grief, and he looked away for a moment, worked to compose himself.

Miriam slid her hand along his arm and placed it over his clenched fist. "I'm sorry. I didn't mean to upset you."

"No, it's fine." He shrugged, turned back to face her. Moisture sparkled in his eyes. She wanted to tell him it was okay to cry, but she wasn't his shrink.

"My past isn't a secret," he said. "Besides, you and me, we've shared a lot—reading auras and Tarot cards, quality time listening to police scanners, tracking Belians, and some impressive first-aid maneuvers."

"Not to mention me throwing up on a regular basis."

He grinned, flashing those killer dimples. "Yeah, there's that."

The sadness around him eased, and the room seemed to grow brighter. He opened his fist, flattened his palm against hers. A current spiked and arced between them, vibrating with energy and strong physical attraction. They stared at each other.

"You have a great mouth," Sean murmured.

He had a great everything. "So do you." *This is one of those moments*, Miriam thought, *where you know exactly what's going to happen next, and there is no stopping it.* Not that she wanted to.

Anticipation hummed between them as they leaned toward one another, as their mouths hovered mere molecules apart and time seemed to stand still. Until finally, finally, their lips came together. And the *wow* factor practically knocked her out of the chair.

One thing about bad boys—they really knew how to kiss, and it was so much more than just tongue action. Sean's large hands cradled her face perfectly, his fingers sliding up into her hair. He knew just how to tilt her head to mold his lips to hers. Knew just the right pressure, how to tease and retreat, and then ramp up the heat with deeper tongue thrusts.

Oh . . . mega wow! She was definitely in. She managed to get onto his lap. He was definitely in, too—and up, for that matter. The kisses became more intense, escalated by roaming hands, and her sweater and bra leaving the scene. Sean was already wonderfully bare beneath her hands, and she took full advantage.

Somehow, they made it to his bedroom, kissing and circling, fumbling with zippers. They finished stripping each other and fell naked across the bed. Sean sat up, pushed her back against the pillows. "You're a natural brunette," he murmured, looking at the dark curls farther down. "Who'd have thought?"

"All you had to do was ask. But I like this disclosure better."

"So do I." He moved his attention to her breasts, cupping one in his hand. "You are one fine lady."

"You're no slouch," she told him, her breathing ragged. That was an understatement. He was amazing. The gods had been extremely generous the day he'd been formed. "Actually," she amended, too honest to play games, "you're beautiful, like a work of art."

He smiled and ran his hand down her body. His gaze

followed it, heated and appreciative, capable of melting steel. As she was mere flesh and muscle, she was currently dissolving into a quivering mass.

Rising to his knees, he slid his hands over her thighs, and pushed them open. He stared at the intimate, moist flesh between her legs with a frank, masculine admiration that melted her even more. His gaze flashed up to her face, molten fire. "Baby, I'm going to make you scream."

She certainly hoped so.

He lowered his head, and that was her last coherent thought.

IT was midmorning Friday before Adam was able to leave San Antonio. Matt was well on the way to recovery, at least physically. He still had an uphill battle with his grief and alcohol addiction, but Sean would be there for him. When Adam left the hospital, both Matt and Sean had been asleep—Matt in his hospital bed with all the medical monitors, and Sean in one of those hard vinyl chairs indigenous to all hospitals.

Adam was fairly certain not all of Sean's fatigue was from lack of sleep; he suspected Miriam White had a role in depleting Sean's energy. He couldn't say he disapproved. Miriam wasn't a conductor, but she had strong psychic gifts and had jumped right in to help them. She had grit and intelligence, and he liked her very much.

Before leaving the city, Adam had done as much damage control as he could, had answered the last of the police questions this morning. It helped that one of his Sentinels was a captain with the San Antonio police force.

That, and the fact that Officer Olvera had been the one firing on the Riverwalk, and David Gains had been the shooter at SeaWorld, made it easier to convince the investigators that Matt Stevens wasn't involved in the shootings.

Which was true, actually, since he hadn't been in control of his body or the Belian at the time.

Now it was on to the next challenging matter—Julia Reynolds. She had managed to catch him off guard—again. No waiting for him to drive her back to Houston, or even for him to return to the hotel room. Just an impersonal e-mail:

Dear Adam, I am returning to Houston today. I need to get back to my classes and resume my life. I think it best that we end our association now, as I don't wish to be further involved in Sentinel activities. Have a safe trip to Corpus Christi. Sincerely, Julia.

Association? Is that how she thought of their relationship? He might not be completely up on current vernacular, but he was fairly certain that when a woman opened herself to a man's touch and then to his body joining with hers as willingly as Julia had, when she called out his name as she climaxed then lay in his arms afterward, allowing tears that revealed her vulnerability—those actions didn't constitute being *associates.*

Try lovers, mates, or to take it one step further, soul mates. He and Julia had been bound to one another long before this lifetime; he was certain of it. That was the only explanation for a Sanctioned having a matched conductor.

She was *his.* That might be archaic and chauvinistic, when he generally considered himself enlightened and egalitarian, but it was a fact. It was also balanced by the fact that he was hers. It was joint ownership, and nonnegotiable. The Universe didn't make mistakes.

But convincing her of that wouldn't be easy. She was independent and stubborn, and she didn't think she had a future with any man. Bennett had done that to her. Adam's hands tightened on the steering wheel as he felt renewed fury. Bennett would pay, at some point in time; the Universe had an ironclad karmic checks and balances system. Adam simply planned to speed up that process.

He took the ramp to Interstate 10, heading for Houston. Julia didn't know it yet, but she had a date with destiny—and with him.

JULIA didn't go to the university until Friday morning. She'd been worn-out when she reached Houston Thursday afternoon, right during rush hour—what fun. The lunch with Dr. Curtis had taken longer than she expected, although she felt the meeting had been a success. So had the defeating-the-Belian-and-saving-Matt mission.

And maybe even the ending-Julia's-twelve-year-celibacy challenge—although she seriously doubted there was much, if any, sex in her future. Especially since she didn't think anything could compare to the mind-blowing sex she'd had with Adam, compliments of the Sanctioned/conductor link.

But she wasn't going to think about Adam anymore. *Put it away*, she told herself.

She was immediately soothed when she stepped off the elevator and headed for the main office of the math department. The familiar décor and sounds and scents surrounded her like old friends. She reached the reception area, and Tami Lang greeted her with a big smile.

"Dr. Julia! I didn't expect you back yet. Adam said you wouldn't be here until next week."

"Did he?" Julia forced a smile on her face, walked over to check her mail slot. It was overflowing. She sighed, tugged out papers and periodicals. "When did you talk to him?"

"On Tuesday, when he called to warn me about your disgruntled student." Tami hailed from Alabama, and her voice held the charm of the genteel south.

"Oh, yes." Adam had told Julia that Bennett was being

tailed 24/7, and about Luke's phone call while she was in the hospital. He'd also informed her he'd called Tami. "I'm sorry about that," Julia said.

"Oh, don't be. I would never give out personal information on any of our staff without specific permission. But your student showed up all right. Said his name was Bill and he wanted to talk to you about office supplies. What a lame excuse."

Julia felt chilled to the bone. She shouldn't be surprised that Bennett had actually been in the math department, since he now knew where she taught, or that he had been on campus talking to her students. But it was still a shock, a personal invasion, and left a sick knot of fear in the pit of her stomach. It took a moment to calm enough that her voice wouldn't shake. "What did you tell him?"

"I told him to give me a minute and then I stepped to the back and called security. But he was gone when I came back. I called the physics department and warned them he might be going there, which Adam also suggested." Tami huffed and went to her desk. "I didn't like that Bill guy. He looked like a criminal to me." She gave Julia a reproving look. "You need to tell me when you have problem students like this."

"Uh, this was something that happened a long time ago. I didn't expect it to be a problem. As I said, I'm sorry."

Tami waved her hand. "Oh, don't worry about it. Students these days. They want good grades just handed to them, without having to do the work. So, how was the funeral? Adam said it was nice."

This was great. It appeared Adam had become Tami's newest source of information. And he probably thought he could pump Tami for details on Julia. She'd rectify that situation as soon as she got her balance and her life calmed down. "It was a funeral," she said. "And I'm glad it's behind me."

Tami's eyes glowed with compassion. "I'm sorry you

had to go through that, but at least Adam was there with you. He's your cousin, right?"

Oh, yes, "kissing cousin" Adam. Julia felt like screaming. Instead, she said, "We're distantly related." And it was going to remain distant. "Is Dr. Moreno in? I met with Dr. Curtis yesterday, and I wanted to share the results of that with him."

Julia had liked Dr. Curtis very much. The woman was quite brilliant and her education and experience were impressive. She was very interested in the position with UH, and Julia would make a positive recommendation to Dr. Moreno.

Dr. Moreno was available, and she had a brief meeting with him. He was in an amenable mood, apparently still charged up about the sizeable bribe—camouflaged as a donation—that Adam had given the department.

Finally, Julia was able to go to her Friday class. Miriam wasn't there, which surprised her. She hoped Matt hadn't taken a turn for the worse, and decided to call Miriam later.

Teaching the class was the highlight of her day. She'd missed this terribly. She was in her element in the classroom, discussing theorems and practical applications, watching the comprehension dawning in her students' eyes, encouraging active discussion. She announced there would be a test next Wednesday, ignored the groans and the whining that her class had been stuck with Dr. Richards for the previous three classes and he wasn't nearly the good teacher Julia was.

"Deal with it," she told the class. "You know my office hours. I'll be available Monday and Tuesday, if you need help. See you next week."

As she packed up her papers and books, several students wandered by to tell her they were glad she was back. Obviously, Richards wasn't a favorite. He was a better theorist than he was a teacher.

After her students were gone, she thought about working

there in her office for a few hours. But the Friday afternoon rush hour had already started and would only get worse. Plus she'd have to face a deserted parking garage, since most staff left early on Fridays. Besides, she had to go home sometime. She'd been fine yesterday evening, hadn't received any more calls from Bennett.

She was scared, no sense in denying it. Maybe even bordering on terrified. But she couldn't—wouldn't—put her life on hold. She'd soldier on, with precautions. She slipped her gun into her coat pocket, where she could reach it quickly, loaded up her case and purse, and headed for the parking garage. There was no way she'd run into Bennett there, not with him being tailed by Adam's people.

Right now, she was grateful for that safeguard, but she'd soon have to tell Adam to call off the watch. He couldn't protect her forever, and Bennett wasn't going away. Sooner or later she'd have to deal with him. But it was nice to feel a little bit safer, at least for the weekend and maybe next week. It gave her time to get her life back in balance.

She saw nothing suspicious on the way to her car, but she breathed a big sigh of relief once she was locked inside and pulling out of the garage. *There is no way Bennett could know where I live,* she told herself. She used her address at the university for her driver's license and vehicle registration. It wasn't legal, but she'd felt it a necessary precaution.

He couldn't very well follow her home if he was being tailed—surely she'd be called on her cell phone by whoever was on watch duty if there was a danger of that. Besides, according to Adam, Bennett was currently using the Metro bus system to get around. So, until such time as she told Adam to back off, she was safe.

Now, if she could just stop thinking about Adam so much.

* * *

I really am clever, he thought, watching Julia exit the parking garage. He'd been to Hoffman Hall on Tuesday, had scoped out the area and knew where the staff parked. He also knew Julia taught a course on Monday, Wednesday, and Friday—compliments of the student who'd shared her phone number.

He'd taken the bus back to the university on Wednesday, but hadn't seen her. Then he'd decided the bus routine was stupid bullshit. He hadn't been able to do anything about it yesterday, because he'd had to meet with his fucking parole officer. What a joke. Look at a list of rules longer than a football field, agree to be a good boy, and salute the goddamn eagle.

He was supposed to start work at the sheet metal plant on Monday, but he couldn't worry about that. He was a man on a mission to get the lying bitch who had put him in jail, and make her pay. Hard to do that when he had to ride the bus.

So he'd stolen a car from an apartment complex four blocks over from his brother's apartment. He'd also been smart enough to take the plates off a broken-down car of a similar make and model from yet another complex and put it on the car he'd stolen, before he drove it anywhere. Less chance of being pulled over by the cops if the plates on his vehicle didn't hit on stolen when they were scanned.

Then he'd parked the car near the staff garage entrance, just out of range of the security cameras. He stationed himself behind a nearby Dumpster, so he wouldn't draw attention. He used binoculars to watch people coming and going, and it had paid off. There she was—bitch Julia. He was surprised to see her limping and using a cane; then, remembering the sound of her leg cracking when he'd smashed it with his hiking-booted feet twelve years ago, he felt a fierce satisfaction that he was responsible.

She was heavier, which made her curvier, sexier. She

probably thought that would attract more men, which stirred his rage. *Whore.* Her face looked pretty much the same, but she'd cut off the long wavy hair he'd liked so well. There would be an extra punishment for that.

Oh, yeah, there'll be a whole lot of punishment.

He ran for his car, started it, and followed her off the campus.

ADAM clicked off his BlackBerry and pushed away from his laptop. He'd spent much of the drive to Houston, and then another two hours once here, dealing with his private investigations agency matters, daily Sentinel reports, monitoring possible Belian activity in Texas, and shifting duties. He had to allow for the manpower he'd delegated to tracking William Bennett, and for the fact that he was currently down two men—Matt and Sean—in San Antonio.

He wanted Sean to stay with Matt until he was steadier. He was grateful Miriam was staying until Sunday afternoon, as she appeared to be a calming, stabilizing force for Sean. She would help see Matt out of the hospital and settled in Sean's apartment. Matt wasn't returning to the house for the time being. There was too much negative energy there. Adam had arranged for the house to be repaired and thoroughly cleaned, but still thought it best for Matt to stay with Sean for a while.

Adam went to the wet bar and poured himself a scotch straight up. He sipped as he strolled to the window and looked out over the Houston skyline view afforded by his suite at the Four Seasons Hotel. It was midafternoon and traffic was already snarled, but then it was Friday.

He stared at the sleek and shiny buildings reaching toward the clouds, but didn't really see them. Now that he'd handled the pressing duties, his focus returned to his most intriguing challenge—Julia. He wasn't sure exactly how to deal with her, a frustrating first for him, as he tended to be very decisive. Oh, he had no doubt of the outcome, but getting there might take some finesse.

Damned if he didn't miss her, and it had only been a day since she rabbited. It wasn't just her sharp-edged mind and wit, her heart and amazing courage he missed, but also her scent, and the feel and taste of her. They'd only had sex twice, and one of those times had been a wild conduction, but already he craved her touch, the sensation of being inside her and claiming her in the most elemental way.

Since he'd always maintained total control over his physical and mental appetites, he found her effect on him disconcerting. But he accepted it, because his meditative visions had shown him this was coming, that it was meant to be. One thing he'd learned in his many lifetimes: Never argue with the Universe's plan. Besides, he wasn't at all unhappy with his fate. Julia, however, probably wasn't going to view their soul mate bond in the same light.

His phone rang, and he walked back to the desk to retrieve it, saw it was from Luke. He clicked it on. "Hello, Luke, what's going on?"

"Bad news, Adam. We have an injured Sentinel, and we've lost Bennett."

"Tell me what happened."

"Bennett walked away from his brother's apartment around noon today, and Davis followed him by car. After they went a few blocks, a kid in a souped-up Charger ran a stop sign and broadsided Davis. He was pinned in his vehicle, and he suffered a broken leg and a concussion, and was unconscious for a while. When he came to, he was in an ER trauma unit. He couldn't get anyone to call me until just now, so I didn't know he was out of commission. We have no idea where Bennett is."

"What's the prognosis for Davis?"

"It's good. They're going to set the leg, then admit him overnight for observation, but don't expect any complications."

"Have you called Julia to warn her about Bennett?"

"Both Marla and I have been trying, but our calls go into her voice mail. Marla said it's probably turned off, since Julia teaches on Friday afternoon, and always turns off her cell for classes. What do you want me to do?"

Adam had a very bad feeling about this. "Let me try to call Julia. If I don't get her, I'll call the math department, and have them hunt her down. I'll get back to you."

But Julia didn't answer, and he got a recording for the department. *Damn it!* That didn't give him any information. For all he knew, Julia was still in class or in her office, but he didn't have that phone number. He tried her at home, didn't get an answer there, either. He grabbed his coat and called Luke as he left the suite and strode toward the elevator.

"Luke, contact university security and have them look for Julia and to stay with her if they locate her. Then get Stamos over to the university. If she's there, I want him to notify me, then relieve the security people and wait with her until I get there. I don't want you to go, because I don't want Marla left alone, and I don't want her at the university, in case Bennett is there. I'm heading to Julia's house now. Call me if you hear anything, and I'll do the same."

"Will do."

Adam clicked off and felt fear chipping at his normal icy control. But he had to remain calm and focused. Julia's life could depend on it.

FOLLOWING Julia was ridiculously easy. She didn't appear to be aware of him, and he was able to stay right behind her. He dropped back a little after they exited the freeway, slowing even more when she entered a subdivision. He stayed well back then, but kept her in sight. When she pulled into the driveway of a modest, beige brick house, he smiled. Home, sweet home, but not for long.

She waited as the garage door started upward. William parked in front of the house next to hers and got out of the car. She pulled into the garage, and he ran to the side of it, which was on the right end of the house. He looked into the garage as the door started down. Julia was still in the car. The driver side was away from him, and closest to the interior door.

He ducked down and scooted in between the right side of the car and the wall. If she came around to the trunk or to his side, he could simply slip around to the front of the car. But she didn't. As the garage door finished closing, she got out, opened the back door on her side, and got her purse, cane, and briefcase. Then she limped into the house.

Elation filled him. He had her now, the lying whore. There were no other cars in front of the house, so he didn't know if anyone else lived here, but if they did, he'd deal with them. He rather hoped to run into her bitch sister again. It had been fun having her witness Julia's punishment the first time. He moved to the door going into the house, waited a beat, then opened it.

He was in a kitchen, small and neat, done in yellow and white, with glossy beige floor tiles. *Aw, isn't that homey?* He heard a high-pitched beeping that indicated an alarm system. He also heard Julia talking to someone and he tensed. Moving silently through the kitchen, he peered around the corner. Julia had her back to him and was moving down a hallway.

"Let me reset the alarm, Ike, and I'll get you some Fancy Feast."

What the—? Hearing a loud meow, he lowered his gaze and saw a large, long-haired Siamese cat following right behind her. Relaxed again. *Just a fucking cat.* She opened a closet door. He came around the corner and moved quickly after her, the thick carpet muffling his footsteps. The beeping stopped, which meant she had cancelled the alarm response.

Before she could reset it, he grabbed the closet door and slammed it back against the wall. She whirled toward him with a startled gasp.

"Hello, Julia," he said.

TWENTY

SHE was terrified. The fear penetrated her bones, her cells, down to her very core. It felt like she was dissolving into a backwash of hideous memories. When Bennett grabbed the door and slung it against the wall, she'd been stunned for a moment, her brain deadlocked in the this-can't-possibly-be-happening mode.

Then reality set in. Adrenaline flooded her body, shock freezing her muscles in rigor mortis mode. Her lungs stopped working; the pounding of her heart roared in her ears. The horror paralyzed her like a deer in headlights. Bennett grabbed her and slammed her against the opposite wall. The pain of that brought her situation home. It also shattered the paralysis, jump started her brain.

She swung her cane at him, but prison had honed him, making him fast. He sidestepped, grabbed her arm, and twisted viciously. She cried out, the cane slipping from her nerveless fingers. He kicked it away. "Bitch," he hissed. "Did you really think you could hide from me?"

She stared at him, her chest heaving. *Oh, God, help me get out of this.*

"Did you really think I wouldn't find you?" he taunted. "That I wouldn't make you pay for what you did to me?"

She made a split-second decision—she wasn't giving in to her fear, wasn't going to cower before this monster. She'd done that twelve years ago. Now, she was made of stronger stuff, forged in the hellfires of pain and a battered psyche. She was a fighter and a survivor. Instinctively, she went for Bennett's ego. He'd react with violence, but rage clouded logic, enabled mistakes. All she needed was an opening to get her gun from her coat pocket.

"No," she said. "I expected you to rot and die in prison, you bastard."

Rage flashed across his face. He backhanded her, slamming her head sideways into the wall. "You'll pay for that, too."

Clenching her teeth against the pain, she slowly turned her head back to face him. She looked straight into his soulless eyes. Instead of fear, she now felt intense hatred. "You're not even worthy of name-calling. You're too low a life-form, below amoeba status."

When he moved in, she was ready, slamming her knee into his testicles. She tried to twist out of his grasp, but he managed to hurl her to the floor. Gasping, he fell back against the closet doorjamb. "You goddamned bitch!"

She flipped over and fumbled for her gun. He rushed her and landed a brutal kick to her side. The agonizing burn signaled broken ribs and ripped a scream from her throat. It took all her willpower to keep her focus.

"You'll pay for that one, too. You can't escape what I have planned." He leaned down, grabbed her coat and yanked.

She cried out again as he jerked her to her feet. *God, it hurts.*

His eyes glittered, feral and insane. "Oh, it will be worse," he promised. "Much worse. The fun is just beginning."

She had to stay calm, had to think. She struggled against the debilitating fear and pain clouding her mind. She had to fight it, had to fight him. *Think, think!* Make him mad, keep him off balance. Get the gun. Bennett dragged her farther down the hallway, and agony screamed along every nerve ending. She bit her lip to keep from crying out, tasted blood.

"Ah, here's the bedroom." He yanked her inside, sent her stumbling. "I could pound you to bloody bits in the hallway," he continued. "But I need more space to do the job right. Besides, the bed is handy. Because before I kill you, bitch, I'm going to fuck you. Every way possible."

No. No! Panic swept through her like a wildfire. Oh, God, she was going to be sick. She couldn't go through that again. She'd shoot herself first. But Bennett was gripping her right arm, the side where the gun was pocketed. She had to wait to get it.

A loud, plaintive meow came from behind them. Ike, demanding his dinner. Bennett swung around. "Fuckin' cat. I hate the damned things." He kicked the cat, sent him flying four feet.

"Ike," Julia gasped, her heart in her throat.

Bennett shot her an evil grin. "Like him, do you? Well, isn't that sweet? Maybe I'll have some entertainment with the furball. Kind of like an appetizer before the main course. But before I make kitty cutlets, gotta make sure you don't cause any trouble." He swung back, smashed his fist into her face.

The blow sent her reeling backward. He punched her again, and she toppled. The force of hitting the floor knocked the breath out of her. Pain flooded her face and ribs, so intense she thought she might black out. She couldn't stop the moans as she curled into herself.

"There, now. That's nice dinner music." He leaned down, pulled a butcher knife from his boot. "Handy that my stupid brother likes to cook. Stocks his kitchen with lots of sharp implements." He walked toward Ike. "Here, kitty, kitty. You piece-of-shit furball."

The horror of his intent broke her. "No," she pleaded. "Bennett—William—please don't do anything to Ike." Tears filled her eyes as she watched Ike slink beneath the bed. This was a nightmare beyond imagining. She couldn't bear it. "Leave him alone, and I-I'll make it worth your while."

"Oh, gutting the cat and fucking and killing you will all be worth my while." Bennett reached under the bed. "Gotcha!"

Ike yowled as Bennett started dragging him out by the tail. Tears overflowed Julia's eyes. She was helpless, lying in a pool of pain. *Wait—the gun!* She struggled onto her left side, fumbled in her coat pocket. God bless concealed weapons. She pulled out her Beretta, clicked off the safety.

"Bennett! Look at me, you scumbag son of a bitch."

He swung around, jerking up a howling cat in one hand, the knife in the other. Fury and insanity twisted his face into that of a monster.

"Go to hell," Julia said. She pulled the trigger.

IT took Adam way too long to get to Julia's house. Traffic was gridlocked, and there wasn't a damned thing he could do about it. He kept trying her cell and home phones, getting voice mail on both. *That doesn't mean anything*, he told himself. She might have forgotten to turn her cell phone back on.

He knew she wasn't at the university. Both security and Stamos had reported her office empty and locked. The security tape of the staff garage showed her getting into her

car and leaving over an hour ago. She could be home, and
screening her calls to avoid him. Or she might be running
errands. Or at the Red Lion Pub, drowning out recent
events—and him.

He tried to remain objective and analyze the situation.
Since Bennett didn't have a car, it was virtually impossible
for him to follow Julia. He might be savvy enough to stake
out the university, get her license plate, and find her address by digging on the Internet. But her address on record
was the university—Adam had checked.

So Bennett couldn't follow Julia or find her home
address—theoretically. Yet all of Adam's internal alarms
were on full alert, his psychic antennae screaming that
something was very wrong. He just didn't know where to
look.

He'd start with her home, and go from there. He finally
exited the freeway then broke all the speed limits getting
through the subdivision. He pulled in her driveway, killed
the engine, and leaped from the Mercedes. She had a solid-
paneled garage door, so he couldn't check for her car. He
strode quickly to the front door, started manipulating the
locks.

The sound of a gunshot inside the house sent a lightning
strike of panic through him. No time to deal with the two
dead bolts. He stepped back, threw out his hand, and blasted
the door with pure power. It shattered, and he stepped over
the debris, drawing his gun. The living room was empty.
He didn't call out. He didn't know the situation, didn't want
to broadcast his presence—although the door blast had already done that.

His heart was pounding, his breathing ragged, very unusual for him. He forced himself to calm and go into full
Sanctioned mode as he focused and searched for Julia's
energy. There—in the rear of the house. He superspeeded
down the hall to the bedroom. Stepping into the doorway,
he aimed his gun into the room.

His heart almost stopped. Bennett was on his back on the floor, gasping for breath. His eyes were glazed with shock and pain. Blood oozed from a hole in his chest, and pooled beneath him. Kneeling beside him, her trench coat dragging in the blood, Julia had both hands clasped around the butt of her Beretta. The barrel was pointed at Bennett's forehead, just inches above it. Her tear-tracked face was battered. Her body was shaking violently.

Adam stepped into the room, lowering the gun. "Julia."

"I'm going to kill him." Her voice was ragged, her eyes wild. "I'm going to send him straight to hell."

He thanked The One she was alive. "You've already injured him. He's down. You defeated him. I think that's enough."

"No!" Hysteria tinged her voice. "Even sending him to hell isn't enough." Fresh tears slid down her face. "He hit me and kicked me. Told me he was going to r-rape me again. Then he tried to kill Ike."

Adam fought back the urge to slowly dismember Bennett and let him bleed out. With great effort, he subdued his own fury. He had to focus on Julia, on what this might do to her. A quick scan of the room showed Ike crouching warily between the nightstand and the wall.

He took a step closer. "But he didn't do either of those things, did he?" Surely Bennett hadn't succeeded in raping Julia this time—she was completely dressed. But if he had—

"No. Not this time. But he-he hurt me." She looked at him, her eyes anguished. "He's a monster. He can't go free again. I have to do this."

Her face was swollen and bruised, and a black eye was forming. She had to be in tremendous pain. Adam's anger resurged. He wanted to pull the trigger himself, but he knew this wasn't the solution. "Bennett won't go free, Julia. He's violated parole, attacked you again. They'll put him away for good this time."

"No, they won't." Her voice rose again. "The system doesn't work. The only way to deal with monsters is to execute them."

And the cost to her soul would be exorbitant. He took another step. He could paralyze her or deflect the gun. But it wasn't his call, since Bennett wasn't an innocent, which would necessitate Adam's protection. Instead, it was Julia's choice. Free will.

"Listen to me, Julia. Killing him is not the way. It will be a mark against your karma, will take a piece of your soul."

"I don't care!" Her finger tightened on the trigger. "You do executions. You kill physical bodies of Belians and send their souls to Saturn."

"We do that only because there's no other way to stop them. If Bennett survives this chest wound, he'll go to prison for the rest of his life. That's hell on Earth."

She shook her head, set her mouth. Pressed the barrel against Bennett's forehead. His eyes widened, and he tried to speak, but was too weak to move.

"I love you, Julia."

She jolted in shock, looked from Bennett to him. "Damn it, Adam! Why are you doing this?"

He took another step and locked his gaze with hers. "Because I know if you kill Bennett, you'll regret it for eternity. And because it's true. I do love you." He meant it. It wasn't just a dictate from the Universe; it was a personal truth.

He could see reason returning to her, warring with her fierce need for vigilante justice. "You're just saying that because you didn't get any sex for two hundred years," she muttered.

Relief loosened the death grip on his heart. "There's that, too." He held out his hand. "You have free will, and you decide how this ends. I'm asking you to choose grace over revenge. To give me the gun."

She hesitated, looked back at Bennett. "I've never hated anyone before, but I hate him. I hate his guts."

"With good reason. But that doesn't mean you should sink to his level. Don't let him destroy your soul, Julia. Rise above it. Give me the gun. Please."

Tears rolled slowly down her cheeks as she stared at Bennett. "Rot in jail," she said to him, then handed the gun to Adam.

He blew out the breath he'd been holding. "Good choice."

Swaying, she wrapped her arms around herself. She was deathly pale, her face pinched with pain. "Yes, well, I think we should go to the hospital now."

She proceeded to pass out, and he moved to catch her. And wasn't it an odd coincidence that as he rose, holding her, his foot just happened to slam into Bennett?

Must be the Universe at work.

JULIA opened her eyes, blinked at the clock. Ten AM? She jolted up in a panic. How had it gotten so late? She never overslept. She had to get dressed and get to the university and—Wait. She looked around the blurred room. Got her glasses from the nightstand, put them on and took in the rich furnishings of the obscenely opulent bedroom. Then it came to her. She was at the Four Seasons Hotel, in Adam's suite, and today must be Sunday.

Turning her head, she saw the dent in the pillow next to hers. Funny, but she didn't recall going to bed last night, and she certainly didn't remember sleeping with anyone—in this case, Adam. Obviously, he'd been up to his woo-woo crap again. It was her own fault, since she had allowed him to bring her to the hotel.

After leaving the hospital yesterday morning, she'd been too wounded, emotionally and physically, to return to her house. Besides, it was being cleaned, and the carpet in her hallway and bedroom replaced, and the front door fixed. Marla was on the hunt for a new comforter set for the bed. Adam had found contractors to do the work at a moment's notice, which wasn't a surprise.

She should have gone to Luke and Marla's house instead, but it had been too much effort to argue with Adam. Friday night had been a blur of pain, ER doctors and nurses, police, Marla and Luke, and of course, Adam. She'd been scanned for internal bleeding, had her broken ribs taped, and kept overnight for observation.

She'd decided Demerol was a great thing, even while swearing off hospitals for the rest of her life. Adam had stayed with her, after convincing Marla he was the best choice, and done his own versions of pain management and healing throughout the night.

Julia spent yesterday here with him. She had to admit he'd taken amazing care of her, channeling more healing and pain relief energies, and ordering in her favorite foods—including Godiva chocolate and vintage merlot. He'd even given her a foot massage. She wished she had a picture of that—she could blackmail him with it. Not that anyone would believe it.

But the best thing he'd done for her was to simply be there. He hadn't pushed her to talk, but had listened intently when she did. He hadn't pressured her in any way, made any more crazy claims about her being his perfect match. Hadn't said he loved her again. That still had her shaken, although she was of two schools of thought about it.

One was that she'd imagined him saying it. She'd been in shock and her memory of Friday's events were murky. The other thought was that he'd said it to distract her and get the gun. Either way, it didn't mean anything. It couldn't, which was for the best.

Then why did her heart feel heavy? She should be rejoicing that Bennett was under guard in the hospital and, when he recovered, would be back in prison permanently. That she'd faced true evil and triumphed. That she could return to her normal routine and the job she loved, and not live in fear. Yes, she should be very happy. *I'm just adjusting back*, she told herself firmly. Right now, she was going to take a shower, tell Adam "thank you" and "good-bye" and get on with her life. And it was absolutely for the best.

She went into the marble and gilt bathroom, took care of necessities, brushed her teeth, and stepped into the gorgeous glassed-in shower. The hot water streaming down on her felt heavenly. She closed her eyes and savored the moment—no stress, no worries, and the joy of being safe . . .

"What do you want for breakfast?"

She jumped and yelped, her eyes flying open. There he was, in front of the open shower door. Her heart felt like a battering ram in her chest. "Damn it, Adam! You scared the daylights out of me." She threw the washcloth at him, and it hit him before falling to the floor, leaving a huge wet area on his black shirt. "The bathroom ban is in force. Go. Away."

"The ban is permanently deactivated. Has been since . . ." He gave her a heated look that curled her toes. "You know when."

That glowing gaze sent tingles through her body. She felt her breasts growing heavy, and flames flowing due south. She definitely had the water temperature too high. "Go away, Adam."

He curled an elegant hand around the doorframe, leaned against it. He looked dark and delectable. "I was ordering room service and came to see if you wanted . . . anything."

Her body temperature shot up even higher, the mercury bursting the top off the thermometer. Oh, man, this was dangerous. *He* was dangerous, and way too tempting. Any sensible girl would hit him over the head with the soap and make a run for it. But when had anything about the past ten days been sensible or practical or even remotely realistic?

Tomorrow, she'd be returning to the real world, to her job at the university. She'd be plain, staid Julia—ordinary, celibate, single lady. She'd already drunk from the sexy-supernatural-male chalice. What was one more sip from the fantasy fountain? Okay, so it was holding up a metal rod in an open field during a fierce lightning storm. But what a charge when the lightning hit.

Even more importantly, she needed a memory to wipe out that of William Bennett. Something clean and good to remove the taint of evil, to reassure her yet again that Bennett hadn't won. *Just one more time*, she told herself. And if she was going to do this, she might as well go over the top.

She took the plunge. "Yes, I *do* want something." Reaching out, she grabbed the front of Adam's shirt and yanked him close. She went up on her toes, tugged his face down, and kissed him.

One thing she liked about Adam—he caught on quickly. He returned the kiss, his tongue dueling sensuously with hers. His hands slid down her wet back, settling possessively over her rear and squeezing gently. The innate chemistry between them exploded into a wildfire. Just like that, Julia was inundated with need so intense, all logical thought evaporated. She tore at his shirt.

"Maybe the bed would be better—"

She yanked him into the shower before he could finish. He stumbled over the raised threshold and against her. The water pelted him, plastering his silk shirt and cashmere pants to some impressive muscles. His Gucci loafers were probably ruined as well. Big deal, since he had more money than God. And she absolutely didn't care about anything but getting him naked.

He didn't seem to care, either. Between heavy-duty kisses, they struggled together to strip off his clothes. "You know," he gasped, "these would have come off easier when they were dry."

"Shut up and take off your pants," Julia panted, tugging at his belt.

He complied, and then he was gloriously, beautifully nude. She wrapped her hand around his impressive length, felt him harden even more. The starbursts flared in his eyes, and he groaned. Heady with her power over him, she stroked and squeezed. With another groan, he grasped her wrist. "We're slowing this down." His voice was deep, guttural, and sexy as hell.

She found herself spun around and facing the wall. Before she could protest, Adam leaned down and nipped her neck, then kissed it. He cupped her breasts, stroked her nipples. Her words dissolved on a moan. She leaned her head back, arched beneath his touch. She felt shockingly wanton and uninhibited, a lightning rod waiting for the strike.

She instinctively widened her stance. He took her unspoken invitation, and slowly, torturously, slid one hand down over her midriff and abdomen, through the curls to stroke lightly. Then he slid a finger inside her.

She felt her legs go weak. "Oh, God."

"Really, you can call me Adam," he murmured, running his tongue along her ear.

"You are so full of—" He moved his finger in and out, and her mind blanked. "Oh!" was all she managed.

Needing more, she tilted her head sideways and up, and he leaned down to kiss her. He seemed so in tune with her, with what she wanted and needed. His tongue mated with hers, imitating the movement of his finger below. She was wet and aching, and certain she was about to disintegrate.

"Adam," she gasped. "Now!"

He turned her around to face him, lifted her. "Put your legs around me."

She did, and he fitted himself to her. Holding her with effortless strength, he slid inside her, deeper and deeper, until he filled her completely and they were fused together, two parts of an amazing whole. A perfect fit.

He braced her against the tile, leaned down to kiss her. Then he began moving and her focus narrowed solely to the sensation, to the building anticipation of a nuclear detonation. There was nothing else but Adam inside her, and the climbing spiral to oblivion. Then the explosion hit with a blinding flash of indigo, and a tsunami wave of pleasure that seemed to last for infinity. Finally, she slumped against him, too weak to move.

"Enjoyed that, did you?" he asked.

"I think I've lost my motor functions."

"Then I'll carry you to the bed." He shut off the water, and keeping them joined, stepped out of the shower. She lay against him, totally drained, as he grabbed two towels. "I could feel your pleasure through the third-eye link," he said, walking into the bedroom.

She made an effort to clear the orgasm fog from her mind. "We were linked? Is that why I saw the indigo color?"

"Yes. So I shared your climax." He disengaged them, lowered her to the bed.

She lay back against the pillow. "Then I must have felt yours—" She looked over, saw Mr. Energizer Bunny was still ready to go. "Oh. Well."

He settled on the bed beside her and stroked his hand down her arm. "I believe I mentioned the Sentinel stamina."

"And here I thought it was just a male-ego fantasy."

He slid his hand over her breast. "I also mentioned it's enhanced by the presence of water."

"I vaguely remember that." Pleasure tingled through her, along with a new rush of desire. She couldn't believe her body was reviving so quickly.

Adam rolled her into his arms and kissed her, and everything else blurred. Only the two of them existed in the Universe. It was slow and tender this time. Between kisses and verbal sparing, they caressed and explored each other. When she was vibrating with need, he slid over her and settled between her legs. "Are you all right with me like this?" he asked.

She looked up into his face, into those mysterious eyes with their starbursts. She saw his concern, his caring. And her heart turned over. He was honorable and strong; he carried enormous responsibilities with intelligence and competence and grace.

He'd given her life back to her, freed her from the debilitating doubts and fears Bennett had bequeathed her. She ached with the knowledge that she and Adam didn't belong together. This wasn't a fairy tale, it was real life. And gods weren't supposed to mate with mere mortals—especially ones as ordinary as she was.

She slipped her arms around him, and drew him close. "This is exactly what I want," she whispered, and leaped into the fire one last time.

ADAM held Julia in his arms, stunned by how profound their joining had been, how perfect and right. Nothing like this had ever happened in the long history of the Sanctioned, but there was no doubt Julia was his soul mate. She completed him, on every level.

Yet he knew she was still holding back from him. The only time she was completely open to their bond was in the throes of passion. He'd like to think that meant he hadn't gotten too rusty in the sex department the past few centuries, but he knew it was more likely the chemistry of the Sanctioned/conductor link.

He'd just have to keep chipping away at her defensive armor. She stirred and moved away from him, slipped out of the bed. She had a classic, curvy body—feminine and mysterious, womanly. He sat up as she walked to the bathroom. "Are you ready to eat?"

She looked at him over her shoulder. "I'm not hungry. I'm going to finish my shower."

He liked her wet. "I'll be glad to scrub your back."

She shook her head. "I think it's safer for me to do this alone. I'm not up to more sex—" She looked at the tented sheet above his lap and rolled her eyes. "Even if you are."

She went into the bathroom and closed the door. She'd put the barriers back up. Frustrated, he got a change of clothes and went to the other bathroom to clean up. After that, he ordered room service. Julia had to eat sometime. And he had to figure out how to tear down her barriers.

He was in the living area, reading faxed reports, when she walked out. She was dressed and had her coat and purse. Her expression was resolute. He sat back, watching her, although he already knew what she was going to say.

"I'm leaving, Adam."

It was a jolt to his system, although it shouldn't be. "Where are you going?"

"Home. I just spoke with Marla. The front door is fixed, the carpet has been replaced, the house is clean, and she has my new bedding. She's on her way to pick me up."

He stood and walked over to her. "Stay here with me."

Emotion flashed in her eyes before she blanked her expression. "I can't, Adam. I won't. This is as far as we can go."

He willed himself to stay calm. "I don't see why."

"Yes, you do. We're not a good match. If anything, I'd say we're completely mismatched. Oil and water. Prime numbers and transcendentals. God and mortal."

"I am not a god."

"You're not truly human, either." She moved in and kissed him on the cheek. "Good-bye."

It took every ounce of willpower to keep from grabbing her and tying her up until she saw reason. But he knew he couldn't force her. His highly tuned instincts told him she wouldn't listen to any arguments he made now. So he let her go—for the time being.

She walked to the door then looked back at him, her eyes glistening. "Have a good life." Then she was gone.

Damn it! She was stubborn and infuriating. Adam went to the wet bar and poured some scotch. As he sipped, he considered the situation. He never failed when he set his mind to something. Julia would see reason, would accept that she was his mate. Hopefully during this lifetime.

He was, however, willing to give her some time. She'd been hit hard, emotionally and physically, these past two weeks. She'd been traumatized by the Belian murders and by Bennett; she'd been hospitalized twice, with some serious injuries. She was understandably damaged and fragile. Forcing the issue of their future together wasn't in the best interests of either of them right now.

He would wait. He would give her time to heal, to call on her formidable will to put the traumas behind her and get on with her life. She was, above all, a survivor, with a steel core of strength and determination.

Yes, he'd give her time to get her balance back. And then he'd simply manipulate circumstances, as he had once before, so that she had no choice in the matter.

Absolutely no choice at all.

TWENTY-ONE

JULIA got through the next weeks, although it was a battle. She alternated between night terrors, unsettling daytime memories, and missing Adam. The first three nights after she returned home, she woke from nightmares, and carried her gun as she checked the house and alarm system. Then she lay in bed, unable to go back to sleep, and thought about Adam, despite her attempts to vanquish him from her mind. His absence from her life was like a physical ache.

But in the tough Reynolds fashion, she pushed forward. Her pain, the hellish memories, her unrealistic yearnings, could all be steamrolled into a level, functioning pavement. *Mind over matter* had been her mantra for so long, it was imprinted on her brain cells. Still, she wasn't above getting help, so she called Dr. Jackson, the clinical psychologist who had kept her sane after the first attack. She'd had several sessions now and was coming to grips with the recent traumas she'd faced.

Thank God for the university and for teaching. Outside

of her family, they were the constants in her life. Her classes kept her focused on lesson plans and exams and grades. Then there was the never-ending paperwork, in triplicate, that a large university demanded, and the departmental meetings, and of course, the politics. There was always work to be done, and Julia embraced it like a long-lost religion. And yet, there was a void in her life, one that hadn't been there before. She'd just have to keep finding more things to occupy her, to dam up the void.

She got off the elevator one Monday morning, glad the weekend was over, although most of her students wouldn't agree. Today was the final exam for her thermal physics course. The semester had ended, and the holidays were just around the corner, but Julia couldn't get excited about them this year. She started down the long corridor, which was currently decorated in a Christmas theme. How convenient that the red and white dancing candy canes on the walls happened to match the UH colors.

She heard people talking and laughing as she approached the reception area, and wondered what was going on. A holiday party, perhaps? As she entered the large open area, she saw at least a dozen people milling around— Tami, Dr. Moreno, Dr. Richards, Dr. Wilson, a number of other professors, several of the graduate student assistants, Miriam, and— Shock speared through Julia as she realized Sean and Adam were also there, at the far end of the room.

Her heart jolted as she stared at Adam, who looked as good as ever in a dark gray suit with a gorgeous gray and lavender striped tie. As if sensing her, he looked over and their gazes locked. Electricity sizzled through her, jumpstarting her heart into a mad rhythm. It was one of those moments where her stunned mind couldn't compute, so she simply stood there.

Tami saw her and let out a good old Southern whoop. "Dr. Julia! You're here!" She rushed over and threw her arms around Julia. "Congratulations! I'm so happy for you, girl." She stepped back and wagged a finger. "I can't believe you didn't tell me about this before now. You little secretive thing, you."

"What?" Julia asked, totally confused.

The other staff members gathered around and started congratulating her, and asking her when the big event would be. She stared at them blankly, wondering if she was dreaming.

"Well, you sure caught yourself the pick of the litter," Tami said and grinned at Adam as he made his way to Julia's side. "Although I'm not sure it's legal for cousins to do this."

"We're very distant cousins," Adam said, slipping a possessive arm around Julia. "Hello, darling."

The assault of sexual energy was immediate, scattering all rational thought while heightening her senses. She felt the heat he radiated, inhaled his expensive male scent. It took all her self-control to ignore the impact—similar to that of a meteorite hitting the Earth—of his nearness and make her brain function. Had he just called her *darling*?

"Legal? Cousins?" She asked, feeling like she was in *The Twilight Zone*. What the hell was Adam doing here? She tried to move away, but he tightened his arm around her.

Tami laughed. "Aren't you the funny one? If I was marrying a man this hunky, I'd be telling the whole world."

Marrying? Alarm bells started going off as some of the mental fog cleared. She glared at Adam, tried again to get free, without success. "What are we talking about here?"

Dr. Moreno—her conservative, uptight boss—actually let out a rusty laugh. "She's such a joker, our Dr. Julia. Getting engaged is a special event. Mr. Masters suggested we might want to have a celebration." He waved what looked like another check. "Your future husband, he is a generous man, no?"

Before Julia could respond, Tami grabbed her arm. "Look over there," she said gaily and gestured to the back wall. Julia glanced over, blinked, and looked again.

There was a huge blue banner on the wall, with the words *Congratulations, Dr. Julia and Adam!* printed on it in red block letters edged in white—the UH colors again. A table had been set up beneath the banner and covered in a scarlet red cloth. A cake and several bottles of champagne were on it. Suddenly she couldn't breathe. The floor felt like it was falling out from under her. She tried to think of something to say, but couldn't seem to force the words from her constricted throat.

"Julia didn't want to tell anyone just yet, but I thought it would be nice to surprise her with a celebration with her coworkers, so she could make the announcement," Adam said smoothly.

The bastard! How dare he just show up after all these weeks, and then pull this stunt? Did he think she wouldn't call him on his colossal lie? She would set the record straight immediately. She would— She looked at the people gathered around her, all smiling and watching her expectantly.

Crap. Did she really want a scene in front of her boss, Tami, her coworkers? She'd worked long and hard for her position here, for the respect she'd garnered. *Crap, crap, crap!* This was insane. Adam was going to be one dead Sanctioned, as soon as she got him alone.

Miriam came over to give her a hug. "Congratulations, Julia—er—Dr. Reynolds. This is quite a surprise, but I'm happy for you." She leaned in and whispered. "Are you all right? Your aura is bright red."

"Oh, I'm just fine," Julia whispered back, between gritted teeth. "I hope you'll visit me on death row." She waited until Miriam stepped back then brought the end of her cane down hard on Adam's foot.

"Ouch! Darling, what—"

"Hello, Sean," she said brightly, doing the same to Adam's other foot. "I'm surprised to see you in Houston." She felt Adam grab her cane.

"Hi, Julia." Amusement in his eyes, Sean coughed behind his hand. Obviously, he'd read the situation correctly. "Matt and I are spending a few days here. Thought we'd catch a Texans game and just hang."

"Maybe Adam can *hang* with you," Julia said, glaring up at the man she planned to murder. *By the neck until dead.*

He smiled back as he discreetly wrenched the cane from her hand, and gave her a warning look. "Darling, I plan to stay by your side all week."

"Oh, that is so sweet," Tami cooed, oblivious to the tension. "Why don't we cut the cake and pour the champagne?" Ever efficient, she hustled over to the table, as Julia struggled for composure. Most of the staff members followed, always ready to eat.

"This is wonderful. Wonderful!" Dr. Moreno positively beamed as he tucked the check into his coat pocket. Since he disliked social events, and people in general, Julia wondered if he'd already been in the champagne. Or maybe he was just giddy over Adam's second bribe.

"Julia!"

She turned and saw her sister and Luke entering the reception area. Marla, with her protruding belly and a glow of happiness, looked especially pretty in a burnt orange sweater and brown slacks. Luke, as always, drew the eye of every woman there. The man was tall and built, with long blond hair and gorgeous blue eyes.

"What are you doing here?" Julia asked with a sinking feeling. Things were going downhill at high velocity. Thank God her parents were on a trip to California.

"Tami called me." Marla gave her an awkward hug, her belly bumping Julia. "She said they were having a surprise celebration for you." She nodded coolly at Adam. "Adam."

"Marla. You're looking good. The baby's due in about four weeks, right?"

"Give or take." Marla glanced around the room, her mouth falling open when her gaze fixed on the banner. She whirled back to Julia. "What the hell—"

"Trust me, it's a total surprise to me," Julia said in a low voice. "One of Adam's tricks."

"Hello, Julia," Luke interrupted smoothly, giving her a hug. "It appears congratulations are in order."

"Oh, I don't think so," she said sweetly. "More like an upcoming funeral."

"This is outrageous!" Marla said. "Adam, what do you think you're—"

"Later, babe." Luke took her arm. "I think we'd better stay out of this." He winked at Julia. "My money's on you."

"But—" Marla sputtered as he pulled her away. He leaned down and said something to her. She clamped her mouth shut, but her expression was mutinous. She glared daggers at Adam.

Julia tried to calm her roiling stomach. This was a disaster. But if she stayed cool, it was salvageable. Engagements got broken all the time. Or she could tell everyone that Adam had met with an unfortunate accident, and been buried beside Aunt Willie—

Whoa! Her gaze had landed on Sean, who was standing very close to Miriam, his hand splayed possessively on her rear. Miriam didn't seem to mind at all. Smiling at Sean, she casually removed his hand, twining her fingers with his. How had Julia missed that bulletin? She wondered if the world had gone mad while she'd been in some sort of trance state, probably induced by the Devil incarnate, Aka Adam Masters.

Tami came over with flutes of champagne. "First two glasses are for y'all. Have you picked out a ring yet?"

"No," Julia said. Make that *hell no.*

"As a matter of fact," Adam slipped his hand into his

coat pocket, "I have a little something for my bride to be." He pulled out a signature blue Tiffany & Co. jewelry box, and Julia's anger spiked. The son of a bitch was playing the game all the way.

"Tiffany!" Tami fanned herself. "Oh, my."

"My sister can't be bought," Marla fumed, starting toward Adam. "If you think you can just force yourself—"

"It's those pregnancy hormones," Luke commented, pulling her back. "They really get you overheated, don't they, babe?"

Marla sent him a murderous look, and Julia knew she had to defuse the situation. She wasn't letting anyone else kill Adam. That would be her pleasure alone. "Marla, it's fine, really. As a matter of fact, I can't wait to see what's in the box." She gave Adam a feral smile. "In private. Just you and me. Why don't we go to my office?"

Tami beamed "Why, I think that's a wonderful idea. Y'all can go be all kissy-kissy and then you can show us your ring. Take your champagne with you."

Julia didn't wait for Adam's agreement; she grabbed her cane from him and limped to the hallway and toward her office. She knew he was following, because she could feel that damned energy. A loud thud sounded behind her, and she turned. Rubbing his shoulder, Adam was staring at Marla, who had the huge Houston phone book gripped tightly in her hands. "You sorry son of a bitch!" She smacked him again, before Luke corralled her. "How dare you jerk my sister around like this!"

At least they were around the corner from the reception area, so no one saw Marla's assault. The astonished look on Adam's face was priceless. Despite the situation, Julia had to smile. Trust Marla to always come to her defense. "Thanks, sister," she said. "But I'll take it from here. I have a cane, a gun, and pepper foam."

Adam sent her a pained look; Luke gave her thumbs up. She spun and walked to her office, going behind her desk as Adam came in behind her. He closed the door with a wave of his hand, and she heard the lock click. That only brought home their differences. Bombarded by a plethora of emotions, she tried to calm herself.

She truly didn't understand any of this. Couldn't fathom why Adam would suddenly show up after almost eight weeks of no contact, and just when her life was finally settling down. Why would he do this to her, stir up emotions she was working so hard to bury? It was a crappy thing to do.

And still she wanted to know why. Logically, there was no way a man like Adam would be interested in a woman like her, unless it was the thrill of the hunt. Wasn't it human nature to want what you couldn't have? Except Adam wasn't exactly human.

He could at least respect her feelings. She'd made it clear she didn't want to be with him. Okay, so she'd told him that after they'd had wild monkey sex in the shower, followed by an encore in the bedroom. So maybe that was a mixed message. But still. Being Adam, he would do exactly what he wanted.

"Are you through overanalyzing the situation yet?"

No matter how annoyed she was with him, his raspy voice did wild things to her libido. She looked at him. He was so fine, tall and broad-shouldered in his classy Italian suit, with that incongruous diamond in his ear. So calm as he waited for her to engage, so brilliant, so powerful, so sexy, so . . . everything.

This was crazy. But she needed to be objective and levelheaded. "Why are you doing this, especially now? You've been out of my life for almost eight weeks, and now," she gestured at the blue Tiffany & Co. box he'd set on her desk, along with his champagne, "this. I don't understand."

"You think I'm stringing you along, appearing every so often to ensure you don't forget me? Staging this elaborate ruse and buying jewelry just to jerk your chain?"

When he put it that way, it didn't sound like a solid rationale, but nothing was making sense right now. "Well, yes, something like that. It's the only . . . logical explanation."

"Julia, fate is not always logical. Neither is love." Adam started toward her, stopped when she raised her cane. He sighed. "All right, then. Let's start with the eight-week hiatus. I wanted to give you time to recover from the traumas of San Antonio, and from Bennett. I wanted you to have time to heal emotionally and physically, before I pushed the issue of our relationship."

Damned if that didn't make perfect sense. And it was actually considerate. Eight weeks ago, she'd have been no match for Adam. Now . . . she still had to harden herself against him. "That still doesn't answer why. *Why* are you doing this, Adam?"

"The correct question would be why are *you* doing this, Julia? Why are you turning away from me, when I know you care? I know you're affected by this attraction between us. Why are you fighting it?"

"It's just chemistry. Pure, ordinary lust, engendered by the Sanctioned/conductor link."

Frustration flashed in his eyes. "You're lying to yourself. There's so much more between us. You belittle what we have when you deny it."

She felt her own frustration, and a whole set of other emotions. She could deal with mathematical equations, but this emotional flypaper was beyond her.

"I'm not trying to belittle anything. I just—" She raked her hand through her hair. How could she make him understand?

"This whole situation is totally, unequivocally illogical! Consider who you are, Adam. You're a superhuman being from Atlantis. You can manipulate energy and battle evil beings. You're responsible for the welfare of dozens of people under your leadership. Your business and your home are in Corpus Christi. You wear designer suits and hobnob with the rich and famous. You slept with Cleopatra, for God's sake. And I—"

She shook her head, waved a hand toward herself. "I'm a plain, ordinary math professor, and I prefer a quiet, uncomplicated life. We're not even close to a match."

"First off, you're not remotely plain or ordinary. You're beautiful, inside and out. And you're gutsy, courageous, brilliant, compassionate, unpredictable, and have a wicked wit." He gave her a heated look. "And you're very sexy."

"That's the Sanctioned/conductor link and two-hundred-year celibacy talking. We're from different worlds, Adam. This can't work."

"Your own sister is happily married to a Sentinel. Don't tell me it can't work."

"I—" She paused, stumped. He had her there. "But you're a Sanctioned. You're far more powerful than a Sentinel, with far more responsibility. It's not the same."

"Julia, you have an amazing intellect. But you're overthinking this. You're my soul mate. Just as importantly, I love you. Does there have to be anything beyond that?"

Didn't there? She was just more confused. She turned and stared blindly out her window. Things had been so much simpler when her sole focus had been teaching and her family.

"Do you know what I think?" Adam said from right behind her, giving her a start. She'd forgotten he was Mr. Stealth.

She turned, finding herself nose to chest with him, and her cane no longer in reach. Then his arms were around her and she was pressed against him. Her knee-jerk reaction was to pull away, but he held her firmly. "Just hear me out," he said against her hair. "Listen to me."

"Do I have any choice?" she sniped against his chest. But she'd be lying if she said it wasn't wonderful to be wrapped in his strength and heat and amazing scent.

"No, you don't, actually. I have a theory about you, Julia. I think you blamed yourself for what happened with Bennett all those years ago. That you felt responsible because Marla got in the cross fire. You second-guessed yourself, overanalyzed like you tend to do. You wondered if you had somehow led Bennett on, somehow given him the wrong idea.

"You took on the blame and have been punishing yourself ever since. That's why you withdrew from the outside world and lived like a hermit. You didn't think you deserved to be happy. You still don't believe you do, which is why you won't accept my love."

The truth in his words slammed into her and cut to the quick. It was hard to argue them when Dr. Jackson had recently suggested the very same thing, when she was coming to that realization on her own. But it didn't change the facts. The old pain, which was always with her on some level, surfaced and rolled through her. With it came tears, burning as they filled her eyes.

"Maybe it *was* my fault," she whispered. "I should have seen Bennett's unhealthy attachment to me, should have done something about it before it escalated to violence. Marla was almost killed. She shouldn't have suffered because I was oblivious to Bennett's fixation on me."

"You know better than that, at least intellectually," Adam said. "Let me ask you a question. When Matt was possessed by the Belian, was it his fault?"

The denial rose quickly. "Of course not. The man was grieving and drinking too much, but he didn't invite the Belian to possess him."

"Then why would Bennett attacking you be your fault? You weren't aware of his attraction to you, and you didn't intentionally lead him on. You didn't flirt with him, or go out with him. You were simply courteous. Right?"

"Well, yes, but—"

"What happened was out of your control. It's that simple. It's time to let it go."

Was it really that easy? But even if she could rationalize blame, it wouldn't change anything. All she could do was embrace life from this point forward. She felt a weight lifting from her soul. Maybe this thing with Adam could work. Maybe she could stop paying Dr. Jackson the big bucks now, since she had her own personal psychoanalyst.

She swiped at her eyes. "What is it about you that makes me cry so much?"

"It's our soul bond." He slid his hand beneath her chin and tilted her face up, gently blotted her tears with his handkerchief. "We feel stronger emotions when we're together."

"So we're back to that."

"We never left it." He pressed a kiss to her lips. "There are two things that should help you feel better."

"And what would those two things be?"

He picked up the blue box. "The first would be for you to put on this ring and agree to marry me."

Panic swept through her. She wasn't ready for a ring, much less a commitment. She was just coming to grips with the fact that she was dating a god, if you could call her activities with Adam dating. "Oh, I don't think we should rush into anything—" The words froze in her throat as he opened the box. *Oh, my.*

Nestled in the satin was a beautiful square-cut diamond in a simple, four-prong gold setting. The band was wider and more contemporary than a traditional engagement setting, and it set off the square stone perfectly. It was simple enough to suit Julia's nonfrilly taste, yet it was elegant. Stunning.

She touched the stone, which had to be at least two carats. Okay, so she was weak. So it was ridiculous that she could be so affected by a large chunk of carbon, that it could so easily weaken her emotional defenses. She'd never been big on jewelry, but getting a ring like this thrilled her down to her staid toes. What a shock to discover she still had girly genes.

"Are you trying to bribe me?" she asked, resisting the urge to rip the box out of his hands.

"Whatever it takes." He removed the ring, took her left hand, and slid it on her finger. Of course it fit perfectly. "Is it working?"

Even though she adored the ring, and—if she were being totally honest with herself—she loved the man, she decided a little payback might be in order. "Oh, I don't know."

"Well, then. Maybe we should move on to the second thing."

She tore her gaze away from the diamond to look up at him. "What's that?"

His eyes took on a heated glow. "Consummating the deal. Right now."

Shock punched through her. "*Now? Here?* Oh, I don't think that's a good idea at all."

He waved his hand and her suit jacket opened. How had that gotten unbuttoned? She felt her bra unhook. "Adam—"

Her slacks, mysteriously unzipped, slid down her legs, followed by her panties. "Adam Masters, stop right now!"

She tried to move away, but he had her pinned against the desk, and her pants were tangled around her ankles. He slipped one hand beneath her bra and stroked her breast, while his other hand cupped her rear. "You'll be calling me a deity shortly."

"We can't do this in here," she gasped as he lifted her onto her desk, took off his coat, and unzipped his pants.

Hearing thuds, she looked around and saw books, papers, telephone, and her calculator levitating off the desk and to the floor. She heard her shoes hit the floor, lost her slacks and panties completely. "Whoa! Wait a minute! This is *not* a good idea— Oh!"

His hand slipping between her legs sent her thoughts spinning into space. She found herself arching back as he lowered his mouth to her exposed breast. This was crazy. Insane. Irresponsible, undignified. What if they got caught? And—

"Oh, God," she moaned as he lifted her hips off the desk and slid inside her. Of their own accord, her legs wrapped around him, and he leaned over her.

"Darling, you're deifying me again." He was way too smug, and she was going to give him hell . . . as soon as they were finished.

She dropped her head back as the sexual link between them swamped her, obliterating everything but the sensation of Adam moving inside her, of the building crescendo that was rapidly approaching.

"I've really missed this," he gasped, sounding a little swamped himself. "We only did it four times—not that I'm counting, or anything—but it's highly addictive."

"Typical male," she managed. "Go without nooky for two hundred years, and you think you're deprived. . . . Oh, do that again."

The phone intercom buzzed from the floor, and Tami's honeyed Southern voice floated out. "Dr. Julia, what are y'all doing in there? Not too much kissy-kissy, you hear? Come on out and join the party."

"We'll be there in a few moments," Adam said, sounding almost normal. And he hadn't missed a stroke. *Impressive.*

"All right!" Tami trilled. "Don't make me come after you, now." She clicked off.

"That . . . was . . . close . . ." Julia gasped. She couldn't worry much about it; she was almost to liftoff. . . .

There was a pounding on the door. "Julia! Are you still in there?" Marla demanded. "What's going on? I hope you kicked Adam's balls into his throat."

Oh, this was a disaster waiting to happen. Julia struggled to think straight. "I'm . . . working on it," she bit out.

She shook her head at Adam so he'd stop thrusting for a moment, but he ignored her. "We've almost come . . . to . . . an agreement. Be right . . . there."

"Are you sure you're all right?"

"Yes. Fine. Coming . . . soon," was all she managed before her world exploded. A scream lodged in her throat. She couldn't worry about that, either. All her focus was on the waves of pleasure spreading out from the epicenter.

It was a while before coherent thought returned. She and Adam were both sprawled across the desk, panting like runners after a marathon. She fervently hoped Marla had walked away before the explosion. She tried to speak, found her voice was hoarse. "Did you paralyze my vocal chords?" she asked Adam.

He nodded. "Just for the moment of . . . impact. I didn't think you'd want your sister to hear you scream."

"Good thinking." She lay there a moment. "Thank you."

"Any time." He rolled onto his side, cupped one hand along her face. "Does this mean you'll marry me?"

"I'll give it some thought. I'll definitely continue to have sex with you. And I'm keeping the ring."

"Can't keep the ring unless we get married." He kissed her until her toes curled. "I guess we'll just have to continue negotiations."

"Looks like," she agreed, her heart swelling with happiness. "Why don't we put ourselves back together and go join the others before Tami has security unlock my office door?"

"Good idea." He stood and helped her up. "But I do like you naked and flushed, Professor."

He couldn't like looking at her nearly as much as she liked looking at him. They got their clothes in order, and returned everything to her desk.

As they started out the door, Adam said, "By the way, I've moved my private investigation agency here. My secretary, Cheryl, agreed to make the move with me. She likes the favorable ratio of men to women in Houston, as well as the very generous salary I pay her."

Another obstacle to their relationship removed. Julia felt her happiness expand. "You'd have to pay her a lot to put up with you," she commented.

"I'm not that bad," Adam protested mildly. He took her hand as they started down the corridor. "I've also bought a home in River Oaks."

It was one of the most exclusive and expensive subdivisions in Houston—what a surprise. *Not.* She did like that he referred to it as a home, not a house.

"You're assuming quite a lot," she said. "And you know what they say about people who assume."

He stopped short of the reception area and looked at her. "I'm not assuming. I *know* you're mine, and you're not getting away from me. You need to start thinking about what kind of wedding you want. Otherwise, you're going to show up for work one day and"—he gestured toward the main area—"find a big surprise waiting for you."

"You wouldn't," she said, but already had frightening images of Tami decorating the reception area with white tulle.

"Yes, I would." He smiled at her horrified expression. "I love you. I know you love me, too. You're going to have to admit it one of these days." He tugged her along to the reception area, where everyone greeted them with cheers, and Tami nearly stroked out over the ring.

Julia felt like she was in a daze, but it was a warm, glowing feeling. And for once, it wasn't so irritating that Adam was right. One day, she'd tell him she loved him. Just not yet—she didn't want him gloating too much.

She knew one thing for certain: Her life was never going to be normal, calm, or predictable again.

But neither was Adam's—she would make sure of that. *Life is pretty darned good*, she decided, enjoying the shocked expression on her sister's face when she saw the ring on Julia's hand.

All she needed now was a bottle of good merlot to top it off. Then everything would be perfect.

Turn the page for a preview of
the second book in Emma Holly's
Fitz Clare Chronicles

BREAKING MIDNIGHT

Available July 2009 from Berkley Sensation!

Somewhere in Europe: December 24, 1933

EDMUND Fitz Clare woke to a darkness so complete he might have been struck blind. He lay naked on his back on a flat steel surface, his immortal limbs as stiff as stone, his belly grinding with hunger. His inability to see—when normally the dimmest light sufficed—inspired a twinge of fear he could not repress: a primitive terror of helplessness. Though he tried to raise a glow in his aura, no illumination came, sure sign that he was as weakened as he felt. He struggled not to panic, but to take in his surroundings in other ways.

He needed all the information he could gather if he was going to get out of here. That he'd best get out, and soon, was crystal clear to him.

The place in which he'd rather pointlessly opened his eyes was cold, damp, and smelled of moldering stone. The cold didn't make him shiver; he was a vampire, after all, and he didn't need to be warm. Nonetheless, the chill was unpleasant. It seemed to worsen the pain in his head, the radiating spears of torment he could hardly think around.

He had the unsettling impression that he'd lost a good bit of time.

He'd been shot, hadn't he?

The question inspired a curious relief. He distinctly remembered being shot—and with iron rounds, the one metal his kind were weakened by. He'd been standing on Hampstead Heath, squaring off with . . . with two young *upyr*, one male and one female. They'd wanted him to kill Nim Wei, the queen of all the city-dwelling vampires. The pair had been rebelling against her rule and had hoped to use Edmund as a stalking horse. When that plan failed, they'd lain in wait for him in the park and had fired on him with machine guns.

What he couldn't remember was what he'd been doing on the heath in the first place.

His fists clenched with frustration, which was when he noticed his wrists and ankles were shackled—by iron, unfortunately. Chains attached the cuffs, probably to the table, allowing each limb a few inches of play. Edmund wrenched against the heavy links, his heart rate rocketing as instincts from another species kicked in. He had a wolf's soul inside him, but with this metal touching him, he wouldn't be able to take its form. Indeed, all his vampire powers were inhibited.

That realization spurred him to fight harder against his confinement, which increased his blood flow, which caused the pain between his temples to surge to sledgehammer blows. He had to force himself to calm, breath by breath, muscle by muscle, until the agony eased enough to let him think again. He was all right; trapped, apparently, and not at full strength, but not in imminent danger. Perhaps he'd been shot in the head. Perhaps one of the rounds was still there. Maybe that was why his thoughts had turned to pudding. His body couldn't push out iron the way it would other poisonous substances.

Edmund wondered how long he'd survive with a bullet inside his skull. Were master vampires vulnerable to brain damage?

That thought was another puzzle piece. Edmund was a master vampire now, an *elder*, as his race called it. He remembered what had triggered the chain of events that led him here, with a flood of relief profound enough to leave him limp. Auriclus, the founder of Edmund's line, had walked into the sun. When he died, his power had been portioned out among his followers, and Edmund's share had pushed him to the next level of potency. He'd been afraid . . . Here his mind stalled again. He'd been afraid of *something* related to his new status. He'd been running away from it when he blundered into his attackers' trap.

He shifted uncomfortably on his cold steel bed, trying to piece the fragments into a sensible whole. He went back to the part he knew: that the sudden increase in power had been too much for him, that it had flared out of his control. He'd feared he might harm someone. He'd been worried about humans, hadn't he? Humans he loved? *Upyr* could love humans, couldn't they?

Threads of fire seared his brain as synapses reconnected, but this time he didn't back off from his attempt. He saw flashes. Faces. Two young human males, one dark, one fair, their arms slung protectively around a blonde girl-woman.

Daddy, she exclaimed, laughing at him. *How could you forget me?*

Time folded back. He saw the girl-woman as a child, no more than four or five years old. Her tiny, warm hand curled around his as real as night. She was alone in the world. They were all alone, and he was saving them. This trio of humans was his family now.

Edmund's eyes were hot, his heart aching.

You've done a good job with them, said another, infinitely dear voice. *You let them all be just who they are.*

He cried out, unable to keep the hoarse sound inside. *Estelle.* Like magic, his beloved's name shuffled the cards of his life into their proper mental place. Sally and Ben and Graham were his family, all of them orphaned in the last great war. Edmund had been passing for human when he adopted them, working as a professor of history at a nearby university. Estelle Berenger was Sally's friend. Edmund had been in love with her almost since he'd met her at fifteen. He'd saved her from being killed by a lightning bolt by leaping between her and the strike in his wolf form. The incident had left her different, as if a bit of his immortal nature had shot into her cells with the energy. She was still mortal, but she had gifts . . . strengths no mortal ever bore.

Estelle was also his fiancée. A moan broke in Edmund's throat as that awareness returned, joy and sorrow mixed like bitter herbs in wine. He and Estelle had just announced their engagement to his family. Edmund had been making love to her, had bitten her for the first time, when Auriclus's power had slammed into him. Estelle had lit up in the backwash, the very blood in her veins glowing like white fire. Edmund hadn't known the secret of the change before he so summarily became an elder, hadn't known his aura and not his blood was the key. When he finally found out the truth, he didn't have the know-how to shut it off. Edmund had thought he was going to make Estelle a vampire, and maybe his family, too, without them having a chance to say yes or no.

Edmund's branch of the *upyr*, the shapechangers Auriclus had founded millennia ago, didn't believe in changing anyone against their will. *That* was why Edmund had fled to Hampstead Heath, to take himself and his new elder powers too far away to influence his loved ones. He'd wanted to protect them.

Which was how he'd gotten himself shot, shanghaied, and chained to a steel table.

Oh, Estelle, he thought ruefully. *How I wish I'd simply stayed with you.*

He only had a moment for the regret.

Another vampire had entered the space he was in. Edmund heard the faintest footfall, sensed the slightest shift in the air. He tried to read the *upyr*'s mind, but found only a blank spot where it should have been. Bereft of any means to defend himself, every muscle in his body coiled.

"*So*," said a deep male voice. The shadow of a German accent gave the word a clean, crisp edge. "You're back with us again. I'd begun to wonder if Li-Hua and I had done too much damage."

"Frank," Edmund gasped, the name rising to the surface unexpectedly.

"And lucid," said his visitor. "That's good to know. Hit the lights, darling."

The order confused Edmund, until he realized another *upyr* must have come in. Frank's female partner, he presumed.

She, it seemed, was amenable to being told what to do. The aforementioned lights exploded in a blaze of brilliant white, blinding him in a whole new way. They were the sort of lights cinema people used, a whacking great bank of them supported by a braced metal pole. When Edmund's eyes stopped tearing, he saw he was in a large, windowless cell, its walls lined with blocks of granite. Mold streaked the stones' chiseled surfaces, the source of the mustiness he'd smelled earlier. He craned his head to see more. The table on which he lay was straight out of a morgue, complete with drains along the sides to let fluids run conveniently out.

The vampire Frank smiled at him. Edmund hadn't caught more than a glimpse of him before the shooting started. Dressed in a dark, double-breasted suit, Frank was very tall, very muscular, and very Teutonic—precisely the sort of male *der Führer* swooned over. His fair hair fell in waves to his warrior shoulders, while his face could have graced a Renaissance painting. His fangs had run out, making his smile a somewhat less angelic sight. Given that the *upyr* was fingering a scalpel in his long white hand, Edmund didn't think he was in for a tea party.

"Tell me when you're ready for me to roll the film," Li-Hua said.

She was a lovely Oriental woman, as slight and feminine as her partner was male. She was dressed in baggy black trousers and a thick fisherman's sweater. The bright red kerchief tied around her neck added to her Bohemian flair. The lights taken care of, she bent to the eyepiece of a motion picture camera on a tripod. Her assurance as she aimed and focused told Edmund she'd done this before.

"Why are you recording this?" he asked. His throat was hoarse from disuse, causing him to wonder yet again how long he'd been at this pair's mercy.

Frank stepped closer. "For fun and profit, of course."

"Profit?" Edmund rasped.

Though he would rather have shown no reaction, he jerked when Frank spread the hand that didn't hold the scalpel across the hollow of his bare belly. As soon as the vampire touched him, Edmund became aware that he could *feel* the bullets inside him, could sense them striving to overcome his recuperative powers. The projectiles were cold, gray things, deadening the flesh around them. There weren't as many as Edmund expected, mere dozens rather than hundreds. Also unexpected was that the skin of Frank's palm was warm, his long, blunt fingers buzzing with a fine tremor.

Clearly, Frank was looking forward to cutting into him.

"You've no idea how fascinating it is to watch an elder heal," he said dreamily. "Your body has been trying to push those bullets to the surface since you were shot. At first I had to slice quite deep to give them a channel out, but now it barely takes an inch or two."

"How long have I been here?" Edmund demanded, suppressing his shudder at Frank's obvious regret. "Where have you taken me?"

"I was most concerned about your head wound," the other man continued, ignoring him. "If Li-Hua or I had a lump of iron in our brain, we'd be drooling wrecks—and never mind the state we'd be in if we hadn't fed in as long as you. You, however, master vampire marvel that you are, are recovering like a trooper. Honestly, I couldn't be more pleased or proud."

"Where *am* I?" Edmund insisted. The younger vampire wasn't trying to avoid his gaze. Taking his chance, Edmund tried to push his will at him, to force him to answer. It wasn't as easy to thrall vampires as humans, but a master should have had the power. Regrettably, Edmund's attempt accomplished only an intensification of the torture in his head. As soon as he released the effort, clammy pink blood-sweat rolled into his eyes.

Frank appeared more amused than offended.

"I don't think I ought to tell you," he said coyly. "In your current state, I don't believe you could pass a telepathic message to anyone, but I'd really rather not take the chance."

It might not have been helpful, but Edmund's temper broke.

"Oh, *do* struggle." Frank approved as he thrashed and growled in his chains. "I'll enjoy this so much better if you fight. So will my beloved, for that matter."

"I'll kill you," Edmund swore through his teeth. His fangs were sharp now, his bloodlust rising with his rage. The flexible steel table made a sound like thunder as he writhed. "If I have to claw my way out of the grave to do it, I'll kill you both."

"We don't want you in the grave," Frank chided. "We

want you hale and hearty and in full possession of your elder power."

Edmund gave his shackles a tug that had the chain smoking on his palms. If he'd been in wolf form, he would have torn out Frank's throat.

"You're insane," he panted, forced by the excruciating pain of holding the iron to unclamp his grip. "You've no idea who you're dealing with."

"Neither do you," Frank said, all playfulness gone. "You will soon, though, once we get on with this experiment." He turned to his companion, gesturing for her to turn the crank that started the film.

When the blade cut into his belly, Edmund didn't bother to restrain his scream.